THE WHITE FEATHER

THE WHITE FEATHER

A Novel of Forbidden Love in World War I England

THE FIRST OF THE CLAYBOURNE TRILOGY

MARY CHRISTIAN PAYNE

The White Feather
First of The Claybourne Trilogy

Garamond typeface used with permission from Microsoft.

Published by TCK Publishing
www.TCKPublishing.com

Sign up for the free newsletter to get news, updates and new release info from Mary Christian Payne:
http://bit.ly/MaryChristianPayne

To Denise for her support

1

It was Lily's Barton's mother who suggested that she apply for the position of private nurse to the Countess of Claybourne - a single act that transformed her life. Lily was not truly a nurse, which is only to say that she had no credentials. But she had assisted her father, Dr. Barton, on his surgeries from the age of sixteen. She'd meant to continue on that path, and had hoped to become a physician herself someday. But Lily's dream swiftly faded when Doctor Barton died of a heart seizure July, 1914, rapidly followed by the loss of her brother, Jordan, at the Battle of the Marne on September 23 of the same year. The war had changed everything.

All of England was elated and filled with patriotism when the conflict began in August of 1914. There was dancing and singing in the streets, and most people thought it would be over by Christmas. But following the Battle of the Marne, in France, it was obvious there would be no quick victory. Both sides were firmly entrenched and it appeared that there might be years of fighting. The country's mood had quickly deteriorated. Lily had little comprehension of why the English were engaged in such a terrible conflict. From her scant knowledge, the immediate impetus for the war happened on 28, June, 1914 when the Archduke Ferdinand of Austria, and his wife, Sophia, heirs to the thrones of Austria-Hungary, were assassinated by Yugoslav nationalist Gavril Princip in Sarajevo. That set off a diplomatic crisis when international treaties, which had been in place over previous decades, were invoked. Germany invaded Belgium, a neutral country, before moving toward France, which led to Britain to declare war on Germany. That was when Jordy quickly ran off to enlist. He left for France as patriotic songs were sung, and flags were waved by the inhabitants of their quaint, Cotswold village. Jordy had believed he would return a hero in short order, and that there would be hoards of girls waiting for him at the station when he came home. Men need courage, of course, and Jordy was no different. Men also need leaders. Unfortunately, the leaders in charge during that time led the men to believe that the war was an honorable undertaking, and that gave the soldiers courage. Unfortunately, it was all a lie. Jordy's courage ended in a filthy, muddy trench with a bullet through his forehead. While it might have benefited Lily to have had more time to grieve the deaths of her father and brother, the need for money to pay for the essentials in life didn't end because of a war. Thus, Lily's hopes of studying medicine had been dashed. Most people thought she was daft anyway, when she said her dream in life was to become a doctor. It was a lofty goal for a lady in the early years of the Twentieth Century - lofty, but not unheard of. Other women had paved the way. Mary Scharlieb, Elizabeth Garret Anderson, and Frances Hoggan were all graduate physicians in the mid to late 1800's in Great Britain. There was no reason that Lily Barton's name couldn't be added to that list. But, she would have to postpone her ambitions until the war ended and the money was put aside.

Elisabeth Barton, Lily's Mum, had seen an advertisement in the village newspaper for a private duty nurse, to tend to the needs of a 'titled lady.' It wasn't difficult to guess that the titled lady was the Countess of Gloucester, Eleanor Claybourne. Surely there was no other titled lady anywhere near *Claybourne-on-Colne*. The advertisement went on to say that qualifications for this coveted position included 'medical skills, and loyalty, in addition to being willing to keep all confidences quite to oneself.' It stated that the 'preferred candidate' would have knowledge of the duties required of a 'ladies' maid.' Elisabeth Barton had shown her the newspaper, and in spite of her sadness, Lily was hopeful at the prospect of working at *Claybourne Court*. Lily's Mum had been a ladies' maid at *Barrow Manor*, a great estate in Southwest England, before she'd married Doctor Tom Barton, and she'd taught Lily what it was like to work in a great house. So there was no question that Lily felt qualified. Her only worry was that she was still very young - only twenty-one - and had no actual experience working in someone's home. In fact, she had no actual experience working at all, except for the aforementioned apprenticeship with her father. But her Mum felt she needed to secure employment as soon as possible, since their funds were shrinking. So instead of medical school, Lily set out to apply for the position her mother had seen advertised. She wrote a neat, professional letter to the address given, and after just three days the butler at *Claybourne Court* rang her. *Claybourne Court* was the ancient manor after which the village was named. It was the seat of the Earl of Gloucester. *Claybourne-on-Colne* was an enchanting hamlet, consisting of the pub, approximately one hundred and fifty cottages, the church, and various and sundry shops. Most of its inhabitants were of the middle class. Lily's parents had moved there before she was born. In 1887 Tom Barton had set up his medical practice just off the High Street and through the years he had become a much loved figure about the village. Everyone waved as he drove by in his carriage pulled by a lovely, old brown mare. He was the first person in the village to buy an automobile in 1908 – a Ford Model T. All the citizens of *Claybourne–on-Colne* turned out to watch as he drove through the town. Lily's life had been a happy one, with parents she adored, and a brother she worshipped. It was hard for her to realize that her father and Jordy were both gone. Nonetheless, she knew what she must do, and did it without complaint. She paid her first visit to *Claybourne Court* the day following her receipt of the telephone call. On that occasion she met Halsey, the butler, and Mrs. Briggs, the housekeeper. Both were very kind to her, and as her fear lessened, she became even more anxious to be hired.

Having already spoken to Halsey and Mrs. Briggs, Lily was invited back to interview with Lord Claybourne, the Earl of Gloucester. She was nervous as she trudged up the hill on that lovely September morning in 1914, hoping that the Earl would approve of her. *Claybourne Court* was an exquisite manor house, built of red brick and golden Cotswold stone. It was covered with thick Ivy vines, meandering their way up its splendid walls. The windows were mullioned, and the roof slate. Roses were still blooming on both sides of the front entrance, in spite of the cool weather.

When she reached *Claybourne Court*, Halsey met her at the door and warmly welcomed her. He seemed less solemn than he had upon her first visit. He showed her to a small receiving room off the great hall, and Mrs. Briggs brought her a cup of tea. Lily practiced what she would say, and tried to remember that she should meet the Earl's eyes when she spoke. She waited only a few minutes. Lord Claybourne turned out not to be what she'd expected. When he entered the room, she was knocked for six. She'd expected him to be a rather portly man, with rotund features and thinning hair. That was the image she'd always carried of an Earl's appearance. Having lived in the village of *Claybourne-on-Colne* her entire lifetime, she thought she knew everything there was to know about the family who lived in the great house. In her enthusiasm she'd forgotten that the old Earl had passed away during the time that her father was tragically ill, that sad summer of 1914. Thus, the man standing in front of her was the Eighth Earl, Lord Christopher Claybourne. He was quite splendid looking. Dressed in the very posh uniform of the *Scot's Grey Cavalry*, he appeared to be in his early thirties, with thick hair of chestnut brown, worn longish, but very cleanly cut. He had superb green eyes, with flecks of blue, depending upon how the light fell. He was tall - quite tall - although Lily was short, so it was hard for her to determine precisely. Broad shouldered and immaculately dressed, she was very, very impressed. Of course, who was she not to have been impressed by an Earl? Lily was dressed in a simple grey, ankle length skirt, and a plain, long sleeved white blouse with a high Victorian neckline. She had borrowed her Mum's cameo brooch. Her auburn hair was neatly done-up in a figure eight, pinned beneath a small proper hat, trimmed with a dainty white feather. She'd been blessed with perfect skin, which was frequently compared to the quintessential English rose. The fairness of her coloring did have pale pink on the high cheekbones, and her eyes, perhaps her best feature, were a remarkable blue-green. She didn't look too fancy, as she knew better than to present for the Earl's inspection looking like a tart. Of course, her appearance didn't make a whit of difference when it came to whether Lord Claybourne would or would not find her acceptable for the position of Private Duty Nurse. Certainly, he wanted a neat, clean, properly attired lady, but he was, and always would be, her employer - nothing more - and she would be expected to be as invisible as possible whenever they happened to be in near proximity to one another.

Lily desperately wanted the employment. She was sitting on an uncomfortable, mud-colored, horse-hair sofa, in the small receiving room, when the Lord of *Claybourne Court* entered. He introduced himself very casually, as 'Christopher Claybourne', and furthermore told her that most people knew him as 'Kit'. Surely he doesn't expect that of me, she thought to herself? She wasn't certain if she should stand, curtsy, or remain seated, sipping the tea that the housekeeper, Mrs. Briggs, had brought to her. She placed her cup on the Victorian marble-topped table in front of the sofa, and started to rise, but he put his hand out to stop her, and said, "No matter. You needn't get up." He seemed terribly nice and she relaxed a bit, but sat very straight, keeping her hands folded neatly in her lap. She tried to make eye contact as she had practiced, knowing that it would not do to act like a shy little mouse. She had a nasty habit of looking at the floor when speaking with people who were far above her socially.

"So, you're the young lady about whom I've heard such nice things from Mrs. Briggs and Halsey?"

Apparently she had passed muster with both the Housekeeper and the Butler. "Yes, Milord. I'm Lily Barton. How do you do?"

"And how do you do? It's a pleasure to meet you, Miss Barton," he replied, as he made himself comfortable at a large, roll-topped desk, sitting against the wall at the side of the room. She handed him her credentials, which included a certificate of achievement from her grammar school, a letter of recommendation from the headmaster at the Public School she had attended, and Red Cross certification, which her father had insisted that she complete. Lily had finished grammar school with excellent performance, and had won a scholarship to *Cheltenham Ladies' College,* located in Cheltenham, Gloucestershire, not far from *Claybourne-on-Colne*. Lily had not boarded, but had been driven by her father each day. Her studies would have culminated in a Bachelor's Degree, and she hoped someday to pick them up again. She had attended for two years, and might have begun Medical School this very month, but present circumstances rendered that impossible.

"So then, can you tell me a bit about yourself? I must say, you're certainly a cut above the average lady who would normally apply for a position of this caliber," he smiled. "Not that you should view that as a negative comment, nor view this position as beneath you, but with your attractive appearance, obvious manners, and strong academic achievements I should think you might land employment more in keeping with your station in life."

"Thank you, Milord," she answered. "I've lived right here in *Claybourne-upon-Colne* since I was born. My father was a physician here for many years, but he died this last summer. Then my brother Jordan was killed at The Battle of the Marne earlier this month. As you have seen, I attended the *Cheltenham Ladies' College* for two years. I had hoped to go on to study medicine, but circumstances have changed. My Mum and I now find it essential that I seek employment. The loss of my father's income, and then my brother's military pay, has had an effect upon our pocketbooks. Perhaps I might be able to find employment in an office, or even a hospital, especially with the war on, and there being such a shortage of workers. However, I would undoubtedly have to travel to London to seek out that sort of position. I was quite thrilled when I saw your advertisement, since this position would be so close to my home. I could see my Mum on off-days. As you must know, there are very few employment opportunities in this village."

Lord Claybourne looked the papers over carefully, and then set them aside on the desk. "You are most definitely qualified. But have you had any actual experience at performing the duties this job requires?"

"Not working away from my home, Milord. But before my parents married, my mother was the ladies' maid to the Duchess de Gurnai at *Barrow Manor*, and she taught me all of the things that she knew about working in a country house. In addition, my father taught me the skills of a first rate nurse, so I believe that qualifies me to serve someone like your wife, who I'm told requires bed rest and special care. As I said, my original plans were to become a doctor, so I'm quite well-versed in medical matters."

"That's excellent, Miss Barton. So, am I to assume that you would be prepared to not only take over the duties of a nurse, but also those of a ladies' maid, if needed? My wife does require a special sort of person."

"Yes. I don't believe that would present any difficulty. I have the knowledge I'd need to act as a ladies' maid. I know I'm well-versed in nursing duties."

"All right. Let me tell you about the position and ask you a few questions, if you don't mind."

"Of course, Milord. I don't mind at all." She was trying hard not to tremble.

"Did Halsey or Mrs. Briggs explain the situation to you?"

"Just that you were in need of a private nurse for your wife, Lady Claybourne. And that she is rather frail. They didn't go into any particulars beyond that."

"Right then. Eleanor, my wife, is with child. She is very frail and quite lonely. We haven't been married a long while. She's American by birth. I brought her here to my family estate from Lynchburg, Virginia - a place on the Eastern seaboard of America. She misses her family greatly, and finds the English climate disagreeable. It seems she took a cold in her chest shortly after our arrival, and the coughing continues. I suppose it's our damp weather. I despise leaving her in the winter months. Let's pray for a mild winter, and hope that perhaps she'll find our English summers more to her liking. The baby is due in April. I'm afraid I won't be here when the due date arrives, for I'll be with the *Royal Scot's Grey's*, probably in France, and I can't count on returning home on furlough. I've held off joining my regiment as long as I can. I'm a member of the Reserves. I attended *Sandhurst* with the sole idea of making my career with the military, but then my father passed away much younger than I ever expected, and that was that. I'm the eldest son, and it's my duty to oversee *Claybourne Court*. Now the war has come. I'm desperately needed, as is every man. Had I known there would be a war, I'd probably have let Eleanor stay in America until this vile thing is over." He paused. "Or not have married at all. We were married last summer in Virginia, where she lived, and immediately came back to England. Now she's here and what's done is done. Naturally, she needs a ladies' maid to perform all of the regularly expected duties of that position - hair dressing, wardrobe needs and so forth. But, up until now she's refused to let me hire for that situation. She is very independent, and prefers to do things her own way. Thus, I want Eleanor's nurse to be a companion to her, and to perform ladies' maid duties when called upon to do so. As I said - she's lonely. Eleanor is young - not yet twenty. I see that your ages are quite near to one another, so you would undoubtedly share common interests. Can you tell me what some of your favorite pastimes and interests are?"

"Yes, Milord." For a moment Lily's mind went blank. She was so terribly nervous that she simply couldn't think. Her mouth was dry and she took a sip of the now cold tea. But once she began, the words rolled off her tongue. "Well, I love to read. I adore animals, especially small dogs, but any dogs, really. In fact, I once considered becoming a veterinarian. I also adore children, so your wife and I might enjoy discussing preparations for motherhood. I take great pleasure in gardening, and also flower arranging. I suppose it's natural that I have a great curiosity about medicine, and helping others. As I said, my father was a physician. I imagine one would say that I have quite feminine interests - clothing, fashion, and the like. Also decorating. I have a love of beautiful things, whether in nature, or in art. Shall I continue?"

"No, I can see that you and Eleanor would get on quite nicely. She is a very restless sort of girl. Do you think that would bother you at all?"

"I'm not certain what you mean by 'restless'."

"I should say that she frequently changes her mind about what she wishes to do. Her moods can vary. Although at the moment she's frail, she can be quite a high-spirited lady. Her frailness and forced bed rest are making her unhappy, and even more restless."

"Are you saying that she likes adventure?" Lily asked.

"Yes. Yes, I would say that. It's one reason that expecting a baby is somewhat difficult for her. She doesn't especially like confinement. Of course, normally that wouldn't be an issue, but the doctors have said that she is in a rather precarious position, in terms of health. This is our first child. She's been told she has to have a lot of bed rest. And of course, no horseback riding. She is a splendid horse woman."

"I can see where that would be hard for her. Perhaps other interests might be found during this period," Lily answered.

"That would be my hope. She was used to traveling a lot with her parents and I worry that being limited to only this home and the surrounding area may be difficult. I have a home in London, but she needs rest, as I said. Even if she didn't, I shouldn't like the idea of her being in London when we're at war. I assume you're aware that if Germany decides to attack us, which is a possibility, London will be a prime target?"

"Yes, of course. I'm happy to be living in the country. May I ask, Milord, would this be a position that requires me to live on the premises?"

"Oh, yes indeed. You wouldn't be considered one of the servants, however. Especially with my being away, I'd rather you be close to her. We've planned a nice chamber on the same floor where our bedchamber is located. If you like, I can have Mrs. Briggs show that to you today."

"You mentioned that you would expect the lady you hire to act as both ladies' maid and nurse to your wife. Has she not had a ladies' maid until now?" Lily asked.

"No. My mother tried to explain to her the way things are done here in England, but she wanted no part of it. She is very independent. She said she didn't want anyone choosing her clothing, or telling her how to style her hair."

"I see. Then I assume I won't be responsible for those tasks?"

"You may be, if she wishes it. I'd like to know that you're capable. As she grows larger with the child, she may change her views."

"Oh, certainly I'm capable. As I said, my mother taught me all of the duties that a top drawer ladies' maid would perform."

"Splendid," he smiled. "May I ask, without becoming too personal, are you engaged to be married or anything of that sort?"

"No, Milord. I was always too busy with school, working with my father, and looking ahead to medical study."

"The only reason I ask is because while I'm away, I'd hope there isn't any disruption in the routine here at *Claybourne Court*. I wouldn't want to employ you, and then have you leave us because of marriage, or having your own child."

Lily felt herself blush. "Oh, no. I've never given those things much thought. Perhaps someday. I'd like to put enough money away to study medicine. I haven't given up all hope of that, but it wouldn't be possible until after the war."

"That's an admirable goal, Miss Barton. I hope you're able to accomplish it. But until then, I think you'll do very well here at *Claybourne Court*."

"Does that mean that you're offering me the position?" Lily was thrilled, but kept her hands folded neatly.

"Yes. I apologize. I sometimes get ahead of myself. Yes. I think you would do quite nicely. Do you have any other questions for me? I'll leave the details regarding wages, off-days, and so forth up to Mrs. Briggs. She'll introduce you to the other staff. I'll expect you to take your meals with Mrs. Briggs, or with Eleanor, if that's her wish. Mrs. Briggs is the primary person who oversees all staff at *Claybourne Court.* If there is ever anything you need, just ask her. She's been with our family for over twenty years. I should also tell you that I have a younger brother who lives in London. He'll probably come and go. His name is Sebastian, and if he makes any difficulty, you're to tell Mrs. Briggs, or Halsey. They'll deal with him."

"May I ask what sort of problems he might be likely to cause?"

"Nothing terribly threatening," he laughed. "He's very immature, and is having a bit of trouble with the fact that as the eldest son, I inherited the title and estate. He's also terrified at the prospect of going to war. Don't pay him any mind. My mother also lives on the property. She is, of course, the Dowager Countess, Lady Cynthia. She lives in the Dower House and doesn't come up to the main house often. When I'm gone, I assume that she'll drop in more frequently to make certain that Eleanor is doing all right. Mother was not pleased that I chose to marry an American, as I'm certain she will only be too happy to tell you. Since Eleanor is so new to her position, she sometimes falters in terms of etiquette and Mother can be quick with her tongue. I believe all of this will change in time. Try not to take sides in their silly, little war, if that's what it can be called. Mother is really a darling and it's hard for her to turn the reins over to a young, inexperienced American."

"I believe I understand, Milord. Shall I meet the Dowager Lady before I begin my duties?"

"Probably not," he smiled. "She's in London at present. I think she's rather glad that she'll be able to resume some of the duties of the Countess, since Eleanor will be laid up during her confinement. Of course, I shall write to Eleanor as often as humanly possible, and also to you. I hope that I can count on you to keep me abreast of anything that needs my attention. I'll be relying upon you heavily for news of what is happening here at *Claybourne Court.*"

"I'll try to keep you informed, Milord," she answered. Finally, she unfolded her hands. "You wouldn't expect me to be telling confidences the Countess shares with me, would you? I don't think I'd feel comfortable with that, Milord."

"No, nothing of the sort. I'm certain Eleanor will be sharing her feelings and thoughts in her letters to me. I just want your perspective on how she is getting on. Oh - and I assume you know that the normal way of addressing you in your new position will be to refer to you by your last name. So, from here on in, you will be 'Barton'. That may take some getting used to. Frankly, I've never liked the practice, but as my mother would say, 'It's the done thing.'"

"I was aware of that. My Mum taught me those points of etiquette, Milord."

"Also – 'Barton', you needn't address me as 'Milord'. That would be correct, except that I'm in the *Royal Scot's Grey's*, and my rank is that of a Captain. So, at least through the duration of this war, I shall be Captain Claybourne."

"Very good, Captain. I'll try to remember that." Lily was much more relaxed than she had been at the beginning of their conversation. She was anxious to meet the Countess, and to actually begin her duties, but was also still nervous, as it was a position she'd never held before.

"All right. Then let me ring for Mrs. Briggs, and have her show you your rooms. If possible, I should like you to start tomorrow."

"Yes. I believe that would be fine. What time would you be wanting me?"

"Early, I'm afraid. I'd like you here to help serve Eleanor's breakfast, which she normally takes in her room about eight o'clock. Is that agreeable to you?"

"Yes, indeed, Captain. I'll pack up my belongings tonight, and be here at *Claybourne Court* by seven o'clock a.m. Will that do?"

"Perfectly. Now, let me ring for Mrs. Briggs, and she can wrap up all of the other details you'll need to know. I'm pleased you'll be joining the household, Miss Barton. I think you're exactly what my wife needs and I'll be leaving with less anxiety about her." He reached out and shook Lily's hand.

"I shall do my best, Captain. I'm very happy to have this position and thank you for your confidence in me," she replied, returning the handshake.

Mrs. Briggs entered the room, and smiled at her. "Did you ring for me, Captain?" she asked the Earl.

"Yes, Mrs. Briggs. I'd like you to show Miss Barton around the house. In particular, show her the rooms we have readied for her. That will be all for today, except for going over the incidentals, such as wages, hours, off-days, and so forth." He got up from the desk. "It's been a pleasure, Miss Barton.

"Thank you again, Captain. Excuse me, but when will you be joining your regiment?"

"Within a week. The regiment landed in France on August seventeenth. Their first contact with the German Army was on the twenty-second, near Mons. There has been a tremendous need for riflemen at the front lines and the *Scot's Grey's*, while a Calvary Unit, have been used almost exclusively as Infantry. At the moment, my understanding is that they're at *Ypres*. The *Scots Greys* have been rotating back and forth into the trenches. Due to the shortage of infantry, the regiment will continue to fill the gaps in the line, fighting in a dismounted role. I don't foresee any furloughs," he smiled. "Any other questions, Miss Barton?"

"No Captain. Thank you again. I promise I won't disappoint you."

"I have no concern about that. I'll turn you over to Mrs. Briggs now." He gathered papers from the desk and left the room.

Mrs. Briggs turned to Lily, and said, "Well, Barton, you appear to have passed his keen eye with flying colors. I'm happy to know you'll be joining our staff. Come, let me show you the lay of the land." She motioned for Lily to follow her. They walked up a broad staircase, carpeted in crimson, stopping on the second floor. She put her fingers to her lips. "Shhhh. Lady Claybourne is in that room," she said, pointing to a closed doorway. "She's resting." They practically tiptoed past, and continued on to another room, three doors away from Lady Claybourne's. Mrs. Briggs opened the door and Lily was led into a lovely room. More lovely than she'd ever dared hope. Her room in the cottage she shared with her mother wasn't nearly as grand. She'd never had one like this. It was all done up in pink florals - wallpaper, bed fittings, curtains. There was even a private bath adjoining it, also decorated in pink. Lily was thrilled. Mrs. Briggs opened a large cupboard, which one could clearly see would fit a wardrobe much, much larger than Lily's. She assumed that it would be holding only her uniforms, and perhaps one day-dress, for off-days. She said as much to Mrs. Briggs.

"Oh, no, dear. As a private nurse, you won't be expected to wear uniforms. Normal day dresses will be fine. If you're engaged in some sort of duty that calls for protection of clothing, you will wear a white, starched apron. The Earl gives a clothing allowance for you to cover six new dresses a year. If you're in need of something now, I can advance you the money."

"Well, I suppose I will need to get some new frocks. I have three day dresses, all of which would be appropriate - dark colors, and simple in design. But, if I'm not to wear the same thing over and over, I shall need at least two more."

"I'll give you five pounds before you leave today. It's early, so you should have time to run into the village and find something appropriate."

"Oh, my. That's just splendid," Lily answered. She'd never dreamed she would be given a clothing allowance. She followed Mrs. Briggs down another flight of stairs, behind a green baize door, to the servant's area. There Mrs. Briggs introduced Lily to all of the other staff, some of which were hard at work, while others drank tea at a large wooden table. Lily tried to memorize their names, but knew it would take a while to keep them straight in her head. There was Cissy and Martha, Parlor Maids; Mary, the Cook; Sarah, the undercook, and two other kitchen helpers, Sally and Molly. There was also a Valet for the Captain, whose name was Michael Richmond. He would be leaving with the Captain when he reported for duty with the *Royal Grey's*. Lastly, there were two footmen, named John Worth and Edward Vyner. In addition, there were outside gardeners, whom she did not meet that day, and a chauffeur, Edward Luther. Later, after the baby came, a nanny would be taken on, and in time, a governess. Everyone seemed very nice, and Lily wasn't intimidated. Most were near her age, or a bit older, with the exception of the Captain's valet, Michael, who seemed quite a bit older. And of course, Halsey, the butler.

Mrs. Briggs led Lily to her small cubbyhole of an office, and asked her to sit down. She offered another cup of tea, and then began to explain about the wages. They were more than she had hoped. Mrs. Briggs said that Lily's off day would be Sunday. She also told her that because Eleanor was in a frail state, Lily would undoubtedly have more extra time, because the Countess rested a lot. During those times, she asked that Lily not leave the grounds of the Court, but that she would be free to read, walk in the gardens, or visit the stables. Lady Claybourne would always tell her when she would be expected back on duty.

It all sounded perfectly clear to Lily and she wasn't worried that she couldn't carry out her duties. If she was worried about anything, it was meeting the Countess, as she had a rather mixed picture from the Earl. She had a hunch that the Countess might be a bit of a handful, but she would play it by ear, and try to become her friend, as much as a private duty nurse and a Countess could ever be friends.

2

After leaving *Claybourne Court*, Lily ran to the village, where she purchased three serviceable black skirts, along with coordinating blouses in white, pale blue, and yellow cotton. They were long sleeved with high Victorian necklines, trimmed with a bit of lace. The dresses she already owned were all long sleeved, shirtwaist styles, made of cotton, in subdued colors, such as grey, navy, or black. Fashions were beginning to change with the continuation of the war. At the beginning, there was still a strong Edwardian influence. Hemlines were creeping upward, and long skirts were ending at the instep. Skirts were fuller and bell shaped. Lily still had money left over from the five pounds Mrs. Briggs had given her, so she used it to buy some new undergarments. After that, she again ran back to the cottage to tell her mother the exciting news. She knew that her Mum would be so relieved that her daughter had found good employment in their home village.

"Oh Lily, what grand news," her Mum exclaimed, placing her hand over her heart. "You'll be close to me if I should ever need you and on Sundays we can still have a regular tea after church."

"Yes, Mum. But, I wonder, now that it's only the two of us, if you wouldn't rather eat out someplace. I'll be earning enough for a special treat once a week, and memories will be a bit sad if it's only the two of us at our big, dining table."

"You may be right, Lily. Perhaps we can do a bit of both - staying at home and eating out."

"Right you are. Let's plan on 'out' this Sunday, since it will be a sort of celebration of my first week on the job. I should have lots to tell you. Now, come to my room with me, while I pack my things. I won't be wearing uniforms, so I'll need to pack a goodly amount."

Together they climbed the narrow, cramped staircase, which led to the second story of the cottage. Upstairs there were three, small bedrooms. One was where her mother slept, and one had been Jordan's. The other, of course, was Lily's. She opened the door to her room, and rummaged around in the cupboard until she found what she was looking for - an old, rather battered valise, but it was a good size and she was certain she could fit everything into it. Then she began to lay various articles of clothing on the bed. First were the three new ensembles, purchased that afternoon. While she packed, she chattered to her mother about the new job.

"Oh Mum, everyone seems so nice. Very helpful. The Earl - Lord - Captain Christopher Claybourne will be off to war soon. He's asked that I refer to him as Captain. He's a Captain in the *Royal Scot's Grey's*. He says he'll be going over to France - poor man. From Jordy's experience we know that it's a dreadful place."

"Yes. There's no doubt of that. Muddy trenches, and apparently no headway on either side. Just a stalemate. It's all so foolish. You'll be taking care of the Countess's needs on your own then?"

"Yes. I'm a bit concerned about that." She reached into a drawer that held her nightwear, and also took her dressing gown off a hanger. She placed the arms flat, next to one another, as she'd been taught, and laid it neatly in the valise. "She refused her husband's offer of a ladies' maid, and I hope she doesn't expect perfection from me in that capacity."

"Surely you'll be very competent at whatever is expected of you," her Mum replied. "A good hair brushing, and helping with choice of clothing isn't overwhelming. I've taught you all of those duties, Lily."

"Yes, I know, and I'm quite good at all of it, if I may so myself," she laughed. "I'm not *really* concerned, but from what the Captain told me, she's going through a difficult spell right now. She's American and is very lonely for her family and home. She's also very high-spirited, and wanting lots of change and adventure. Yet, with a baby on the way, she's been told that she must have almost complete bed rest. The Captain said the baby is due in April, so that will mean about six months. Apparently, she's in delicate condition."

"I'm sure you'll do fine, sweetheart. I do hope that you're able to become friends. It would be good for the both of you."

"Yes. Well, I rather doubt a private nurse would ever become true friends with a Countess. I'll have to walk a fine line, you know."

"Of course. Perhaps there will be others at the Court you'll be friendly with as well."

"Perhaps," she answered, as she packed her toiletries. "I liked them all." She paused and looked around at the room. "All right. I believe that does it," she exclaimed, as she snapped the valise shut, swung it off the bed and set it on the floor by the doorway "Now, I'd best be getting on to bed, Mum, as I have to be there at seven o'clock in the morning. I don't want to start off late."

"Will you be wanting to eat here in the morning?"

"No. No. You rest. I'm sure I'll have tea at *Claybourne Court.*"

They put their arms about one another and embraced. "Then you be having a good week, my sweet girl. I'll be thinking of you and looking for you on Sunday."

"And I'll surely be here, Mum. Now, don't you work too hard this week. There will be time to clear out everything later." Jordan's room still had to be gone through, but up to then it had been a task too filled with sorrow.

They hugged again and said 'goodnight', and her Mum closed the door to Lily's room.

The next morning, she was awake at four o'clock. The excitement that filled her was simply too great to allow sleep. She descended the stairway, and made herself a cup of tea. She tried to be very quiet, as it was so terribly early, and her Mum needed the rest. Her mother had experienced so much heartache of late, and Lily hoped that with her wages from *Claybourne Court*, there would be no need for her to go out to work too. There had been a decent amount of money put back when her father died, and they were receiving a small pension for Jordan's military service, which added to their income. It had been years since her Mum had worked out of the home, and Lily didn't want to see that happen now. The cottage was unencumbered, since her father had paid cash when it was purchased. So that resolved one large living expense from her Mum's worries. With Lily's quite impressive wages from *Claybourne Court*, they should have no financial worries.

Lily sat at the old, scratched kitchen table and thought about what her new life would be like. Would she be able to be a proper companion for Lady Claybourne? After all, Lily was, by nature, an introvert. She didn't care for meeting new people - felt all undone by such circumstances. However, once she learned to know others, she generally warmed to them. She had a very kind, generous spirit. She was certain that's what would happen in this case. It was only the beginning moments that frightened her a bit. She greatly admired Captain Claybourne, which meant that Eleanor must be the sort of person she would also admire. Lily had never known anyone from America. She'd studied about that country in school, and even had a vague idea of where Virginia was located. She remembered that there were mountains and valleys, and that it was a lovely spot. She looked forward to learning more about the Countess's homeland. Lily checked her timepiece, and decided that it was time to leave, if she were to allow herself the enjoyment of not having to rush on an autumn day.

She left the cottage and followed the same route she had taken the day before. Her Mum was sending the valise by hired cart later in the day. There were wildflowers blooming by the roadside and the trees were still in full leaf, yet they had turned to their annual red, russet, and gold. It was a splendid, blue, English day and Lily's spirits were high. Reporting for duty on a new job was an exciting event. She reached *Claybourne Court*, set in extensive parkland and backed by gentle, rolling hills.

Lily rapped on the large front door. The lesser servants were expected to use the door in the back of the house, but she'd been told to use the front entrance. The doorway opened and Halsey stood in front of her, ready to welcome her to *Claybourne Court*. She entered the great hall, where a breathtaking staircase swept down to the marble floor. Portraits, tapestries, and fine pieces of furniture nearly overwhelmed the senses. There was a sculpture gallery containing magnificent specimens from classical times and a library, which had an especially fine collection of books. She followed Halsey to Mrs. Briggs' small office. When she saw Lily, she rose from her desk, smiled and shook Lily's hand, saying that she was very glad to see her.

"Please sit down, Barton. Would you care for some tea and a fresh scone?"

"Oh, indeed I would, Mrs. Briggs. That's very kind of you," Lily answered. "I left our cottage early, so as not to wake my Mum, so there was no stopping to prepare breakfast."

"Will a scone and tea be enough, then? I could have Mary prepare a proper English breakfast for you."

"Oh no, Mrs. Briggs. I'm not such a big eater. A scone and tea would be lovely."

She rang the kitchen, and within ten minutes Lily had her meal. As she ate her scone, Mrs. Briggs prepared Lily for the day ahead. "Now, I shall take you to meet the Countess, and then leave you alone with her to become acquainted. Her husband always checks with her the moment he returns to *Claybourne Court* after a day in London, so have her dressed and in the chair by the window at five o'clock. Of course, he'll be leaving soon, but until I tell you differently, you're to follow that regimen every day. If she asks you to lace her up, remember she is expecting a baby, and we don't want to do anything that might interfere with her condition. Even if she tells you that she thinks her dress should fit more snugly, pay her no mind. She's quite a vain one. She's used to being independent, and may balk at someone else trying in any way to assist her. Try to include her in decision-making. Also, she has a little dog which she treats as a human." She laughed heartily, and Lily tilted her head to the side, curious as to her meaning.

"She treats the dog like a human?" Lily echoed.

"Yes. That's the truth. I suppose she's lonely, and the dog serves as a companion to her. Lord Claybourne allows her to do as she wishes with the animal. If it makes her happy, that seems to be the only thing that matters. Apparently you told him you liked small dogs, so I'm assuming you won't have any difficulty accepting her love of the Spaniel. Its name is Virginia, after her place of birth. We all call her Ginny."

"I see," I answered. "No, I won't have any difficulty with the dog. I adore animals."

"Well, this one is extremely spoiled, but I'm sure you'll manage."

Lily finished her tea, and together they climbed the staircase to the Countess's room. Mrs. Briggs knocked briefly, and then opened the door. "Lady Eleanor, I've brought someone for you to meet. She will be your new nurse." A head rose up from the pillow and blankets.

"Oh. Will you be caring for me, then?" a voice asked.

"Yes, indeed, Milady. I hope we'll get along together very nicely."

Eleanor Claybourne was lovely. Strikingly lovely. She had long, golden curls that tumbled down to her shoulders, and very large blue eyes. Her skin glowed, as though lit from within, although she appeared to be somewhat pale. There was no question that she was in a delicate way. Her face was too narrow, from missing too many meals Lily conjectured, and her arms were definitely too thin, in spite of the fact that she was already showing that she was with child. Lily thought that she would set to helping put meat on the Countess's bones. Surely it couldn't be good for her not to take proper nourishment when she was expecting a baby.

Mrs. Briggs said that she had duties to attend to, and left the room. Lily was alone with the Countess, and could think of nothing to say. The little dog she'd heard about, popped its head from the covers, and began to bark.

"Hush, Ginny. This is our new nurse, Barton. She's come to care for us," Lady Claybourne said, petting the little brown and white dog on the head. It was a St. Charles Spaniel, and Lily lost her heart at once.

"Oh, may I pet her, Milady? I'm so very fond of dogs. She is a real beauty."

"Certainly. Go right ahead. But, I must warn you, Ginny is not terribly fond of strangers. If she growls, you might want to step back. She's been known to nip."

Lily reached over and let the little dog sniff her hand. She held the palm up, and gave Ginny plenty of time to adjust to her presence. Finally, Ginny's tail began to wag. Then Lily put her hand on her head, and scratched behind her ears. Ginny closed her pretty, brown eyes, and looked to be perfectly happy with Lily.

"Well, I am totally astounded. She doesn't take eagerly to strangers. You must have a magical way with animals. Her full name is Virginia, but I call her Ginny."

"Yes, Mrs. Briggs told me about her. No, not magical. I just try to be very patient with them, and show them that I can be trusted. Dogs are such loving creatures. I adore them, Milady, and I believe they have a lot of love to give in return, if one respects them."

"Well, I *am* impressed," she answered. Her manner of speaking was different than any Lily had heard before. It was a soft, drawn out intonation. Lily thought it was very pretty. Later, she learned that all persons from the American South spoke in such a fashion.

"It's time for my morning coffee, I think," the Countess exclaimed. Just at that moment, there was a knock on the door and it was Molly from the kitchen, carrying a large silver tray. She handed it to Lily, and she managed to place it on the bedside table, while she straightened Lady Eleanor's bedding, and set up the bed tray to accommodate dishes from the silver tray. There was toast, oatmeal, cut-up fruit and coffee. She ate very little, feeding most of the toast to Ginny, and a good bit of the fruit.

"Would you prefer something different on your tray tomorrow," Lily asked. "Perhaps a scrambled egg?"

"No, this is sufficient. I'm not a very large eater. I know that the baby needs nourishment, but I just have very little appetite."

There was silence. "Have you ever had a baby, Barton?" she asked of Lily.

"No, Milady. But, I'm mad about children. I think it's a very happy thing to look ahead to. Just imagine. Next summer at this time, you'll have a little one to walk over the grounds with, and enjoy summer afternoons reading stories."

"Hopefully, I shall be able to return to London by then. Pushing a baby around in a pram doesn't excite me greatly. Yes, Barton, summer will return and the trees will be trimmed in green. New songs will be taught to the birds, and flowers will bloom beautifully. But, summer means very little to me in this faraway, strange land. I long for the sun of home. I long for the banks of the Shenandoah. I feel like a caged bird."

Her voice sounded so melancholy and Lily felt dreadfully sorry for her. Tears welled in her eyes, and were about to stream down her pretty, but pale cheeks. "Virginia sounds like a beautiful place," Lily answered. "Perhaps in time, you'll find that English summers have their own special beauty."

"Don't you see, Barton? I gambled my freedom away. What good is a lovely summer, if one is trapped in a place they abhor? I'm afraid in this world of strangers. Everything is so different. I miss my home, and my sisters and brothers - my entire carefree life at Lynchburg."

"Yes, Milady. I can understand how difficult that would be. When did you arrive in England?" Lily asked.

"We were married last June in Lynchburg. Oh, Barton, it was a glorious wedding. The English think that they are the last word in etiquette, but in the South - the southern United States - there is nothing lovelier than a wedding that takes place on a sprawling Plantation like *Cloverhill* - my family home. Well, my former home. And to marry an English Earl. Well, all of my friends were green with envy. Who could blame them? That doesn't happen often. Father raises fine thoroughbred horses, and my husband - well, then he was just an Earl visiting from England - came to *Cloverhill,* wanting to see our horses. Not only did he purchase a fine stallion, he carried off the prettiest girl in the County as well. I know I sound vain, Barton. Well, I *am* vain, but it is the truth. Of course Kit might have had any girl he desired. I only wish we might have stayed in Virginia." There was silence again. She had grown animated when describing the happiness of her marriage, but Lily wondered if that happiness had already fled. She pushed her tray back, and Lily took it from her, placing it on the side table. It was not Lily's job to return trays and the like, but she didn't mind. If no one had come to claim it by the time Lily left the room, she would carry it to the kitchen herself.

"Do you think you will be able to return for a visit to America after the baby comes, Milady?" Lily asked.

"I doubt it very much. Here England has gone and involved itself in a war. I doubt that I'll be able to return home until after the trouble has all come to an end. Who knows how long that will be? Now, Kit will be leaving for some Godforsaken place in France, so I won't even have him and he's the reason I gave up my home to begin with. Now my health is very precarious. The doctors say I must rest during the entire duration of my pregnancy. I've been so discontent. I weep a lot. There has been no one to whom I can pour my heart out. But, now I have you and I do hope that we shall grow to be good friends."

"Yes. I hope that too, Milady." However, it still seemed a difficult line to walk, trying to be a friend as well as a nurse to a Countess. Lily helped her into a dressing gown, and then over to the chintz covered chair near the fireplace. Even though it was October the huge fire roaring in the fireplace made the room very warm and stuffy. The little Spaniel, Ginny, hopped down off the bed, and then hopped back up to her mistress's lap. "Did Mrs. Briggs tell you that one of your duties will be to give Ginny her walks?" asked Lady Claybourne.

"She didn't mention it, Milady, but I'll be more than happy to do so. You'll just have to tell me if there are regular times for her outings."

"I like her to go outside four times a day. In about an hour would be fine. And then again, about four o'clock. After her dinner at about 7:00, and before her bedtime, about 10:00 at night. Will that suit?"

"Perfectly fine, Milady. Does she have a lead and collar?"

"Yes. Look over in the basket by the bookcase. Yes. There. You see them?"

Lily found them quite easily, and placed them on the mantle, so she could reach them quickly when the time came. "Milady, does the doctor allow you to take fresh air in a rolling chair? If so, perhaps I could wheel you about the grounds. It's quite lovely outside for October, unusually warm. The flowers are still beautiful."

"No one has suggested such a thing. If there isn't a chair, we can get one. I'd so love to be able to go outside. I've been caged up here for over two months now."

"Oh, Milady, that *is* a long while. I do so hope that your doctors will give their permission." Lily frowned.

"Yes, would you please find out for me, Barton?" Lady Eleanor looked at her expectantly.

"Indeed I shall, Milady."

"Will you help to dress me now, Barton? I so hate looking like a fat, dowdy frump. I don't like asking your help. But, I'm not supposed to do it myself. I don't understand why, since I'm not that far along. But I am showing a bit. It isn't that. My doctor is afraid I could miscarry."

"Oh, Milady, I'm happy to. And it could never be that you're fat and dumpy. That could never be. You're a beautiful woman. I've always felt a woman who is expecting a baby is lovelier than any other."

"Oh, Fiddle, Barton. I've heard that all of my life. I've probably even said it to others. Now that I'm expecting myself, I know how silly that really is."

"I'm sorry you think it's silly, but I really do feel that way."

"I apologize, Barton. I'm just feeling very sorry for myself. Forgive me. Let's get me dressed."

"That's fine, Milady. Do you have a choice of apparel for the day?"

"Ummmm." She placed her finger on her chin, and pursed her lovely lips. "Yes. Let's try the green muslin. Long sleeves, high collar, and of course, no waist." She laughed a little.

Lily opened her cupboard, and saw hundreds of dresses hanging there. Of course some were probably fashions she'd had before her present condition, but still – Lily had never seen so many clothes in one place. It wasn't difficult to find the dress Lady Eleanor described. All of the maternity clothes were hanging in one location. Lily extracted the dress, and laid it upon the bed cover. "Is this the correct one, Milady?"

"Yes, that's it. So dreary. I'll be so happy to be able to wear a lovely dress with a waistline again."

Lily didn't answer. It seemed clear that the Countess was in a negative mood. Lily asked her where her undergarments were kept, and she pointed to a chest by the door. Lily found a loose fitting slip, and some silk knickers.

"Let's get you into the bath now. Or, are you more accustomed to having someone bathe you in your bed?"

"I can no longer bathe in the tub. The doctor doesn't allow it. So, you'll have to bed-bathe me."

Lily was happy that her father had taught her the fundamentals of such care, and after she'd helped Lady Eleanor back to the bed, she went about getting a pan of warm water, and a bar of lavender soap. She washed her gently and modestly, and rinsed her with clear lavender water.

"No one has used that before, Barton. That's lovely. Did you bring that with you?"

"Yes, I did. I think it makes one feel so fresh and feminine."

"It definitely does. Thank you."

"That quite alright, Milady. Now, let's get you dressed." Lily helped her stand, and then slipped the dress over her head. It was lovely and she looked exquisite.

"Shall we do your hair now?" Lily asked.

"Yes, I suppose. I've been doing it myself, but as long as you're here . . . It makes so little sense, since I've nowhere to go."

Lily sat her down in a chair in front of a dressing table, and unpinned her thick locks. They tumbled down her back in a waterfall. Lily thoroughly brushed it until it crackled, and then pinned up the sides and back into a Gibson Girl. The style was a bit dated, but since the Countess was not going anywhere special, Lily felt it was becoming and would do.

Lady Eleanor reached up and loosened a few tendrils about her face. She truly looked lovely.

"Do you want to go back to you chair now, Milady?"

"Yes. And please bring me my lap desk. I'd like to write a letter to my family."

Lily found a lovely, French lap desk sitting on a chair, and brought it to her. Then she instructed Lily where to find her stationery, pen and ink. The stationery was heavy vellum in a crème color. It had her name and title engraved at the top - *Eleanor, the Countess of Gloucester, Claybourne Court, Claybourne-on-Colne, U.K.* Lily tried to imagine how anyone could be unhappy when they had everything the Countess had; a handsome husband, who seemed to dote upon her; beautiful clothing; no worries about money; the excitement of a baby to look forward to; an incredible, age-old mansion, and a bevy of servants to see to her every want and need. For a moment, Lily felt a bit angry with Lady Eleanor. But, then she remembered that the Countess was very young, and was far away from the family she loved.

"If you would take Ginny for her walk now, that would be splendid," she suggested. "I'll be busy writing for quite some time. When you bring her back, I'll probably be ready for a lie-down before luncheon."

Ginny came to Lily very easily. She buckled the dog's collar, and snapped on her lead. Lady Eleanor gave Ginny a kiss goodbye, and they were off on their walk.

3

Lily took the dog out the side door from the kitchen, and discovered that there was a large fenced area there, probably designed for the dog to run when she wasn't on a lead. They stopped, so Ginny could do her business, and then went through a large wooden gate that led to the rolling grounds surrounding *Claybourne Court*. The little dog was beside herself - sniffing the grass, and biting petals off the flowers. Lily laughed aloud, as Ginny scurried to and fro among the shrubs and plantings, and rolled on her tummy atop the green grass, her long ears flapping in the breeze. Lily could already see that the dog was covered with debris that she had picked up along the way, and knew she would require a good brushing when they returned. Lily didn't mind in the least, as it provided her with something to do. As Ginny calmed down after her frantic running and tugging at her lead, they were able to walk more sedately and Lily admired the lovely plantings. There were masses of roses climbing up the side of the house on an enormous trellis. The fragrance they gave off was divine. There was an old bed of *David Austin* roses planted to the right of the front entrance and she stopped to smell their glorious scent. As she stood with a lovely pink rose in her hand, she heard a voice behind her. "Are you enjoying Claybourne's prize roses, then, Barton?" It was the Earl, or rather the Captain. Lily jumped at his surprise greeting.

"Oh, I didn't expect you, Captain. Home early, are you?" she asked.

"Yes, Miss Barton. Since I'm to leave in such a short while, I've been trying to spend as much time with the Countess as possible. I see you've met. How are you and Ginny getting along?"

"She's a darling, Captain. I think we've already become friends. Your wife was surprised that we took to one another so quickly."

"And, how are you and my wife getting on?"

"Very well, Captain. She does seem very lonely and frail. I shall try my hardest to be a good companion to her."

"Excellent. Now, let me take over the walking of Ginny and I'll return her to my wife. If she wants a lie-down, I'll go down to my library and work on some papers. Then I'll return and have dinner in Eleanor's room. It will be a nice surprise. You won't have any need to return until time to prepare her for bed. Enjoy the fine weather. Acquaint yourself with our beautiful grounds. There's a gazebo in the back, and stables. You might want to wander down and meet our splendid specimens of horseflesh."

"That sounds wonderful, Captain. Are you certain the Countess won't mind?"

"Yes. She likes it when I surprise her like this. I've brought her a nice gift - a very fine piece of jewelry. I'll let her show it to you."

"Right then. I'll be off and I'll return to her this evening. If you should need me, I'll only be gone for a short spell. Then I'll return to my own room. You can ring me there."

"That will be fine, Miss Barton. Enjoy your afternoon."

He disappeared into the house, and Lily strolled in the direction he'd said the stables were located. She'd no idea that the grounds were so massive. There was even a small, artificial lake, with benches near the edge. Elm, Ash, Birch and Willow trees were scattered about haphazardly, to give the impression that they had simply sprouted there, but it was perfectly obvious that a very artistic gardener had carefully positioned them. Lily couldn't imagine that the Countess didn't find the setting serene and peaceful. It was hard to believe that her home in Virginia could possibly have been any more delightful.

Soon, the stables came into view. They were housed in a long, low building, with a high-pitched roof and painted a gleaming white. Lily entered through the gate entrance in front of her. There were eight stalls, holding the same number of spectacular horses. A young man whom she took to be the stable keeper approached her. "Might I be 'elping you, Miss?" he asked.

"Not really. I've just come to look about. I'm Lily Barton – 'Barton' to the staff. I'm the new ladies' maid to the Countess. His Lordship told me I might come and visit the stables. What beautiful horses he has."

"Yes, Miss. 'Ere, I'll show you about. Down to the far end, you'll be finding the newest addition. 'Is name is Spark of Fire. He come over from America."

"Oh, he must be the horse his Lordship brought back when he married the Countess," Lily replied.

"Yes, Miss. 'E's a corker, that one. I'll be workin' with 'im while Lord Claybourne is abroad. Needs some calmin' down. Next to 'im is our old Sugar in the Morning. She's the oldest of the lot."

She was a white mare, with beige markings on her face.

"And 'ere we 'ave Miss Katie. She's a Welsh pony. Sweet to look at, but wants 'er own way. Stubborn. Next to her is our darlin' Taffeta. She's the best temperament of all. If you're ever wantin' to ride, it's her I'd recommend. Never throwed nobody in her life." He took a lump of sugar from his pocket, and gave it to the chestnut mare. Lily reached up and petted her velvet nose. She already knew she'd fallen in love with the horse.

"And what are the others named?" Lily asked.

"Next stall over is Wesley. Wesley's a good one. We bred 'im last year to Miss Isabelle, and you'll be seeing the result in the last stall."

Wesley was gorgeous. He was quite a large horse - a Bay, with dark, brown coat and a black mane and tail. Lily walked to the next stall over, and there was Miss Isabelle, a very pretty horse with fine legs and a white stripe down her nose. She was mostly brown, but there was some white mixed in. In the last stall was the little filly the stable boy had been referring to. They had named her Sprite because she was high-spirited, and had come so quickly. She was a pinto - brown and white like her mother, with more white. Lily reached out and petted her nose too, and asked if she could have some sugar lumps for all of them.

"Sure can, Miss. I carry 'em about just for such purpose." He gave her a handful.

She walked back down to the first stall, gave one to Spark of Fire, and continued on to the end, where Sprite was lucky enough to get two. Lily turned to the stable boy and asked, "And what shall I call you, Sir?"

"Don't be calling me no Sir." He laughed. "I'd think you was daft. Me name's 'Oward. 'Oward Eden."

"It's awfully nice to meet you, Howard. I hope to be seeing more of you."

"I'm 'ere in the stables most all time. I even sleep 'ere. If you got time on an off day, I'll put you on 'Taffeta', and let you go round the ring."

"I'd really love that, Howard. I've never ridden a horse before, but I'd like to learn."

"You'll be needin' to. Her Ladyship is a champion rider. She'll be wantin' you to go with her on a ride soon as the babe comes."

"Well, then I shall be certain to come have you give me lessons," Lily answered. Howard was a funny, little man, with bright red hair, and rather prominent teeth. She knew she was going to like him, and definitely planned to learn to ride. She said goodbye to him, and wandered back to the house, where she went directly to her room. Gingerly, she lay down on the bed. It looked so neatly made up she hated to ruin it. Lily didn't think she was tired, but it wasn't ten minutes before she was fast asleep.

Lily had never needed anybody or anything to wake her up. She always told her parents that she had a clock in her head, because she was always certain to wake before an appointed time. So, true to form, she woke at four o'clock on the dot. She went into the loo and washed her face and hands. They smelled like horse. Then she changed into a second, fresh dress and proceeded to the Countess's room. The door was closed, and she knocked. It was the Captain's voice. "Come in, Miss Barton. You're a tad early, but better early than late."

He was sitting on the side of the bed, next to his wife. "I hope I'm not interrupting anything. I thought I should check back with the Countess, to see if she's needing anything," Lily said.

"No, I'm not, Barton, but come see what my lovely husband has brought to me."

Lily walked into the room, and Lady Eleanor held out her wrist, which was adorned with an exquisite sapphire and diamond bracelet. "Kit says that it matches my eyes," she smiled.

"Oh, Milady, it's just splendid. How kind of him." Lily turned and smiled at the Captain. "Yes. It does compliment her eyes. Now, aren't you cheered up a bit by such a gift?"

"Yes. Yes, I am. I've been so dreadfully melancholy. His gift has cheered me enormously."

"I'm so glad, Milady."

"I'm going to have my lie-down now, Barton, so you won't have to return to me until about 9:00, when it's time to prepare me for bed, since Kit will be having dinner with me."

That's fine, Milady. I'll be back then. Enjoy your rest, and your dinner."

Lily left the room, and stood outside in the hallway for a moment. She couldn't decide what to do next. It was not considered appropriate for her to go into the drawing room, so her only choices were to go back to her own room, to Mrs. Briggs, or to the kitchen, where she really wasn't supposed to be either. Finally, she decided to return to her room and read. She'd been told that she was welcome to borrow any book she wished from the library, and after she finished the one she was reading, she planned to start on all of the wonderful classics she'd seen there.

Lily had just settled herself into a comfortable chair, when there was a knock at the door. She straightened her skirt, and opened it. There stood the Captain.

"Hello, Miss Barton. I'm sorry for interrupting, but I really must speak with you."

"Of course, Captain. Of course. Please come in."

He came into the room, and sat down in the chair she had just vacated. Lily pulled a small stool across from him. He ran his fingers through his hair and sighed.

"I haven't told Eleanor yet, but I'm going to have to leave to report to my regiment tomorrow." His voice almost broke, and Lily's heart jumped. He took a deep breath and continued. "I was at the War Department today, and they told me that I'm to take command of a unit of soldiers. There have been so many causalities, and I'm desperately needed. Eleanor will be horrifically upset. I wanted to tell you first, so that you could be prepared. I'm sure you're already aware that she can be very emotional. I wish there were a way that I could send her to her parents for the duration of the war, after the baby comes, but there simply isn't. I'm counting on you to be her brick. Please write to me, at least monthly, and if you can, weekly. I just want to keep up-to-date on how she's progressing."

"I'll be glad to write to you weekly, Captain. More often if it seems necessary. Please. Try not to worry about her. You have to defend your Country. You have an important job to do. I'll do anything I can to help her. I asked her today if she would be interested in having a rolling chair, so that I could take her outside for some sunshine and fresh air. She said she would dearly love that. Is there a chair available, Captain, or a means for getting one?"

"I shall have one delivered tomorrow, Barton. I think that's an excellent suggestion. I should have thought of it before now. She says she is already very fond of you and I'm so relieved to know that. If there are any other things you think we need to keep her comfortable and happy, just tell Mrs. Briggs. She'll take care of anything. I shall tell her that I've given my permission for you to make all decisions regarding the Countess."

"Thank you, Captain. Has she made any plans for preparation of a nursery? I believe that's another thing that might interest her, and keep her busy. She and I might discuss furniture choices, colors, and so forth. I'm certain that the shops will be happy to send photos of baby cots, and swatches of fabric for windows and bedding to *Claybourne Court.* I can take care of the ordering, or visit the shops. She can be wheeled into the room to watch the progress."

"Excellent, Barton. You're a true treasure. I don't know which room she's chosen for the nursery, but do discuss it with her. Also, she will want one of those fancily decorated, rounded cradle-like things by our bed for the first weeks of the baby's life. Do you know what I'm talking about, Barton?"

Lily smiled. "Yes, Captain. It's called a bassinette, I believe."

"Yes. I couldn't remember the name. That's it. Discuss that with her, too."

"I shall, Captain. I promise that everything will be lovely, and completely ready when the little one arrives. Is there anything I can do for you, Captain? I mean, for you personally?"

"No, Barton. The army takes care of all of my needs, and I shall have Michael Richmond, my valet, with me. Seems rather odd to have a valet when one goes to war, doesn't it? A bloody strange way for one to live. Sorry, Barton, that was impolite. I just believe that the English aristocracy is going to have to open their eyes and realize that when we're involved in such a miserable situation, none of us should try to pretend we're still in our secure, privileged world. But, it is the way it is, and so Michael will accompany me."

"I'm certain he wants to do so," Captain.

"Yes, I imagine so. Although, I think he'd rather be fighting for his country, too."

"This is his way of fighting for England, don't you think?"

"Yes, I suppose. Well - Take good care of yourself, Barton. I believe God sent you to us just in the nick of time. I'll be looking forward to your letters."

"Will you still be dining with the Countess in her rooms this evening, Captain?"

"Yes, of course. I'll also help her prepare for bed. I'm going to sleep in her room tonight."

"Very good, Captain. Shall I see you in the morning?"

"Yes, Barton. But, I won't be able to speak privately with you. Mrs. Briggs has the physician's number and also that of a midwife, although I prefer the doctor. So does Eleanor. I'm happy that you have nursing skills. I hope you might be able to assist when the time comes."

"I would be honored, Captain. Please don't worry. I've assisted my father on births many times. When you come home, you'll have a healthy, lovely baby."

"That's a happy thing to look ahead to," he replied. "It will keep me going in those cursed killing fields." He rose from the chair and readied himself to leave.

"Oh Captain. Please don't say that. You'll come through this - I'm certain of that. I firmly believe that when one is in a terribly difficult situation, God lifts you up and gives you the strength - he takes you to a place and makes you stronger than you were before, and you endure." She had tears in her eyes. She reached out her hand to shake his, but he took hold of it, and pulled her to him, holding her for a moment. It wasn't a romantic gesture. Lily believed he simply felt that a handshake was much too formal at such a time. There was only that one, brief moment. Then he smiled at her and left the room.

Lily sat down on her bed. She was actually shaking, but couldn't have said why. His touch had lit a fire inside her. She'd never felt so strange. Of course he was a very attractive, extremely nice gentleman. But, it wasn't like Lily to go off her head over a married man - and a member of the gentry, at that. She thought for a few minutes, and came to the conclusion that it was simply the emotion associated with his need to fight in such a gruesome war, and to leave his lovely home.

Before she was even dressed and ready to go to the Countess, Lily heard heart-wrenching sobs coming from Lady Eleanor's room. Of course, she knew what the problem was. He must have told her he was leaving. Had he told her the previous evening, she most certainly would have wept the whole night through, so he had decided to wait until the very last moment. Lily could hear her cries and moans, and then his voice, murmuring comforting words. She knew he must be feeling helpless. She hurriedly dressed, and went to the Countess's room, where the sounds of anguish were much more pronounced. Lily knocked, rather timidly. The Captain answered, "Please come in." His voice was filled with despair. She entered the room. He was sitting on the edge of the bed, and the Countess had her head buried on his chest. Her tears were soaking his tunic and he had his arms around her. "Oh, Barton! Kit is leaving for France. I can't bear it. How can I live through this? I want to go home. I want to go to Virginia. I hate England. I came here because of him, and now he's leaving." She sobbed hysterically, and pounded her small fists against his chest.

"Shhhh, be still, darling. You don't mean that. You'll grow to love *Claybourne Court* as much as I do. It's our home. It will be our child's home. Please try to think about it in those terms. You aren't a child any more, Eleanor. Of course, you'll always love your parents, and the place you grew up. But, you have a new home now. And a new family."

"I have *no* family. You are going off and leaving me. I like your brother, Sebastian, but he'll soon turn eighteen, and then he'll have to fight too. Your mother corrects everything I do. She isn't warm and loving, like my own mother."

"Darling, mother is *very* loving. She's just British. You'll learn to adjust to the fact that we British aren't emotional people. We don't show our feelings as much as Americans do."

"Well, I don't have to get used to it. I don't like it. Everything here is strange and odd. And, now you won't be here."

"I'll be back. I promise."

"You can't promise that. I could be left here all alone, with a baby. How could I survive?"

"Eleanor, I need you to be strong. I wish I didn't have to go. But, thousands of men are fighting and dying every day. I have honor and love for my Country too. Freedom is important to me. You must start realizing that I have a responsibility to England."

"Oh, what idiocy. Men are such fools about war. Nothing is ever settled by war."

"Perhaps. But, darling, please, pull together. Barton will be here to see to your needs. She will be with you when the baby comes."

"Ooh, Baby. Baby, Baby, Baby. You care more about this baby than you do about me. The only reason you married me was to get yourself an heir."

"Eleanor, you know that's silly talk. There are hundreds of girls right here in England I could have married if the purpose was only to get an heir. It was you that I fell in love with. You know that."

She began to sob ever more loudly. "I don't know anything anymore. I only know that you're going away and I don't know when I'll see you again. I'm to be left alone in this place I hate."

"Eleanor, you won't hate England once you're able to get out more. I know this is a terribly difficult time for you. But, it will be over soon. Then you'll be able to ride again, and get out - meet people - enjoy life more."

"How am I to enjoy life, when you aren't here, and there will be no parties or balls to attend, because all of the men are away fighting this stupid war?"

"Oh, Eleanor, there are other things in life besides parties and balls. You'll learn that, after the baby comes. Please try to pull yourself together. It's dreadfully hard for me to leave when you're so upset. I want to go into battle with the memory of your smile. Please try."

"No, I won't try. Why should I smile? I've nothing to smile about. Go if you must, but don't expect me to be happy about it."

Lily stood and watched this fiasco, and couldn't help growing more and more angry at Lady Eleanor's childish behavior. She was acting like a very spoiled, young girl, and showed no consideration whatsoever for her husband's feelings. Lily was beginning to see that the Countess was an exceedingly immature, self-centered young lady. Eleanor continued to weep, and to beat on her husband's chest. Finally, the Captain turned to Lily.

"Miss Barton, I really must leave, or I'll miss my train. Can you come over here, and sit with Eleanor? Please stay with her throughout the day. As you can see, she's terribly distraught."

What Lily could see was that Lady Eleanor didn't care if he went away feeling miserable and downhearted. It was no way to send a soldier husband off to war. Lily could have slapped her. However, she did as he requested, and moved near the bed, sitting down in the chair closest to the Countess. The Captain kissed Eleanor once more, with great passion, then turned and left very quickly.

Lady Eleanor was screaming at the top of her lungs. "If you leave, I'll not be here when you return," she howled.

What a beastly threat to make! Lily tried to calm her down. "Milady, please try to calm yourself. This isn't good for you, nor the baby. The Captain has no choice but to go. I know it's difficult for you, especially at such a time, but he needs all of the support we can give him. This is a dreadful war. Men are being killed every moment. You don't want his last memory of you to be one that causes him despair?"

She continued to sniffle. "No. But, I'm more important than a stupid war. I suppose you're correct, Barton. Has he left the house yet? If not, call him back and I'll try to say a proper goodbye."

Lily opened the door and raced down the stairway, and found the Captain standing in the great hall, looking dreadfully sad, waiting for his valet, Michael, and the chauffeur, Edward.

"Oh Captain. I'm so happy that I caught you. Eleanor is sorry she was so overwrought. She wants to say a proper goodbye to you. Have you time for a quick jaunt back up to her bed chamber?"

His face lit up. "Yes, yes, of course. Oh, thank you so much, Barton I knew you could bring her round." He rushed up the stairway, and Lily remained down below. Five minutes later he returned, just in time for his departure. His face was much happier, although still filled with despair. "She seems much better. I don't know what you said to her, but she did promise she'd write, and would try not to complain, and she did tell me she loved me."

"Of course, she loves you Captain. She's still a young girl, as you've said yourself. She'll adjust."

"You do think she wants this baby, don't you, Miss Barton?"

"Not want a baby? Captain, babies are the most precious gift God can give. Babies are life renewing itself. Every woman in the world wants a baby."

"Yes, that's the way you feel, but I'm not certain about Eleanor. I just have to hope that once the child arrives, she'll discover motherly love."

"Of course she will, Captain. Now, you get on to the station. You don't want to miss your train. We'll all be sending you our prayers. God Speed."

He smiled, and kissed her hand. "Thank God for you, Miss Barton." Then he turned and Michael picked up his bag. They were off to war.

4

Lily climbed the staircase and went back to the Countess. She was lying with her head pressed into the pillow, still weeping. Lily got a cool cloth, and poured lavender water over it. Then she returned to Lady Eleanor and asked that she lie face-up. She placed the cloth on her forehead, and requested that she just lie still, and take deep breaths. Eleanor did as Lily asked. There was silence in the room for quite some time. Finally, she appeared to be much calmer.

"Is he gone, Barton?" she asked.

"Yes, Milady. He and Michael have left for the station. I imagine they're on the train by now."

"Oh, how shall I ever bear it? I do love him, you know. Life will be unbearable without him here with me."

"It will be difficult, Milady. But, not unbearable. We shall think of ways to pass the time. The Captain ordered a rolling chair to be delivered sometime today. That will perk you up. We also need to begin to prepare for the baby's arrival. You and I can work together on designing a nursery. Won't that be fun?"

"I suppose," she answered, with a lack of enthusiasm.

"Let's try to look ahead and be optimistic, Milady. I know it isn't easy for you, but I'm here to make it easier."

"Sometimes I ask myself 'who is Eleanor Claybourne?' I've asked myself that question over and over, and the only answer I can give is that I don't know," she sniffled.

"Why, Milady, Eleanor Claybourne is an enchanting Countess, who is the wife of one of the most renowned Earls in the realm. She's lovely, and sweet; an intelligent lady; a great horsewoman. She has everything a woman could dream of having. God has been very good to her."

"You don't understand, Barton. I believe Kit married me, knowing that I was so young, hoping that he would be able to mold me into what he wished a wife to be. I don't want to be molded. People here expect me to change. I don't want to change. I was born on a plantation in Virginia. I'm a Southern Belle. Here in England, nobody even knows what a Southern Belle is. Instead of being told what a lovely creature I am, which is what my Daddy always told me, here I am criticized for not behaving properly."

"How are you criticized, Milady?"

"For instance, all I ever hear from my mother-in-law is that 'it has always been like that,' when I ask her why I must do something in a certain manner. I continually draw her disapproval. I make what she terms 'inexcusable blunders.'"

"Such as . . . ?"

"Such as asking a valet to get me a glass of water. Or requesting that the parlor maid lace up my dinner dress, when Kit is out of hearing."

"Yes - well - there are quite rigid rules about such things in English society. In time, you'll come to understand it all."

"No, I doubt that. It all makes no sense to me. At home it didn't matter which of our house servants I asked to get me a glass of water. It wasn't as though everyone had an assigned role that no one else could play."

"I imagine someday that will change here in England too. But for now, it would be better if you tried to learn to adhere to them. It's just the done thing, Milady."

"What does 'the done thing' mean?"

"It just means that this is the way things have always been done."

"Well, I should prefer to do things the way they were always done when *I* was growing up."

"I understand your feelings, Milady. But, I have to say that such an attitude is sure to cause you further upset. The Captain married you because he believed you would make a splendid Countess for his beloved home. You don't want to disappoint him, do you?"

"Oh, no Barton, I don't. I'm just very confused. I have begun to wonder if I made a terrible error when I decided to marry him."

"Oh, Milady. You shouldn't be saying such things. I know you don't mean that."

"Well, yes, I do. You see, the greatest mistake I ever made was doing something with no idea of the real reason I did it."

"I'm not certain I understand what you mean?"

"Now, when I look back on my marriage, I think I was swept off my feet by Kit's good looks, his English title, and the jealousy of all of the other girls in the County. It was terribly exciting. I was the center of attention, and loved that. But, I didn't really think about all of the rest. I never looked ahead to what it would be like to leave my home, move to England, and learn a whole new way of living. I didn't realize that people change every moment, but that what we do in the past doesn't change at all. In other words, I am not quite such a silly little girl as I was when I married Kit, just for all of the attention and excitement. And, now, what I did has been done and it can't be undone."

Lily was appalled. These sorts of things were not discussed. Even if that is the way she felt. How could she not see how wonderful her life was? But, Lily was her nurse, not her close friend, and she couldn't lecture on her exceedingly immature thoughts. She decided to change the subject to something she really needed to tell her, but dreaded. It would probably end in another round of tears, or worse yet, a tantrum.

"Milady, I understand that the Captain's mother and his brother have returned from London to say their goodbye's to him, before he joined his regiment. I imagine they'll be wanting to call upon you before the day is out."

"Oh, Fiddlesticks! I can't abide his mother. His brother isn't as bad, as at least he has a sense of adventure about him. He's promised to take me for a ride in his new Hispano Suiza automobile, after the baby arrives."

"Isn't that a quite dangerous motor car?"

"Well - not if the person driving knows what to do. Sebastian has raced autos. The Hispano Suiza is one of the most expensive autos in the world."

"Well, I suppose that would be something exciting to look forward to, Milady. But, certainly not before the baby comes."

"Oh, no. The baby always had to come first," the Countess replied, in a sarcastic tone.

"Why don't we order your breakfast tray, and then bathe and dress you, so that you'll be ready to receive guests. I'll tell Mrs. Briggs what time would be appropriate if you wish."

"Yes. I guess I shall have to see them. But, not until afternoon. Tell then to come by about two o'clock. Then I can have a lie-down after they've left. I'm sure I'll need one."

Lily left her room, and walked briskly down to Mrs. Briggs' office. She was sitting behind her desk, going over a list of figures. "I'm sorry to interrupt, Mrs. Briggs, but I wanted to discuss the Countess's schedule for the day. I understand that Lady Cynthia has returned from London, and that the Captain's brother, Mr. Sebastian, is also visiting. The Countess said it would be acceptable for them to pay her a visit about two 'clock this afternoon."

"I'll let that be known to both of them. Unfortunately, she should have waited until they requested a visit with her." Her mouth was a firm line.

"Shall I tell her that, or simply let it pass?"

"Let it pass. She's acted like such a spoiled creature this morning, I don't want any more uproar. The Dowager Lady heard the spectacular scene she made - everyone in the house could hear it. She is not at all pleased, and will probably tell the Countess just that."

"Oh, Lord Have Mercy, I hope not. It's taken all morning to calm her, and if she feels criticized by her mother-in-law, I'm afraid it will all start up again."

"Well, none of us is in a position to tell Lady Cynthia what should and should not be said to the Countess. You've not met her yet. She is truly a good person, but she doesn't brook much nonsense. She is not terribly fond of having an American for a daughter-in-law and the Countess's behavior this morning won't have helped her standing."

"What about Mr. Sebastian?"

"Mr. Sebastian is as immature as the Countess. He won't give a whit what she did. He thinks most things in life are amusing. I shouldn't pay him any mind."

"Shall I meet either of them before they pay a visit to the Countess?"

"I think it would be best. I'll arrange for a small get-together in the drawing room, for a late morning tea. Would that suit your purposes?"

"Whatever suits theirs, Mrs. Briggs."

"Fine. Shall we say eleven o'clock? That's two hours hence. Will that give you time to complete your duties with the Countess, and change into a fresh dress?"

"Yes, I'll make certain that there is time."

At eleven o'clock, Lily descended the staircase, dressed in one of her new black skirts, and a pale yellow, Victorian blouse, trimmed with lace. She wore her mother's cameo brooch at her throat. She'd re-done her hair into a properly smoothed bun, and touched her lips and cheeks with a tiny bit of pink rouge. As she entered the drawing room, there was an older lady sitting on the sofa and, a well-dressed young gentleman standing with one hand in his pocket, and one arm on the fireplace mantle. The Lady Cynthia rose, and gave Lily her hand. Lily gave her a slight curtsy. She wasn't certain if she should have done so, but it didn't seem an enormous breech of etiquette if it was any at all. "It's a pleasure to meet you, Miss Barton," the Captain's mother said. "I am Cynthia, the Dowager Lady of Claybourne. You may address me as Lady Cynthia."

"How lovely to meet you, Lady Cynthia. The Captain speaks so highly of you."

She was a truly lovely, elegant lady, but one could tell immediately that she was no shrinking violet. She had totally grey-white hair, worn in an upsweep, with combs holding it in place. Her dress was beautiful Edwardian poplin, in a pale grey, trimmed with bits of lace at the collar. She wore several strands of pearls. Her face was devoid of lines and wrinkles, and if it weren't for her hair, she would have looked much younger. As it was, she seemed to be in her late fifties. Her figure was still trim and attractive. It was clear that she had great self-esteem, and Lily could immediately sense why she and the Countess might cross swords.

"Thank you, Miss Barton." Then, turning her body toward the fireplace, she said, "and this is the Captain's brother, Mr. Sebastian. Thank Goodness he isn't of age yet to be in the military. Worrying about one son in this ghastly war is quite enough."

"I'm sure, Lady Cynthia," Lily replied. Sebastian was very handsome, in a different sort of way from his brother. He had darker hair, and wore a fine, three piece suit. There was an air of recklessness about him. Lily would have guessed his age to be about seventeen, although his manners put him at an older age. But, one could see that he was still an adventuresome boy.

"Won't you sit down, and join us for some tea?"

"Thank you, Milady."

"How are you getting on at *Claybourne Court*," she asked.

"Very well. I enjoy my work tremendously. Of course, I'm very new. This is such a splendid home. Everyone has been most agreeable. I have no complaints whatsoever, Lady Cynthia."

"I'm happy to hear that. Do you not even find complaint about the Countess Eleanor?"

"No, Lady Cynthia. She has much growing yet to do. I recognize that. She is also very homesick and lonely. But, I'm trying my best to help her overcome those feelings."

"You are much more generous than I would be. I think she needs a good spanking. I cannot imagine why Kit saw fit to go as far as America to find himself a bride. Any girl in Great Britain would have made a better bride. I don't know that she cares for him, as she should. She doesn't seem to understand the responsibility she carries as a Countess."

"I understand, Lady Cynthia." It was difficult for Lily to engage in such a conversation. She was well aware of her duty not to break any confidence that had been shared between the Countess and herself, yet when speaking to the Captain's mother, she also knew that she should never argue, or challenge her viewpoint.

"In any event, I shall give her a strong piece of my mind today when I speak to her. I'll have no more scenes like she displayed this morning."

Sebastian broke into the conversation. He had moved from the fireplace to a chair, which sat to the left of the sofa. "Oh, Mother. Give her some room to breathe. She's very young. I think I would go daft if I had to sit in this house - actually in one room - all day long. She isn't used to such confinement."

"Well, she had better accustom herself to it. She has duties she should be performing, even though confined to her bed until the birth of her child. She could be going over the menus each day with Mrs. Briggs, and discussing other household matters. I still continue to perform all of the duties of the Countess when I am here at *Claybourne Court*, which isn't proper. Now that Kit has gone to France, I shall be spending much more time here, and I expect her to start acting like one expects a Lady to act."

"I understand, Lady Cynthia. Perhaps you speaking to her will bring about a change in her attitude?" Lily commented.

Tea was served, along with some of the wonderful scones the cook made, and they all stopped chatting long enough to enjoy such a treat.

"How long will you be staying, Mr. Sebastian," Lily asked.

"Not long, Miss Barton. I just came to see my brother off to the war. I find the country so terribly boring. London is much more delightful."

"My dear son, when a Country is embroiled in a war, as England is at present, there should be no place that one thinks of as delightful. You should be ashamed of yourself for thinking of wanting frivolity and fun when your brother could die."

"I'm sure I shall find myself in his position at some point. I intend to live life while I can. I wasn't born to mourn the living. Of course I worry for Kit. But, he's always landed on his feet, hasn't he?"

There appeared to be a tone of some envy there. Perhaps it was what the Captain had told her that first day she'd spoken to him, about Sebastian being unhappy that the eldest brother had inherited everything.

"And, where did you grow up, Miss Barton," Sebastian asked Lily.

"Ironically, right here in *Claybourne-upon-Colne*, Sir. I was actually born here. My father was a physician."

"Ah, a local girl. How interesting. Do you still have family here?"

"Yes, Mr. Sebastian. My Mum lives in the village. My Father died last summer and I had a brother who was killed at the Battle of the Marne. That's what forced me out to work."

"Well, we're very glad that you were available to come to us at *Claybourne Court*," The Lady Cynthia said." I have had nothing but praise of you from all quarters."

"How nice. I do so enjoy it here, and it's not even a full week yet."

"You came to us at an eventful time," she added.

"It's usually dull as dirt here," Sebastian added.

"Sebastian, how nasty. That is not the truth. Not everybody needs constantly to be going and doing, and getting into some scrape or another."

"I'm quite a calm quiet person, Mr. Sebastian. So, the country suits me perfectly. I love the peace and serenity of the Cotswold hills."

"Well, then you should find *Claybourne Court* much to your liking," he replied.

Lady Cynthia placed her teacup back on its tray, and Lily followed suit. "Well, I think I'd better see to any tasks Mrs. Briggs can use help with. It's been lovely visiting with you, and I'm glad you're happy here. If you ever need me for anything, don't hesitate to ask." She stood up, and shook Lily's hand and that ended the meeting. Sebastian shook her hand as well, and left the room before Lily did.

5

At two o'clock, Lily deliberately went to her room. She left the door somewhat ajar, as she was curious to hear what took place during the conversation between Lady Cynthia and Countess Eleanor. She didn't have to wait long.

The first voice Lily heard was Lady Cynthia's, and she was *not* happy. "Eleanor, I have had just about all I intend to put up with from you," she exclaimed loudly. "You are a spoiled, selfish, girl with no understanding of our culture and your responsibilities. I heard the scene you performed for the entire household this morning. Your husband, who tries everything in his power to show his love for you, was leaving his home to go to France, where he will be engaged in some of the worst fighting that has ever taken place in the history of our land. He should have departed with the knowledge that he had the support and love of everyone in this household. But, the most important person in his life, although I am certain I cannot say why, gave him no consideration or care at all. All you were interested in was your own whining and bawling. You need a good shaking, and if you weren't expecting a child, I should like to do just that. What do you have to say for yourself?"

Lady Eleanor was weeping, but she still raised her voice and fought back. "You don't frighten me in the least, Lady Cynthia. If Kit heard the way you are speaking to me, he would be most angry. You have no right to use that tone of voice with me. *I* am the Countess in this household. Not you. I wish you would stay in your own Dower house, and leave Claybourne Court to me. If you are an example of what a proper English Countess is like, I should never want to become one."

"Leave the management of *Claybourne Court* to you! How absurd. You haven't the slightest idea of the proper English etiquette required to run this lovely home. If you had sense, you would be letting me teach you the things you need to know. I don't like to argue with you, Eleanor, and I am not trying to make you frightened of me. But, it is nearly impossible to witness your selfish behavior, and not reach a point where one simply has to speak out."

"Speak out if you must, but don't expect it to do any good. Kit fell in love with me the way I am. I have no reason to change. He wasn't upset with me this morning. He understood that I was frightened to see him go, and to be left alone here in this strange land without him. Can't you see that the only reason I am here is because I married him, and now he isn't even here?"

"Oh my dear girl. Do you ever think of anyone except yourself? Things happen in life that are beyond our control. Do you think Kit wanted to leave you to go to France? What silliness. He has been called to do his duty, and he has done what any honorable Englishman would do. You should have backed him one hundred percent."

"In other words, you think I should have lied? Why am I supposed to pretend that I won't be miserable without him, when of course I shall be?"

"Oh my dear young lady. You have so terribly much to learn about life. I cannot abide this conversation any longer. I shall be in the Dower house if anyone should need me."

"Very well, Lady Cynthia. I don't expect I shall be needing you," Eleanor retorted.

Lady Cynthia threw a glaring glance at her daughter-in-law, and left the room, with the door open. The next to appear was Mr. Sebastian. Lily could hear his footsteps in the hallway. Big, heavy footsteps. Certainly those of a man, not the feminine, small slippers that Lady Cynthia wore.

"Hallo, dear sister. Did I just witness an altercation between my sweet mother and you?" Sebastian laughed.

"You might say so," responded Eleanor.

"Don't pay her a whit of attention. She's an old bat, even if she is my mother. She doesn't care for the fact that we young people are now running the world. She wishes things to stay as they've always been, and of course, they can't and won't. She is angry because Kit married you, when she had full control of *Claybourne Court* before that. She prattles on so about Kit and his honorable duty to go to war. Well, of course, I suppose there is some truth to that. He did attend *Sandhurst*, the Royal Military College. He has already served with the *Scot's Greys'*, once before. Now he holds the rank of Captain. Captains won't be in near the danger that the poor chaps who enter service without a commission will be. When you next see a listing of the dead and wounded, see how many Privates are listed, versus Officer Ranks. And just what is it that everyone expects you to do? Just sit here, day in and day out, lamenting your soldier-husband, fighting for his Country in France? I think the whole muck-up is foolishness, from beginning to end. There is nothing going on in France except a disgusting stalemate between our men and the beastly Germans. There's nothing that will convince me to go out there and fight for God and Country."

"But, Sebastian, how can you not go? Once mandatory conscription begins, and I've heard that could be soon, you will be of age to go. There is nothing you can do to stop it."

"Right you are about one thing, Eleanor, old girl. I'll turn eighteen this month. But, you'll never see me in one of those damned uniforms."

"How do you intend to keep from going? You'll be given a white feather for being a slacker."

"No. Not with an injury that keeps me from being found fit for duty," he answered, laughing.

"What injury? You have no injuries. You're in perfect health, as far as I know?"

"Well, don't you worry your pretty, little head. You'll be finding out soon enough, I daresay. Now, when is your time of confinement over? I'm frantic with wanting to take you for a run in my new Suiza."

Lily couldn't see into the room, but she heard Lady Eleanor clap her hands together. "Oh, wouldn't that just be too fun? The baby is due in April so it's still such a long time. I'll have a nanny, so as soon as I've recovered I can come with you on your adventures."

"Then I'll be certain to be fit and ready by July," he replied.

Lily couldn't imagine why Sebastian was sounding as though he knew that he was going to fall ill, or meet with an accident. It was a very peculiar conversation. She also knew that Captain Claybourne, unlike many other British Officers, didn't expect the boys who fought under him to do anything that he didn't do himself. He was in the fight just as much as any other soldier. The Captain himself had told Lily that, but he hadn't wanted his wife to know, for fear she would worry more. Lily didn't think Lady Eleanor was worried in the least about him.

After the row that morning, and then again with her mother-in-law, Lady Eleanor showed such a total lack of respect. Lily was beginning to like her less and less. She just didn't seem to have any regard for anyone else. She seemed more excited at the prospect of going 'joy riding' with her brother-in-law than in learning how to be respectful to her elders and how to adapt to the British way of doing things. If she continued such behavior, Lily didn't think she would find herself with many lady friends, as her American background was a detriment from the start. In order to win over her English counterparts, she needed to ask their help, and keep in the background until she was much more polished, and had an understanding of proper decorum. But, as her nurse, Lily couldn't tell her those things. She wondered if she'd ever even listened to her own mother.

The door to Lady Eleanor's room closed silently, and Lily could hear no more conversation. Yet, Sebastian hadn't left yet. She was certain of that. Perhaps they were speaking more softly. Surely, there was nothing else they could be involved in. Was there? Lady Eleanor was three months gone with child. No man, not even Mr. Sebastian, could be the sort who would enter into any kind of affair of the heart with an expectant mother. And his brother's wife to boot. No, Lily refused to consider that. But, she did reach the conclusion that it was time for her to knock on the Countess's door, and remind Lady Eleanor that it was time for her afternoon lie-down.

She walked down the hallway, and rapped lightly. She could hear soft laughter, but then Mr. Sebastian said that she should come in. She stepped inside the doorway, and was dumbfounded. Lady Eleanor was supine, lying on her front side, while Sebastian rubbed her naked back! Lily's first impulse was to raise her voice, or to run to get Lady Cynthia. Even Mrs. Briggs. The problem was, none of those people held any sway at all with either the Countess or Mr. Sebastian. She was certain that there would have been another huge kerfuffle, but a fat lot of good it would have done. So, she kept her voice level, and entering the room, she suggested that it was time for the Countess to have a nap.

"Eleanor's back was hurting her. She was complaining to me of severe pain, so I told her I would massage it for her. I hope you find no problem with that, Barton," Mr. Sebastian drawled, in a lazy voice.

"No sir. No problem. It's just that it's past time for the Lady to take her lie-down. She's supposed to take a lot of rest, and she's had quite an emotional day. So, if you don't mind, perhaps you could find something else to do for a bit. Perhaps you'd like to join her ladyship for dinner, or give her little dog Ginny her afternoon walk?"

"No, I'm not much for walking the dog. I think I'll go and have my own lie-down, Barton. What do you think, old girl? Would you like me to come back and join you for dinner?" He asked Eleanor.

She turned over, and pulled the bed covering above her chest. Lily couldn't tell if she had clothing on at all. "Yes, Sebastian, that's very kind of you. I think I would like my lie-down now. Perhaps you would be so kind as to walk Ginny for me, Barton?"

"I'd be happy to, Milady." Lily answered. She gathered up the Spaniel's lead and leash, reached down, picked up Ginny, and left the room.

She walked Ginny for about fifteen minutes, but her mind was not on the task. How was she expected to handle such a conundrum? She was nearly the same age as both Mr. Sebastian and Lady Eleanor. She certainly had no ranking in terms of age, which at least Mrs. Briggs, or the Lady Cynthia could lay claim. In addition, she'd been hired to act as a companion to the Countess, not as a watchdog, or warden. What would the Captain expect of her in such circumstances? Perhaps there was nothing for her to be getting into an uproar about. Perhaps this was the normal manner in which the Countess interacted with her brother-in-law. It seemed awfully hard to believe, however. If, indeed, that were the case, Lily certainly understood clearly why Lady Cynthia was so terribly angry earlier in the day. It wasn't Lily's wish to contribute to any further upset in the house, but she also didn't want to be taken as a fool by the Countess, for allowing such improper behavior to occur right under her nose. Lily decided she would wait until the next time she had an opportunity to speak to Lady Eleanor alone, which would probably be when she was readying her for bed. She would think of some way to broach the subject without another one of Lady Eleanor's temper tantrums.

Lily brought Ginny back inside of the house, and silently let her into her mistresses' room. From what she could tell, the Countess was resting quietly. Lily gently closed the door, and found her way to Mrs. Briggs' office. She was glad to see that the Housekeeper was resting in her chair with a cup of tea. She asked Lily to join her, and she was happy to do so. Lily accepted a nice, hot cup of tea, and leaned back in the chair facing the desk.

"Ahhh, this feels marvelous. It's been quite a day, hasn't it?" she commented.

"Indeed it has. I understand Lady Cynthia and the Countess had quite a tussle. Were you privy to that?"

"Oh, yes Mrs. Briggs. It didn't seem to make a whit of difference to Lady Eleanor. She spoke back to her mother-in-law like she was a servant."

"That isn't unusual, Barton. She's quite a handful. My biggest concern is what her behavior will be like after the baby is born, and she's free to come and go as she pleases."

"Yes. That concerns me, as well. Mrs. Briggs. Am I expected to be a part of her shenanigans? I don't exactly know how I'm to handle this."

"What sort of shenanigans are you referring to?" Mrs. Briggs asked.

"Well, for instance, she's already mentioned to me that Mr. Sebastian has some sort of fancy sports car. It's supposed to be very fast. She is jerking at her chain wanting to go for a ride in it. Of course I told her that it couldn't be considered until after the baby came. And she agreed, somewhat sarcastically. But, what happens then?"

"She's a grown woman. None of us have the right to interfere with her comings and goings. She can do whatever pleases her. But, no, I don't think that the Captain would expect you to take part in such silly, reckless play."

"If I discover that she's doing something that I feel is inappropriate, shall I simply handle the situation with her, or am I to seek out assistance?"

"Oh My. How inappropriate?" Mrs. Briggs inquired.

"I wasn't going to say anything. I'm not certain it's anything to be alarmed about, but then perhaps it is. I knocked and went in to tell Lady Eleanor that it was time for her afternoon lie-down, and that Mr. Sebastian needed to take his leave, and she was lying face down on the bed, with her back unclothed, and he was umm - well - he said he was massaging it, because she was having pain."

"*That,* Barton, is quite inappropriate. However, if you want my opinion, I think she does these things just to cause everyone in the house to fret. She's angry because the Captain is gone to war, and she's acting like a child. Perhaps she believes that if she causes enough trouble, he'll have to return. She's very manipulative, that one."

"In that case, I'm glad I spoke to you. It might be best not to call attention to it, if that's what she's hoping for. I think I'll choose to ignore it for now. Let's see what comes next."

"Yes. Wise thinking. I'm glad you talked to me about it. Don't ever hesitate to do so. I don't want to see you leave your position because you get so fed up with her behavior. The Captain is counting on you so much, Barton."

"I understand that, Mrs. Briggs. I promise you needn't worry about that. I need my job too much to let this sort of thing send me off looking for another position in London."

Lily finished her tea, and went back to her own rooms. There she paced the room for a good half hour. How had she managed, in just under three days, to get herself into such a muddle? She truly loved her job, and wanted to do right by the Captain, who seemed like such a fine man. It was hard for her to imagine how he'd ever found himself head over tail for the spoiled little girl down the hallway. Lily supposed it must have been her appearance, for she certainly was lovely. Lily doubted that she'd shown the side of her that tended toward sulking and outpourings of tears before the 'I do's' were said. In any event, though she was a lovely girl, she really had a terrible need to grow up a bit.

6

Captain Kit Claybourne, Eighth Brigade, 2nd Regiment, *Royal Scot's Grey's,* was lying on his back, in 'No-Man's Land'; that dreadful stretch of mud and blood soaked land which lay between two strings of barbed wire, separating the German from the British trenches by only a matter of yards. It was night - a black, cold, rainy night - and he lay half in and half out of a crater that had been formed when a German grenade whizzed over him, just missing decapitation, and throwing shrapnel everywhere, hitting his helmet and knocking him unconscious from the force of the blow. When he came to, there was silence all around. His head was fuzzy for a moment, and he had to think where he was. Then it all came back. He'd been leading a unit of his men over the top, into no-man's land to charge the German trenches. As a Captain, he had no duty to even *be* on the battlefield. Most of the officers billeted in lovely old French Chateaux in the area, and only walked the trenches to check on the men under their command. But, Captain Claybourne believed in not asking his men to do anything that he wasn't willing to do himself. He raised his head slowly, and tried to see through the smoke, which still hung in the air from the bombardment, and the mist of the rain. He could see no one else. At least, no one else alive. There were bodies strewn everywhere. Not five yards from him was a man with no head. Two others lay a bit beyond that, their intestines glistening in the moonlight, where they had spilled from their bodies, when hit. Obviously, they were dead. Was there anyone alive? It didn't appear so. Where was the British trench? In the darkness, it was very difficult to see, and he was still confused from the probable concussion he had sustained. He lay there a few more minutes, trying to get his bearings. Then he heard a sound.

"Oi – Captain. Are you alive?" came a voice from the trench toward which his feet were pointing. Obviously, it was one of his men. It was suicide to speak loudly, so the man was scarcely speaking above a whisper, but Captain Claybourne could just make out his words, and understand that the British trench was only a few yards in front of him. He began to crawl slowly and stealthily across the ground. He was terribly thirsty, but he couldn't abide the thought of drinking from the filthy water that had accumulated in the craters dotting 'No Man's Land'. Just a few more yards, and he would be safe in the trench. Then he could have a drink of clean, canteen water. He was shivering all over from the cold, and probably from shock. "Captain. Captain. Is that you?" The voice called again. Captain Claybourne knew now that it was one of the men in his regiment. He answered back, in a very low voice.

"Yes, it's me, Claybourne. Whistle when I'm next to the trench." He continued the seemingly endless crawl. There was a loud explosion from the German side, and he burrowed his head into a muddy crater, lying very still. Shrapnel flew everywhere. He wasn't able to tell if he was hurt or not. He continued slithering across the mud, and then heard a whistle. It was the man in his unit, telling him he'd arrived safely. Arms reached up over the side and helped to pull him inside of the carved out furrow of dirt that had been serving as home since his arrival at Ypres. There were yards and yards of such trenches, some with boardwalks, more without. He slid down the side and onto the floor of the filthy trench. Two of his fellow *'Scot's Grey's'* helped him shed his haversack, and removed his tunic. Blood was flowing from a hole in his left arm. Tom Holiday, a Private, reached inside Claybourne's tunic, and removed his medical kit. He tore open the Captain's shirt, and scrubbed at the wound with flannel doused in Lysol. The pain was excruciating. Then Tom poured iodine into the wound, and covered it with a clean bandage. The blood was still flowing freely. Tom took a strip of cloth from the torn shirt, and used it as a tourniquet, wrapping it tightly above the ghastly wound, cutting off the blood supply from the artery. That was all to be done until the stretcher-bearers arrived on the scene and removed Captain Claybourne to a Causality Clearing Station behind the lines. Claybourne took the blanket Tom had given him, and curled up in a ball on the muddy floor of the trench. He was still shaking, and cold all over. Nevertheless, he fell asleep quickly.

The next he knew, he woke in the Clearing Station at *Etaples*. It was daytime, and nurses were scurrying to and fro in every direction. Oh how wonderful it was to see a woman again! He had been living for weeks now with his regiment, and had nearly forgotten how calming and gentle a woman's touch could be. There was no sexual overtone to such a feeling . . . just the appreciation that came from the feeling of a gentle, smooth hand on his forehead. He looked around the room. The walls were a grimy pale blue, and there were rows and rows of beds with soldiers in each one. All were wounded. Some had terrible burns, and others were clearly absent a leg or an arm - or both. One man's jaw had been blown away. Another had a deep gash on his cheek. Captain Claybourne looked down at his own arm. There was little to observe, since the arm was in a cast. He was relieved to see that it was still there. A nurse walked briskly to his bed.

"Ah, Captain Claybourne. Have you enjoyed your rest? Welcome back to the world of the living. You are at the Causality Clearing Station at *Etaples*. You were wounded rather badly, but the doctor was able to save your arm. We've given you extra blood, as you lost a considerable amount before the stretcher lads arrived. All in all, you are in quite good form. How are you feeling?"

"I'd like some water, Nurse. How long have I been here? I don't remember anything after I was pulled back into the trench. Will I have full use of my arm again?"

"Yes, Captain. Here, let me help you with some water." She lifted his head a little way off the pillow, and let him drink. His mouth was terribly dry. "You've been here two days, sir. It's lucky your mate had the good sense to place a tourniquet on that arm. I'm afraid you would have bled to death. To answer your question, the doctor believes you will, indeed, have full use of your arm again. We'll keep you here for a week, and then you'll be moved to a base hospital at Brielen to recuperate until the arm is totally ready for you to return to battle."

"Damn! Then it isn't a Blighty?"

"No, sir," she laughed. A Blighty was an injury that was bad enough to remove a man permanently from the field of battle, but not so serious as to render him disabled for life. When one received a Blighty, they didn't have to return to the fight. But, Kit Claybourne hadn't received a Blighty, and he would be going back.

His first visitor, besides Michael, his valet, who was billeted in a châteaux near *Etaples,* was Tom Holiday, the Private from his regiment, who had helped to pull him over the side and into the trench, and had tended to his wound until the stretchers arrived. "Sorry about your arm, Captain, but I wouldn't mind pinching that pillow from you, Sir," Private Holiday laughed, as he approached Captain Claybourne's bed.

"Well, well, Tom. I owe you some bit of thanks. If it hadn't been for you, I'm not sure I'd be here at all, let alone with a nice, soft pillow. You saved my life, you know."

"I just did my duty, Captain. I wasn't having you bleed all over the trench."

Captain Claybourne laughed. "Seriously, Tom, I'm very grateful to you. Was it you who gave me the whistle to tell me that I had reached the trench? I just scarcely remember that."

"Yes Sir. That was me. When we got back from the raid, we counted up the men, and you wasn't with us. We thought you'd had it out there. But, then I got hold of a periscope and looked out across 'No Man's Land'. I seen you movin'. Course, I didn't know it was you then. That's why I called out your name. Do you remember that?"

"Yes. Just barely. That's when I started crawling in the direction of the trench. I wasn't sure what direction to go in till then. I must have made some noise, because the Huns let go with a massive grenade. I didn't know that I'd been hit. I was so cold that my arm just felt numb. Then I spotted the edge of the trench, and there you were to help pull me in. I sure remember that, and your fine work in bandaging and putting a tourniquet on my arm. They've told me here that if it hadn't been for the tourniquet I would have bled out right there."

"You'd a done the same thing for me, Sir. It's just a soldier's job."

"Well, you did it well, and I'm going to recommend you for the Military Metal."

"Jeeze, Sir. I don't deserve no bloody medal." Tom Holiday looked embarrassed, but proud.

"You may not think you deserve it, but I do, Private Holiday. Now, no more arguing."

"Well, what's the verdict, Sir? Is it a Blighty? Or will you have to be returnin'?

"No Blighty, Tom. I'll spend some time here, and then on to a Base Hospital at Brielen. After that, I'll be back with my regiment. Do you think you can make it that long without me, Holiday?"

"Yeah - we'll all make it, some -how," he laughed. Perhaps I can get meself a Blighty while you're gone."

"I hope you do it up better than I did," Claybourne answered. "So, how are things progressing at Ypres?"

"Pretty awful, Captain. But, I think the Brits are holdin' their own. It's hard to tell with this trench fightin'. I'm rotating to the back lines for the next two weeks, thank God."

"By the time I return, you'll be about ready to be brought back up. If I have to pick a soldier to fight by my side, I'd pick you, Holiday."

"I appreciate your faith in me, Sir. Well, I got to be getting' back to my post. I'll tell the rest of the boys that you're comin' back. They'll be glad. Not too many Captains fight with their men."

"Tell the boys I'm looking forward to seeing them, Holiday. And, try to keep safe."

Kit lay in his bed and thought about the horror of this war. He'd completed schooling at *Sandhurst*, and had enlisted with the *Scot's Grey's* back when he was a young, eager Lieutenant in 1908. He's loved the Calvary, and was proud of serving his country in the *Scot's Grey's*. But, this war was a thing apart from what he'd ever thought battle meant. He thought about the water in the trenches, through which he'd waded, alive with a multitude of swimming frogs. Red slugs crawled up the side of the trenches and strange beetles with dangerous looking horns wriggled along dry ledges and invaded the dugouts in search of the lice that infested them. Dead bodies were strewn everywhere one looked, some with maggots crawling all over their corpses. The sounds of the gun roar was never ending, and some of the men had a hard time controlling their nerves. Particularly the very young. He wasn't a

Calvary officer anymore. They'd taken away his horse early on, and assigned him to an Infantry unit. He realized now how much he'd come to depend on that beautiful grey mount for a feeling of safety. Now, his only weapon was a Lee-Enfield Rifle and a bayonet.

He turned his thoughts to home. England. Gloucestershire. Daffodils, hyacinth, and roses. *Claybourne Court*, with its red brick and golden sandstone. And, Eleanor. Oh, God, Eleanor. Thinking about his wife should have brought feelings of love and longing, but instead he was filled with anxiety at the thought of her. It was getting so that every time he received a letter from her, he dreaded opening it. She hadn't the slightest conception of what war was like, and what's more, didn't care to learn. Her letters were one hundred percent concentrated upon herself - her boredom, her dissatisfaction with her appearance, her dislike of his mother. On and on it went. He understood that she was young, but so were a lot of the wives who were married to soldiers he was fighting with. When their letters arrived, the men were thrilled, and some even cried at the sweet concern their loved ones showed. Perhaps when the baby arrived, things would be different. That was his fondest hope.

While he was laying in his bed deep in thought, a nurse brought a packet of letters to him. It was the first time he'd ever received so many at one time. Probably they had all caught up with him. He laid aside the one from Eleanor, and also the one from his brother Sebastian. There was another from his mother, and one from Eleanor's nurse, Miss Barton. He opened hers first.

Dear Captain Claybourne,

I hope this letter finds you well and safe. One hears such dreadful stories of the conditions under which you are fighting, and it causes grave concern. I am writing in an attempt to keep you informed as to the conditions here at Claybourne Court, as you requested of me.

The Countess has calmed considerably since your leave taking. She is still far from happy, but I have managed to persuade her to use the chair you ordered, and we have been going on outside walks. They seem to raise her spirits greatly. We take Ginny along on our treks, and the little dog adores the fresh air and green grass to run about. Yesterday, I took the Countess down to the stables, and we visited the horses. I've grown to have warm feelings for Howard, the stable boy. Don't misunderstand. Not romantic feelings. He always gives me handfuls of sugar lumps to give to the horses. 'Miss Taffeta' has become my favorite, and after the baby arrives, Howard has promised me that he will teach me how to ride her. The Countess is ever so ready to be able to ride again. She is really just potty over the horses. I suppose that's because of her father owning a breeding farm. She keeps speaking of riding Spark of Fire, the stallion you brought back from Virginia, but I wonder if that horse is ready to be ridden. Howard says 'No.' I wonder how I'll handle the Countess if he tells her she must ride another in the stable. This is nothing for you to worry about, Captain. I shall work it out.

Your mother visits frequently and so does your brother. I have grown quite fond of your mother. She is a lovely lady. I now see what you meant when you said your brother Sebastian was a bit immature. Still a child in many ways, but a harmless one, I think. He's been fretting lately about the fact that the Government may be placing conscription in order. I am sad to say that I am not certain he will make a very fine addition to the armed forces.

That is all of the news from Claybourne Court, Captain. I do so hope that you are in good health. At first everyone said that the war wouldn't last until Christmas, but now everyone is changing tune. Wishing you God Speed.

Yours Affectionately,

Lily Barton

He smiled as he read her letter. She was extremely articulate, and wrote a fine hand. In addition, she seemed to want to show her concern for his wellbeing and to brighten his day with little tidbits of news about *Claybourne Court*. She was right. Sebastian was not cut out to be a soldier.

The second letter he opened was from his mother.

Dearest Kit,

My goodness how I do miss you, and your sound, intelligent thoughts. The only illogical thing I think you ever did in your life was to marry that fool girl Eleanor. I certainly have no desire to cause you concern, but that wife of yours is almost more than I can handle. I told her after you left that she was a spoiled brat, but it made no difference to her. She just said that I didn't scare her a mite. I'm coping with her - mostly by ignoring her - but it will be awfully nice to have you home again. I think she does things to purposely aggravate me. I have joined a group of ladies who are knitting socks and jumpers for you boys overseas. We meet all day, two days a week. I'm glad to have something to do which makes me feel like I'm contributing in some way. That lovely girl, Barton, who you hired to be Eleanor's nurse is also doing her bit. While she has quiet time, she also does knitting, and contributes it to the lot to be sent to boys in France. She is really a dear girl. So mature for her years, and just lovely in every way. I don't know why Eleanor couldn't be more like her. Imagine me comparing your wife to her nurse!

From what I hear, things do not go terribly well in France. I do worry for you, my son. You are my heart and soul, and I couldn't cope if I lost you. So please take care and remember I think of you often.

With Love,

Mother

It sounded like his mother was having difficulty with Eleanor. He supposed while he had the time, during recovery, he would try to write to his wife and rattle some sense into her head. He held out little hope for such a thing to happen, however. He opened the third letter, from his brother:

Dear Kit,

I hope things are going well for you out there in France. Better you than me. There is talk that the government is going to implement conscription, and I cannot bear the thought of my having to put on a uniform. What in the Hell do you do for women out there? Of course, that probably doesn't matter to you, what with being married and expecting a baby. Speaking of which, your lovely wife has become quite large. One would scarcely know it was Eleanor. She is not happy with the way she looks! I do try to be of help to her, and to Barton, by giving her back rubs and the like. Barton is a Savior. She takes Eleanor outside most every day, when the weather is nice, and has her interested in decorating a room for the baby. Seems like dull stuff to me, but of course, it's a woman's thing.

I'm enjoying my new Hispano Suiza. It drives like a dream, which it should for the price I paid for it. But, as I always say, you only live once. I can have all the girls I want just by driving by and waving from the car, but it doesn't do much good when there is nowhere to take them. England's society life has become as dead as dead can be. All of the men are away fighting this miserable war, and that leaves very few to attend parties. God, I hope it all ends soon. On top of that, they are rationing food items, and even petrol, so that makes for an un-enjoyable life at the moment.

Well, I do hope you're holding up, old Sod. I'll write again in a week or so.

Fondly,
Sebastian

Now there was an example of a young man who was incapable of thinking about anyone but himself, Kit laughed. "God, I hope he doesn't join the military," he said aloud. What a beastly addition he would make to the troops. The last letter of the day sat on the table by his bed. Of course, it was Eleanor's. Rather depressingly he opened the envelope:

My Darling Kit,
Oh how I long for you to be here with me. I am so dreadfully unhappy, and wonder sometimes if I can bear one more minute of your absence. Isn't there some way you can get furlough to come home for just awhile? Wouldn't they let you come if they knew you had a wife who was in desperate need of you?
I know that you are supposed to be doing an important job for the Country, but I can't see why one man, more or less, makes any difference. Especially one who is married and has a child on the way. You have only been away for two months, and it seems like a year.
Barton has been a Godsend, I must admit that. She does make every attempt at keeping my mind occupied. She has been taking me outside in that chair you ordered for me, and I do so like to be able to breathe in fresh air. Unfortunately, I will soon be so large, and then I won't even be able fit comfortably in the chair. Perhaps we will have a long autumn. And then a short winter. Come April, I'll find myself with a baby, and undoubtedly you still won't be here. What woman in her right head would ever have a baby if she thought her husband wouldn't be there with her? Not only that, but I can't even have my own mother by my side. But, at least after the baby comes, I'll be able to return to a more normal life. Sebastian says he will take me for a ride in that splendid auto of his, and perhaps we can visit London. I've also thought about taking Barton to Bath with me, so that we can enjoy the warm waters. Perhaps there is more going on in Bath.
We have started to decorate the baby's nursery. I decided upon the room at the far end of the hallway, as I don't wish to be woken by a crying child at night. The room is large, and there will be space allotted for the Nanny to sleep. I have also decided that I have no intention of feeding the baby my own milk. I have heard from other women that allowing such a thing will ruin the shape of one's breasts. So, I shall make arrangements for a wet nurse when the time nears. My little Ginny is as

precious as ever. She is simply the light of my life. I don't know how I would endure without her. Anyway, the baby's room will be all white. That way, if it is boy or girl it will do. Once the baby comes, and I know which it is, I shall add pillows, stuffed toys, paintings and so forth in the proper color - blue or pink. I do so hope that you are here to see it, but I doubt you will be. Several men from the village have already been killed out there in France. Of course, they weren't Officers, so I'm sure that does make a difference. They say that officers are very rarely injured.
There is really nothing else to tell you, right now. Things here are just about as bad as they can be.
Love,
Eleanor

"Well, now there's a letter to cheer a fellow up", Kit thought to himself. My God, did the woman have no conception of what he was going through? He wasn't even certain he should let her know that he had been injured. She would only start haranguing away at trying to use his wound as a way to get a furlough. Perhaps after the baby comes, she'll become more considerate of others, he thought. It was the one rail he hung all of his hopes upon. It was the only reason he could think of for the tremendous change in her outlook on life since their marriage. My God, would he even have thought of marrying her if she'd been like this when he met her? She'd been very sweet, thoughtful, and filled with interest about him, and *Claybourne Court.* Now, everything was about *her.* He was also concerned about Sebastian. The boy was such an immature fool. Thank God he had no intentions of volunteering for the military. Perhaps the war would be over by the time conscription came into being. A nurse came over to his cot and interrupted his thoughts.

"Captain Claybourne, you're being transferred tomorrow morning to the Base Hospital at Brielen. The ambulance will be here at eight o'clock, so we'll be wanting you up early, so that you can have your breakfast before you leave."

"Thank you nurse. I'll be looking forward to it, although I must say you people here at *Etaples* have been splendid."

"Thank you, Sir. We do try our best, but with so many wounded coming to us, it's hard to give the attention we'd like."

Kit looked up, and saw Michael, his valet, approaching his bedside. "Well, good to see you, Michael. How are things since our last visit?" Kit asked.

"Well, Sir, I have a request. I'm not allowed to tend to you properly out here in France. I don't like doing nothing more than sitting around that fancy French mansion, with a bunch of other valets. At least they're busy, taking care of their employers, who are all high-up Officers. I've come to ask your permission for me to resign my position as a Valet, and join up with the other soldiers. I want to do my bit too, Sir."

"I hate to see you go, Michael. But, I understand your position. Of course, you have my permission. The only thing I'll ask is that you return to me after this damned thing is over and we're all back in England."

"Yes, Milord. I should want to do that. I thank you for being so accommodating. I wish you great luck, and I hope to see you again along the way."

"Yes, Michael. Thank you for your excellent service to me. Good luck in your new spot, and God Speed." Kit and Michael shook hands, and Michael turned and left the Clearing Station.

7

Kit lay in his trench, trying to become accustomed to the quiet that reigned supreme. The artillery guns had stopped their horrendous thunder, and everything was very still. It was Christmas Eve, and he couldn't help but be homesick. He'd received a package of knitted wool socks from his mother, and also one with a knitted jumper in it from Lily Barton. Sebastian sent photos of his automobile, and Eleanor, true to form, sent a bottle of his favorite shaving lotion and a new razor. The bottle was broken. His arm still ached from his wound, but all in all, he was physically fit to be back in the trenches.

German troops began decorating the areas around their trenches earlier in the evening. Nobody thought much of it. All of the soldiers were nostalgic for past Christmases, so it was no surprise that the Germans would feel that way too. They began by placing candles on their trenches and on small Christmas trees. Then they continued the celebration by singing Christmas Carols. It wasn't much longer before Captain Claybourne's regiment began singing Carols too. The two sides continued by calling Christmas greetings to one another. It was downright peculiar. Soon, thereafter, there were excursions across 'No Man's Land' where small gifts were exchanged, such as cigarettes, candy, buttons, food and alcohol. Later, some of the men even engaged in a football match, north of Ypres. Since Captain Claybourne was an officer, he should not have participated in such odd behavior, nor allowed it to continue. But, he was not about to report his men to his commanding officer, and there seemed little harm in both sides remembering that there was such a thing as Christmas spirit. The poor boys had enough of the roar of guns the other 364 days of the year. Let them share a moment of peace on that one night. By the next day, the battle continued, and it was as if the impromptu truce had never occurred.

Life in the trenches was almost unbearable. This was not war as he had been taught. It was a horrendous mixture of tedious monotony punctuated by moments of sheer terror. Once the British Expeditionary Forces were able to reorganize and take part in the Battle of the Marne, where Lily's brother had been killed September 1914, the *Scots Greys* had shifted from covering the retreat to screening the advance. Eventually, the advance of the B.E.F. halted at the Battle of Aisne, where British and German forces fought to standstill just short of the Chemin des Dames. After being pulled from the trenches at the Aisne, the *Scots Greys* were sent north to Belgium as part of the lead elements as the British and Germans raced toward the sea, each trying to outflank the other. With the cavalry reinforced to Corps strength, the *Scots Greys* and the rest of the 5th Cavalry Brigade were transferred to the newly formed 2nd Calvary position.

As the front became more static, and the need for riflemen on the front line more pressing, the *Scots Greys* found themselves being used almost exclusively as infantry. The regiment was almost continuously engaged from the start of the First Battle of Ypres until its end. A Battalion would serve a spell in the front line, then spend some time in the support lines, then in reserve, and then they would be allowed a period of short rest, before returning to the front line again. A day in the front line trenches started before dawn. Everyone was woken and ordered to fix bayonets or climb onto the fire step to ward off any enemy dawn raid. Both sides practiced the 'stand-to' procedure up and down the line, and both knew that each other did this. But, dawn raids did occur. Afterwards, it was breakfast and weapon cleaning time. Breakfast was usually bully beef or other tinned food and was brought up in containers from the field kitchens. In some areas rum was issued to warm up the troops. After all work was done, including repairing duckboards, refilling sandbags, repairing and reinforcing the walls of the trench, the soldiers could relax a little. Many would take advantage of quiet periods to snatch a bit of sleep or write letters home. It was only at dark that real action began. Some of the most dangerous jobs on the front line meant going out into 'No Man's Land.' Being out there, a soldier felt very exposed. The slightest sound would alert the enemy and the entire area would erupt in a fury of flares and machine guns. 'No Man's Land' was a wretched, deadly area. However, it was necessary for patrols to go out there to repair barbed wire, check on enemy movements, recover equipment and retrieve wounded or dead comrades. Death was a constant companion. Disease was rampant. Rats and lice infested the trenches in the millions. Drawn by all of the dead bodies, rats were absolutely everywhere, and they were despised.

Back in England, the mood at *Claybourne Court* was not festive. Eleanor was now five months along in her pregnancy, and continued with her complaining. Sebastian came home to spend the holidays with his mother and sister-in-law, but his mood was dreary as well. The rumors kept flying that the Government was going to put conscription into effect. Although it would take another year before such a thing actually occurred, Sebastian continually obsessed about it. Lady Cynthia was totally fed up with Eleanor's whining, and Sebastian's immaturity, when she had a son who was fighting for his Country and his life in France. The only person she didn't mind being around was Lily, and Lily would be spending Christmas in her own home in the village.

Lily too, was tired of the mood at *Claybourne Court.* She looked very much forward to being with her mother for the holiday. The twenty-fifth fell on a Friday, so Mrs. Briggs had given her Saturday off too, besides her regular day of Sunday. It was the first time she'd had three days in a row to be home with her Mum. She arrived at the cottage on Christmas Eve. She'd stayed at *Claybourne Court* long enough to settle Lady Eleanor, and take Ginny for an evening walk. Mrs. Briggs told Lily to go along home, and that she would see to Ginny's ten o'clock walk.

Bursting through the door of the cottage, she hugged her mother tightly. "Oh, Mum. I've three whole days to spend with you. Isn't that grand?"

"Oh yes, Lily. It will be such a nice Christmas. I've invited William Morris and his son, David, over for Christmas Dinner. David's been mustered out of the military due to a leg injury. I thought it would be nice if we had some friends to share the holiday dinner with us."

Lily could see that the big dining table was set with her Mum's best china and silver. There was also a small, decorated tree in the parlor. The cottage looked like it used to before her father died. William Morris, a chemist, was a widower from the village. He and his wife were once close friends of Lily's parents, Elisabeth and Tom Barton. Mrs. Morris had died shortly before Dr. Barton, leaving William as a widower. He had a son, David, whom Lily had known for years.

"That's a lovely idea, Mum. I'm sure Mr. Morris gets lonely at these holiday times. He'll probably welcome a good, home cooked, Christmas dinner and David must be trying to readjust after being away at the Front," Lily commented.

"Oh, I know they both will be glad of a nice visit on Christmas. We can all attend church together after the meal, and a rest. Now, come here and hang your coat up my sweet girl. How did you leave things at the Court?"

"Oh Mum, the mood's really quite dreary, especially for the Holidays. I had hoped that the Captain might have been given a furlough, but that wasn't to be. He wrote me a letter last week, and said that there was no hope for such a thing, and that the fighting just goes on and on."

"How is his wife coming along?" Elisabeth asked, as she poured tea into two cups, and handed one to Lily.

"Not so very well, Mum. I do work hard to keep her amused and smiling, but it's not easy. She's still so lonely for her Mum and Dad in Virginia. It's probably a good thing that there are no passenger ships going to and fro, or I feel certain she'd be on one."

"Surely she wouldn't leave her husband, when he's fighting at the front?"

"I hate to say so, but I think it's a distinct possibility. I just keep praying that after the baby comes, she'll have a change of attitude. I'm almost certain that's what the Captain hopes too."

"It's not really for me to say, since I've never even met her, but she seems like an odd one to me."

"Oh Mum. She's very young to have married and come across to England. Then the war came and now she's alone, expecting a baby. I just don't think she ever dreamed it would be like this."

"Well, you'd think her mother might have prepared her. It sounds to me like she thought it'd be great fun to marry an English Earl, and make all of her friends jealous. That's even what you've told me. Don't you ever wonder if she ever even loved the Captain?"

"Yes, Mum, I do wonder that. She seems so disinterested in him. There he is, fighting with all his heart and soul, in that ghastly battle at Ypres, and she just shows no concern at all. She says that Officers never get killed. I don't know how she came about that knowledge?"

"I don't know either, but it's a fool thing to say. Does the Captain still write to you regular, like?"

"Yes, well, every few weeks or so. I write to him and keep him up-to-date on happenings at *Claybourne Court*, and then he'll reply to my letters. It's hard for me to write to him. I don't like to tell him how dreadful the Countess is acting. I think his mother tells him, because he always seems to know what things Milady has said or done, and it wasn't me who's told him."

"Well, Miss Lily it's time we wind it up for the night. We'll be rising early in the morning in order to have dinner ready for William Morris and his son."

"That's fine with me, Mum. I'm awfully tired. Now, don't forget to wake me when you get up. I want to help with every bit of the meal."

They hugged one another, and said good night, as they climbed the narrow stairway to the bedrooms.

Bright and early on Christmas day, Lily put on her dressing gown, and descended the stairway, where she found her Mum already in the kitchen. She was hard at work whipping cream for fruit salad. Lily set about cutting apples and bananas into slices, and opened a can of tinned pineapple. She mixed them all together, and when Mum finished with the cream, she put the whole bit in a bowl, and folded everything together. Then she sprinkled some powdered sugar into the mixture. After dipping her finger to see if the taste was to her liking, she nodded her head, and put a cover over the bowl. Just before they served it, she would add some marshmallows. For now, the bowl went into the icebox.

Meanwhile, her Mum busied herself with rubbing a paste of herbs over the outside of a large, standing rib roast. Then she placed it in the oven at a high temperature. It would be turned much lower in fifteen minutes, and then allowed to cook until it was the desired inner temperature. She had already calculated when everything needed to be finished in order for them to sit down and eat when the Morris's arrived. It would be ready to be carved at just the proper time. The Morris's were invited for half after twelve. Lily peeled potatoes, and put them into a large kettle on the stove, so that they could be cooked and ready to be placed around the roast, where they would take on a lovely browned appearance. She also readied carrots to be laid next to the roast toward the very end of the cooking time. Mum had already prepared a lovely trifle for dessert, and it too was chilling. At eleven o'clock, she disappeared back up the staircase, and changed into the dress she'd purchased especially for the Holiday. She so rarely bought anything new, but decided she could also use whatever she chose as a dress for her duties at *Claybourne Court*. The shops had very few items to choose from. Ready-to-Wear clothing had only just become available before the war began, and now the village dry goods store was unable to obtain a large supply, due to the need for all factories to turn out uniforms for the thousands of soldiers who were fighting. Finally, she settled upon a sailor midi dress, with a calf-length skirt in navy blue wool, and a navy and white midi top, with a low, navy knot. She slipped the dress on, and breathed a sigh at the freedom she felt at no longer having to wear a corset. She brushed her long auburn hair, and wound it into a figure eight, pinning it at the back, but allowing a few curls to escape by her face. She added court shoes to her ensemble, and returned to the kitchen, where she donned a starched, white apron. Her Mum was the next to disappear up the stairway to change into her Christmas Day dress.

She was very conservative in her clothing choices, and still favored Edwardian shirtwaists, with black skirt and white blouse. For the first time in ever so long, Mom had begun to care about her appearance again, after the loss of Lily's father. She took time brushing her still thick, lovely hair, and swept it up into her usual Gibson Girl style. She turned around and peered at herself in the mirror, and was satisfied with her appearance. She did not look like she was the mother of a twenty-one year old daughter, or of her deceased soldier-son, who would now be twenty. Down the stairs she came flying, to finish up the meal preparations, before the Morris's arrived. Lily was busy pouring off fat from the roast, and readying the ingredients to make Yorkshire pudding with au jus. Her Mum put the carrots on the stove to begin cooking, so that they could be placed next to the roast for the last few minutes, to absorb the flavor of the meat. A few moments later, the roast was taken from the oven, and set to the side. A couple of spoonful's of the roast fat was added to the pudding cups, followed by a mixture of flour, eggs and milk, and the oven temperature turned to very high. The puddings came out fluffy and lightly browned, looking delicious. Mum decided she would let William Morris carve, as it was traditionally the man's responsibility, and it was ever so nice to have a man joining their table. The meal was very close to being served.

Both of them removed their aprons, and smoothed their hair. Their faces were flushed from the high temperature in the kitchen, which leant lovely color to both sets of cheeks. Lily put the tea-kettle on, and readied four cups. She would offer tea before the dinner. A wonderful fire was roaring in the parlor fireplace. She so enjoyed being home with her mother, and couldn't help but wonder what this day was like for Captain Claybourne. Of course, he had to be missing the lovely dining room at *Claybourne Court*, and the immense decorated tree that stood in the drawing room. She wondered how Lady Eleanor was enjoying the day. Or *if* she were enjoying it. For weeks now, all Lily had heard were stories about Christmas at *Cloverhill*, her family's home in Virginia. Nothing at *Claybourne Court* compared. Lily thought to herself that in some ways it was better that the Captain wasn't home. She wondered if he would have grown as weary hearing about *Cloverhill* as Lily had.

Her thoughts were interrupted by rapping at the front door. Her Mum again smoothed her hair, and answered the door. There stood William Morris and his son, David. Mr. Morris was better looking than Lily had remembered. He must have been about fifty years, and had brown hair, with quite a good bit of grey. His eyes were very blue. He wore what was obviously his Sunday best suit, and carried a bottle of wine, a lovely bouquet of flowers, and a box of *Cadbury* chocolate fancies. His son, David, stood next to him, on crutches. Lily hadn't known that David lost a leg in the war. His pant leg was pinned up to the knee, where the stump would be. Her heart went out to him. She concentrated upon not letting her face show any surprise or sadness.

"Come in, come in," chimed her Mum. "We're so happy you could join us for the holiday."

David went ahead of his father, maneuvering rather well on the crutches. Lily led him to a comfortable chair, and reached out her arms to take the crutches, as he made to sit down. She then offered him a cup of tea.

"Oh, thank you, Miss Lily. That sounds lovely. I got so used to drinking gallons of tea at the Front. Now, I never seem to get enough."

"I have the kettle on, David. I'm sure it's ready. Let me fetch you a cup." She scurried away to the kitchen, where she had lined up the four cups. In the meantime, her Mum was overwhelmed by the thoughtful hostess gifts William had presented to her.

"My goodness, Will. I'm knocked for six! Where did you find such lovely blooms in December?"

"The local flower shop had them. I was surprised too. Perhaps they grow them in one of those glass houses that keep the cold out."

"Yes, I'm sure. And then, you've included chocolate fancies - *Cadbury's* no less. William, I'm stunned. I can't remember the last time I was given chocolate candies. And, my land sakes, wine too! You are so terribly thoughtful. Thank you so much." She called to me, "Lily, come see what the Morris's have brought us." Lily came back into the parlor, carrying a cup of tea, which she carefully handed to David. After he took it, she turned and walked over to where her Mum stood with Will Morris, still just inside of the doorway.

"Oh, Mr. Morris. How very generous of you. I doubt anyone else in the village has fancy *Cadbury* chocolates, flowers and wine too. I work at *Claybourne Court*, and I'd be truly surprised if such things can be found there. You've gone way overboard, but we're ever so thankful. Please come in - give me your coat, and let me get you a cup of tea. David is already enjoying some."

Will Morris shrugged out of his coat, and hat, and handed them to Lily, and she, in turn, placed them in the cupboard. Then she went back to the kitchen and returned with Will Morris's cup of tea. He was already seated on the sofa, which fronted on the fireplace. Lily made one more trip and brought the teapot into the parlor, setting it on the tea table. Her Mum was seated next to him. Lily took the last chair, across from the sofa. They all sat quietly sipping the tea, and enjoying the fire.

"How long have you been back in England, David?" Mum asked.

"Not very long, Mrs. Barton. I was wounded at Ypres. Spent some time at a base hospital, and then at the Prince of Wales hospital here in England, recuperating. I'll be returning after Christmas, to be fitted for an artificial leg, and learn how to get about on it."

"What a dreadful thing to happen to you," interjected Mum. "But, thank the Lord you're alive, and back with us. I lost my son, Jordan, you know, at Marne They never even found his body."

"Yes, Ma'am, I know. I'm mighty angry about the Jerry's taking my leg, but I'm so glad to be out of it, that it's almost worth it. It's a horror out there."

"The gentleman I work for, Lord…I mean… Captain Claybourne is at Ypres. His wife says that officers never get involved in the actual fighting. Is that true, David?"

"Not really, Miss Lily. I know of many officers who fight with their men. Most feel that they don't want to ask anything of their men that they wouldn't do themselves. The higher-ups are less likely to fight - Majors, Colonels and the like. But, Captains mostly do."

"That's what I feared. The Countess won't listen to anyone who says differently. I think she would prefer not to believe that her husband could actually be fighting the real battle."

"Could be, Miss Lily. Doesn't he write to her and tell her of his exploits?"

"He writes to her, but never says anything about how dreadful the conditions are, or what exactly he's involved in. He mostly shows his concern for her in his letters. At least, that's true of the ones that I see, and the ones that she shares with me."

"He writes to you too?"

"Yes. Before he left, he asked me to keep him abreast of his wife's progress. She's expecting a baby. He's very concerned about her. He hired me to be a ladies' maid, and also a companion to her. It's a fine line to walk."

"I imagine so, Miss."

Mum interrupted, telling us that it was time for the meal to be served. She asked Will to carve the roast, and he responded with alacrity. Poor man. It was obvious that he missed having a wife and home where he could do all of the chores that a married man was expected to perform. He and Mum disappeared to the kitchen, and Lily helped David to stand and retrieve his crutches, so that he could move into the dining room. Will carried in the roast, while Lily and her Mum brought in the puddings and other side dishes. Finally, everyone was seated at the table, and a prayer was said in thankfulness for the lovely meal, but also in remembrance of those who couldn't be with them on that Christmas day, 1914.

They sipped the excellent wine, and delighted in the sumptuous meal. Lily was glad that her mother had invited the Morris's. It made for a much nicer Christmas. Mum seemed very pleased with her company, and it crossed Lily's mind that her mother had a bit of a crush on Will. Well, it was going on a year since they'd lost her father. She knew her Mum was lonely, and it was obvious that Mr. Morris was as well. Lily would be happy if she could stop worrying so much about her Mum. Will seemed like a lovely gentleman, so she had no objection to the possibility that a liaison might develop between her mother and him. On the other hand, she was somewhat concerned that David Morris was showing quite a lot of interest in *her*. He was a very nice boy - actually very good looking, in spite of his missing leg. He had light brown, shiny hair, and dimples that showed when he smiled. Lily didn't know why she felt like she wouldn't welcome his attention. Certainly, there was no one else in her life. She just didn't feel that she was ready to become involved in any sort of relationship with a man. She admired his courage and bravery, and thought him a very nice person. She just wasn't attracted to him in that way.

The four of them finished their dinner, and enjoyed some Port in front of the fire before it was time to go to the village church for Christmas services. It was not a long walk, and Mum strolled next to Will, while David limped along on his crutches next to Lily. It was quite cold out, and their breath came in visible puffs. There was little conversation, as it took David all of his energy to make progress on his crutches. The path to the church was rocky and dotted with potholes, so it took strict attention in order to avoid accident.

Lily was glad when they reached the small, village chapel. The church was draped with greenery, and the ceremony was filled with carols. When they all emerged from the meaningful service, it had begun to snow. Great, wet flakes descended from the sky, and the bells in the church tower rang. It was a perfect Christmas setting. For just a moment, Captain Claybourne's handsome face appeared in Lily's mind. She wished he could be sharing the beautiful Christmas Eve in his English village. She tried to turn her attention back to David Morris. He was saying something to her.

"I wouldn't want you to be thinking I'm being forward, Miss Lily. I've had such a nice time this evening, and I can't help but wonder if you would agree to walk out with me on your off days?"

"Well - David - I only have the one off-day. Sunday. I rather like to keep that day special for Mum. Otherwise, I wouldn't see her often."

"Well, would you be spending your off-night back at *Claybourne Court*, or do you stay at your Mum's cottage and return to Claybourne in the morn?"

"Mostly, I stay with my Mum overnight and return in the morning." Lily's heart was sinking, as she couldn't think of a decent way to turn him down without hurting his feelings.

"Well, then, couldn't you spend the day-time with your Mum, and walk out with me in the evening? We might go for tea in the village."

"I suppose that would do," she answered. "I think not every Sunday though, David. Perhaps you and your father could join Mum and me on various Sundays. Why don't we talk again after you're home from the Prince of Wales?"

"That'll be fine. I'm very happy to know that you'd be willing to see me on and off."

"Yes, that would be fine, David. Do ring me when you return from hospital."

They continued, walking in silence back to the cottage, where father and son took their leave. Lily and her Mum went inside, and set about returning the cottage to normal.

8

Nothing changed much at *Claybourne Court*, as the weeks and months progressed into the New Year. Eleanor continued to whine, Lady Cynthia continued to look at Eleanor in disgust, Sebastian continued to complain non-stop about the possibility of conscription, and Lily tried to walk the fine line between being a companion to the Countess, and being her employee. There were some adaptations in Lily's personal routine. She began to walk out with David Morris on an occasional Sunday evening, and enjoyed his company more than she'd thought she might. He was very thoughtful and considerate, and had a good sense of humor. They talked little of the war. He didn't seem to want to dwell on that time in his life, and Lily certainly couldn't blame him. He had his artificial limb fitted, and moved back to *Claybourne-on-Colne*, where he worked in the chemist's shop with his father. Everyone in the village knew and liked him. His father, Will, also became a steady companion to Lily's Mum, and she suspected that sooner or later they would make an announcement. When she spoke to her about her feelings for him, she never went into great detail, but told Lily that she had grown very fond of him, and had forgotten how nice it was to have a man in her life. Lily was happy for both of them, but was not ready for that sort of companionship in her own life.

Sometimes, on afternoons, when she walked Ginny, she strolled to the stables, and visited with Howard. She learned to stop by the kitchen and fill her pockets with sugar lumps, or apples, so she always had a treat to offer to the horses. They became her friends, and seemed to expect something wonderful from her when she came around. She loved to run her hand over their velvet noses. Howard taught her how to groom them, so if she had the time, she'd brush, comb and smooth their coats and manes until they shined. She looked forward to the summer, when she would learn to ride. There was no question that Lady Eleanor was more than ready to resume her favorite pastime, and Lily was anxious to join her. She even purchased a riding habit, so that she would be ready when the time came.

On January 19, 1915 a perfectly ghastly event occurred. Two Zeppelin airships silently cruised in over the East coast of England and bombed Great Yarmouth and King's Lynn. These silent killers carried the flaming sword through the skies hundreds of miles above the battle lines, striking terror among the non-combatant populations of their cities. Shrieking bombs crashed through the roofs of sleeping civilians in the dead of night, bringing their toll of death to innocent people. The two raids, on 19 January, killed nine people. The fact that unprepared civilians were killed was beastly, and the fear that the German action caused spread from city to town and from village to hamlet. British citizens were terrified about when a zeppelin raid could next occur. There were no shelters prepared for people to flee to safety, and the best one could do was run and hide in a basement or cellar. Although the damage was slight, compared to the horrors that were taking place in the trenches in France, the sense of collective intimidation was astounding. The Germans succeeded in their tactic to frighten Englanders. But, instead of folding with fear, Brits found a way to minimize any more damage that such evil weapons could bring about. From that time on, they were instructed to black out any lights that shone at nighttime, thus making it nearly impossible for the air ships to hit their intended targets. That maneuver didn't stop the attacks completely, but made them much less frequent than they might have been, and lessened the damage.

April finally arrived. Lily was always so happy when spring once again returned to her beloved land. On the velvet lawns of *Claybourne Court,* daffodils bloomed in wild profusion. Hyacinths, tulips and forsythia followed.

Soon there was a mass of color. The trees began to leaf out in vivid green, and the cotton-tailed rabbits could be seen scurrying through the soft grass. April meant the end of winter, but more importantly, its arrival meant that Lady Eleanor's waiting time was over. The baby was due any moment, and they all waited with baited breath. The due date came and went, and everyone was on edge. Tempers flared over nothing. Lady Cynthia held her tongue, and allowed the Countess to whine incessantly. Sebastian stayed away from the house, as suddenly it held little appeal for him. Lily stopped taking her off-day, for fear that she wouldn't be nearby when the Countess needed her. Finally, on the night of April 15, Mrs. Briggs woke her and said that Lady Eleanor's pains had started. She immediately rang the doctor, since they weren't about to take any chances that the baby might arrive before there was professional help available. Lily wasn't terribly concerned, since she had attended the delivery of many a child when helping her father in his surgery. Usually, he and Lily would travel to the expectant mother's home, and perform the delivery in the woman's own bed.

Lily dressed quickly, and briskly walked to the Lady Eleanor's room. She was lying on her back, crying and moaning. "Oh dear Barton, I'm so glad you're here. If these pains grow any worse, I shall die."

Of course, Lily knew that no such thing was about to happen. In fact, she was in the very early stages of labor. The pains would grow much more intense before the night was over. However, she wasn't about to tell Lady Eleanor that. She filled a basin with water, poured in some lavender water, and sat down beside her. Dipping a flannel into the solution, she bathed her forehead and murmured words of encouragement. "Everything will be just fine, Milady. By this time tomorrow, you'll have a lovely baby. Try to be calm, and take deep breaths. Mrs. Briggs has rung the doctor. I'm sure he'll be here shortly. Tell me when each pain comes, so that I might time how far apart they are."

The pains were still very spread out and, Lily's experience told her it would be hours of labor. The most important thing she could do was to try to keep her as comfortable as possible, and not let fear take hold. In between the pains, Lady Eleanor was quite all right, but when another wave hit, she wept and cried out for her mother. Lily did feel badly for her. She surely would want her own Mum if ever she gave birth. Probably an hour passed, and the pains grew steadily more forceful. She switched from crying out for her mother, to damning Captain Claybourne. "Damn Kit. He got me into this mess! Ahhhh, and then he left me here alone! I didn't want a baby. He knew that. I know there are ways of preventing this. A girlfriend - Ahhhh - once told me of something called a French letter. If I know about them, why doesn't Kit? Ahhhh - he wanted to make me pregnant. All men think about is producing an heir. I shall never forgive him for this."

"Shhhh, Milady. It won't help you to become upset. You'll feel differently once the baby arrives. All woman go through feeling like this when their time comes."

"No, I won't feel better. I wish I'd never married him. I think - Ahhhh - that he just hopes that a baby will keep me from wanting to be and act young. I never should have married someone so old. He's boring. Ahhh."

Lily so hoped the baby would hurry and make its appearance. The Countess was getting on her nerves. She never seemed to know when to be circumspect. Lily did not want to hear about her personal feelings regarding the Captain, and thought her very nasty to be speaking about him in such a fashion. Lily admired him greatly, and couldn't believe Lady Eleanor didn't realize how fortunate she was. Who knew what he might have been going through at that very moment, but whatever it was, it was surely no better than the Countess's difficulties. At least Lady Eleanor knew that her trouble would come to an end, and that she would have a lovely baby after it was finished.

The doctor finally arrived. He was a bit abrupt with her, and said that he could hear her whining all over the house. Then he washed his hands, and examined her. After that, he rolled his sleeves down, told her that it would be awhile yet, and assured her that he would stay. Lily asked Mrs. Briggs to fetch him a cup of tea. He went to the drawing room, and settled himself with the *London Times*. Lady Eleanor, having been chastised by the doctor, stopped her wailing for a bit, but as the pains increased, so did her vocal protestations. Finally, the physician returned to the room, and once again examined her.

"All right, Lady Eleanor. The baby is crowning, and when I tell you to push, I want you to bear down as hard as you can." This went on three or four times, and with each push, the Countess screamed at the top of her lungs. At long last, the baby made its appearance. It was a little boy, and Lily couldn't help but think about how thrilled the Captain would be. While he was fighting in the trenches for his life and his Country, a new being had been brought into the world - a lovely son who would eventually change the Captain's life. The doctor smacked the infant on the bottom, and he let loose a healthy cry, that almost equaled his mother's. The doctor laughed, and said he'd obviously inherited his lungs from her. Then he handed the tiny life to Lily, while he went about taking care of the last bit of delivery. Lily wiped the baby clean, and smoothed his hair, of which there was a great amount. It was brown, like his father's, and his eyes were a lovely blue. It was hard to know whether they would be more like his mother's or his father's. All in all, he was a beautiful baby. Lily swaddled him into a white blanket, and laid him on his mother's chest. She put her arms about him, but it seemed the gesture was more an attempt to keep him from rolling onto the floor, then a true cuddle of love. The doctor looked up, and told her to place the boy at her breast, so that he could begin learning to feed. Lady Eleanor looked aghast.

"No doctor. I have no intention of breast-feeding this child. I shall not have my breasts ruined because of his gnawing. I shall have a wet nurse. This should all have been arranged before. Now what are we to do?"

"You *will*, indeed, breast feed him," retorted the doctor. "Lady Eleanor, we are in a war in this Country. There is a shortage of everything, including milk. This child needs milk from his own mother's breast to help him grow healthy and strong, and to assure that he will build immunity against disease. I do not want to hear any more nonsense from you. Most mothers are thrilled to breast feed their babies. Whether you are or aren't, *that* child needs nourishment, and *you* will provide it."

The Countess began to weep again, but she didn't protest. She unwrapped the infant's head, and placed him at her breast. Tears were streaming down her face. It would have been nice to think that they were tears of joy, which they should have been, but it was obvious that she was very unhappy. She resembled a young girl who had been scolded for being naughty. She didn't look down at the beautiful child in her arms, but bit her lip and turned away, as though she couldn't bear to watch him suckle her breast. Lily believed the child could sense his mother's mood, for shortly after he began to cry - pitiful wails.

"Now what's the matter with him?" the Countess asked.

"There's nothing the matter with your son, Lady Eleanor. But, you are showing him no affection. It is as though he were trying to nurse from a marble statue. He went around to the side of the bed, and righted the baby in her arms. Now, cuddle him, Lady Eleanor. You do know what 'cuddle' means, I assume? Or don't they believe in cuddling in America?" He was being very sarcastic.

"Of course I know what 'cuddle means'. I'm just very worn out. After all, I've just gone through a ghastly birth. Why can't he sleep for a while, and then I might be more ready to cuddle him, as you wish?"

"Lady Eleanor, you are a very exasperating young lady. This is your son. Your own flesh and blood. Do you not care if he needs to be fed? You did not go through a ghastly birth. In fact, it was one of the easiest births I have attended, and I have delivered hundreds of babies. I might add that you are the only mother I have ever seen who does not seem to have the ability to naturally love her child. Now, I repeat. Put the child to your breast, put your hand under his beautiful head, murmur loving words to him so that he knows he is cared for, and he will do very nicely."

"The Countess looked at the doctor in astonishment, but did not argue. She followed his instructions, and soon the baby was suckling sweetly, with his tiny eyes closed, his hands balled into miniscule fists and a look of contentment on his face. "All right, Lady Eleanor, That's more like it. Let him nurse until he begins to turn his head away. Then you will know he is full. Then he can sleep and so can you. Until the next time he needs a feeding."

"How often will he need feeding?" she sniffled.

"Every few hours. Don't expect to be getting a lot of sleep these first few weeks." She began to sob, but the doctor paid her no mind. He turned to me. "Now, Miss Barton, that is your name, is it not?"

"Yes, Doctor," Lily replied.

"Since there is no nanny present, and the mother seems not to know the first thing about babies, I am hoping that you will be the one to help her learn. Are you capable of doing that?"

"Yes, Doctor. My father was a physician. I've cared for many babies, mostly in illness, but I won't have any trouble with the new Viscount. I look forward to caring for him."

"Yes. Well, I'm happy that there is someone in this home who knows about infants." He turned back to Lady Eleanor. "Countess, this child's father is fighting in the trenches in France. We owe him a healthy son when he returns. That must be your only concern. Once his father is home, you may go back to concerning yourself with your appearance. Until then, your son should be your only interest. Do I make myself clear?"

"Yes, Doctor," she answered, not at all happily.

"Good. Then I shall take leave of you. I'll stop by in a day or two and I hope to see great improvement in your mothering skills."

With that, he exited the room. Lily was left to cope with the Countess's flood of tears. The baby continued to nurse, and she did keep her arms about him, but she wept harder and harder. In between sobs, she tried to speak. "I've never been…spoken to so… rudely… in all my life. That man has no…bedside manner. He has no… right to say such terrible things…to me. I am a Countess. He practices a trade. I shall tell Kit that we need a new physician." The tears were dropping on the baby, and Lily was concerned that he would end up soaked through. He turned his little head to the right, and Lily made the decision that he probably had nursed long enough. She reached down, and took him into her arms. He was such a tiny little bundle, and so warm. It was inconceivable that Eleanor wasn't potty over him. She laid him in the bassinette that had been readied by the side of the bed. Then she turned her attention to the Countess. She dipped a flannel in warm water, cleaning her breast, and then she buttoned the nightdress. Finally the tears dried.

"There, now Milady. You're very tired. You have a lovely baby boy, and now you need rest. You'll see things very differently after some sleep. Do you have any thoughts about what you want to name the new Viscount, Milady?"

"Kit wanted him named after his father, Winford Edward Claybourne. We'll call him 'Win.' Now let me go to sleep." She turned over on her side and Lily dimmed the light.

Lily shook her head, and leaned over to make certain 'Win' was sleeping soundly and safely. He was a darling baby, and she already adored him.

She went downstairs, and made a stop at Mrs. Brigg's office. It was very early in the morning, and Lily wasn't certain she would be awake. But, there she was, sipping her usual cup of tea, anxiously awaiting news of the baby's birth.

"Oh, Barton. Thank you for coming to me. I had hoped you would. Has the little one arrived?"

"Yes, Mrs. Briggs. A beautiful baby boy. The Countess says that the baby is to be named after the Captain's father, Winford Edward Claybourne. It's a rather nice name, I think."

"Yes. Yes, indeed. I suppose they'll call him 'Win.' That's what Captain Claybourne's father was called."

"Yes, that's what the Countess said."

"How is Lady Eleanor doing? I could hear her clear down here. I think the servants could hear her in the downstairs rooms. Lord, that lady has a set of lungs."

Lily laughed. "Yes, that's what the doctor said. He was very strong with the Countess. He didn't take any foolishness from her. She didn't want to nurse the child, but believe me, she did."

"Didn't want to nurse her own child? What on earth is the matter with her? Is she showing any affection toward him?"

"No, Ma'am. It distresses me. Perhaps she's just worn out, but you know how we have all hoped and waited for the baby to see if the birth would improve her temperament. I'm not seeing any improvement as yet. She's sleeping now. Let's see how she is upon waking. The trouble is, the baby will wake for another feeding, and I feel certain that Lady Eleanor will go into a tirade. The doctor is extremely stern about the baby being nursed. The Lady doesn't like that at all. She wanted a wet nurse."

"A wet nurse? And where would she be thinking that she'd find a wet nurse? You know, I believe some of these ideas come from the fact that she was raised on one of those American plantations. I know all of that terrible fighting about slavery is mostly over, but many people who own large estates still have a great many servants who live on the grounds. Over there, they probably always have someone on the premises who has given birth, and they hand the baby over to her."

"Yes, I'm afraid that's true. She'll just have to get used to nursing the boy, at least until he can be weaned onto a bottle. But, the doctor was most firm about there being a war on, and milk not being in huge supply. I must be on my way, Mrs. Briggs. I need to let the Lady Cynthia know that she is a grandmother, and that the child has been named after her deceased husband."

Lily continued on to the first floor, and before she could open the door and get ready to walk to the Dower House, the Lady Cynthia came out of the drawing room. She looked as if she had only just awakened. Rubbing one eye, she said, "Oh Barton. Do tell me. Have I a grandchild?"

"Indeed you have, Milady. A lovely grandson. Perfect in every way. He's sleeping soundly at the moment, but if you'd like, I'll bring him to you when he next wakes. He's been named Winford Edward Claybourne, after the late Earl. The Countess says he'll be known as 'Win.'"

"I am happy that she kept to that choice of a name. My deceased husband would be so proud. Oh, I should love it if you could bring him to me when he wakes. I shall stay here in the big house. We don't need to be taking the little one outside just yet. How is my daughter-in-law holding up?"

"She's also sleeping. The doctor said it was an easy birth, but I suppose no woman who experiences labor would agree with that statement. Certainly not Lady Eleanor," I smiled.

"No, certainly not her. I could hear her screaming for her mother down here. What's more, I could hear her saying dreadful things about my son."

"Oh, Milady, she can't really mean such things. She has a tendency to become rather hysterical. You know."

"Yes, I certainly do. Well, enough about her. Kit needs to be informed. Do you think telegrams are delivered at the front?"

"I rather doubt it, Milady. It would probably be best to write a letter. I know it will take longer, but I don't think a telegram would be much faster, considering that the person making the delivery would have to be sent to the trenches."

"Yes. You're undoubtedly right. I'll write him a letter. You might want to as well, since you were present when his son was born and can describe his features."

"I'd be happy to do that, Milady. I'll go and do so right this minute."

Surprisingly, Lady Cynthia reached out and embraced Lily, saying how much she appreciated her being there to help them through the ordeal. She wasn't normally given to such a show of emotion. Lily told her that she was very happy to have been a part of such an event, and then excused herself to go to her room.

Sitting down at her small writing desk, she gathered a pen and paper, and wrote the letter to Captain Claybourne. It was difficult to know exactly what to say, or how to phrase it. Of course, the most important part of the letter was the news about his son. Lily didn't see any need to concern him about the behavior of his wife. She desperately hoped that as time progressed Lady Eleanor would become a loving mother, and by the time he came safely home, he would find an affectionate wife and an adoring mother.

9

Captain 'Kit' Claybourne sat in his trench, smoking a cigarette and reading his mail. He first opened the letter from his mother. He knew that Eleanor's time had come, and he suspected that the news the letter contained would tell him if he was a father. There was no letter from Eleanor, which didn't surprise him much. He took the sheet of crème colored stationery, engraved with the Claybourne Coat of Arms, out of the envelope:

Dearest Kit,

Well, my fine son, you are now a father and I am a grandmother. Eleanor was delivered of a lovely baby boy early this morning. He has been named Winford Edward Claybourne, as you requested. I've not seen him yet, but Barton has and I have asked her to write to you and tell you her impressions. The doctor was with her throughout and he said it was not a difficult delivery. I am not certain that Eleanor would agree with that statement. However, it is now over, and your wife is sleeping soundly, with your son beside her in the bassinette. Barton has promised to bring him to me when he is awake. I so wish you could be here to share this happy moment with your family. Someday we will explain to 'Win' all that was happening when he entered the world. They say this is the 'war to end all wars,' so hopefully he will never know the horrors that you are experiencing. I keep up-to-date daily on the events in France, and although I don't know exactly where you are, I assume you are in the thick of it. I long for the day that you walk through the doors of Claybourne Court and meet your son for the first time and I pray that that time isn't far off.

As usual, Barton was a brick through all of this. You made a terribly wise decision when you chose to hire her. She seems to have a soothing effect upon Eleanor. If I had been blessed with a daughter, I would hope that she might have had Barton's sweetness. She is seeing a fellow in the village. He is the Chemist's son, and was injured at the beginning of the war. He accompanies her to church every Sunday and I see them there together. He is quite good looking. I do hope she doesn't marry and decide not to work out of the home anymore.

And so, I shall close for now, so that I can post this today. I do hope that you are well. Please remember that I think of you every moment, and pray for your safe return.

With Love,

Mother

Kit put his head into his hands, and ran his fingers through his hair. My God, he thought. I have a son. Winford Edward Claybourne. He re-read the letter, folded it, and returned it to its envelope. Then he reached down and put it in the bundle of other letters he had saved. He kept this one on top, as it was the most important of all, and he knew he would want to read it again and again. Next, he opened the second envelope. His mother's letter had already told him that Barton was going to write, so he knew it would be from her. Indeed it was. The paper was a pale pink, which reminded him of her. It had the initial 'B' at the top of the page:

Dear Captain Claybourne,

I am so pleased to tell you that you are the proud father of a beautiful, baby boy. I was there when he arrived, and I already adore him. He is truly a mirror image of you. I am anxious to hear what you mother's impression is, because she will have known you as a baby, and will know if I speak honestly. He has a great deal of hair. It is a very pretty brown. I would call it chestnut. Of course his eyes are blue, but I cannot tell whether they will be dark or light. His features are perfect. I looked him over very carefully, knowing you would want to know every detail. The doctor weighed him, and he is 2.72 Kilo, and 48.26 Cent. He has all ten fingers and toes, although they are very, very tiny. He has long lashes, and his lips are a lovely pink -almost as though he were wearing lip rouge, and they are a lovely shape, rather like a rosebud. All in all, he is a splendid baby. I held him immediately after he was born, and then he began to nurse from your wife, and there wasn't any grizzling at all. She is still having to adjust to the nursing, but did very well. Originally she thought she wouldn't nurse, but the doctor changed her mind, which is good, because he said it is much healthier for the child. It is starting to be very warm outside, so after a few weeks, we shall put him in the pram, and stroll across the grounds. I think the fresh air will be good for him. I intend to try to convince the Countess to change the color in the nursery to a pretty blue. She thought all white, originally, but now that we know it is a boy, it only seems right that the color match his gender.

I shall quit rambling. Congratulations on becoming a father. Everyone here prays for your safety.

Warm Regards,

Lily Barton

Kit was so touched by Lily's sweet letter that tears actually welled in his eyes. He glanced quickly to each side, to make certain none of his mates saw him. It appeared that no one had. He saw his friend Tom Holiday crunched down in an uncomfortable position, trying to get some sleep. He was still awake, so Kit whistled to him, and motioned for Tom to join him. Once he reached the place where Kit sat, they were able to whisper to one another.

"What's up with you, then?" asked Tom.

"Nothing much. Except that I've just received word that I'm a father and have a son."

"Well, my God, Mate, that's spectacular news. And what's he to be named?"

"Winford Edward Claybourne," Kit replied. "A bit highbrow, perhaps, but it's after my father."

"It's a nice name. What'll you call him?"

"Win. A perfect name for a baby born in the middle of this mucked up mess."

"You're right about that. Too bad we can't go to a pub and have a few pints. Here, I have some rum in my flask. Do you want a nip?"

"Ah - why not, Tom? Here, fill it up," Kit answered, handing him a tin cup.

They sat and drank their rum, and talked far into the dark, starry night, wondering what life would be like when Win grew up, and hoping that he would never have to watch friends be torn apart by ghastly grenades and enemy bombs.

When the morning of April 22 broke over the trenches, which ran perpendicular to the German forces near Gravenstaffel, a small village near Ypres, Kit felt a bit hung-over. He was relieved that there had been no fighting during the night. At least that was something. The day that he'd learned that his son was born, no one in his regiment was killed or wounded. He would have to remember that. But today was a new day, and tonight, another night. His boys were weary. So was he. One more week, and they would be rotated back behind enemy lines for two weeks, before they were brought forward again. It just went on and on. The weeks spent in the trenches were, of course, the worst. They had received new reinforcements from the Canadians and the Algerians, and it was terrific to have a brand new contingent of fresh soldiers, but unfortunately they were not battle hardened, and consisted primarily of businessmen, lawyers and other middle class men. Since he was an officer, Captain Claybourne was tagged to command this regiment of soldiers. Little did he know that he was about to be a part of one of the worst battles in the Great War.

It started much like other battles. The Germans waited until sunset, and then began heavy bombardment of the British, Canadian and Algerian troops. Soon, however, there was a new wrinkle. A strange olive-green cloud rolled over the Algerian position, to the left of the first Canadian Division. Kit's men began to panic as the cloud came near. It was a cloud of death, and the light north-easterly breeze blew it toward them. In only a moment, true death was upon them. Many became disoriented. Others fled in disbelief. As the night deepened, they were terrorized and ran blindly - stumbling - falling - gasping for air, and collapsed, their chests heavy with the agony and the slow poison of suffocation. Hundreds fell and died; others lay helpless, foam covering their suffering mouths and their bodies convulsing with sickness and nausea. They would die later. A slow and lingering death of unbelievable agony. The night air was tainted with the acrid smell of chlorine that caught at the back of the men's throats and filled their mouths with its metallic taste. The German troops had released 110 pounds of chlorine gas. It produced flooding of the lungs - an equivalent death to drowning only on dry land. The effects were numerous. Splitting headaches and agonizing thirst were only two. If a soldier drank water, he died instantly. Along with these symptoms came a knife edge pain in the lungs and the coughing up of that ungodly greenish froth from the stomach and the lungs. It all ended in death. The color of their skin turned from white to a greenish-black and yellow, and eyes assumed a glassy stare. It was a monstrous way to die.

Kit didn't run from the gas, but toward it, which resulted in his heading away from the cloud. Even those who stood their ground, were in a better position, because eventually the gas passed over them. He had been taught at *Sandhurst* that in case of such a horrific attack, the best protection was to urinate into his handkerchief and hold it over his mouth and nose. A Canadian chemist confirmed this theory that the ammonia in the urine acted as a deterrent to the effects of the gas. Word was passed down the line to follow this tactic. Kit called for volunteers to attempt a counterattack. Eight men responded. They counterattacked the German position with bombs and managed to capture three Germans Officers, 102 men and 500 yards of their trenches. Kit was badly injured in the eye, when a German attacked him with a bayonet, and missed his abdomen, but went straight into his eye. All of his brave volunteers were injured in one way or another, and would later receive medals for the heroism. Kit was given the Victoria Cross. But, no medal would help him to forget the horrific sights he saw on that unbearable night. That was only the first of six engagements in the battle for Ypres, and Britain had lost 59,275 men. It was almost more than the mind could comprehend.

He was taken to base hospital at Boulogne after that siege, and given treatment. His worst injuries were to his lungs and his face. There was little that could be done to help aftereffects of the gas attack. Mercifully, Kit didn't suffer nearly the agony that so many other men did. It was their miserable deaths and not his own injuries that caused his own disability. He thanked God for the rest of his life that he had been lucky enough to live through the horror of April 22, 1915. From that point on, he definitely believed that naming his son, 'Win' had protected him in the midst of such fear and torture. At the end of all three battles of Ypres, which didn't come until November 6, 1917, when Kit Claybourne was far out of it, the total number of causalities for both German and allied soldiers was 850,000 men.

While Kit lay in the Base hospital, recuperating from the ordeal at Gravenstaffel, he received word that he was going to be sent home. He was deeply depressed and suffering from Shell Shock, which is what they termed the nervous condition resulting from intense and horrific battle. He had also lost that eye, when attacked by the bayonet in the German trenches. But, when he looked around at the other beds in the hospital, he felt guilty to be as healthy as he was. The physician in charge had told him that he would be kept at Boulogne for another week, and then sent to a hospital closer to home, near Calais, France. After approximately another two weeks of recuperation there, if all went as planned, he would be taken by ship back to England. Immediately, he wrote a letter home. He addressed it only to Eleanor, as he knew she could tell the others, and he didn't feel he had the strength to write several reports of what he had been through.

April 28, 1915

Somewhere in France

Dear Eleanor,

I have survived what is being called one of the worst battles of the war, to date. I won't mention the location, as the censor's would only clip it. All I can say is that it was the horror to end all horrors. I am in a base hospital at present, and have only now received the news that I am to be mustered out and relocated home to England. I needn't tell you how delirious with happiness I am. And yet, there is a sense of guilt at having to leave behind so many of the brave men I've fought with. I pray to God that they'll also find themselves back in their homes soon. I have been awarded the Victoria Cross, and will explain the details when I see you. It is a marvelous honor, but I would give it up in a moment if it would bring back those who didn't make it. From what I'm being told, I shall be moved within a week to another hospital, closer to where I shall depart for England. I may be there as long as two weeks - perhaps more - but, I am hopeful that I'll find myself at Claybourne Court no later than the first week of June. Perhaps, much sooner. I'll try to send a wire when I board ship.

I haven't even had time to write and tell you how delighted I am about our son. I'm sure it was an ordeal for you, but now it is over, and we have 'Win.' It was on the news of his birth that I sustained this injury. All of the mates in my regiment said that 'Win' is a lucky name. It certainly was for me, as I am still here, and looking forward to holding him for the first time. So often I have prayed that he will never have to experience anything like this beastly war. Miss Barton wrote and told me all about our beautiful baby. She was very detailed and factual, so I feel as though I have already seen him. It will be interesting to see if the picture I hold in my mind is anywhere near reality. I hope you are recovering nicely from giving birth to him. What a wonderful gift you have given me, Eleanor! I hope to hear from you before I leave hospital. Please share my letter with everyone else, including Miss Barton, and of course, my mother.

I look so forward to holding you in my arms. I do love you so, Eleanor.

Kit

Six days later, he found himself in a rather nice base hospital near Calais. It turned out that the Medical Doctor in charge of the facility, Captain John Garrett, was a former classmate of his from *Sandhurst.* They had been close friends and it was wonderful to see a familiar face. John had seen papers telling him that Kit would be arriving, so he was waiting by the bed when the stretcher bearers brought him in.

"My God! John Garrett. So you ended up out here too! It's great to see you, old chap." Kit reached his arm out and shook Dr. Garrett's hand. "Sorry for not using your title, Doctor. I was so surprised to see you."

"No harm done. I'm delighted to see you, Kit, or Captain Claybourne, whichever you prefer."

"Kit, of course. How long have you been in France?"

"Since the beginning. They're short on doctors, so there wasn't any question about what I had to do."

"Yes, I felt the same way. Now I'm glad to be going home, but I feel guilty about leaving so many men behind. I know a lot of them won't make it. They'll never see England again."

"Yes, I know. But, don't you be feeling guilty. From what I understand, you did your bit at Ypres. Victory Cross, no less."

"Yes. Well, they aren't very choosy about who they award those things to."

"Hey, come on, Kit. I have all of your papers here, so don't try to give me a story about how you really didn't earn it. You went a far way beyond the call of duty. I'm proud to call you a friend."

"Thanks, John. Sometimes, in the heat of battle one does things without really thinking. All of the men, or at least a good number, were running away from that damnable green cloud of gas. For some reason, I ran toward where it had originated. It turned out that was wise, since the cloud continued floating over the trench I'd escaped from, and further toward the men who'd chosen to run that direction. Since I was running right into the German trenches, it seemed logical to scoop up a bunch of Jerry's and take them with me. I only wish that one bastard hadn't got me with his bayonet."

"Yes. Let me take a look at that eye. You're lucky he didn't slice your neck off, or stab you in an artery." John took the bandage off his eye, and peered at it with a lighted instrument. Then he gently probed the area around it. "How badly does it still hurt?" he asked.

"Ouch! That was sore, when you pushed by the edge. But, I don't have much pain. At first I did. It was bloody awful. But, half way through my time in the last hospital, it improved a lot."

"Good. It looks like they did a good job there. It looks clean, and is healing nicely. If you want to, later you can think about an artificial eye. Personally, I think they're a lot of trouble to mess with. I'd settle for an eye patch and be done with it."

"Yes. That's been my thinking too. God, I hate returning home with this wound. My wife will go bonkers."

"Oh, surely not. I've seen so many horrific things - men with no arms and no legs - and their families have welcomed them with open arms. Do you mean she'll be repulsed, or do you mean she'll feel horrible to see that you lost an eye?"

"I hate to say it, but I think she'll be repulsed."

"Come on, Kit? Who did you marry anyway? She can't be that lacking in empathy."

"Well, perhaps she won't be, but I'm not optimistic. I married a girl from Virginia in the States. She's a beautiful woman - one of those 'Southern

Belles' you hear about. Her father has a famous horse breeding operation. I went to view the horses, and met Eleanor in the process. Before I knew it, she had a wedding planned. It didn't take long. Of course, I was over the moon in love. She *is* a sensational beauty. Long blonde hair, big blue eyes. And just so sweet that butter wouldn't melt in her mouth. But, *that* was before we married and I brought her to England. She's very young - only twenty - and I don't think she really understood what marrying an English nobleman and moving to England meant. I thought she'd make a splendid Countess for *Claybourne Court*, but I'm seeing very little sign of that yet. Anyway, I shouldn't be going on like this John. When I went off to France, she was pregnant, which was hard for her. I hated leaving her in that condition without her own family near. She loathes my mother, and about the only person she cares for is the nurse I hired for her before I left for France."

"Damn Kit, I'm sorry to hear this. Perhaps when you return home, she'll have a new attitude. Has she given birth yet?"

"Yes. Ironically, on the fifteenth, right before the night of the second battle of Ypres, where I was injured. A boy. We named him Winford Edward, after my Dad, but we'll call him 'Win'."

"It's a fine name, Kit. That should give you something terrific to look forward to. I'd like to be returning to a son I'd never set eyes upon."

"Are you married yet, John?"

"No. I met a wonderful girl a couple of years ago - also a doctor. There aren't many of those, you know. But, she was brilliant, beautiful, and kind. I was just crazy over her. She served in the war too, at a base hospital near St. Omer. She was killed when the Germans bombed it."

"Oh what a tragedy, John. She sounds like a lovely girl. I'm so sorry for you. Where did you meet?"

"In medical training, of course. We both attended the University of Edinburgh. She was from near you - a town called Barrow Gurney. Very small. She grew up there. She wanted us to establish our own practice in a village. I wasn't quite as keen on it, but to tell you the truth, after this war, I think I'd like to work in a peaceful, quiet environment."

"I can certainly understand that. I'm looking forward greatly to enjoying the solitude of *Claybourne Court*. I don't care if I never see London again. I think most of the boys who've fought feel the same. After nothing but the roar of German guns, quiet is a rare commodity."

"Your medical file mentions that you've suffered from some shell shock? I don't see any evidence in talking with you. Has it improved?"

"Yes, it has. But, I still have bouts where I wake in the night yelling and screaming, cold with sweat. My hands also shake at times. You get a funny feeling, you know. A tingling sensation, and a rapid heartbeat'

"Well, you're describing classic symptoms of shell shock. I don't think yours are so severe that they will interfere with your life to any large degree. Getting back to peace and solitude is going to help a lot. You need a lot of rest. I hope your wife understands that. Some of this can be a holdover from the gassing, although thank God they didn't use nerve gas on you. Chlorine was it?"

"Yes. A bloody awful green cloud of it."

"Let me listen to your heart and lungs," John said, as he placed the stethoscope on Kit's chest. There was quiet while he listened to the sounds of Kit's breathing and his heartbeat. "Okay, mate. Everything sounds pretty damned good to me. Heart's nice and steady - a bit rapid, but that's to be expected. Your lungs sound clear, so if the gas got to you, it doesn't seem to have done any permanent damage. I'd say your eye is your most severe wound, and it could have been a lot worse. I'm not trying to minimize it Kit. I surely wouldn't like to lose an eye, but it beats a slew of other injuries by a mile. I'm going to write to your family - that's simple protocol - and I'll explain your wound, and make certain that your wife understands what your needs are."

"God, thanks John. That makes it easier for me. I haven't wanted to tell them about it, yet I think everyone should know what to expect. Especially Eleanor. How long do you think it will be before they let me out of here?"

"Not very. Let's see, today's the third of May. I'd like to watch the eye for a couple of weeks or so, and if nothing unexpected pops up, I'll release you. Now, I'm going to let you rest and get situated, and I'll be back to check on you this evening." John patted Kit on the shoulder, and strolled away from his bed, to see another patient.

Kit slept for most of the afternoon. When he woke, the hospital was in a complete uproar about something. Had there been something that had happened near the base sight? Everyone was talking to everyone else, and he was able to overhear comments being made about the brutality of the Germans, so obviously it was something about the war. It didn't take long to learn that on that very day the Germans had torpedoed the British passenger vessel the *Lusitania.* She had been struck by a German U-Boat as she made her way from New York Harbor *to* Liverpool. A total of 1198 passengers and crew-members lost their lives. It was a brutal act by the Germans and one which everyone suspected would cause great trouble down the line.

He woke fully when a nurse laid a letter on the table by his bed. After she'd left, he rolled over and reached out for it. It was from Eleanor. Eleanor's letters did not have a tendency to make him feel more calm and rested, yet he knew he had to read it:

Dearest Kit,

Well, I needn't' tell you how over the moon we all are to know that you are coming home. I actually wept when I read your letter. At long last my prayers have been answered, and I won't have to be so lonely anymore. It has been such a terrible nightmare. Perhaps now I can get back to feeling the way I did when I met you. Your mother is acting like the King is paying us a visit. She is potty over the fact that you're coming home. Of course, I am happy too, but there is such a thing as acting with decorum. I was a bit upset by the fact that you wrote from a hospital and apparently have been released because of some sort of injury. I hope it isn't anything too gruesome. They certainly wouldn't release you if you still needed any care, would they? When you return, I want to start doing all of the things we planned before this ghastly war interrupted everything. I want to go to London, and stay in our home there, and see all of the new plays, as well as Art Gallery Openings. I also look forward to horseback riding again. I shall make certain that your riding habit is in proper shape.

Once you return, we'll need to set about thinking of a nanny. For the time being, Barton has been looking after me, and also caring for the baby. She says she doesn't mind, and has really taken to little Win, but it's inconvenient for me when I need her, and she is busy changing a diaper. I don't know how she can bear to do such a loathsome task. I have weaned him, and he now takes a bottle. Oh what a fight I had with the doctor about that, but I won in the end. Now, Barton gives him his bottles, and I am able to sleep though the entire night. Having to get up several times a night was ruining my complexion. I am so glad that we had a boy right off, as I can tell you unequivocally, I shall not have any more babies. You will just have to find some way of preventing me from becoming pregnant, or I'm afraid your fun in the bedroom is over. I know there are ways though, because I had girlfriends in Virginia who told me so. At least you have a son and an heir, which is the main thing.

I have been enjoying being able to fit back into regular clothing. I had the dressmaker complete several lovely ensembles, so I shall be all ready to show them off when you return. I kept my figure through this ghastly childbearing episode, so you needn't worry that you have an overweight, ugly wife waiting for you at home. Sebastian says I am prettier than ever, and I don't believe he is jesting.

The one other thing I wish to talk with you about before you return is how much time you plan on spending with the baby. I do not think it is good for him to be fawned over, and anyway, he gets plenty of that from your mother and from Barton. I want to establish a regular schedule, whereby he will be brought to you at the end of the day, for perhaps a half hour of play time, and then again in the morning for the same amount of time. He's not to grow too dependent upon you, for I intend to have him off to boarding school as early as they take them. I am writing later today to see at just what age that will be. I suppose they have to be toilet trained before then. Oh, well, Barton will probably adore it.

And so, I will be looking forward to seeing you. I am still too frail to come to the station, but I imagine Sebastian, your mother and perhaps even Barton will be there to welcome the hero home.

Love,

Eleanor

Kit sat back in his bed and laughed. Clearly, it was time to change his approach with Eleanor. She was completely incapable of thinking about anyone but herself. Well, she was going to learn that there were two people in this marriage, and that they also shared a son. He certainly intended to see his boy more than a few hours in a day. He suddenly realized that her attitude had completely killed the feelings he'd once had for her. He would begin to make the rules in his own home, and Eleanor was going to have to abide by them.

10

Lady Eleanor sat in the drawing home at *Claybourne Court*, unfolding a letter she had just received from Captain John Garrett, the physician in charge of the base hospital near *Calais,* where Kit was being kept until his release to come home. She had received a wire that very morning from Kit himself, telling her that he was boarding the ship from *Calais to Dover*, where he would be taking a train to *London.* From there, he would take another train to *Claybourne-on-Colne.* He expected to arrive about five o'clock p.m. In the meantime, this letter from the base hospital had arrived. It must have been written while Kit was still there. She took the page out of the envelope, and read it through:

My Dear Lady Claybourne,

As the physician in charge of your husband's case at this base hospital, I am writing to inform you about his injury, and to give you my recommendations about any further restrictions that should be placed on him in the immediate future.

As Captain Claybourne has informed me, you already have news that he was injured at the Second Battle of Ypres. This was the worst battle of the war to date. We are very fortunate that your husband is alive, as men died by the thousands. Captain Claybourne was given a hero's medal for his splendid service at Ypres. He received the Victoria Cross for his courageous bravery. Unfortunately, in the course of his brave action, he received a bayonet wound in his left eye, by an enemy combatant. The bayonet rendered his eye inoperable, and the doctors were unable to save it. Therefore, Captain Claybourne is reduced to the vision of only one eye, and will be wearing a patch over the other eye. He is adjusting wonderfully well, and although he will never have the sight one enjoys with two healthy eyes, he is able to see very well with his right eye, and will adapt over time. I have told him that if he wishes, at some point later, he can look into an artificial eye. He does not show much interest in doing so at this time.

For the most part, he is in excellent shape. He suffered some shell shock at Ypres, which is most common. This was the first battle when poison gas was used, and his smart thinking saved him from a gruesome death. I have examined his lungs, and they appear not to have been damaged, and his heart rhythm seems fine. He reports that he does suffer occasional nervous spells, and has difficulty sleeping. Again, this is very normal for a man who has been through trench warfare. He was also injured by a bullet wound in the arm, earlier in the war. That injury seems to have resolved itself, leaving only residual stiffness. My recommendation is that he have calm, quiet recuperation. Let him get used to his eye injury at his own pace. He may not want to read, or write for a period of time. I advise his sleeping without his eye patch, as the elastic that holds it in place can be uncomfortable. Primary, Lady Claybourne, I cannot stress enough that he must be made to feel that this injury in no way takes away from his attractiveness. It is important that he still feel that he is the whole man that he was before he became involved in this conflict. I must add that I am acquainted with Kit from Sandhurst, and know that he is a true gentleman. He will not want to be any bother to you, or anyone else in his household, but I think it important that he not be made to feel rejected in any manner. He needs the comfort and love that only a loving wife can give. I also understand that you have been blessed with a new child recently. The baby should be the best tonic for Kit. Let him spend as much time as he wishes with the child each day. This will help to heal his soul.

I admire your husband greatly, and remain ever your servant,

John Garrett, M.D. RMC, Captain

"Barton!! Barton!! Where are you? I need you at once. Barton!" Lily heard Eleanor's voice up in the nursery, where she was rocking baby. One would have thought that the house was on fire. She was bellowing at the top of her lungs. Lily put Win back in his cot, and ran to the stairs.

"Where are you Lady Eleanor? What's happened?"

I'm down here in the drawing room. Come here quickly." Lily took the stairs two at a time, and found Lady Eleanor sitting on the camel backed sofa, sipping a cup of tea. There were tears streaming down her cheeks, but that alone wasn't unusual. "What is it Milady? What's upset you now?"

She threw the letter at Lily and ordered her to read it. It landed on the floor by the sofa. Lily bent and retrieved it, and read it though twice. Finally she spoke.

"Oh, poor Lord Claybourne. What a tragedy. But, Milady, it might have been so much worse. What a kind man Doctor Garrett must be to have taken the time to write such a thorough letter. You must thank him for it, Milady."

"Thank him for it! Thank him for writing me a malicious letter intended to ruin my life by ordering me about. Ha! He deserves no thanks from me."

"I don't understand Milady? Aren't you glad to know ahead of time what to expect, and how to give the Captain what he needs while recuperating?"

"Of course not, Barton, and neither would you be if this were your husband whom the doctor was speaking of."

"Why ever wouldn't I be, Milady? I truly don't understand."

"Because, Barton, it clearly says that Kit is going to sleep without that dreadful eye patch. Am I to awake in the morning to an empty eye socket? I don't think I could bear something so grotesque."

"Oh, Milady, no. He's the one who's lost an eye. He needs your love and sympathy. You certainly mustn't make him feel as though you are repulsed by this change in his appearance. Surely you understand that Lord Claybourne would never treat anyone who'd suffered such a wound with anything but kindness."

"Well, Barton I *am* repulsed. I didn't marry a man with one eye. Do you think that would even have been feasible? The prettiest girl for miles around, marrying a defective person?"

"Milady, the Captain is so much more than just an eye. I'm distressed to hear you speaking this way. Perhaps when he arrives, you'll see that you don't feel that way at all. Let's just wait and see."

"I don't think I can pretend, Barton. I cannot imagine letting him touch me, let alone share a bed with him. And, did you read what that doctor said about having to take the stupid eye patch off at night? Oh, I am very certain that would put me in a terribly romantic mood," she said snidely. "God, Barton, I cannot cope with this."

"Milady, I am walking out right now with a lovely gentleman from the village, named David Morris. He lost a leg in the war. He now has an artificial one, and it doesn't bother me in the least. Nor would it, if I were married to him."

"Well, Bully for you, Barton. Walking out with him is a lot different than sharing his bed. I'm not so certain you could bear that."

"Well Milady, I spend many off-days helping him to learn to walk on the new leg, and we practice taking it on and off until we get it right. I've seen where it was amputated, and it doesn't bother me at all."

"Well, Barton, you are simply not as frail a person as I am. Your father was a physician. After all, you were used to seeing God knows what as you grew up. I led a much protected, sheltered life until I came to England."

"Yes, Milady. I understand that. But, we're discussing your husband, whom I know you love very much. You certainly don't intend to throw away the loveliest gentleman I know, because of a trivial change in his outer appearance?"

"I didn't say that I was going to throw him away. But, I'm certainly not going to follow all of this *Doctor's* recommendations. He will, indeed sleep with that patch on. And I just thought of something else. What if we were making love and it came off? Oh my God, Barton. I'd die."

"No, Milady, you wouldn't. Please think about his feelings. It's a difficult enough thing for him to have gone through. He needs to know that everyone at home loves him as much as ever."

"Oh, how you *do* go on, Barton. I have feelings too, you know."

"Yes. Milady. Well . . . he's arriving today, or this evening isn't he? I should prepare his room for him."

"Yes, do. I don't think he needs to sleep with me until he's had time to adjust."

"Whatever you say, Lady Eleanor," Lily answered. She was sure her feelings showed in her voice. She was acting like a ghastly, spoiled little girl, which wasn't anything unusual, but Lily thought that perhaps with the Captain's return, her attitude might change. Apparently that wasn't going to happen.

"Well, Milady, I have to go and tend to Win, so I'll leave you to your own thoughts. Do try to think about what the Captain has been through. I lost a brother at The Battle of the Marne, and I would give anything to have him back, regardless of his condition." With that, Lily turned on her heel and ascended the grand staircase. Win was sleeping soundly in his nursery. Lady Eleanor had transferred him to his own room as soon as he was fully weaned, which didn't take a lot of time. From that time on she had seen scant little of him. Lily took care of all of his needs, from bathing, dressing, and changing nappies, to warming his bottles and feeding him. He was an adorable baby, and Lady Cynthia remarked over and over about how he looked so much like Kit had when he was that age. She said she would never have been able to tell them apart. Lady Eleanor was not made happy by such comments, and did what she could to stay away from Win when Lady Cynthia was nearby. Lily held Win and rocked him, trying hard to keep her feelings under control. What sort of mother couldn't show love to a baby? There surely was something amiss in Lady Eleanor's emotional makeup. However, Lily was not in a position to speak freely to Lady Eleanor - Not if she wanted to keep her job. And she did. She expected to hear that her mother and Will Morris would be marrying soon, and knew when that day came she would be delighted. But, during the few times that Lily and her Mum had discussed such a possibility, Mum made it clear that she and William would move to his cottage. That meant that either Lily must be able to pay rent or purchase the cottage from her Mum, or she didn't know where she would go. Therefore she needed her wages. She knew she could find another position in London, or perhaps even at another country house, but the thought of leaving tiny Win brought tears to her eyes. She was already far too attached to the child. Once Lord Claybourne returned home, she prayed that things would right themselves. David Morris had already made overtures to her about marriage too. She thought him a fine gentleman, but she did not love him, and knew she could never marry without love.

The train pulled into the station at *Claybourne-on-Colne*, along with the usual screeching of brakes, and bellow of steam. Kit threw his haversack over his shoulder, put on his cap, and readied himself to disembark. Home. What a wonderful word that was. Home. In just a few minutes he would walk through the gates at *Claybourne Court*, and back into his beloved home. It was such a world removed from the filthy, mud caked and blood soaked trenches of France. As he stepped down from the train, there waiting at the station was his mother, his brother, and Lily Barton. He hadn't expected her, but was very pleased to see her lovely face. Of course, Eleanor wasn't there, but she had said as much in her last letter. His mother threw her arms about him, and hugged him tightly.

"Oh Kit, you're home. My precious son. I haven't rested well since you left. Oh, how wonderful it will be to have you back where you belong. Now, let me look at you. Well. I think that eye patch gives you the look of a dashing hero. Of course, you are one. Kit, we were so proud to learn that you'd received the Victoria Cross. Now, don't you try to tell me that it was nothing, because I know better. Very few men receive one." Lady Cynthia hooked her arm through her son's, while Sebastian took his haversack. "Eleanor is waiting at home. She is still a bit frail, although I certainly have difficulty understanding that, since I was up and about very shortly after I gave birth to both of you boys."

"Everyone is different, Mother," Kit answered. "I'm so very anxious to see my son. Miss Barton, from the description in your letter, I know I'm going to be over the moon with pride."

"Yes, indeed, Milord. He's just the best little baby you could ever hope for. I have to admit that I've fallen a bit in love with him myself. I've had a bed moved into the nursery, and that's where I sleep most nights."

"In the nursery? Miss Barton, may I ask why you choose to do that?"

"Well, Milord, if he wakes during the night, and needs to eat, or has a wet nappy, I'm right there to take care of him."

"Shouldn't that be Eleanor's responsibility?"

"Well - it would properly be a nanny's responsibility, but we haven't one, and to tell the truth, I really don't want one."

"Isn't it a lot of work to care for a baby and also be Eleanor's ladies maid?"

"Not so much, Milord. If I feel the need for a nanny I'll tell you so. Don't take Win away from me now. I've grown so attached to him, and he knows me so well. I think it would distress him to have to become used to a nanny."

Sebastian interrupted the conversation. "Well, say then old boy, was it beastly out there in the trenches?"

"Rather, Sebastian. It's hard to think that just over the Channel it's an ungodly Hell. I'm terribly thankful to be out of it, but I 'm guilt-ridden at having had to leave so many good men behind. Most of them won't be lucky enough to leave there alive."

"As bad as that, is it? How much longer do you think it will go on?"

"Well, right now it's escalating, and most of the officers are calling it a war of attrition, meaning that we'll all keep shooting, throwing grenades, and blowing one another to bits until there isn't anyone left to blow up."

"My God, Kit. If it's that bad, I simply can't be sent out there."

"The British haven't put conscription into effect yet, but I think it will come to that. If it does, then, you're bound to be called up."

They reached the car and Edward, the chauffeur, opened the doors. He put Kit's haversack into the boot, and Kit climbed into the front of the automobile. They all got into the back seat. "Welcome home, Sir. We're all awfully glad to see you back at *Claybourne Court*. It's been strange not to have you with us", Edward said, as he backed the big Daimler out of the parking spot.

"Thanks Edward. I can't tell you how good it is to be back. One forgets how lovely England is in the summer. I look forward to a few peaceful months at home, before I tackle any actual work."

"What sort of work, Milord?" Lily asked.

"Miss Barton, the running of an estate the size of *Claybourne Court* is an enormous amount of work. Mother has been making all of the major decisions since I've been gone, but now she can get back to her normal life, and I'll return to seeing that the estate is kept in it's prime, so that Win will have his inheritance."

"I see, Milord," Lily replied. "I thought perhaps you meant you were going to be in London or someplace else."

"No. I hope to live out the remainder of my day's right here at *Claybourne Court*. If I never had to leave here again that would be fine with me."

"Whoa, Old man. Eleanor will have something to say about that. She has all sorts of plans made for a social life in London, and even travel abroad once the war ends."

"Well, Sebastian, Eleanor has a lot of ideas that I'm not in favor of," Kit replied. She and I are going to have a serious discussion when I get home."

"Good Luck, you poor sod."

"Sebastian, where *did* you pick up such language? You weren't raised to speak in such a fashion. If you *must* sound like a dock worker, please do so out of my hearing." Lady Cynthia was not at all pleased.

"Sorry Mother. Didn't mean to offend you. I just was trying to convey to Kit that his wife expects that he'll be ready to hit London with her."

"He'll be doing nothing of the sort," answered Lady Cynthia, with a firm expression.

"For now, don't you think we should all concentrate upon how nice it is to have the Captain home again?" Lily added.

The car climbed the hill to *Claybourne Court*, and early evening sunlight cast shadows about the entrance to that spectacular home. Trees swayed in a light breeze, and flowers bloomed in masses. Kit remembered that when he left it was fall, and he's prayed he'd live to see spring and summer again at his beloved home. Now, here he was. It was hard to believe that the filth and stench of the trenches he'd so recently left behind were really not so terribly far in distance, but were a lifetime away from the calm and serenity of his home and village. The car came to a halt, and he exited the left door. Eleanor was standing at the front of the massive entrance doors. His breath caught when he saw her. He'd forgotten her extraordinary beauty. She was dressed in a brown and pink striped silk dress, with long sleeves and a lace high collar. Her hair shimmered in the setting sun. Kit had forgotten how tiny she was. He took two steps at a time, and ran to the doorway. Grabbing her in his arms, he smothered her face against his uniform jacket. "Oh my darling, Eleanor. How I've longed to see you – to feel your arms – to smell your sweet fragrance." He covered her face with kisses, still holding her closely. "Eleanor, Eleanor, I'm home. Everything will be all right now. We have our precious Win - I have you. Now we can begin our new life together."

She pulled away from him, and stared up into his face. She focused straight upon his eye. Then she looked away, at the ground.

"What is it, Eleanor?" Are you upset by my injury?"

""Yes. Yes. You don't look like the man I married. I married a man with two lovely eyes. Not a patch. You look like a pirate. It's gruesome."

"But, Eleanor, I'm still the man you married. Surely you can't mean what you're saying. I love you so much. I could never stop loving you over something so trivial."

"Trivial? You think losing an eye is trivial? It changes your entire appearance. I need time to adjust to this. I feel as though I don't even know you. I don't know what to do. I suppose it hurts you for me to go on in this way, but I can't help it. You look frightening. Surely, you don't expect me to be seen in public with a one-eyed man?" She started to weep, and then screamed. "Oh, none of you understands. It would have been better for you not to have come home at all than to appear here looking like some sort of highwayman." She turned and ran from the front of the house. No one knew where she was going, and frankly, no one cared. She ran around the side of the house and disappeared. Lily suspected that she was heading for the stables. She had been looking for an excuse to go riding, and now she'd found it.

Poor Lord Claybourne looked crestfallen. It was the last thing he had expected. Lady Cynthia was seething, and even Sebastian looked like he could wring her neck. Lady Cynthia ran to Kit's side, and put her arms about him. "Don't pay her any attention, Kit. She's making this all about her, as usual. Come, let's go into the house, and meet your new son. Eleanor will return when she's ready to act more like a wife who is ready to welcome her husband home from the war."

"I'll go in search of Lady Eleanor," Lily said. "She's been nervous and distraught. I'm sure she didn't mean what she said, Milord. Lady Cynthia is right. Go and meet your adorable son, and I'll make certain the Countess is all right."

The rest of them entered the house, and Lord Claybourne had a stunned look upon his face. His shoulders were erect, and he was trying hard not to let Eleanor's atrocious behavior affect him, but there was no question that it must have hurt unbearably. This was not the sort of homecoming he had envisioned.

Lily scampered across the lawns toward the stables. Sure enough, she could see the pink stripe of her day dress in the distance. She was talking to Howard. It looked like they were arguing. As Lily came closer, Howard spotted her, and called out, "Miss Barton. Lady Eleanor be wantin' me to saddle Spark o' Fire. I says I can't do such Ma'am. 'E's not broke yet. I needs to work more with 'im. 'E'd throw 'er for sure."

"Howard, since when do you give the orders around here?" Eleanor said. "I want to ride Spark of Fire, and I shall. I am an excellent rider. I need to get away. I need time to think. I always think better on horseback."

"Lady Eleanor, then please take one of the other horses. You haven't ridden for quite a spell, and Spark of Fire is not well broken yet. Howard knows what he's talking about. There are several others who would make good companions."

"Oh, Barton, as much as I like you, you don't know a thing about riding. Now, I am going to take Spark of Fire. She threw a saddle upon the horse, and wrestled him around until she got a bit into his mouth. He was prancing, pulling, and kicking, all the while whinnying.

"Please Lady Eleanor. Don't. Please listen to me. Your husband is up at the house, worried about you, and desperately longing to see you. Please calm down and come with me."

"That man is not my husband. He's some stranger with a patch over his eye. My Kit was handsome and perfect. I cannot bear imperfect creatures." She jerked her arm away from Lily, as she tried to pull her back from the horse. Then in one swoop, she was on the horse's back, and cantering across the meadow toward the woods. Lily put her head in her hands. What was she to do? Part of Lily felt like letting her go, and not caring whether she was thrown and injured, or even killed. She was so fed up with her, and her spoiled ways. She turned to Howard.

"Howard, what can we do?"

"I'll take Wesley and go after 'er. She's acting like a bloody fool, if you'll be 'scusing me, Miss Barton. You wait back here. When I catch up with 'er, I'll put 'er behind me on Wesley, and lead 'Spark o Fire' back, if he ain't broke his bit. Just you sit tight. She didn't 'ave a big 'eadstart. I'll find her."

Howard quickly saddled Wesley, and took off at a fast gallop, following in the direction that Lady Eleanor had gone. As he emerged from a clearing in the wood, he could see her ahead, still cantering at a wild gate, but holding on. Damn fool was trying to ride him side- saddle, which he'd not been broken for. He was bucking, and shying sideways, and she was trying to hold the reins. Suddenly the horse came to an abrupt stop at a particularly fine looking growth of thick clover, and Miss Eleanor wet flying head over heels above his head. She landed in a pitiful, twisted lump on the ground. Howard was quick to dismount, and ran to her side. She was unconscious, but breathing. He gently picked her up, being careful not to make any injuries worse, and lay her over Wesley's back. Then he resettled the bit and rein on Spark of Fire. He swung himself onto the back of Spark of Fire, throwing off the saddle, and riding bareback, while holding on to the reins of Wesley, gently walking him beside him as he rode Spark of Fire. He kept a close eye on Lady Eleanor, to see if she awakened. There was no movement, and he prayed to God that she wasn't badly injured. It wasn't too long before they rounded the bend back to the stables, where Barton waited, pacing nervously.

She ran to Howard when she saw him approaching. "Oh dear God, Howard. Is she all right? Where did you find her?"

"Laying in the pasture. Spark of Fire found some clover to 'is likin'. Miss Eleanor went flying over his head. I'm going to lift 'er down and put her in the stable. You be running to the 'ouse and get 'elp. I'll watch 'er."

Lily took off a mile a minute. In the course of running, she lost a shoe, but didn't stop to retrieve it. Her hair flew lose from its pins and she could feel perspiration marks under her arms. She burst into the kitchen doorway, where Cissie and Mary were in the process of preparing a welcome home meal for Lord Claybourne. Both of the footmen, Edward and Thomas were sipping tea at the large communal table in the eating portion of the large kitchen. "Oh, please, someone come help. The Lady Eleanor has taken a bad fall from one of the horses. Howard has brought her back to the stables, but she's unconscious. I need two strong men to help bring her back to the house," Lily cried.

Edward and Thomas jumped to their feet and threw their cups down. "Lead the way, Barton. We'll fetch her. Polly, run tell Halsey what's happened, and have preparations made. Fetch the doctor." The three of them headed back out of the door, and ran as fast as they could back to the stables. There they found Howard, sitting by Lady Eleanor, who lay on a bed of fresh hay, covered with a horse blanket. He was pressing a rag to her head. "What's her situation?" Howard," asked Edward.

"Ain't good. She still ain't awake. She's taken a good 'it on the 'ead. I can feel a lump on her fore'ead."

"Well, let's get her back to the house, where she can have a doctor. Fine way to greet a husband come home from the wars," Thomas muttered.

Lily ignored his comment, although she completely agreed with him. Poor Lord Claybourne. What a miserable homecoming. Lady Eleanor had managed, as usual, to turn attention to herself. The three men gently picked up her and, between the three of them, managed to find a somewhat comfortable position to carry her. Lily trailed next to them, still soothing her forehead, and talking to her. She was breathing and her eyelashes fluttered from time to time, but she did not open them. When they reached the house, Halsey and Mrs. Briggs met them at the back doorway, and told them to bring her into the library. They didn't want to take the chance trying to move her up the stairway. Mrs. Briggs had prepared a bed of sorts on the leather sofa, with a pillow, and a nice cashmere blanket. They gently laid her down. No one had informed His Lordship, Lady Cynthia or Sebastian. They were all praying she would awaken before that became a necessity. After a few moments, she began to moan, and turn her head to the left and right.

"Ohhh. My head hurts dreadfully. Is my neck broken?" she whispered.

"I don't believe so, your ladyship," answered Edward. "But you took a bad fall from a horse. Lie still now, until the doctor arrives, and we'll know more."

"Oh me God, at least she's alive," breathed Howard.

"Yes. Thanks to you, Howard. That was quick thinking," answered Edward.

Lily hurried to the drawing room, and found Kit, pacing the floor. With trepidation, she told him about Lady Eleanor's accident. He had been through so much upset, in such a short period of time that she wasn't certain the news even registered. Since Eleanor was so horrified by his appearance, he wasn't certain whether he should go to her or not. He asked if Eleanor was injured, and Lily told him it was nothing very worrisome. Kit sighed, and threw himself down on the sofa.

In a short time, there was a knock at the door of the library. It was the doctor, accompanied by Mrs. Briggs, and the rest of the family. "What in the world is going on in here?" the doctor asked, in his gruff voice.

""She took a bad fall from a horse, Sir. "

"She's scarcely dressed for riding. No wonder she fell with all of these damn fool skirts. Trying to ride side-saddle was she?"

"Yes, on a horse that hasn't yet been broken," Lily replied.

"This woman is more trouble than she's worth," he muttered. Then he began to examine her. He pushed and prodded, bent her legs and arms, and turned her head left and right. He asked her to follow his finger with her eyes, and proceeded to pepper her with questions about her name, date of birth, dwelling place and name of husband. She answered all satisfactorily. "It does not appear that she has a concussion. Still, I would like you to make certain that she doesn't fall asleep for several hours. Someone will have to stay with her, and if she dozes off, gently shake her and make sure she stays alert. There's to be no foolishness like this again. She might have killed herself. Isn't it enough that we have men dying in the trenches by the thousands, without fool women falling from horses that aren't fit to ride? I'll leave you something for pain, but I don't want her to have it, unless she is really in terrible need of it, and then not too much. I'll stop by tomorrow to see her. You boys did a good job of getting her to the house. Let her rest here a bit, and then carry her up to her room. She may eat, but only lightly. Tea and toast perhaps." He shook hands with *Lord Claybourne*, who had made the decision to go to the library and check on Eleanor. Kit thanked the doctor, and he exited through the rear door.

Kit immediately went to her side. He began to smooth her hair back from her forehead, and murmured endearments to her. She lay with her eyes closed, lapping up the attention. Then she opened her eyes and looked into his face. There was complete silence, and then she screamed at the top of her lungs. He jerked his hand back from her, looking puzzled. "Get away from me. Get away from me. I'll not have some one-eyed monster taking care of me."

"Eleanor! I don't care how badly you have been injured, you will not speak to my son like that in this house," shouted Lady Cynthia. "I abhor you. You spoiled, cruel girl. As soon as you are able, I want you out of this house. I have a son who has returned from France with wounds. He needs peace and quiet, and he is not going to get it as long as you are here. I'm completely fed up with you." She turned to her son. "Kit, this will not do at all. I shall not stand by and listen to this foolish, little chit say rude and unkind things to you. I mean it. Some arrangement will have to be made. When she is ready to return to *Claybourne Court* and act like the mature mistress of a stately English country house, it can be discussed. Until then, I want her out of here, while you are recuperating."

Kit put his head in his hands. "I know you're right, Mother. I don't think I can take anymore of her wicked tongue at the moment. Perhaps she's just in shock, but until she is quite well again, I think it best that she go to London and stay in our house there."

"Who will accompany her? She can't just be set lose in London. Lord knows what sort of trouble she'd be likely to fall into," his mother sniped.

"I'll accompany her," Lily answered. "After all, that is my job, isn't it? "

"Oh Barton, I hate to place such a burden on you," Lord Claybourne responded. "And what about Win? From my understanding, you have been his sole caretaker. This will mean that he must become accustomed to a nanny."

She felt tears well in her eyes. "Yes, poor little thing. I should hate the thought of that. Don't you think perhaps Win could accompany Lady Eleanor and me to London?"

"I don't think I could bear that,' Kit answered. "I've only just met him. It's seems terribly unfair that I should have to give him up so quickly."

"That baby is going nowhere," Lady Cynthia pronounced. "He is my son's only child, and he deserves to know his father. God knows the mother doesn't give a whit about him. And, I'm not in favor of Barton accompanying Lady Eleanor to London. She loves Win, and he loves her. It will be a terrible upheaval in the household. I should prefer making Barton the nanny, and sending one of the other servants along to London as a companion to Eleanor, or hiring someone new."

Lily heaved a sigh of relief. The last thing she wanted was to have to accompany Lady Eleanor to London.

"I intend to be spending a great deal of time at the London townhouse in the foreseeable future," commented Sebastian. "I suppose it wouldn't be proper for me to accompany Eleanor?"

"No, it most certainly wouldn't, although you are her brother-in-law," answered Lady Cynthia. "We shall find another ladies' maid for her in London. Then, if you care to be present, it won't look so terribly improper.

Barton will stay here to care for Win. If Eleanor should come to her senses, after Kit has had time to recuperate, we shall discuss logistics then. Has anyone any objections to such a plan?"

Everyone looked at one another, and then down at Eleanor. She had a cat-like smile on her lovely lips. She had gotten precisely what she wanted.

11

By the middle of July 1915, Lady Eleanor was settled in the family's cheery townhouse at 10 Dover Street in Mayfair. A new ladies' maid had been taken on, whose name was Edith Woods. She seemed competent, and was about Lily's age. She was a London girl, so perhaps she really was a better choice. Lily only met her twice, during the interviewing process, with which Lady Cynthia and Mrs. Briggs asked her to assist. She and Lady Eleanor seemed to get on splendidly and Lily had an inkling that they would be eminently suitable to one another.

The weeks leading up to Lady Eleanor's move were fraught with tears and more unkind words. Lady Cynthia, for the most part, stayed in the Dower house, and did not interfere. She really was totally fed up. Lord Claybourne seemed heartsick. He had looked so forward to coming home to *Claybourne Court*, and never in a million years had he envisioned the nightmare that awaited him. He was a strong man, and did not show a lot of emotion, but it was clear to even a casual observer that he was very downhearted. Lily's heart ached for him. The only bright spot in his entire existence at that time was his little boy. He and Win took to one another immediately. Lord Claybourne spent hours and hours in the nursery, rocking the baby, and singing him little songs, as well as war ditties. He was perfectly at ease changing nappies and feeding bottles, and Lily was not certain how much she was actually needed. Except that, every time she tried to get other chores accomplished, Win cried and cried.

Lady Eleanor appeared to have little interest in the fact that she was leaving her sweet son, for who knew how long? She went into his nursery and kissed his forehead, and said things like 'poor baby,' but Lily never saw her hold him. She didn't believe Win really even knew that she was his mother. She had a hunch that by the time Lady Eleanor came to her senses, and realized what she had done to her life, it would be too late. Win would never be as close to her as he might have been, and it was difficult for Lily to believe that Lord Claybourne would be either. He stayed out of Eleanor's way as much as possible, until the morning before she left. Sebastian was driving her to London, and she was all packed. First, she asked Lily to come up to her room, and of course, Lily did so.

"Barton, thank you for coming," she remarked as Lily entered her room. Eleanor was dressed in a lovely crème traveling suit, with a slim, ankle-length skirt, and matching jacket, trimmed in black braid. Her hat was swathed with white gauze, and decorated with masses of white flowers.

"You look lovely, Lady Eleanor," Lily said.

"Yes, well hopefully that won't go as unnoticed at my next destination as it has here," she replied.

"I'm not certain I understand, Milady?"

"Oh come, come Barton. Surely it's obvious to you that no one here appreciates anything about me. Whether it's my clothes, my appearance, or my many charms. That is why I'm being sent off to London, as a spoiled child might be."

"Well, Milady. It has been a difficult time. I wish things were different. I've enjoyed working for you, and I shall miss you."

"And I you, Barton. You are the only person here at *Claybourne Court* who has been kind to me."

"Oh, but Lady Eleanor, surely you don't include your husband in that group?"

"I most certainly do. He is the one who wants me gone. You find me another woman on the face of the earth who wouldn't react the way I did when first seeing that the man she fell in love with had only one eye. I'm sorry, Barton. I know it sounds crude, but I'm absolutely revolted at the sight of him. And, I cannot see anything that will change that. Have you seen these men who walk around with artificial eyes? My God! They look nothing like the real thing, and only stare in one direction. They're positively frightening. So, the prospect of that holds no hope. He would still take that ghastly thing out at night, and I should faint if I had to look at an empty eye socket."

"There really is no point in discussing this any further. It appears that the decision that has been made is going to best for everyone, at least for the time being," Lily responded.

"Yes. I imagine you think I'm a dreadful person for leaving my own child. Actually, you see, I don't see it that way at all. I do feel sorry for Kit. He didn't ask for any of this, any more than I did. The very least I can do under the circumstances is to leave his son with him. I was never cut out to be a mother. Not really. I do have a fondness for Win. He's a sweet baby, but babies take altogether too much time, and at this point in my life, I simply don't wish to devote myself to caring for a baby, even with a nanny. And, of course, I know that he will be in splendid hands. You are really a born mother, and I know you'll make Win into a good man, like his father."

"What are your plans, Lady Eleanor, long-term, or do you know?"

"Oh yes, I'm fairly certain I know. I haven't any intention of telling Kit now, as I do realize he doesn't need any more shock, but when he is better and this rotten war is over, I intend to return to Virginia. I never should have left to begin with. It was a terrible mistake. I can divorce Kit rather easily when back in my own Country. Win will be fine, and I imagine Kit will re-marry one day, to someone a bit more able to stomach war wounds."

"Does your Country not frown upon divorces? Won't you be a social outcast if you do such a thing?"

"Oh, Barton, the world is changing. In my Country, I don't believe I'll run into too much difficulty. I have dear friends, and they will understand my circumstances. It was all a dreadful mistake."

"What about Ginny? Are you taking her with you?"

"No, I'm not, which rips my heart in two," she said. It was the first show of emotion on her part. "I'm leaving her here, and I want your promise that you will make certain she has all of the love I gave her. I would take her, but I don't think she would be happy in London, and then when I go back to

America, there would be difficulty, as my Country requires that you quarantine an animal if you bring it in from abroad. I simply couldn't do that to her. So, please be kind to her, and give her lots of love and petting. I'd appreciate it if you would occasionally write and tell me how she is doing." Not one word about Lily writing to tell her about her estranged husband or her infant son!

"Of course, I'll do so, Lady Eleanor. I do hope to hear the occasional word from you, too."

"Of course, Barton. Now, I want you to have this as a reminder of our friendship." She handed Lily a small box, wrapped in plain white paper, with a blue bow upon it. Lily unwrapped it, and was stunned to see that it was the incredible bracelet that Lord Claybourne had given to her before he left for France. The one fashioned of sapphires and diamonds.

"Oh, Lady Eleanor, I can't accept this from you. This was given to you by your husband on the eve of battle. It should always be a keepsake of yours. I have no place to wear such a lavish piece of jewelry, and even if I did, it would be cruel of me to let Lord Claybourne see that you had given it to me."

"You needn't let him know that I gave it to you. Just don't wear it around him. If you don't feel comfortable wearing it, save it and give it to Win someday for me."

"Yes. All right, Milady, I'll do that," Lily answered, dumbfounded.

Eleanor gave Lily a perfunctory hug and said, "I do hope we see one another again. It's been a pleasure knowing you Barton." It was obvious that Lily had been dismissed.

After Lily left the room, she saw Lord Claybourne enter. The door was ajar, and she could hear their conversation quite clearly.

"Hello, Kit. Come to say goodbye, have you?"

"Yes, at least for a time, Eleanor. It's very difficult for me to know how we reached this place in our marriage. You know I love you, and would do anything not to have this separation."

"Well, you can't get a new eye, can you, Kit? I don't mean to be so abrasive, but I'm just being honest. Perhaps there are some women who could handle such a trauma, but I'm not one of them. Look at me, Kit. I'm young, and vibrant, and life is just waiting for me to take hold and live it. I'm beautiful, Kit. You yourself have said so often enough. Can you imagine me being seen in public with a deformed man? Oh – Oh –I know you aren't truly deformed. Not in the manner of someone who was born that way. But, nonetheless, I don't really see the difference. Do you think I would have married you if you'd been missing an eye? My God, Kit. I'm certain that you can find some nice woman who will have that sort of nurse-type instinct, and won't mind a whit about your missing eye. I'm just not the proper wife for you."

"Are you saying that you don't believe we can ever put our marriage back together again?"

"Oh Kit, I don't know. Eyes to me are so expressive. They are the windows to the soul. How am I to see your soul, if you only have one eye, and most of my time would be spent trying not to look at the missing one?"

"Eleanor, you are a cruel, merciless woman. If I had known when I married you that this was what you were like, I would never have given you a second look. I'm afraid to say that you are not beautiful. Not the way it counts. Beauty is more than a pretty face, and a nice silhouette. Kindness, empathy, compassion – those are all aspects of beauty. You have an enormous amount to learn Eleanor. Do you think I would even want to live with a woman who finds me repulsive? To tell you the truth, I find your attitude repulsive. Disgusting. I've never known anyone like you, and I hope never to again. Now, go to London, and enjoy yourself with whomever you wish. I am perfectly aware that you undoubtedly plan on sailing back to Virginia after the war ends. I'll let you take care of all legal necessities regarding dissolving our marriage. Until then, of course, I am your legal husband, and should you be in need of anything, I shall be here for you. But, I have no great desire to see you again."

With that, the door to the room opened, and Lord Claybourne strode out into the hallway. Eleanor slammed the door to her room. Lily's own was partially open, and he saw her, sitting at her writing desk.

"Oh, my dear Miss Barton. I'm sorry you probably heard that. I just couldn't contain my anger any longer. I have come quite close to loathing that creature. It sounds dreadful, of course, speaking about the mother of my son in such a way, but she doesn't appear to have normal feelings. I'm glad she's leaving. I hope I never see her again."

"Oh Milord. What a conundrum. I have to agree with you. I certainly cannot understand Lady Eleanor. She has everything a woman could ask for, and yet she seems bent upon saying such cruel, evil things, and throwing everything that's really important in life away from her."

He put his head down, and bit his lip. Lily saw him reach up and touch the eye patch that he wore. "If it hadn't been for this damned wound . . ."

"Oh no, Milord. That is absolute foolishness. You look quite dashing with your eye patch, and any woman who would walk away from a marriage because of such a trivial thing is not normal. If you want my honest opinion, I believe that Lady Eleanor wanted out of your marriage long before you were ever wounded. I think the moment she arrived in England, the happiness and joy she felt at making all of her friends green with envy because she married an English Earl, suddenly disappeared into the past. She woke up and realized what she had done. I think from the start she began to seek a way to get out of the situation she had created. Your wound only gave her the excuse she needed. No woman who really loves a man would think one iota about your wound. I've known men who lost legs, arms – whole faces – and their wives have stood by them and are just thrilled that they are alive and home with them. I'm certain you have too."

"Yes, I have. This war has produced thousands and thousands of casualties that make mine pale in comparison. If two people really love one another, then it's what's inside that matters. Eleanor has no understanding of that."

"I'm sorry to say it, Milord, but I don't believe Eleanor has ever been in love. I'm not certain she has the capacity for love."

"You could be very right, Barton. Well, let me tell you that I thank you immensely for all you've done to smooth the way for me. I'm terribly grateful that you won't be going to London with her, and that little Win will still have you. You're doing a marvelous job with him thus far, and I'm delighted that you'll be the one who cares for him as he grows. God Barton, I hope you don't go fall in love, marry and leave us. If you decide to marry someday, I can understand that, but I wish you'd promise me that you'll continue on at *Claybourne Court*, even if you have a family of your own."

"I haven't any plans to marry anytime soon, Milord. I think I'd find it very hard to leave the young Viscount, and everyone in this lovely home. That, of course, includes you, Milord."

There was a protracted silence. Lily looked down at her shoes. It was an awkward conversation. The truth was that unless she could ever find someone as decent and fine as the Lord, she couldn't imagine herself ever wanting a husband. And the chances of that were slim.

The week after Eleanor departed for London, Lily's mother married Will Morris. Lily was delighted for her, and she seemed marvelously happy. They were married in the small, ancient village church, and she wore a lovely summer suit. Will seemed beyond himself with glee. Lily had a small reception for them at her Mum's cottage, where they enjoyed a cake and tea, and even some champagne. Then they were off on a wedding trip to Windermere, in the Lake Country, for two grand weeks.

Before they left, it was decided that Mum would keep her cottage for at least one more year. Lily was so pleased, as it meant that she would have someplace to go on her off-days, if she wanted to be alone. Mum would not be living too far away, since Will's cottage was across the bridge, on the other side of the town, but, sometimes, on an off-day, she liked to just have the peace that comes with having a day all to oneself. Lately she had been feeling a bit undone in her head, as she realized she was entertaining confusing and inappropriate thoughts about Lord Claybourne. Lily knew with certainty that there was no way any relationship could possibly develop between them. The social difference was just too wide. Practically forbidden. She wondered how wise it was for her to continue working in such close proximity to him, knowing such feelings were developing. She spent long hours considering what else she might do, if she were to leave *Claybourne Court*. The thought of leaving Win brought tears to her eyes, as she loved him so dearly, and knew he loved her. But, the longer she stayed on, the worse it would become. Now that Eleanor was gone from the house, it sometimes seemed almost too much temptation to be alone there with Lord Claybourne. Not that she didn't trust him, for she did. He was a thoroughly decent gentleman. She was more concerned that she didn't trust herself. It was getting harder and harder to be around Kit, and not accidently slip and say something that would alert him to her feelings. She made the decision to stay through the year, and re-evaluate how she felt after that.

In the meantime, the summer drifted by slowly at *Claybourne Court*, as Lord Claybourne recuperated, and Win grew into a chubby legged little boy. Summertime was so peaceful there and it was hard to think about the brutal war that raged on. Nothing seemed to be accomplished, and there was a nasty stalemate that went on and on. Lily was so thankful that his Lordship was out of it. One noticed when walking on the street in the village, that there were few young men to be seen, and those who were there showed clear evidence of already serving their time. David Morris was more eager than ever to spend time with Lily, now that both of their parents were married and she did like him a lot, but never enough to think of marriage. She knew the time was approaching when she would need to make her feelings clear to him. She did not want to be accused of leading him on, and wished he could find some other nice girl in the village. God knew there were many who were longing for husbands.

Lily finally took her riding lessons from Howard, and she and Taffeta seemed as though they were meant for one another. She was gentle, and non-threatening and Lily learned to trust her to know what to do. First they were walking, then trotting, then cantering around the ring and finally Howard began to take her to the trails for longer outings. The trails wound back into the wooded area that grew very dense and thick with large trees, and it was so peaceful to ride Taffeta there on warm summer days. Other times she rode down by the artificial lake, and let Taffeta graze while she dreamed about how beautiful the world could be. Ginny ran behind them, always happy, rolling and digging, doing the things that dogs love best. She was such a precious, outgoing little animal, and now, when nighttime came, she sneaked into Lily's room, and slept by the side of her bed. If there were a storm, or other worrisome sound, she often found Ginny with her head buried beneath Lily's blankets. She'd returned to the room she had originally occupied at *Claybourne Court.* Win still needed nighttime feeding, but she was accustomed to that, and if she heard him cry, she was there instantly. Her heart nearly broke when she thought about the poor little baby, and how his mother had in actuality deserted him. It was beyond Lily how any woman could do such a thing.

They heard nothing from Eleanor throughout that lovely summer. Seeming to be well established in London, Sebastian occasionally brought news of her, but nothing of great import. Lily wondered if her parents knew that she had all but abandoned Lord Claybourne and her son. Perhaps they just assumed that the Claybourne's were spending time at the London townhouse as a family. Lily often wondered what sort of people they were. It was hard to imagine that any parents could have raised such a totally self-absorbed daughter.

One afternoon Lord Claybourne, Win and Lily took a picnic lunch down to the summerhouse. Lily spread a blanket on the summerhouse floor, and placed Win upon it, along with a goodly amount of his playthings. Lord Claybourne carried a basket of food prepared for them by Mary. It was a splendid day, quite warm for England. Lily wore a lightweight shirtwaist in pale pink muslin, with a small straw hat, festooned with tiny pink roses. It tied under her chin. Win wore a little white baby gown, for those were the days when even little boys wore dresses until about aged three. The Lord was also dressed casually, in lightweight trousers and a white linen shirt. He had rolled the shirt to his elbows. Ginny was with them too, and she scurried about, sniffing and digging, happy to be in the sunshine. They fed Win, and then Lily held him a bit, until he fell asleep in her arms. They laid him down on his blanket and he seemed content enough to sleep for hours. Then his Lordship and Lily ate the lovely luncheon prepared for them. It was very rustic, with wonderful French bread, great slabs of cheese, fresh fruit and cold, sliced chicken. Mary had also included two bottles of chardonnay wine, which Lily would never have thought of drinking at that time of day, but since Kit – which is the way she now thought of him- seemed pleased that Mary had tucked it into the basket, Lily decided that she, too, would partake. There were two crystal wine glasses, and he poured them each a glass. They leaned back against the round railing and savored the moment.

"This is something I never dreamed I'd do again, when I was at Ypres," he commented.

"No, I don't imagine so. These must be the kinds of dreams men in the trenches have when they're away from home and fighting in such filthy conditions."

"You're absolutely right, Lily. A man wonders if he'll ever see home again."

He had called her Lily. She was a little startled and didn't quite know how to react. He had always been very proper with her, although he was the only one in the family who always called her 'Miss Barton' instead of just 'Barton.' However, referring to her as 'Lily' was an entire departure. It was probably a slip of the tongue, but she felt she should call attention to it.

"Milord, are you aware that you just referred to me by my given name, 'Lily'?" she asked.

"Yes, now that you mention it, I am. I hope I didn't offend you?"

"Oh no, not at all. It just startled me. We are, after all, gentry and nanny, and it's not common, that's all."

"Lily, I don't feel comfortable referring to you as Barton, as if you were some sort of serving wench. 'Lily' is a lovely name, and I see no reason why I shouldn't address you as such."

"It doesn't bother me in the least, but it would rather be like my referring to you as 'Kit', instead of Milord. Don't you see? It just isn't the done thing."

"I grow very tired of the done thing, Lily," he smiled.

She was silent, not knowing how to respond.

"Now, I've made you ill at ease," he commented. "I don't mean to. It's just that I think of you as a dear friend, and I hope you think of me in the same way, Thus, I see no reason why we cannot be Lily and Kit to one another.

"You know very well why," she answered.

"You mean because others would find it inappropriate? Well, bother others. I care for you Lily. At least when we're alone, I shall call you by your lovely name, and I hope you'll reciprocate by calling me 'Kit'." He finished his glass of wine, and reached out his arms to her. She knew she shouldn't do it, but the wine had gone to her head, and so had Kit. She let him take her into his arms, and hold her. She could feel his heart beating against her breast. She clung to him for a moment. Lily had dreamed of such a divine moment. She knew he had been terribly lonely for so long. Not since before the war had he held a woman in his arms. She could feel him shaking a bit, and she was as well. Then he tipped her head up to his, and placed a very soft kiss on her lips. She kissed him back, but gently, and tentatively, without passion.

"I don't frighten you do I, Lily?" he murmured in her ear.

"No. I realize that you've been very lonely. I suspect that I'm acting as a stand-in for another more acceptable person."

"Lily!" he cried, as he held her away from him. "You are not a substitute for anyone. I wish I had met you before I met Eleanor. I never would have married her. You're the sort of woman I should have married. Warm, kind, sweet, and gracious. You're much more a lady than Eleanor could ever be."

"I think you flatter me, Sir. But, even if those things were true, you leave out the fact that I am also a nanny, and you are an Earl. We live in a world that doesn't accept such differences. It is forbidden."

"Lily, I am not now, nor have I ever been, concerned with what the world thinks. I wasn't raised to think like that. Did you know that my mother was a tradesman's daughter?"

"Lady Cynthia? You can't be serious?"

"Yes. Very. Her father owned a shop in London. So, is that so different than your father having been a physician?"

"No, I don't suppose so," she answered. "But I'm simply not a part of your world."

"You fit into my world very well, Lily. Even my son seems to know it."

He pulled her back toward him, and this time the kiss was deeper and longer. Lily ran her fingers through his hair, and kissed his cheek – his forehead – his eye. Yes, the one covered by a patch.

Tears trickled from his other eye. "My God, Lily, I wondered if any woman could bear to come near such an abhorrent place."

She placed small kisses all around the area. "I have no fear of your wound, Kit. It's just a part of you. And everything about you is very precious to me."

"Oh God, Lily, I'm so in love with you, I can scarcely bear it." He tightened his grip on her, and smothered her with his kisses. "Tell me you love me. Please. This isn't some foolish summertime dream for me. I've thought of you for so long. We'll find a way to be together, I swear. I'll move mountains to make that happen."

"Oh, I do love you, Kit. I'm not as optimistic about the future as you are, but perhaps that's because you're the one who would have to bear the nasty comments, and rude remarks people would make, if we were to really decide to be together."

"You let me worry about that, my sweet Lily. That isn't even a concern of mine. The most important thing is for Eleanor and me to obtain a divorce."

Lily removed herself from his arms, but kept hold of his hand. "How difficult would that be, since she has left you?"

"We would have to live apart for two years, before the courts will consider 'desertion' as the grounds."

"Oh, that seems so long."

"She can't go anywhere until the war is over anyway. Since the *Lusitania*, there have been few passenger ships crossing the Atlantic. Our best hope is to pray for a quick end to this war."

"I pray for that every night as it is," she smiled.

Win began to make grizzling noises on his blanket, which brought an end to their truly astonishing afternoon. Lily was glad that it was a Saturday, for the next day would be her off-day, and she definitely needed time to think. They gathered up their belongings and headed back to *Claybourne Court*. He kissed her once more, before they got near the house. "I promise you, Lily, this will be resolved. I want you to be my wife."

Lily was in a daze. In the course of an afternoon, they had gone from Milord and Miss Barton, to Lily and Kit. He seemed sincere. He wasn't the sort of man who wasn't sincere. If it had been Sebastian, she wouldn't have believed a word he said, and would have known it was all a ploy to get into her knickers. But, Kit wasn't at all like that. It was clear that he meant every word he said. There wasn't any question regarding how she felt about him. He was everything she'd ever dreamed of, and more. It wasn't his social status, or his money. In fact, she wished that weren't even an issue. If they did work things out, and she married him, she couldn't imagine becoming the Countess of Claybourne. She wasn't at all certain that she could cope with such responsibilities. The difference between Eleanor and Lily was that Lily would be willing to listen to whoever wanted to give her instructions. That seemed like such a long way off, and such a remote possibility, that she didn't give it a lot of thought. The whole thing was surreal.

She retreated to her bedroom, after settling Win in his, and giving him a bottle. There she sat on the bed, trembling a bit, and wondering if everything had really happened. Where did they go from here? It had definitely been a watershed moment. She couldn't imagine going back to an employer-employee relationship with him, but it was also hard to envision anything else. Certainly in front of the staff, they had to be very circumspect. Lily disliked subterfuge, and was not a good liar. Her best hope was to avoid him as much as possible. Yet, she wanted to see him with all of her heart. Oh what a muddle! She bathed and changed clothing for dinner. Then Kit did another wildly unacceptable thing, which frightened her dreadfully, and also thrilled her at the same time. He sent word through Mrs. Briggs that he would like Lily to join Lady Cynthia and him for dinner that evening. Lily had never been accorded such an honor. Wasn't that like telling the entire household that she had been elevated to a higher realm within the sphere of *Claybourne Court*? She wished she could ask him what in the world he was thinking, but he had gone to the stables to check on the horses. So, she dressed in her best tea-length gown, of lilac with a full crinoline over a bell shaped skirt. She washed her hair and arranged it a bit differently, with a few tendrils loose around her face, and the top swept up into a knot. She even added a bit of lip rouge. Looking into the mirror, she saw that she appeared quite fetching. When the dinner bell sounded, she descended the staircase, and Kit was at the bottom waiting for her, in full evening dress. She was scarcely able to speak. He was so handsome. He put out his arm and she took it, and together they walked into the drawing room. Lily had, of course, spent time in that room, but it was not a regular place for a nanny. It was so elegant. Lily particularly admired the color scheme of pale pink and green furnishings, on light colored Aubusson carpeting. It was a cheery room. Kit led her to a large shell pink sofa in front of the marble fireplace, and seated her there. Then he rang for Halsey, and ordered two champagne cocktails. He handed one to Lily, and she sat, still as a rod, sipping it slowly, and wondering what came next. Soon, Lady Cynthia joined them. She requested a gin and tonic, and expressed delight in seeing Lily's presence.

"Why, hello, Miss Barton. How lovely that you could join Kit and me for dinner. It's usually just the two of us, and while I do love my son immensely, a twosome can become dreary after a time. I'm sure you'll liven things up."

Had Kit told her of the change in their relationship? She was always friendly to Lily, but she seemed to be even more so on that evening. Lily was very nervous.

"I've shared with Mother some of what we discussed earlier today, Lily," Kit said, as though he had read her thoughts. Lily looked aghast. "Don't be alarmed. Mother is very discreet, and completely on our side. He turned and smiled at Lady Cynthia. "She has never been pleased about my marriage to Eleanor, as you well know, and looks upon you with much greater favor."

"Yes, but . . ." Lily didn't know how to respond. She felt he was playing a reckless game.

"Don't worry, my dear," replied Lady Cynthia. "I don't intend to shout Kit's feelings for you from the rooftops, but I cannot imagine living under the same roof and pretending to go about business as usual. I've never been one to lie and sneak. So, then, let's have things out in the open, within certain proprieties. Everyone in Christendom knows that Kit and Eleanor are separated, and it is only time before he is rid of her for good. There is nothing untoward about having one's nanny share the dining table now and again. The servants all adore you, and there is no question that they would prefer having you as their mistress to having that terribly spoiled girl."

"I just feel very uncomfortable, Lady Cynthia. I'm not at all used to such splendor. I don't want to send tongues wagging about me. If I should ever need a reference, this would not give a proper picture."

And, what, my dear, should you need a reference for? I don't intend to let you out of my sight, until all of this is settled. Of course, your Sundays will still be yours to do as you wish," Kit smiled.

Lily sighed, and drank the rest of her champagne. The three of them entered the grand dining room, and she felt she was being looked at with judgmental eyes by the enormous portraits of Claybourne ancestors which glared from the walls. Kit showed her to a chair to his right, and held it out. She settled herself as comfortable as possible, and spread her napkin in her lap. Then she took a sip of water. Suddenly she was parched. She noticed that neither Lady Cynthia nor Kit had unfolded their napkins. Then she remembered that it was the footman's responsibility to spread the napkins. She silently picked hers back up from her lap, folded it, and placed it back on the table. Her face grew pink. Neither of her dinner companions seemed to notice, which was probably only their good manners.

"Miss Barton, do tell me about more about yourself, dear. I know so little, really. Everyone speaks so highly of you."

Lily cleared her throat. "I grew up here in *Claybourne-on-Colne*, Milady. My father was the physician here. I adored him. I trailed behind him constantly, and hoped one day to be a doctor myself. He was in favor of my aspirations, and we planned on someday owning a practice together. I acted as his apprentice. But, then he died, and my dreams died too."

"Well, perhaps you will now have new dreams to replace the old," Lady Cynthia smiled.

"Yes, perhaps," Lily answered.

Edward, one of the footmen, shook out the napkins and spread them on each person's lap. Halsey presented the first course of the dinner, and Lily waited to see if he would look astounded that she was sitting at the table with the Dowager Duchess and the Earl. She saw no reaction on his face, but that was probably due more to his strict training than anything else. Neither did the footmen bat an eyelid when they saw her. She relaxed a bit. It was a lovely Court Bouillon, and Lily thanked her Mum, silently, for teaching her the proper way to eat soup. A salad course followed, then Cornish hen, then Rib Roast, with all of the trimmings, and a simple dessert of iced cream. Any one of the courses would have been enough. But it was lovely.

"I still feel a bit improper dining with you," she commented. "It doesn't seem right somehow."

"Lily, someday I hope that you will be the Countess here, and I want to introduce you to our way of doing things. For now, no one need know of our feelings for one another, besides Mother. There is certainly nothing inappropriate about our dining with the woman who has almost exclusive care of the next Earl of Claybourne. It can be explained, if need be, as a perfect time for us to come together, in order for you to bring us up on Win's progress."

"Yes, I can see that," Lily replied. She liked the idea. "All right. That makes me feel infinitely better. But, I hope we shall really do so. It's important for both of you to be included in his everyday activities and his growth. I agree that this presents a good time for me to bring you up-to-date."

"There you see," Lady Cynthia smiled. "Problem solved."

"If you are dining with others –company and the like – I would rather not be included in such affairs, if that is acceptable to you," Lily responded.

"I think that will be perfectly fine, Lily, and you'll probably enjoy yourself much more than we will," Kit laughed.

And so a new routine was born, and every night, after Win had been tucked in, she dressed in a more formal gown, and presented herself for dinner with Kit and his mother. She found that she looked forward to these occasions immensely, and believed it was very beneficial for them to be kept abreast of the happenings in Win's life. Naturally, the thought of a special evening with Kit was thrilling to her, as well. Lady Cynthia could not have been nicer, and Lily was certain that the dining experience at *Claybourne Court* improved immensely when the new arrangement went into effect, and Lady Eleanor was far away in London.

12

On September 8, the German's sent one of their deadly, silent ships directly into London. This was a much worse attack than the last had been. Houses and buildings were struck. Eleanor had just returned from a West End play, when the devastation hit her townhouse. She took cover in the basement, which probably saved her life, but the home was in ruins. The attack killed 22 people and injured 87. It accounted for the worst loss, in terms of cost, of all of the attacks during the war. Eleanor, of course, went bonkers. While other stoic Englishmen, went about a thorough search of the area, and assisted in the emergency aid of those who were injured, until the ambulances could arrive, Eleanor Claybourne ran back and forth in front of her townhouse, screaming and weeping. A kindly neighbor helped to settle her down, and got in touch with Kit at *Claybourne Court.* She carried on incessantly about the loss of a lot of the lovely things in the home that has been destroyed. "My wedding china; the Sterling tea service, priceless paintings; the Sterling flatware; on and on she went. Those who had lost loved ones could not have cared a whit that her precious Waterford Crystal chandelier had been smashed to bits. She finally sat on what had been the front steps, and moaned. That is where Kit found her, when he arrived, in the chauffeur driven Daimler. She wore a pale blue, formal gown, which had been her choice for the theater that evening. Her hair was askance, and one shoe was missing. When she spied Kit, one would have assumed that they were the dearest of husband and wives. She ran to his arms.

"Oh Kit, Kit darling. Hold me. I was so frightened. I'd only just removed my gloves when this gigantic explosion sounded. I ran for the cellar, tripping on the narrow, steep stairs, but I made it. That's why I lost a shoe. Anyway, there was smoke and flames, and I used my handkerchief to cover my mouth. I hid in a corner of the basement, until I heard people's voices, and no more of the horrid, loud detonations. Oh God, Kit, I thought the world was coming to an end."

He held her against his chest, but made no move to kiss her. "The world has not come to an end, Eleanor. You are perfectly fine. Now try to calm down. You aren't hurt at all. Of course the house is a total loss, but insurance will take care of that."

"But, Kit. Nothing can ever replace all of the priceless objects that were lost. My incredible Sterling silver, with the hundreds and hundreds of pieces of fruit carved into one single knife handle. And, oh! All of my gowns. What shall I do for clothing?"

"You'll replace it, of course. Just be glad that you're alive, Eleanor. Anything else can be replaced," he sighed wearily. After what he had seen at Ypres, this seemed very trivial indeed. "Come, get into the car. You're shivering all over. Why in God's name are you dressed in such a flimsy garment?"

"I'd attended the theater with a friend. I'd only just returned home."

"Did you friend not wait to see that you had made it into the house safely, and were all locked up for the night?"

"Well – he was in a bit of a hurry. He's married you see, and did not want to be seen by anyone who knew him."

"Ahhh, yes, I certainly do see," replied Kit, with a sardonic smile.

"Now Kit, it was nothing like what you're thinking. He's just someone I met at an afternoon tea at Lady Leedy's last week. He is an older man. I have no interest in him other than as a friend."

"May I be so bold as to ask this gentleman's name?" Kit asked.

"He is a Duke. The Duke of Painswick. It was just a friendly assignation. His wife loathes the theater, so I said that I would accompany him."

"No matter, Eleanor. Climb into the auto." She finally did as she was asked.

"Wherever are you taking me? I can't go to a hotel in this frightful state."

"No, you can't. I'm taking you back to *Claybourne Court*. I warned you about the dangers of being in London during wartime, but you wouldn't listen. You know that I preferred to lease a cottage in the village. Well, you have no choice now. I am still your legal husband, although you'll never know how much I wish that were not so. It's is my responsibility to look after you."

"Well, perhaps it won't be so bad at *Claybourne Court*. I've grown rather weary of London. Every man I see who is anywhere near my age is disfigured in some gruesome way. Your patch actually looks rather handsome, now that I've seen so many other injured men."

"Look, Eleanor. Don't get too attached to C*laybourne Court* or me. Until this war is over, you will be under my wing, but I have not changed my feelings for you. And I rather doubt you have changed yours for me. I suspect that you've taken a good look around you, and realized that things weren't as bad as they seemed. It will take a good while to make repairs to the London townhouse, and you will have a lot of time to be occupied with replacing all of the precious items you lost, but please don't bother me."

Eleanor slumped down in the back seat, and pouted. There was a time when he would have thought she had a pretty pout, but now all he saw was a spoiled, selfish brat. "That look is not going to work, Eleanor, so you might as well stop trying to influence me through sulks. Besides, why don't you concentrate upon seeing your son?"

"Oh my son! He doesn't even know me."

"And whose fault is that? You have never lifted a finger to show him that you love him. In fact, I'm not at all certain that you do love him."

"Oh, what a cruel, beastly thing to say. Of course I love him. But, I told you that I'm not a 'baby person.' When he can have a conversation with me, I'm sure I shall find him quite entertaining."

"Eleanor, if you were a man, I'd slap you for that comment. Now, I'd simply appreciate you not saying another word until we reach *Claybourne Court*." She curled up into a ball on the back seat, and sniffled throughout the journey.

Soon the lights of the house came into view. The outside gaslights had been turned off, so as not to alert German airships of a fine target. The car made its way around to the back, where the garages were located, and the passengers got out of the car.

"Well, we might at least have entered by the front doors, instead of like servants," Eleanor sniffed.

"I want the car garaged as quickly as possible, Eleanor, There is a war on, in case you've forgotten, and you've only just escaped a bomb dropped from a Zeppelin."

She hobbled her way to the back entrance, with only one shoe on her foot. Kit supposed he should have put his hand under her elbow, but was loath to do so. When they entered the kitchen, Mary was at the door, along with Halsey and Mrs. Briggs. They were very solicitous, and she was given a hot cup of tea, and a warm blanket to put around her shoulders.

"Where am I to sleep?" she asked forlornly.

"I suppose in your usual room. I'll be staying in my own room, as always."

"You mean I shall have no comfort, after the ordeal I have been through tonight?"

"Eleanor, you will have your little dog Ginny. She seemed to be comfort enough for you before." With that, Kit turned and left the room. Eleanor sat in silence, sipping her tea. After a few moments, Lily came into the room at a brisk pace, saying she was in need of Win's bottle. She came to an abrupt halt when she saw Eleanor at the table.

"Well, I certainly didn't expect to see you here, Lady Eleanor. Has something happened?"

"You might say so, Barton. The house in London was totally destroyed by a Zeppelin raid. I'm lucky to be alive. I've lost all of my belongings. Can you imagine? I really haven't the foggiest idea what I shall do. I'm to stay here, but no one at *Claybourne Court* appreciates me at all. I don't see how I can live with a man who treats me so mean."

"I should imagine you will have to, Lady Eleanor. I would follow Kit's advice if I were you."

"Yes, I suppose," she murmured. "I wonder if Sebastian will stay here too."

"Was he living at the townhouse in London, too?" Lily asked. "And didn't you have a ladies' maid there? Where is she?"

"She's run off somewhere. Fear, I suppose. She said she was going to the country. I doubt I'll see her again. Yes, Sebastian was with us most of the time. Occasionally he visited friends in other parts of the Country. He wasn't there when the Zeppelin raid came. Since my ladies' maid is gone, I'll be needing you again. Obviously, there's no question but that you're the one I want, Barton."

"But, Lady Eleanor. I'm now Win's nanny. Win would be very upset if I stopped caring for him, and so would I."

"Well, you can do as you did before – just continue on with Win, and also assume your duties with me."

"Lady Eleanor. That isn't remotely possible. Win was a tiny infant when I assumed responsibility for both him and for you. He is five months old now, and needs my attention. That was a terrific drag on me before. In fact, I didn't realize it, until you left. I don't feel that I could possibly do that, now."

"Well, then, we'll just have to find another nanny for Win. I obviously can't exist without a ladies' maid."

Lily was stricken. Surely she wouldn't be expected to take over assisting Lady Eleanor. If it came to that, she would have to refuse. But, she knew that Kit would not let it happen. Win was the most important person in the world to him, and he knew how very much he loved Lily. "I suppose we will just have to let Kit – sorry – Lord Claybourne decide what to do," Lily stammered.

"Oh? So it's 'Kit' now? That is the second time during this conversation that you've referred to him that way. How inappropriate, Barton. Did my husband ask you to call him by his given name?" Her eyes narrowed.

"No. No. That was a slip of the tongue. You were referring to him as Kit, and I wasn't thinking."

"I don't believe I referred to him at all, Barton. Yes, I imagine it was a slip of the tongue, but I wonder if that isn't because it's how you think of him."

"Lady Eleanor, that is ridiculous. Your husband is my employer. I have a lot on my mind at the moment. I simply wasn't thinking. I would never disrespect Lord Claybourne by neglecting to use his title. Now, I need to get Win's bottle ready, so if you'll please excuse me . . ." Lily fetched the bottle, placed it in a pan of warm water, and tested it on her arm. Then she wrapped it in a warm flannel, and went back to Win's room.

At the first opportunity, Lily had a chat with Kit. She had to be very careful now that Eleanor was back at *Claybourne Court.* She seemed to watch Lily's every move. Lily believed that Eleanor had a sense there was something different about Lily's relationship with her husband, and with Lily's position in the house, in general. The day after Eleanor's return, Lily rose at nearly dawn and waited until she heard Kit's footstep on the upper landing. She scurried across the hallway, and tugged on his sleeve. He smiled, and started to speak, but she put her finger to her lips. "Shhhh. We need to talk alone," she whispered. He motioned her to follow him, and she did, as he led her to his library on the lower level. After they were in the room, with the door firmly closed, he laughed.

"Now, just what is all of the mystery, Lily?" He moved to kiss her, but she put her arm up and pushed him away.

"No, Kit. This is serious. I ran into Eleanor yesterday, when preparing Win's bottle. I'm afraid during our conversation I slipped and called you 'Kit'. I'm terribly sorry. It just happened. I think I made a good excuse, but Eleanor looked very suspicious. Also, she is adamant that I should return to being her ladies' maid and that you will hire a new nanny for Win. So help me, Kit, I'll leave this house before I go back to caring for Eleanor."

"You are not going to be Eleanor's ladies' maid again. That is out of the question. I'll not have a new nanny for Win. My God that woman has nerve. I didn't even want her back in this house. I didn't know what else to do with her. I've been thinking about it all night. If she returns, then my grounds for a divorce have disappeared, because we have to be apart two years in order to claim desertion. I know she really doesn't want to be here. She was so anxious to leave before."

"Will Sebastian be staying here too?"

"I assume he will, for a while. He really has nowhere else to go. Although, frankly, I can't imagine him staying here too long a spell. My brother hates country life even more than Eleanor does."

"Kit, perhaps I'm just being a silly woman, but I don't trust Eleanor. I wonder if she hasn't had her fill of London. There really are no young men to entertain her, and tell her how lovely she is. Perhaps she's decided she shouldn't have been so hasty in her decision to leave. If that's the case, she may want to try to make a go of your marriage now."

"Yes, Lily. I've had the same thoughts. I even confronted her with them. She did say that London wasn't as much fun as she'd thought it would be, because of the shortage of young men." He put his arms around Lily. "I love you, and that's all there is to it. There is nothing she could do to woo me back to her. I'm dead set against a marriage to her, and want out at the first possible opportunity. Don't you worry about such an impossible thing. I'll do whatever needs to be done to make her understand that this marriage is over, and that the only reason she is allowed to stay here is because I am trying to be considerate. She can write to her parents in Virginia and they can send her some money to lease a house or flat. If necessary, I'll provide the means. Now, stop your fretting." He kissed her longingly, and then told her to leave the library first, after which he would follow along in a few moments. She did as Kit asked.

Sebastian arrived at *Claybourne Court* the following evening. One always knew it was him by the loud screech of the tires as his Hispano Suiza roared into the driveway. Entering the house, he threw his driving cap on a nearby chair in the hall, and called for his brother. "Kit! Kit! Where the devil are you? Kit!"

"Stop bellowing like a cow. I'm right here," Kit answered, as he entered from the library. "What brings you to the wilderness?"

"I suppose you know all about what happened to the London house? It's a total disaster. Where in God's name has Eleanor gotten herself off to? I can't seem to find her at any of her usual haunts."

"She's right here, Sebastian. Edward drove me down and fetched her when it happened. She's fine. She was at the theater, and it happened just as she'd returned home."

"That must have been some fright."

"Oh, to hear her talk, it was like being on the Titanic. I've already had an insurance man out. It will all be taken care of. She's most concerned about her clothes. I told her it would be a good excuse to buy a new wardrobe, which seems to have perked her up a bit."

"Well, I see things are no better where the two of you are concerned."

"Did you think they would be? I want her out of my life, Sebastian. Did you think I could ever forget the ugly things she said to me when I returned from France? My God, man, there is no question about her feelings. I never should have married her."

"She has a wicked little tongue, that's for certain. But, then she can be charming too."

"She's lost any of the charm I once saw in her. She's a foolish, selfish little girl. I so wish she could go back to Virginia. Damn this war."

"Don't you think for the sake of Win the two of you should make an attempt to reconcile? My poor, little nephew should have a mother."

"Eleanor is not a mother. I don't want him to grow up with the idea that all women are like her. He needs to understand about kindness, compassion and real love. Eleanor can't teach him those things."

"Who can?"

"What do you mean, who can? A lot of women could. Most women, in fact. But, before I can even start to think about that, I have to divorce Eleanor."

"Dear brother, I have a suspicion that you already have someone else in mind." He threw himself down on the sofa in the drawing room. "Am I to be allowed in on the secret?"

Kit sat down across from him. "I have no idea what you're talking about. I don't know where I'd have the chance to meet anyone else. I've been here at *Claybourne Court* ever since my return from France, except for the trip to London to retrieve Eleanor."

"Yes. Well, perhaps there is someone at *Claybourne Court*?"

"What are you talking about?"

"What about the beautiful Miss Barton? She'd fit the bill quite splendidly, but for her rather common roots."

"Sebastian. That's a rotten thing to say. Her roots, as you put it, are as good as the next person's. Her father was a physician. But why all of the talk about Miss Barton? She is a lovely girl, and a nice one too, but she is Win's nanny. That's all."

"I've heard some talk from the servants. She's been joining you and Mother for dinner at night in the dining room. Rather unusual for the nanny of the house, eh?"

"Oh, God. How servants will go on. Yes, Mother and I have asked her to join us for the evening meal. It's a fine way to keep abreast of everything that's happening in Win's life. I don't want to miss out on anything. He is my entire world. Mother's too, really. Well, of course, she loves us, but Win is her first grandchild, and the heir to *Claybourne Court*. So, there's nothing out of the way with our having a meal with his nanny. I'm surprised that you would listen to any gossip."

"Sorry, dear brother. It just sounded a bit peculiar. Now that you've explained it, I can see that it's nothing very titillating."

"Believe me, Sebastian, you'll be the first to know when I've found a new wife. And, I'd appreciate it if you wouldn't spread this gossip any further. All I'd need is for Eleanor to get some fool idea like that in her head."

"Don't worry. I'm more concerned about how I'm going to escape this conscription thing if it happens." He crossed his feet, which were leaving marks on the pale pink sofa. "I've been handed white feathers on three occasions. I don't like being demeaned, and made to feel like a coward."

Kit ran his hand through his hair. "Little brother, I think you'd better come to grips with the fact that you're going to be fighting for your Country. Unless you plan on crashing that delightful automobile of yours, and sustaining some ghastly injury, you are going to be covered with mud in a trench somewhere in France before the year is out."

"I can't do it, Kit. I mean it. I really can't. What if I lost an eye, like you? Or even worse?"

"Then you'd go on, you bloody fool. Just as I have. What if every man in the country were as shallow as you are? We'd all be speaking German by now."

"What if I just tell them that I don't believe in war? I don't, you know."

"Sebastian, you don't believe in getting wounded, or having to be uncomfortable, and eating less than gourmet food. Your beliefs about war have nothing to do with anything. Now, please, just grow up, and realize that you have a duty to do. No one I knew in France wanted to be there. But, we stayed, and did what we had to do. So will you. The greatest fear is fear of the unknown. Once you've actually experienced it, the worst will be over. Do you remember Shakespeare's famous quotation, 'A coward dies a thousand deaths, the brave man dies but one?' That perfectly sums it up. It's time to be a man, Sebastian." Kit was irritated. He thought of all of the chaps he'd known in France, and not one had a cowardly bone in his body. He saw them blown to pieces in their attempts to cross No Man's Land, and fight to save fellow comrades when only one arm remained on their own bodies. His spoiled brother was acting like a fool. It was hard to understand how both he and Sebastian had come out of the same family. They were so vastly different. Of course, they always had been. Sebastian, from the time he was a young boy, liked to hunt, ride, and fish. None of those things held enormous interest for Kit, who only learned to excel at them because such skills were expected of an eldest son. The truth was, he abhorred killing. The first time his father had taken him fox hunting, and the blood of the fox had been smeared on his face as a sign of his having reached adulthood, he was nearly sick. He saw nothing manly about shooting a placid deer with a deadly rifle. The only skill he had conquered and actually enjoyed was horseback riding, which is why he had joined the *Scot's Grey's* after *Sandhurst.* But, even then, when in battle, he found no joy in seeing men and horses fall dead in the heat of battle.

Sebastian got up from the sofa, and sauntered out of the room. "I'm going to go for a ride in my auto. I feel out-of-sorts," he said, as he slammed the heavy front door.

"Watch out for a white feather," Kit called snidely, as he heaved a heavy sigh. Everything was so terribly undone. What was he to do about Eleanor? How long would he have to wait until he could make Lily his wife? Should he write to Eleanor's father? He couldn't imagine what good it would do, and he suspected that the only answer he would be given was that she was Kit's wife, thus, his responsibility. He leaned his head back against the winged back chair, and closed his eyes. Soon, he was fast asleep.

13

"Kit! Oh my God! Kit! Where are you?" It was Lady Cynthia's voice, and she was clearly beside herself with upset. It was the first time Lily had ever heard obvious tears in the Dowager Countess' voice. Lily was in Win's room, changing a nappy, when she heard the commotion.

Kit was still asleep in the drawing room, but his mother's frightened voice brought him abruptly awake. "Mother, I'm in the drawing room", he called, standing up. "Whatever is the trouble?"

Lady Cynthia ran into the drawing Room and fell into Kit's arms. She was truly sobbing. "Mother, Mother, what in the world . . .?"

"Oh Kit. It's Sebastian. He's been in a terrible accident. He was apparently out driving that damnable automobile of his, and he crashed it into a tree."

Kit gently removed her arms from around his neck, and sat her down on the sofa. Then he rang for Mrs. Briggs, and asked for a glass of water for Lady Cynthia. "Try to calm down, Mother. Now, tell me what happened, so that I know what to do."

"He apparently went out for a drive in that car of his. He wasn't that far from home. He was taking the turn from the bottom of the hill, and he must have been going too fast. There is a large Oak tree there. Do you know where I mean?"

"Yes, yes. Go on."

"Well, that's it. His car smashed headlong into the tree. The ambulance lads were called, and he is at hospital. They've just rung. Mrs. Briggs answered and they asked to speak to a member of the Claybourne family. I was standing almost next to her, so she handed it to me."

Kit rang for the chauffeur and went to the closet to throw a jacket on. It was a raw, windy day, and there was a light mist.

"My God, my God, this is my fault. I gave him the idea. How could I have been so stupid? I should have known he'd do it. He would have done anything to get out of going into the army. Damn, damn, damn. Oh please God, let him be alive. I wasn't being serious. Stupid, idiot boy."

Lily ran down the stairway, after placing Win back into his cot. She caught Kit just as he was about to leave. "Kit, what's happened now? I could hear you clear upstairs in Win's room. What are you so upset about? I heard your mother's voice, too."

"Yes, she's lying down in the drawing room. That damn fool brother of mine has crashed his auto into a tree. He's in hospital. We'd been discussing the possibility of conscription before he left to go for a ride. I'd been quite unkind. Said it was time for him to grow up, and that there was no way he would get out of serving, short of driving in his car into a tree and sustaining an injury that was bad enough to keep him out."

Lily put her head in her hands. "Oh no. But, Kit, you can't blame yourself. You didn't know he'd be foolish enough to do such a thing."

"No, but I never should have said it. I knew he was depressed when he left. He said as much. Said he was all undone. I should have kept him from going. I was just so tired of hearing about his fears over having to fight in the war."

"Of course you were. We all were."

Suddenly, Eleanor's voice interrupted their discussion. She was on the stairway. "What are you saying about Sebastian? And why are you having any sort of conversation about my brother-in-law with Kit, Barton? What are you even doing down here? I heard Win grizzling upstairs."

"I-I'm sorry, Milady. I was putting a nappy on Win, when I overheard a commotion down here. I ran downstairs to see if everything was all right."

"And is everything all right?"

"Well, no. I'll let you and Lord Claybourne discuss it and I'll return to Win. I'm sorry I interrupted Milord. I was overtaken with concern."

"What's happened to Sebastian?" Eleanor asked, as she cast a nasty glance at Lily.

"I haven't time to repeat all of this. He's in hospital. There's been a car wreck. I'm on my way now."

"I'm coming with you," she demanded.

"I don't want you with me, Eleanor. I'll call when I find out how things are. Stay here and keep Mother company."

"No. I'm coming, and that's all there is to it. I am still married to you, in case you've forgotten. Sebastian is my brother-in-law, and a good friend."

The Daimler pulled up in front of the house, and Kit hurried out and got in. Eleanor ran behind him and jumped in beside him. Not a word was spoken on the way to hospital. A couple of times she tried to speak, but he held his hand up in front of her mouth, making it clear that he did not want to hear anything from her. When they arrived, he jumped out of the back door, and slammed it, leaving his wife alone in the rear seat. By that time Edward, the Chauffeur, was out and beside the door. He opened it for Eleanor, and she ran to catch up with Kit.

"Kit, please stop acting so horrible. I haven't done anything to you. Can't I be concerned about Sebastian too?"

"You can be anything you want to be, Eleanor. But, don't expect me to forget how repulsed you are by people with only one eye. Defective people. I hope Sebastian isn't disfigured in any way. You have nowhere to run off to if he is. I guess you'll just have to stay at *Claybourne Court* and bear it."

He was walking very rapidly, and she almost had to run to keep up with his pace. It was hard to talk, because she was nearly out of breath. "Oh Kit, you're being silly. I was shocked when you first came home from France. I'd never seen anything like a missing eye before. After all, you know what a sheltered life I'd lived. Also, I'd just had a baby. You know doctors say that women get all foolish in the head a lot of the time, after having a baby. I didn't mean to hurt you. Can't we just put it behind us now? I'm sorry. Now, there, does that make you feel better? I don't usually say 'I'm sorry' to anyone."

Kit stopped in the hallway, just outside of Sebastian's room. He turned to Eleanor, and tried to speak in a soft voice. "Eleanor, I do not care if you're sorry or not. I don't want you back in my life. I don't know what you are up to, but I don't trust you for one second. You don't want to put this behind us because you love me and want our marriage to work, nor because you love Win. You have some scheme cooked up in your devilish head. Now, leave me alone, Eleanor. I'm going to see my brother. If you care to see him after my visit, feel free, but I don't want you in the room when I'm in there."

Eleanor began to weep, and Kit completely ignored her. He left her sitting on a chair in the dimly lighted hallway, as he opened the door to his brother's room.

Sebastian was lying on the bed, nearly as pale as the white bedding. His head was thickly bandaged, as were his eyes. One leg was propped in the air on a traction line, in a cast. The rest of his face was bruised badly.

"Sebastian. Sebastian. It's me," Kit whispered. "Can you hear me?" There was no answer. Kit walked closer. He reached out and ran his hand down his brother's arm. "You won't have to go to France, old boy," he said, as tears streamed down his cheek. He sat down in the chair by the bedside and tried to pull himself together. How could this have happened? Had his brother always been so lacking in courage? Kit had assumed he was simply young, and having anxiety attacks like every man did when faced with the prospect of going to war. But, Sebastian was truly different. He has been petrified. Preferring to end up like this in a hospital bed, rather than fighting in a trench in France. He'd tried to let Kit know, but his mien was always that of a flippant youngster, and there was no way to take him seriously. Well, Kit took him seriously now. He put his head in his hands and wept. Deep, heart wrenching sobs for the brother who had trailed around behind him all of his life. He wept for the fun they'd had as boys, and for the pain that his mother was about to experience. There was a gentle knock on the door, and a physician in a white coat entered the room. Kit stood and shook his hand. The man introduced himself as John Goodman, Sebastian's physician. Kit, in turn, told him who he was.

"Let's go over here into the corner and have a bit of a chat," the doctor suggested. "I don't like to talk too close to the patient. Even though we may think that they are unconscious, there is really no way of knowing that."

Kit followed Dr. Goodman over to the far corner of the room. "What is his condition, Doctor?" Kit asked.

"Well, you can see for yourself, it's not good. Frankly, Lord Claybourne, I will be surprised if he lives through the night. His heart stopped once while on the table in surgery, but we were able to massage it back into rhythm. He was thrown through the windshield of the vehicle. His eyes were damaged severely by glass fragments. If he lives, he will not see again. But, worse than that, are the brain injuries that he suffered. Since his head went right through that windshield, it was cut in several places, but then he landed right on it, on cobblestoned pavement. Of course, we have no way of knowing just what the inside of his brain looks like, but he surely suffered severe damage. As you can see, his right leg was broken in three places. Again, should he live, he will never walk properly again. I cannot be certain what internal injuries he may have suffered, but from the yellow tinge to his skin I suspect there is liver damage. All in all, the picture is not good."

"Is his breathing normal?" Kit asked.

"Yes, amazingly, it is. Apparently, there wasn't any lung damage. But, I implore you not to get your hopes up. Of course, miracles do happen, but that's what I fear it would take in this instance."

"Shall I make certain the other members of my family are notified?"

"Yes, indeed, and the sooner the better."

Kit extended his hand, and the doctor shook it. "I'm dreadfully sorry, Your Lordship. I wish there was more I could do."

"Thank you for all you have done. Excuse me now. I'll need to call my mother."

The doctor left the room, and Kit followed out to the desk in the hallway, where a nurse stood watch. He ignored Eleanor completely as he left the room. She trailed along behind him, trying to find out what was going on. Kit asked the nurse if he could borrow her telephone to ring up his mother, and of course she acquiesced.

Mrs. Briggs answered on the first ring, and handed it directly to Lady Cynthia.

"Kit, how is he? What do the doctors say?" she asked.

"It's not promising news, Mother. He's badly hurt. There is doubt as to whether he'll make it through the night. I'm sending Edward with the car, to pick you up. I think you should come as soon as possible."

He could sense that her voice was about to break, but true to form, his mother remained strong and told him she would see him shortly. When he hung the telephone receiver in its cradle, Eleanor grabbed hold of his jacket.

"Kit! Is Sebastian going to die? Oh my God, tell me that isn't so."

"It does not look promising Eleanor. If you want to see him, I'd suggest you go into his room now."

"Is there blood? Does he look terrible? I won't get sick, will I?"

"Damn it, Eleanor. I don't know if you will or not, and furthermore, I don't care." He turned and walked to the far end of the hall, and left her standing alone.

After a few moments, she seemed to gather her nerve, and tiptoed to Sebastian's door. She peeked her head around the doorframe, and then abruptly retreated. Putting her head into her hands, she began to weep, and cried out "Oh Kit, he looks so horrible. I don't think I can stand it."

Kit didn't even bother to turn around. He had already made up his mind that he was sending her home when the car returned with his mother. There was certainly no way he intended to make it through whatever lay ahead with his dimwit of a wife hovering about making inane comments.

Before long, Lady Cynthia arrived. Kit hugged her, and told her to go on into the room, because he had to speak with Eleanor before he sent her home. Lady Cynthia nodded her head, and briskly walked to Sebastian's room. Eleanor slowly walked over to her husband and asked him if he would accompany her in to see Sebastian.

"No, Eleanor, I shall not. And, you are not about to go near his room. I have no intention of putting up with your hysterics and foolishness. I want you to gather your things, and go straight back out to the car. Edward will take you home. You are to go directly to your room, and do not start gossiping with the servants. They will be told everything when the time is proper. I also would like you to have Miss Barton sent back here by car."

"Barton? Why should Barton be allowed to come to the hospital? She isn't a member of the family, and she doesn't even particularly like Sebastian."

"Perhaps. But, I want her here, and so will Mother. They've grown quite close. Miss Barton has nursing skills and is well versed in medical matters. She will be a good person to have nearby."

"Well, you bastard! So you *are* having an affair with Miss Barton! I knew it! That's why you won't make any attempt to reconcile with me. Well, we'll just see about that. If you think that little nobody from nowhere is going to take away my position, and my son, you can just think again. I shall write to my father and tell him everything. I don't intend to give you up so easily."

"You will do as I ask, Eleanor. And I don't want to hear another foolish word about my having an affair. I've practically forgotten what making love to a woman is like. The last time I did was when you got pregnant with Win."

"I'll just bet, you liar." She slapped him hard across the face, and flounced off toward the stairway. The nurse came bustling up to him.

"Are you all right, Sir? I'm sorry, but we really cannot have scenes like that in the hospital."

"I know, nurse, I apologize. It won't happen again. She has returned home. I'm going into my brother's room now. Please send a woman named Miss Barton in as soon as she arrives."

Kit walked back into Sebastian's room. His condition hadn't changed, and Lady Cynthia was sitting in the bedside chair, with her cheek touching his. She was murmuring tender, loving words to him. Kit walked over to her, and rubbed her shoulders. Time seemed to stand still, and yet the clock on the wall steadily ticked the minutes away. Finally, he heard rapid footsteps, and then Lily's lovely face appeared in the doorway. He was so glad to see her. She walked silently over to him, and took hold of his hand. "It's bad, I know," she said.

"Yes," he answered. Lily kissed Lady Cynthia on the other cheek, and went back to standing next to Kit, still holding his hand. The room was a tableau of grief, as they all stayed in the same positions for what seemed like hours. Finally, at 4:40 a.m., without regaining consciousness, Sebastian passed away. Everyone's tears were exhausted. The doctor came in and listened for a heartbeat, and there was none. All three of those present kissed him again and the blanket was pulled up over his face. They left the room and went home to plan a funeral.

The night after the services for Sebastian everyone went to bed early. It had been an utterly exhausting day. Eleanor had sobbed through the majority of it, and Lady Cynthia began to wonder if she had been in love with her youngest son. If she had been, it didn't matter now. He was gone, and everyone would have to carry on. Kit had ignored Eleanor during most of the rites, and the preparations leading up to them. It was, of course, necessary to sit with her during the services, and to at least be civil to her afterwards, when the house was filled with mourners. Eleanor made the most of this necessity, by clinging to him, and saying over and over to friends and neighbors how dearly she loved him and how terribly sad everything was. She vowed to countless people that she would do her best to see that Kit was given all of the comfort and love that he needed.

Lily did not attend the reception after the funeral. She made the excuse that Win needed her, and shut herself into the nursery. She had already had to witness the sham that Eleanor was acting out at the church, and she couldn't take any more. While she knew that Kit wasn't the least bit swayed by Eleanor's counterfeit behavior, deep inside she had some concern that Kit was very vulnerable at the moment. There was no question that Eleanor had some sort of scheme in mind. Lily only hoped that Kit's grief wasn't so enormous that it might overcome his usual rationality.

When all of the lights were turned low, Kit wearily made his way to his son's room. Win was sleeping, with his arm around a toy dog. Kit stood and watched his tiny chest move up and down as he breathed. Kit was spent. It was still impossible to believe that he would never see his handsome, laughing brother's face again, and he still blamed himself for what had happened. He'd been too wrapped up in trivial matters, and hadn't given Sebastian the time he should have. He should have been able to see the fear that was practically paralyzing the poor boy. Now Kit was lost in thought, going back over every word of their last conversation, when the door to the nursery slowly opened. He didn't even hear the slight creak as it swung inward on its ancient hinges.

Eleanor was wearing a pale pink nightdress, fashioned in a sheer, gauze-like fabric. It left nothing whatsoever to the imagination. Her hair was not done up, but rather hung down her shoulders in platinum waves. Her lips shone with a deep, pink rouge. He sensed her presence when she was directly behind him. Whirling around, he was nearly face-to-face with her, and their bodies were almost touching. He started to say something in a low voice, so as not to wake Win, when she reached up on her tiptoes and put her arms around his neck while she pressed her lips to his, all the while stroking between his legs. She could feel that he was aroused. He kept his arms by his sides, and tried to push her away, but she continued the stroking, and then very deftly began to unbutton his pants. He didn't want what was happening, and yet his body was rebelling against his wishes. With one hand inside of his pants, she took hold of his hand and placed it on her breast. He could feel the hard nipple through the nightdress. Swiftly, she slid out of the gown, and stood naked, begging him to take her. He was about to push her away again – harder this time, before he lost all control of himself and the situation. She was whispering "Take me, Kit, take me. I'm your wife. I love you."

The door opened and the light came on. Lily Barton entered carrying a freshly laundered pile of Win's nappies. She took about three steps into the room, when she realized that she wasn't alone. Turning, she saw them both. Eleanor was stark naked, and making moaning sounds. Lily thought she might be sick. They were both so engrossed in what was happening, that they didn't even stop when the light came on. A moment later, Kit found that he was staring straight at Lily's horrified expression. He called her name, but it was far too late. She threw the nappies down, and ran as fast as she could to her own room.

Kit slumped against the wall, and put his head in his hands. "Get out of here Eleanor – Just get out of here, before I harm you."

"But, Kit, I could tell you wanted me. I was only trying to give you what you need."

"I do not need you, Eleanor. Once and for all. I do not want you. I don't love you. If I ever did, you killed those feelings. Now, get out!"

She turned and slipped her nightdress back on, while he kept his head buried in anger and grief. What in the Hell was he going to tell Lily? She would think he'd instigated a seduction of Eleanor- that he still loved Eleanor, and had been lying to Lily. What else could go wrong in his life? Eleanor silently left the nursery, weeping, and Kit went to the small single bed in the corner – the one that Lily had used when Kit was just a tiny baby.

He threw himself down on the bed cover, and buried his face in the pillow. He knew he should go after Lily – try to explain – put things right. But, he was exhausted, and could not face any more emotional turmoil. First he would sleep, and then he would have a long talk with Lily.

Meanwhile, Lily pulled her old valise from underneath the bed, and threw clothing into it. Then she swept everything from atop the dresser, and added it to the jumble she'd already packed. Grabbing the handle, she ran down the stairway, and to the door. Edward Luther lived in a small flat above the carriage house, and she hurried to that spot. Banging on the door where the stairway went up to his sleeping quarters, she called his name over and over.

He finally came to the stairs, and asked what she needed. "Please, oh please take me to my cottage in the village. I know it's late, and I'm terribly sorry, but I really must be gone."

"Course I shall, Miss Barton. You hold on just one tick. I'll be ready to go."

She paced up and down the graveled drive, taking deep breaths, and trying to erase the ugly scene from her mind. How could this have happened? Supposedly Kit didn't love Eleanor. He said he couldn't stand her. Had all of her fake actions at the funeral convinced him that he still had feelings for her? That was very hard to believe. Lily was still a young girl, and still a virgin. She had no understanding of a man's body, and the way it sometimes let arousal override sense. She didn't understand that it had been nearly two years since Kit had held a naked woman in his arms, or had a woman touch him intimately. In her mind, the only reason for two people to be in the position she had found Eleanor and Kit in was because they were about to make love. She knew nothing of pure, raw sex, or the hold it could have on a man. Or even of the comfort it could sometimes give to a person who was grieving. The way it reminded a person that he or she was still alive, when someone else wasn't. Most importantly, she didn't know that Kit had not allowed the situation to get out of hand, and that he had flatly made it clear to Eleanor that he wanted nothing to do with her.

Edward came down the stairs from his quarters, and opened the carriage doors. Then he backed the Daimler out into the driveway, and stopped. Opening the door, he exited, and helped Lily into the rear seat.

"I really am very sorry, Mr. Luther. I simply have to leave here immediately, and I had no way to get to the village except to wake you," she said.

"No reason to be sorry. I'm glad I can help. Just sit back and I'll have you there in nothing flat."

When they reached the village, Edward asked directions about how to reach Lily's cottage, and she told him. Soon, she was stepping from the car, and Edward was walking up the pathway, carrying her valise, while she fumbled for her key. Finally she found it, and opened the door. Edward placed the valise inside, and asked if there was anything else she needed.

"No. I'll be fine now. Thank you so much." Edward began to walk away, after wishing her a goodnight. "Oh, Mr. Luther, wait. There is one favor I would like to ask of you."

"Yes, Miss. Whatever I can do."

"Please, if the Earl should ask where I've gone off to, don't tell him."

"Well, Miss, I'm afraid I can't make such a promise. I can't lie to my employer. I'll try to avoid giving him details, but that's the best I can say."

"I understand, Mr. Luther. I shouldn't have asked. Goodnight again, and thank you."

Lily turned, closed the door to the cottage, and broke into anguished tears.

14

She felt sick inside. It was impossible to think that she'd seen what she had. But, it was no hallucination, and no mistaken identity. It was Kit and Eleanor, and it was not innocent. Kit was every bit as involved as Eleanor. What on Earth were they doing in Win's bedroom, acting like two animals in heat? Why didn't they stay in their own private bedroom? Did Eleanor hope that Lily would walk in on them? That seemed possible. But, it was hard for Lily to believe that Kit would have wanted such a thing to happen. Eleanor, yes. It would have suited her purpose. But, a man has plenty of time to get away, if he isn't interested in the naked lady standing in front of him. Lily had seen Eleanor's nightdress, such as it was, lying on the floor of the nursery. So, she had been wearing it when she entered the room. Then that meant that Kit had plenty of time to exit while she was undressing. Why did he stay? The only explanation that made any sense was that he didn't want to leave, and he was just as eager for making love as Eleanor was. Had he been lying to Lily all along? He may have been somewhat attracted to her, but after all, Lily had to remember how totally foolish it was for her to believe that Kit had meant it when he said he wanted to marry her. Lily, a private duty nurse, ladies' maid, and nanny versus Eleanor, with her wealthy Virginia upbringing and astonishing good looks. Also, the two shared a child together. How foolish

Lily had been. She wiped the tears that were falling down her cheeks in torrents. She felt like she might faint.

She went into the kitchen and made herself a cup of tea. Then she rang her mother at the cottage she shared with her new husband. Will answered the telephone, and it was clear to him that she had been crying.

"What's the matter, Lily, luv? "You're sounding awfully blue."

"Oh, Will, I am blue. May I speak to my mother please?"

"Course you can. Wait just a tick."

There was a short pause, and then her Mum's sweet voice was on the line. "What sort of trouble are you having, Lily?"

"Mum, can I come and stay with you and Will. I'm all undone over something that happened tonight at *Claybourne Court.* I need to talk to you. I'm at our old cottage now, but I don't want to stay here. You'll understand why when I talk to you."

"Of course you can come to us," her mother replied. "Will can be there in two shakes of a lamb's tail to collect you."

Lily thanked her Mum, and rang off. She sat on the sofa in the living room, watching the clock tick the minutes away. It wasn't even five minutes before she heard Will's car in the drive. Peeking out of the curtains, she looked through the window in the front room, to make certain it was her stepfather's auto. It was. She left one light on in the hall, and turned the others off. Then she picked up her valise, and went out of the door, making certain it was locked. When she arrived at her Mum's cottage, Will carried her valise, and she ran to the door, which her mother held open. "Oh Mum, I'm so glad to see you," Lily cried, as she let her mother fold her into an embrace.

"Lily, what's wrong? Something dreadful has happened to you. Come, sit down and let's talk about it."

"Oh Mum. It's such a long story. I've told you about my relationship with Kit – about how it has deepened, and that he's said he loves me. Well, everything has been wonderful, and I truly thought that as soon as Eleanor left to return to America, he would be marrying me. But, everything has turned upside down. Two days ago, his brother Sebastian drove into a tree and died. Perhaps you heard about that."

"Yes. Everyone in the village talked about it. It was tragic."

"Yes. The family believes he did it on purpose to avoid having to go into the military. He was terrified of the war. Shortly before the accident, he'd tried to talk with Kit about his fears, but Kit was tired, and really just fed up with Sebastian's constant worry about having to fight. He wasn't terribly kind to Sebastian. After his brother died, Kit blamed himself. So, he has been terribly troubled and downhearted over that." Lily paused, and took a sip of the water her mother had given her. "Anyway, Kit went up to the nursery to be with Win. I gathered a pile of clean Nappies from the downstairs, and carried them up to the nursery. When I opened the door, Eleanor was naked in Kit's arms, and they were kissing. Not only that, but Eleanor had her hand . . ." She couldn't finish the sentence. She straightened her back, and took a deep breath. "She had her hand inside of Kit's pants. They were unbuttoned. It was shocking. I threw the nappies down, and ran out of the room. I went to my own room, gathered my belongings and begged Edward, the chauffeur, to take me to the village. Of course, he did. That's when I rang you."

"Oh Lily. How awful. But, surely you don't believe that Lord Claybourne was simply leading you on? You said he was such a nice man."

"I don't know what to think, Mum. I feel like such a fool."

"Perhaps you should have given him a chance to explain it to you," her mother replied.

"Oh no. I can't bear the thought of even looking at him. It was such a horrible scene, Mum. I need some time to think. May I stay with you for a while? I have to get my mind straight. I must decide what I'm going to do. I can't go back there."

"Lily, now that Will and I are married, there is no need for you to work to take care of me. If you want to leave *Claybourne Court*, then do so. But, what will you do then?"

"I'm not sure. That's what I have to think about. I won't stay here too long. A month perhaps. Two at most. Enough for me to sort it all through and decide my future," Lily answered.

"Yes, of course. What do you want me to say if Lord Claybourne should ring you, or worse still, come to the cottage?" Elisabeth Barton seemed very nervous about the entire ordeal, and couldn't help but hope that it might still be worked out.

"I don't want to see him or speak to him. Just tell him the truth."

"Oh, Lily. He sounded like such a nice chap. Are you certain you won't even give him a chance to explain?"

"No, Mum. What he did was wrong. He should never have led me to believe that he cared for me, if he still had feelings for Eleanor, which it's certainly obvious that he did. I don't want to hear any more lies. I'm so embarrassed now I should die."

"Well, I'll leave it to you, Lily. I hope you know what you're doing. You were so very fond of him,"

"When I thought he was speaking the truth, Mum. I could never abide a man who isn't honest. Now, if you don't mind, I'm terribly done in, and really would just like to rest. Which room do you want me in, Mum?"

"Will and I are the only ones here. There are two other bedrooms. Why don't you take the larger of the two. The one at the end of the hallway. Do you know which I mean?" her mum asked.

"Yes, I'm sure I do. I'll find it." Lily put her arms around her mother, and gave her a hearty embrace. "I love you so, Mum. Thanks so for being here when I needed you."

"I'm glad we were both here, and that you thought to come to us. Now, get along to your bed, and try to rest. I'll check on you later. If there is anything you need, just ask."

Lily climbed the stairs to the bedrooms. The cottage was larger than that which she had shared with her parents and Jordan, and it was very cozy. She found the room at the end of the hallway, and entered it. It must have always been meant for a guest's room, for it was done up in lovely shades of pale yellow, with a white duvet and pretty matching curtains. Will had unpacked her valise, and hung all of her dresses in the wardrobe. Her toiletries were lined up neatly in the adjoining bath. Lily washed her face, brushed her teeth and brushed her hair. The, she turned down the cover on the inviting bed, and crawled in between the cool, crisp sheets. It felt so good to be with Will and her mum. She would have a rest, and then spend some serious time deciding what she was going to do with her life.

For the first week, Lily stayed barricaded in her room, not wishing to see or speak to anyone. Finally, she reappeared and tried her best to summon her usual sunny disposition, but it wasn't easy. Her mother and Will were extremely understanding and didn't ask questions or intrude upon her thoughts. And thinking is primarily what she did. Her thinking primarily still consisted of asking herself questions. How could she have been so foolish as to think that an Earl would ever want to be married to a girl from her class? Had she been living in a dream world? She'd known he was married. Why on earth did she put herself into such a position? Finally, she realized that there weren't any logical answers to any of her questions. She felt guilty for simply disappearing and not speaking with Mrs. Briggs, Halsey or any other staff member. Most of all she felt guilty about running out on Win. What would Lady Cynthia think of her? Twice she picked up a pen and began to write a note to her, trying to explain, but there didn't seem to be any way to put her feelings and reasons into writing. What difference did it make anyway? She would never see any of those people again.

She stayed longer than she'd intended. Her mum and Will begged her to stay through the holidays, and she finally agreed. It was a sad affair, even though they tried very hard to make it happy. David was there with the girl he was about to marry, Jane Marshall, who seemed lovely. But Lily could only concentrate on what the future held for her. Kit did ring her parent's cottage and asked to speak with her, but she refused the call. He made several attempts, but finally gave up. After three months of almost continual thinking, along with making numerous phone calls, and writing letter after letter, Lily finally reached a decision. She was going to join the V. A. D.

The Voluntary Auxiliary Detachment had been formed in 1907 by the Red Cross and the Sisters of St. John as a means of providing free help to hospitals. Now that the war had come along, they were invaluable. In the beginning, there was a requirement that women under twenty-three years could not go abroad as a V.A.D. Later, as nurses become in very short supply, the rules were altered to allow any woman twenty-three years old or older to go to the hospitals abroad if they'd had three months experience working in a British hospital in the United States. She applied for the V.A.D., and was accepted immediately. She was sent to Hatfield in Hertfordshire, home to the magnificent palatial manor house of the same name. It was owned by the Duke of Salisbury. The Duke offered his lovely home to his country for use as a military billet. Lily was assigned to the Cottage Hospital, close to Northcutts, near the railway station in Hatfield. The hospital was operated by the V.A.D. She was under orders to keep in her pocketbook a letter from Katharine Furse, the Commander in Chief of the V. A. D. It stated; '*You are being sent to work for the Red Cross. You have to perform a task which will need your courage, your energy, your patience, your humility, your determination to overcome all difficulties.*' Every V.A.D. volunteer was to carry this document. Thus, it was never far from her person.

15

Although she had plenty of experience performing the duties of a nurse, she took her orders very seriously, and even if she had learned to do something differently than the method used at the Cottage Hospital, she always followed the V.A.D.'s methods. Lily was very good at her tasks. She performed them with precision and good humor. She never complained of fatigue, and always accepted whatever assignment she was given with a smile. As a result she received very nice reviews from the nursing matrons. Although she had joined up to get as far away from Kit and *Claybourne Court* as possible, she found that she loved the feeling of giving to others, and the camaraderie of the girls in her unit. All were from middle and upper class families, and they formed a close bond. Everyone was of equal rank when it came to applying their nursing skills in a hospital setting. In particular, she became friends with three girls immediately. One of their names was Madeleine Brooks, a very pretty girl, from an upper-class background. Her father was the well-known owner of a large department store in London. Maddie, as she was known, was a darling girl. She resembled a pixie, with wide blue eyes, and an impish nose. Her hair was light, and styled in the traditional bun, which all of the girls wore. One could scarcely see a nurse's hairstyle anyway, as it was always covered by a crisp, white hat, with points at both ends. Their uniforms were also white - starched cotton, long-sleeves, and a neat shirtwaist front. Lily loved her uniform, and made every effort to keep it immaculate. Another friend she became very fond of was Penelope Paulson, whom everyone called Poppy. She had bright red hair, and an infectious grin. Her sense of humor was wonderful and she kept the group in stitches. Her third, and perhaps closest pal was Gena Weatherford. Small and lovely, she was a complete innocent and the others enjoyed playing pranks on her. Lily took her under her wing, and saved her from the worst of their tricks. Gena was from a titled family in Hertfordshire. Her parents had been angry when she volunteered for the V.A.D., saying it was beneath her dignity to expose herself to the filth and evils of war. Nonetheless, Gena had followed her own desires. She was very strong, intelligent and independent, and she and Lily took to one another immediately.

The four of them quickly became a close-knit quartet, and Lily was so happy to have friends with which to share her inner feelings. All of the girls worked terribly hard. The cases that were overseen at the cottage hospital were those men who were in the recuperative phase, so it wasn't an unpleasant assignment. Lily spent a lot of time reading to them, and writing letters to their loved ones. They often needed assistance with feeding and bathing, and the nurses performed those duties as well. None of them had seen a man naked before, so at first there was some giggling and a bit of fear, but after a while it was just another duty to perform. The men were so thrilled to have a woman's soft hand upon their brow, and it made all of the girls feel good to know they were appreciated.

The three months flew by. Before she knew it, Lily was being given her orders. She was to travel to France, and take up her post at *Aubigny,* which was a Casualty Clearing Station for the wounded, in central France. It was situated about ten kilometers behind the front lines, so unlike the cottage Hospital in Herefordshire, she would be exposed to some of the worst cases, as they came straight to her Clearing Station from the front lines. Now she began to understand just how horrific the war really was. It nearly overwhelmed her, but just like everything else in life, after being exposed to the worst cases, she began to adjust and calm herself when a new boy was carried in on a stretcher, with his abdomen blown open into a gaping wound and his entrails outside of the body, the poor man trying to hold them inside.

One night, when it was relatively quiet, she took a candle and walked from bed to bed. There was row upon row of them, ten on the right, and ten on the left. As she walked down the aisles in the Clearing Station, she could never have imagined the sights she witnessed. Her heart ached at the pitiful sight of these pathetic soldiers, most of whom were permanently disabled by the brutality of war. Drugged with morphine, smelling of foul, putrid, gangrenous limbs, she wasn't certain she was up to this task. Some of the men had lain with gaping wounds in their abdomens, praying to die – praying to live – until they were discovered by the stretcher-bearer chaps. Some of them died cursing and raving; some died quietly, in a drug-induced haze; most died crying for their Mums.

When a man died, Lily pulled off the blood soaked sheets, put fresh ones on the bed, and turned it down properly, as she might have for a guest at the Savoy. A new patient would take the dead soldier's place, in a matter of moments. He would either be patched up sufficiently to return to battle, only to be wounded again, or he would die. A very few survived their wounds, and were sent to a base hospital, such as Calais, where they would recuperate and be mustered out. They would be free, but a very different life awaited them. Lily often thought of Kit, although she didn't want to. Now she understood the horror he had endured. She realized how strangely fortunate he was only to have lost an eye. How would Eleanor have greeted him if he'd returned with no arms and no legs? She hated what she was seeing, but she was glad to be there to hold a hand, read a letter, or just help a desperately wounded man make it through a cold, lonely night, filled with agony and fear of death. Her decision to enter the V.A.D. had turned out to be a wise one. After gaining an understanding of the horrors taking place in France, her difficulties with Kit seemed trivial. Her Mum wrote to her often, and sent news of Kit. He had finally been to see Elisabeth, and tried to explain that he loved Lily, and could not live without her. Finally, he brought a letter that he asked to be forwarded to her. Elisabeth would not give him her location, for fear he would travel there, and convince her to come back. When the letter arrived, Lily turned it over and over in her hands for a good while. She even put it under her nose and sniffed it to see if she could find a hint of Kit on the paper. But, in the end, she tore it into tiny pieces, and threw it away with the medical trash. There was absolutely nothing he could have said that would convince her that he loved her. She waited until her regular work day was complete and then she walked out and sat down outside of the Nissen hut that served as a ward for the injured soldiers. The Clearing Station was made up of rows and rows of such huts, painted green. Most were filled with wounded soldiers, but others were designated for surgery, and still others were sleeping quarters for the staff.

Lily's hand shook as she lit a cigarette. Sure enough, she had taken up smoking now that she was in France. All of the other girls smoked too, and she would have felt an outcast If she hadn't. Besides, the cigarettes seemed to calm her nerves. Her mind traveled back to Kit's letter. Should she have opened it? And, what difference would it have made if she had? She was sworn to do her duty as a V.A.D. nurse, and she intended to keep that vow. It was very hard for her to trust Kit, at any rate, even though she knew he might sound very sincere. But, until Eleanor was gone from *Claybourne Court*, and a divorce was finalized, she would be asking for heartache, if she showed even a miniscule of belief in him. So, rather than try to explain her conflicting feelings, she decided to make every effort to forget the letter. It was more difficult to forget Win. Whether Kit had told the truth or not, his honesty made no difference in her love for that precious, little boy. She thought about him often, and prayed that he was being well-cared for.

Gena came out and sat down next to Lily. "Care for a fag?" asked Lily, offering her pack of cigarettes. Gena shook her head. It was rare if she accepted one. Gena leaned back against the building. "You've been rather quiet since the post arrived. Letter from Kit, by any chance?"

"Oh, yes, Gena," Lily sighed.

"What did it say then?" Gena asked.

"I ripped it up and threw it away", Lily replied.

"Oh, no Lily. Why did you go and do such a thing? Weren't you at all curious to see what he'd written?"

"Yes, I suppose I was," Lily answered. "But, I don't intend to let him sweet talk me back into his arms. I made a terrible mistake. I never should have become involved with him. After all, Gena, I knew he was married. What was I thinking?"

"Sometimes it's sort of nice not to have to think every minute," Gena smiled as she reached up and undid her hair. "I feel like a rat," she laughed.

"My hair needs a wash, and I must find time tonight. I pray we won't have any casualties brought in." She shook her hair out, and it fell to her shoulders. It was astounding to see the difference between a neat, little bun, and masses of golden curls. She took a small brush out of her uniform pocket, and ran it through the long tresses. Then she pulled it back and re-did the bun. "There, now I look like a professional." She giggled.

"You always look like a professional, Gena, and you're always gorgeous. I'd kill to have your hair."

"Lily Barton! Who has thicker, shinier hair than you? And a complexion to match?"

"Well, yes, it's all right, but I like the blonde curls," Lily cried. "Anyway, I wish I could be more like you, Gena. As far as not thinking every minute. But, you see, when I tried that, it completely muddled up my head," Lily laughed ruefully.

"I know, Love. Let's see where things stand when this God awful war is over." Gena stood up, brushed off her uniform and went back into the hospital. Lily snuffed out her cigarette in a puddle of water, and followed. They were preparing for a heavy load of patients to be brought in, probably the next night. There was word that the Allied forces were about to strike at a place called The Somme. Everyone predicted it would be one of the worst battles of the war.

16

They started working the next night, and never stopped for two weeks. The surgeons continued operating day and night with two tables in continual use. They received seventy-five cases the first night and twenty-seven operations were performed. There were only eight nurses, including Lily. Most of them had been together since Hatfield. The less severely hurt men were sent on to other base hospitals, so that space could be kept available for the most acutely injured. The battle took place on either side of the Somme River. It was the worst day in the history of the British Army, with over sixty thousand casualties. And that day was only the beginning. The Battle of the Somme was better known as the Somme Offensive, and it constituted several battles, which lasted until November of 1916, and when it was all over, more than one million men were wounded or killed. The nurse's duties were expanded considerably. They assisted the surgeons, disposed of amputated limbs, and helped make certain that the operating facilities were kept clean, even it that entailed mopping up blood. Lily held down arms and legs that were sawed off, cradled screaming soldiers in her arms, and tried to bring a measure of peace to those who were dying. She often forgot whether it was day or night. They only stopped for a quick bite to eat, and often that too was forgotten. A cemetery grew up around the hospital. The nurses always marched along behind each boy who was buried, trying to bring some dignity to his demise.

Finally, in November, the horror ended. When it did, the British and French forces had penetrated six miles into German- occupied territory, taking more ground since the Battle of the Marne, where Jordan was killed in 1914. Even so, it was a horrific loss of life. The war was turning out to be one of attrition. How many Anglo-French troops would remain when it all ended, versus the number of German troops? Lily sometimes wondered how much more she could take. However, that attitude brought on even worse feelings of guilt. While the terrible ordeal that the nurses faced was beyond description, it was absolutely nothing when compared to the suffering they witnessed every day. It was incomprehensible that human beings could brutalize one another so viciously. It all seemed so senseless.

Though the Battle of the Somme came to an end, the war continued. There was continuing action at Verdun, and other French locales. Lily and her friends had a bit of rest, with fewer men brought in after the Battle of the Somme. They were all near a breaking point, and the surgeons too were to the point of extreme exhaustion. The only thing that kept them going was the knowledge that lives were being saved, although not nearly as many as they wished. At Christmas, 1916, they celebrated with some champagne brought back to Camp by a doctor who had been on furlough to Paris. Everybody drank out of paper cups, and small gifts were exchanged. Then they gathered together and sang carols. It was a bittersweet Christmas Eve, and each one of them prayed for an end to the long, ghastly war.

Lily's Mum wrote to her weekly. The war was taking its toll in the homeland too. The whole country was under the jurisdiction of the Defense of the Realm Act. It gave the government wide-ranging powers during the period of war, such as the power to requisition buildings or land to be used for the war effort. The law was intended to prevent invasion and keep morale high, but as time went by, the British people became war weary and tired of restrictions placed upon their lives. Such trivial activities as flying a kite, building a bonfire, buying binoculars, and feeding wild animals bread were outlawed. In addition, alcoholic beverages were watered down and pub openings were changed from one o'clock to three thirty, and six thirty to nine-thirty p.m. The streets were conspicuously empty, mostly because there were very few young men left to stroll the sidewalks. Those who were seen most often bore the signs of battle. Missing arms and legs were commonplace. Women were working in the factories, and petrol was harder to come by. And yet it seemed to go on and on. Her mother never mentioned Kit or *Claybourne Court*, and Lily was sometimes tempted to ask if there was any news from that quarter, but she'd made up her mind never to have anything to do with him or his home, and she was hell bent on holding to that promise.

Toward the middle of Lily's time at *Aubigny,* a new physician was transferred to her unit. The moment she heard his name, she knew who he was. *John Garrett.* He had once written a letter to *Claybourne Court.* The letter that had started so much heartbreak when Eleanor read it and learned that Kit had lost an eye. Her actions seemed even more terribly foolish now. When Dr. Garrett entered the hut, which held rows of beds filled with recuperating soldiers, Lily excused herself from the group of nurses, who were looking in his direction, and walked over to the doctor. She introduced herself, and then told him what she remembered.

"I'm familiar with your name, Dr. Garrett. I was a nurse at *Claybourne Court* in Gloustershire when Lord Claybourne was your patient. You wrote a letter to his wife, describing his disability and giving instructions for his care. I know you must have written hundreds of similar letters, so you may not remember. My name is Lily Barton, and now I serve with the V.A.D."

He shook her hand. "Of course, Miss Barton. I've known Kit Claybourne since I was at *Sandhurst.* I consider him a good friend. I remember that he was concerned about what his wife's reaction would be to his injury. Did it go well?"

"No, not at all, Doctor. I'm sorry to have to say that, but his wife, Eleanor, became extremely upset when she saw him. She said some terrible things, and then ran off and got into a horseback riding accident. She wasn't seriously injured, but all attention in the household turned away from Lord Claybourne and toward his wife. It was very sad."

"I'm not surprised at what you tell me. He shared with me his concern that she wouldn't be compassionate."

"She's a very narcissistic person, Dr. Garrett. But, they have a baby boy and I believe Lord Claybourne is making every attempt to make it a happy marriage."

"I can imagine living in that sort of household wouldn't be easy. Is that what moved you to join the V.A.D.?"

"Yes, partly," Lily replied. "It was a very complex situation. I'd rather not go into the details."

"I understand," he replied. "If you should ever need to talk, don't hesitate to call upon me. Remember, I'm a doctor, and anything you tell me would be confidential."

"I appreciate that. Perhaps some time when it's quiet here, I'll take you up on that".

Dr. Garrett shook her hand again, and told her how nice it was to have met her. Then he continued on, introducing himself to other members of the staff. Lily was knocked for six. She remembered the day Dr. Garrett's letter had come in the post, and she'd found Eleanor sitting on the sofa in the drawing room, calling Lily's name and looking stricken. Lily wondered if it might help her to talk to the doctor about everything that had happened after that. The entire kerfuffle seemed so inconsequential when compared to the dreadfulness of war. She could never bring herself to bring up her own heartache to someone who was trying to cope with hundreds of dying and wounded men every day.

Gena joined her after she too had met the new doctor.

"He's a dish," she laughed. "I wonder if he's married."

"No, I don't believe so. Kit once told me that he'd had a great love – a female doctor, who was killed when the Germans bombed the base hospital where she was attached. Really, just a ghastly story."

"Oh dear, yes. I wonder if that was very long ago," Gena mused.

"Three years back, I think. Probably shortly after the war began."

"Hmm. Perhaps he's ready to start over again."

"Gena! What a cheeky thing to say. He's very much a gentleman. I know that. I know you come from a titled family and would fit into his world, but wait to see if he shows any interest," Lily remarked.

"Oh of course, Lily. I'm not going to throw myself at his head. I just wanted to get the lay of the land. I may not be his type at all."

"And then again, you may be," Lily smiled.

The months rolled by, and there was a lull in the fighting. Everything was at a stalemate. Lily wondered if it would ever come to an end. And she wondered what she would do when that time came. She was almost afraid to return to *Claybourne- on-Colne.* If Kit was still there, and she assumed he was, how could she keep from eventually running into him? Someone in the household would learn that she had come home. The thought of seeing him again frightened her, as she knew that she still had strong feelings for him. She wished now that she hadn't acted so rashly when she'd seen Eleanor in his arms. Perhaps she should have let him explain. But, it was far too late now. She suspected that he had reconciled with Eleanor, and for all Lily knew, they could even have another child. She thought about resuming her studies after the war ended. She still had all of the money from her wages at *Claybourne Court,* and her Mum had been sending her more than she needed ever since her enlistment in the V.A.D. She thought there might be a chance that she had enough saved that she could go back to following her dream. But, the war hadn't ended, and no one knew when it would.

17

On April 6, 1917 a great turn-about occurred. The United States of America declared war on Germany. Everyone knew that now it would be just a matter of time. The American soldiers would bring fresh blood to a weary war, and there was a definite feeling of optimism. They came in droves. Whole regiments filled with what were being called the 'doughboys'. The British and French troops were in bad shape, and there was great happiness when the Yanks arrived. There was never a shortage of blown-up bodies that needed to be rushed to medical care. Even very young men looked old and tired. After nearly three years of living and dying inside a dirt trench, they were more than ready to see help arrive. There were new nurses too. Finally the hospital huts weren't so short staffed. The American soldiers were typically what the British always thought they would be – cocky and brassy, and not fit for polite company. Nonetheless, they knew how to fight, and that was all that mattered. The American girls were terrific however, and they all made friends very quickly. All of the British nurses learned to use American slang, and soon Lily, Gena, Maddie and Poppy were saying "Oh Swell" and "Gee Whiz." For the first time since Lily joined the V.A.D., she had hope that the awful bloodshed would soon come to an end. But, even with all of those new soldiers fighting on their side, it still dragged on. The only difference was that more and more battles were being won by the Allies.

One sunny afternoon in the spring of 1917, Lily was sitting on the bonnet of an ambulance, smoking a cigarette and enjoying the lovely weather. It seemed peculiar to her that flowers could still poke their heads through blood soaked soil, and that what trees remained were leafing out once again. Tears welled in her eyes as she pictured the rolling lawns of *Claybourne Court,* and remembered the day that she and Kit had taken Win to the summerhouse for a picnic. That was the first time he'd kissed her. That was when everything had changed. Closing her eyes, she could still feel his lips upon hers, and at that moment she knew that it hadn't all been a dream – or an evil game that Kit was playing. He had meant it. He had loved her. Her tears began to fall harder.

"Why is a beautiful lady sitting on the bonnet of an ambulance, weeping," a male voice asked.

Lily opened her eyes, and Dr. Garrett was standing in front of her. He took a cigarette out of a new package, and offered one to her. She accepted it, and he lit it for her, followed by one for himself. "Tell me what's causing you such pain, Lily. I can't have my best nurse feeling so blue. Has someone hurt you?"

"No, John. It's me who did the hurting. And now I regret it something fierce."

"Do you want to talk about it?" he asked.

"Perhaps it would ease my pain. I've so seldom spoken about it to anyone."

John pulled himself up onto the bonnet, and sat down next to her. "All right, Nurse Barton, tell me your troubles," he said, in a mock professional voice.

Lily swatted him on his arm. "If you aren't going to be serious, I won't tell you anything," she warned, smiling.

"I'm serious. I do really want to hear what's making you so sad. You need to unburden yourself. Come on, Lily."

"All right, then. Well, it all goes back to when I worked at *Claybourne Court.* I believe I told you that I'd worked there when we first met."

John nodded, and took a drag on his cigarette.

"It's hard for me to tell this. I don't know where to begin."

"Just start at the beginning, Lily. When did you go to work at *Claybourne Court*, and what were the circumstances?" he asked.

"I went to work there as a private nurse to Lady Eleanor, the Countess of Gloucester, Lord Claybourne's wife. She was expecting her first child. That was in the fall of 1914. The Earl was getting ready to leave England and join the *Scot's Grey's* in France. He wanted someone to look after Lady Eleanor. She was frail and confined to bed rest by her physicians. She was very new to England, and didn't care for it. She was extremely lonely and depressed. My mother was a ladies' maid long ago, before she married my father, at *Barrow Manor*, in Somerset. She knew a great deal about the proper behavior for a person living in a great house, and of course, she'd taught me. I'd also trained with my father, who was a physician. In addition, I'd attended college for two years, hoping to go on and eventually become a doctor myself. I may have told you that before. I don't remember."

"No, not that part. You have had a lot of medical training," he commented, while slapping away a fly. "You only told me the part about working at *Claybourne Court*. Excuse my asking, Lily, but you have quite an impressive background. Why would you agree to go to work in a private home? Surely you could have found employment that was more in keeping with your education and upbringing."

"Yes, I could have. But, *Claybourne Court* was within walking distance from my home. I wanted to be close to my Mum. My father had died only a few months previous, and then my brother was killed at the Battle of the Marne in September. Mum and I were worried about expenses. It was a good position, close to home."

"That makes sense. All right, so what happened there to cause you to be weeping now?"

"Oh, John, it was utter turmoil. Lady Eleanor is a spoiled young lady. At first I thought we would get along, but before much time passed, I realized how ghastly she was. I could go on and on with tales of her abhorrent behavior, but I won't bore you. Suffice to say, she was not pleasant to be around. But, I had promised the Earl that I would watch over her, at least until his return from France, and I try to keep my word to people. I was there when the baby came in April of 1915 – baby Win." Lily got a far-away look of tenderness and love in her eyes. It was clear that she adored the baby. "I assisted with the delivery, and just thought he was darling. Lady Eleanor appalled me when she refused to nurse him, and really simply turned over his care to me. She didn't seem to have any motherly instincts. I slept in his nursery with him, so in effect, I was both baby nurse, ladies' maid and private nurse to the Countess."

"I can't believe it. Lily, are you daft?" he asked, looking astounded.

"You might think so," she answered. "But, no. I loved the baby, and I'd promised Lord Claybourne."

"Go on," John prompted her.

"Well, finally Lord Claybourne came home. He arrived shortly after your letter was delivered by the post – the same day. The Countess was fit to be tied. When she learned that he'd lost an eye, she lost her head. There was a terrible uproar. And, in the midst of all of that, her husband appeared. She acted so horrific that I won't even repeat some of the things she said to him. She ran out of the house to the stables, and jumped on the back of the wildest horse they owned. Of course she was thrown. Poor Lord Claybourne was really crushed by her behavior. I wanted to slap her. Anyway, to make a long story short, she packed herself off to their home in London, and left Kit and Win. I stayed too. She hired a new ladies' maid in London. I suppose it's not a surprise that Lord Claybourne and I became very close. Very close. He told me he loved me. He promised marriage as soon as Lady Eleanor could be shipped back to America, and they divorced. Of course I believed him. I was terribly in love with him. Don't misunderstand. There was nothing of an intimate nature – well – you know . . ."

"In other words, your relationship wasn't sexual?" John asked.

Lily blushed. "Oh no, no. Nothing like that. We kissed, of course, but nothing further."

"Lily, it's beyond me how a top drawer nurse can be shy about the most natural of human urges. Women confound me." John smiled and shook his head.

"Well, that's just the way I was raised, John. But, to make a long story short, Eleanor returned to *Claybourne Court*, right about the time that Kit's brother Sebastian died in an auto accident. Naturally he was devastated. After the funeral, when everyone had left, I picked up a pile of nappies from the downstairs, and brought them up to the nursery. When I opened the door –

well – Eleanor was in his Kit's arms, and they were kissing. Need I add that she was naked?"

"Oh my God! That doesn't sound like Kit at all. He's one of the finest men I've ever known. There has to be more to the story."

"I don't know. I quickly packed my things and left. I haven't seen or spoken to him since. I joined the V.A.D. a few months later. He wrote me a letter, which he gave to my mother to mail to me, but I tore it up."

"And, now you're sorry you did," John said.

"Yes, I suppose so. But, don't you see, I could never trust anything that he said? I didn't want to hear his excuses. I can't imagine what they would be. Now I believe that he was just lonely, and hadn't been near a woman for such a long time, and perhaps he thought he cared for me, because I was kind to him and loved his son."

"Lily. That's rubbish! Kit Claybourne could have any woman in the land. I've seen the girls he used to walk out with. All of them stunners. Kit was never the sort of fellow who took advantage of his position or his appearance. He's as decent as they come. I think you misunderstood what you saw."

"Do you really think so, John? If that's true, do you think there's any hope that we could work this muddle through and reunite?"

"Lily, I don't know what the state of affairs is now. Is he still married to Eleanor? If not, has he met anybody else? I just don't know what to tell you on that score. But, I will say this. When this damned war is over, you need to get yourself back to *Claybourne-on-Colne* and find out what his situation is now. Perhaps it's not too late."

"Thank you, John. Oh, thank you so much. I did need to talk to someone about this mess. I shouldn't have doubted him –should have at least given him a chance to explain."

There was silence for several moments. "John-you don't suppose that you could . . ."

"Lily, if you'd like I might be able to . . ."

They were both speaking at once. They laughed. "You go first, Lily," he said.

"Well, I was just wondering if you could write to Kit. Just to catch-up. To learn what's happening in his life? I wouldn't want him to know that you were writing on my behalf . . ."

"Lily, I couldn't do that unless I had your permission to at least mention that you are here at Aubigny. I'd tell him we'd met, and become friends. That it made me think about him, and wonder what was going on in his life. How would you feel about that?"

"Oh, John, I don't know. It seems so transparent. I don't think I'd want you to mention me."

"Then let it rest for now. There will be time for you to learn what you need to know when the war is over," John replied.

"All right, John. I don't want to do anything too rash right now. But, I'll keep you informed if I hear anything from home."

Again, silence overtook them. The breeze and sun were wonderful. It was so lovely to sniff the fresh air, and feel the warmth, after the stuffiness and often unpleasant odors emanating from the surgical hut.

"Lily. Would it be impertinent for me to ask you about your good friend and fellow nurse, Gena? I know she's an excellent nurse. Second only to you," he smiled. "But, what's the story with her personal life? Is there a man?"

"Oh ho! John Garrett, now I know why you came out here to talk to me," Lily laughed.

"No, of course not. Remember, you were the one who was weeping."

"I'm only making fun. Gena is a wonderful girl. They don't come any better. No, there isn't any man. She's beautiful, as I'm sure you know, so she's had her share of admirers, but no one special. To be honest, since you're the one who's asked, I think she is a bit keen on you."

"Really? How very interesting," John smiled. "That's nice to hear."

"Gena comes from a titled family, who were greatly angered when she volunteered. But, she has a strong desire to help others. She is the most unselfish girl I've ever known. I hope her parents figure out that she's very special, and stop their silliness. Do you want me to mention that you could be keen on her?"

"No. Nothing like that. I was just curious. Perhaps if we both get a free day at the same time, I'll ask her to have tea with me in the village."

"I think she'd love that, John."

18

For the soldiers who fought in the Battle at Passchendaele, or the third Battle of Ypres, it became known as the Battle of the Mud. On July 17, 1917 the Allied forces began a heavy artillery barrage, launched at the German forces, and it lasted for ten days. Just as with previous attacks, there was heavy bombardment before an Infantry attack. The Germans were fully prepared, since they knew such bombardments were always followed by Infantry. As a result, the Allied forces made only small gains. In the early days of August, the area was saturated with the heaviest rainfall that had been seen in thirty years. The scene became a swamp. Tanks got stuck, soldiers found roads impassable, and they could scarcely walk across the fields. Craters formed from past shelling were filled with water, so there wasn't even anyplace for the soldiers to hide. On November 6, 1917, Passchendaele Village was finally taken by the Allies, but the price was very high. For the sake of a few kilometers, the British lost 310,000 men. Once again casualties from the fighting at Passchendaele were appalling. More amputated arms and legs; more gaping holes in abdomens' more missing hands; and death by the thousands. With more physicians and nurses, the task was made somewhat easier, but the operating rooms were still in use round the clock. There was nothing easy about nursing in World War I France. One never became used to the heartbreak and sorrow, and the boy's crying for their mothers. More than once, soldiers begged Lily to give them an overdose of medication and let them die. None of the staff could blame them. While nobody could have done it, they all prayed for the end to come quickly for many casualties.

When the battle was over in November, everyone was exhausted. Several of the staff were given three days furlough. It wasn't long enough to get to one of the ports in order to be transported back to England and then return, but they wanted so desperately to get away from the wounded, and the screams of dying soldiers for even a long weekend. The group got together, and finally decided they would travel to Paris. It was about a five-hour trip by train which made it doable. Lily had never been to Paris, nor had Gena, but Poppy and Maddie had spent considerable time there. In fact Maddie had studied art there. A group of the doctors decided to go too. John Garrett, Roy Porter, Michael Hewitt and Bill Phillips were making the journey with them. While this wasn't strictly forbidden, it had to be arranged somewhat surreptitiously. It still was not considered proper for the girls to travel with unmarried men. Lily thought it was complete rubbish. Sometimes the reasoning in society was somewhat strange. These women had seen everything that was imaginable in life. They were more mature than women twice their age. And, of course the physicians were the equivalent of brothers at that point. However, rules were rules, and they followed them, or faced dismissal or, at the very least, punishment of some sort. Lily, Poppy, Maddie and Gena would take a different train to Paris than the physicians, arriving at completely different times. In addition the first train would deposit the girls at Versailles. Each wanted to tour the spectacular palace there, and then they would grab a later one into Paris.

You would have thought that they were going on the Grand Tour of Europe, they were so excited. It had been such a long time long since any of them had slept in a comfortable bed, and enjoyed a deliciously soothing bath. And the mere thought of good food made their mouths water. When the day finally arrived, Lily counted her money over and over. She had plenty saved, since she'd had absolutely nowhere to spend it since her arrival in France, except for paper, pencils, cigarettes, and occasional candy or chewing gum. They'd held a small meeting and decided that they would reserve rooms at the elegant and quite recently opened Plaza Athenee, located on the plaza Montaigne. The men were put in charge of that detail. They had splurged and booked the Prestige suite for the girls, and the deluxe suite for themselves. The girls' accommodations had two bedrooms off a main drawing room, as well as a dining room and three full baths. The men's suite was a bit less formal, with mahogany paneled walls, but by no means less extravagant. Lily wondered if she might feel a bit out of place, and shared her concerns with Gena.

"Gena, I've never stayed in this sort of hotel. I hope I don't make a complete fool of myself-you know, use the wrong utensil or get confused on when to tip."

"No fear. I've not been to Paris, but I've been at other grand hotels in Italy, Switzerland, and London. They're all the same. I'll keep an eye out for you, but I know you'll do fine. That sort of hotel has exceptionally well-trained staff. It would be a terrible breech of etiquette for them to let you know if you did make a mistake. People make them all of the time. It's nothing to fear. If you made it through living at *Claybourne Court*, you'll survive the *Plaza Athenee*. There's one thing you should always remember, Lily. Good manners are nothing more than making the other person feel comfortable. That applies at home or in a hotel."

That assuaged Lily's feelings of unease. Of course, while *Claybourne Court* was an elegant country house, the Claybourne's were not a stuffy lot, and treated the staff much more leniently than most. She doubted that most great houses allowed the nanny to share the dining room with them. It would also have been unheard of. Similarly, she knew there was probably no great house in the land where the Earl picnicked with a staff member. No matter. Lily was on pins and needles waiting for the big day. Things were in a stalemate on the European Front, so it was the best time to be leaving. In addition, American nurses would be filling their posts. The morning of December 17, they boarded a train at the village of *Aubigny,* which went directly to *Paris,* with a stop at *Versailles.* The men took a similar train from via *Sur le Mer* and *Abbeville*, and then on to *Paris.* Because the girls were stopping at *Versailles*, the men expected to check into the hotel first. Lily was to ring their room upon arrival. They packed lightly, for after all, there was little to take. Each girl had a traveling dress, and one evening outfit. They all planned on purchasing some clothes in Paris, albeit not at the luxury boutiques. 'Ready to wear' had become very obtainable, and one was able to go into a shop or store and buy an article of clothing right off of the rack. They were at the Station in *Aubigny* early, eagerly awaiting the arrival of the train that would take them to the 'City of Lights'. It seemed difficult to imagine that not so far from all of the death and destruction, a vibrant city continued with its business. Lily wondered if the same thing was true in England. She had heard that the big stores, like *Harrods* and *Selfridges* were as busy as ever. When they boarded the train, soldiers were crowding the aisles.

Lily leaned back in the comfortable seat, and watched out the window as the train speeded by the France she had come to know; bombed out areas, and miles and miles of craters; the dead remains of trees and stumps, where once there had been forests. And blackened ruins of farms and homes, destroyed by fire. It made her very angry. It was such a waste. Such a bloody waste. Finally, she fell asleep.

She woke when the conductor made the announcement that *Versailles* was the next stop. The four of them gathered their gear and stepped from the train. There was quite a large group of people getting off at *Versailles,* most anxious to tour the magnificent palace that had seen so many moments of history played out within its walls. The guide led them to a side entrance and after buying their tickets, they were allowed inside. The magnificent *Chateau de Versailles*, one of the most beautiful examples of Eighteenth Century French art, began its life as one of Henry the XIII's hunting lodges. His son, Louis IV, transformed and expanded it, moving the government of France to *Versailles* in 1682. Each of the three French kings who lived there made improvements and expanded its beauty. At the dawn of the French Revolution, just steps away from the palace of *Versailles*, the founding act of French democracy took place. The girls were filled with awe as they gazed at the opulence of the magnificent chateau. The Hall of Mirrors, the Chapel, and the Royal apartments – all were astounding. They were so glad that they had taken the time to schedule a visit during the short furlough. After the tour was over, they took photos outside of the palace, and wandered around the grounds. Then it was time to board another train to make the trip to *Paris.* Their excitement grew with each turn of the engine's wheels. When they arrived at the *Gare du Nord*, they gathered their luggage, and hurried to exit. It was still not late in the day, and they hoped to enjoy some sightseeing before the sun set. As they stepped from the train, they were astonished to see John

Garret, Bill Phillips, Roy Porter, and Michael Hewitt, the doctors who had made the trip too, standing on the platform.

"Oh my Gosh, what a surprise. We didn't expect to see you until we got to the hotel. It's so good to see you." Lily hugged each of them. Gena stayed behind, a bit shy. She had never hugged a man she didn't know quite well. Poppy and Maddie were over the moon with excitement, both at the men being there to meet them, and at being in *Paris*. They hailed two cabs and everyone crawled inside. Lily noticed that John was sitting in the back with his arm around Gena's shoulders. Gena's cheeks were bright pink. Lily had no particular interest in any of the fellows. She was only glad that they had men to escort them around Paris. She didn't know whether Poppy or Maddie were interested in any of the men, but if so, it was good to know none was married. Of course, she did know that Gena was keen on John Garrett and that he had an interest in her.

The taxis drove them to the *Plaza Athenee*, where they got out of the car, stretched their legs, and headed for the lobby. The men had already checked in, so only the girls approached the registration desk. Poppy went up to the counter and gave their names.

"Yes, of course, ladies. We have assigned the Prestige suite to you. I hope you'll enjoy your stay with us." He reached for the keys, and took down four. Handing one to each of them, he smiled, as if that was all there was to it.

"Don't you need our signatures, or a one night deposit?" Poppy asked.

"Oh, no, no Mademoiselle. Your rooms are already paid for. You are registered under the name of Doctor John Garrett."

"Oh-but there must be some mistake. Dr. Garrett is a friend, and he traveled here with us, but the group of doctors he is with are responsible for their rooms, and we ladies are responsible for ours."

"I would suggest that you discuss this with Doctor Garrett," the desk clerk responded.

"Oui. Yes. I guess that would be best," Poppy stammered. The others, who stood behind her, were puzzled. They exchanged glances with one another, and followed the bellman toward the elevators. "The hotel obviously misunderstood when we wrote for reservations. John will be able to straighten it out," Maddie said.

They got off on their floor, and walked down the hallway to their room. John and the other doctors had taken their luggage up with them. The bellman opened the door and stood to the left while the ladies all entered. He showed them each of the rooms, and the baths. Gena gave him a tip, and he wished them a pleasant stay, as he closed the door. They all looked at each other dumbfounded. The rooms were more than they'd ever imagined. The drawing room had a dove grey sofa, with two pale, pink, velvet, French chairs facing it, across a lovely tea table. There were magnificent draperies framing floor to ceiling windows. They were swooped back, so that exquisite sheers showed beneath them. The draperies were dove grey velvet on the outside, lined with taffeta in the same pale pink. The same draperies adorned the bedrooms, and the duvet comforters on the beds were also pink. The baths were large, and lavishly appointed with large tubs, and gold fixtures.

"I think we've just landed in heaven," said Poppy.

"I'm going to run a delicious bath," cried Gena. "I feel like it's been years since I've had a true bath."

"Me too," said Maddie as she headed for the second bath.

"I'm going to ring John and find out what's going on with the room bill," said Lily. "I'll probably go down to his room." She picked up the elegant French telephone, and asked for Doctor Garrett's room. The operator rang it, and quickly a male voice picked up. "Is John in? This is Lily Barton."

There was a pause, while whomever had answered brought John to the telephone. "Hello Lily," John's voice said, as he came on the line. "Are you all getting settled?"

"Yes. Gena and Maddie are already in the bathtubs. Poppy is spread out on one of the beds. Everything is so unbelievable. But, John, we're all a bit confused. When we checked in, the man at the desk said that our bill was already taken care of. How can that be? He told me that I needed to speak with you about it."

"Yes. There's no confusion, Lily. I'm paying for the lot of us."

"What. That wasn't the way it was supposed to be. We never discussed that, John."

"I know, Lily, and if we had, I know you would have turned down my offer. So, I just made arrangements with the hotel."

"John! We're talking about an obscene amount of money. I wasn't raised to accept gifts like this from a man. None of us were. We can't allow it," argued Lily.

"Now Lily, that's childish. I want to pay back my nurses for the wonderful work they've done. I couldn't have made it through all of these months without your help. Please don't argue with me. I'm very able to afford it, and just think of it as a well- deserved gift."

"Well, I don't know, John . . ."

"Lily, I do know. Use the money you were going to spend on accommodations to go shopping. I know how ladies love to shop, and there's been scant possibility of that in *Aubigny*."

"Oh, John, you are too good. I'll tell the others, and see what they think. Can you honestly afford it?"

"Lily, I'm the second son of an Earl. I've never told you that, because I saw no need. That's one reason Kit Claybourne and I had so much in common at *Sandhurst*. We were both sons of Earls. So, yes, honestly, I can afford it."

"My God! I didn't have any idea. You aren't stuffy and full of yourself – not in the least."

"Not all titled people are. You know that, Lily. Was Kit full of himself?"

"No. He was – well – he was wonderful."

"All right. You see. Now, make plans for a shopping trip this afternoon, and tell the others to buy a lovely gown for a fancy dinner at *La Tour d'Argent*."

"*La Tour d'Argent*! Isn't that the most expensive restaurant in Paris? You can't mean it."

"Yes, it has that reputation, although it's equally well known for its food, Lily. Yes, I mean it and it's my treat. Now don't argue. I've made reservations for eight o'clock."

"Oh, John. How thrilling. I'll tell the others. Is it very fancy?"

"Whatever you wish. Certainly a dinner dress at the least."

"Oh. This is so exciting. I have to go and tell the others. Shall we meet in the lobby at seven thirty?"

"Right on, Lily. See you then."

They rang off, and Lily called out to the other girls. "You aren't going to believe this. Dr. Garrett – John- is paying for the hotel. Did any of you know that he's the younger son of an Earl? I surely didn't. I knew he came from a good background, since he attended *Sandhurst,* but imagine, his family is titled!"

Poppy came running in from the bedroom. "Lily. What splendid news. Do you think it's all right if we let him pay for all of us?"

"He says he wants to pay us back for all of the hard work we've done. I tried to argue, but he wasn't having any of it. He said it was a gift from him to all of us."

"Well – I guess it's not improper to accept a gift, but it's a very large one."

"Not only that, but he's taking us all to *La Tour d'Argent* for dinner tonight. He told me to tell everyone that should use the money we would have spent on the hotel, and go on a shopping spree. We will need something to wear to such a top drawer restaurant."

"Lily, this is just too exciting. We need to hurry and get to the shops. Have you any idea where we should go?"

"I've never shopped in *Paris.* Let's ask Maddie. I think she has."

Maddie and Gena both came into the drawing room, dressed in the robes the hotel provided.

"I heard the news. This is spectacular. What a weekend this will be. I never dreamed that he was from the gentry, "said Gena.

"Who is?" asked Maddie.

"Dr. Garrett. He's the second son of an Earl. I wonder what he's doing over here in France, fighting this dreadful war," wondered Poppy.

"I know there was a terrible shortage of doctors. Also, I've known other titled people who have fought." She thought of Kit Claybourne. "Even the Prince of Wales is in the military," Lily added.

"Maddie, you've been shopping in Paris before, haven't you? Where would you suggest we go, to find dresses for tonight?" Lily asked, changing the subject.

"Let's go to *Printemps.* It's at the corner of La Havre and Boulevard Haussmann. It's a gorgeous art deco department store. They have lovely clothing, and good prices," Maddie suggested.

"Right, then. Let's be dressed in fifteen minutes, and meet in here," said Lily.

They each scurried off to one of the bedrooms. Gena and Lily were sharing, and Poppy and Maddie were in the other. They were all ready at the appointed time, and eagerly took the elevator to the lobby. There, the doorman got them a taxi, and off they went to *Au Printemps*. It was a large, imposing department store. In spite of the war footing, it was quite busy. They entered and found their way to the Women's Fashion Department, where each began to search the racks for the sort of dress that would be appropriate for dining at *La Tour d'Argent*. A very nice French sales lady assisted them, and luckily Maddie could speak French much better than the others, so she helped with translation for her friends. They had a wonderful time trying on a multitude of dresses, and each finally settled on something lovely for a night out in *Paris*. It had been so long since any of them had shopped, and each was surprised at the change in styling. Skirts were shorter, above the ankle, and they were looser fitting. There was no longer a need for corsets, which Lily had known was true just before she joined up. Since it was November, there was quite a selection of holiday dresses. Lily preferred pastels, but most of the colors were reds, greens, blues, and gold. Sooner or later each of them found what she wanted. Lily settled upon a crème-colored dress of delicate cashmere, with a skirt of soft pleats and a tucked top; tunic in style. It had long sleeves and a V-neckline. She bought crème court shoes and stockings to match. They were all astounded to find silk stockings! Poppy selected a green silk gown, with a tiered shirt and organdy sleeves. Maddie picked a red taffeta, with an ankle length tulip skirt and short sleeves, topped with a stylish jacket with puffed sleeves. Gena chose a gold tea gown, which complimented her lovely hair. It had a small waistline and a flared, tiered skirt. There was a higher collar, trimmed with lace and lace again at the bottom of the long sleeves. Each girl was terribly excited with her choice. They checked their watches, and found that they still had plenty of time before they had to be back to the hotel. They were so glad now that they had taken the earliest morning train. They decided to have their hair done, since there was a salon right in the store. What an incredible treat, after over two years of washing their hair in a bath-sized sink at the base. They took the elevator to the salon, and were fortunate to be able to book appointments immediately. Each one of them was taken into a private room, so no one could see what was happening with the other. After two hours of being washed, trimmed, massaged, styled and pampered, one by one they emerged. The first three, Lily, Maddie and Gena looked sensational, with clean shining hair, done up in French twists. Then Poppy sailed out of the room with her hair cut into a bob! She looked so different, that it was a bit of a shock. Different but splendid. Of course it would have been Poppy, who'd dared to do such a thing. Bobs were just starting to be seen, but none of the others had dreamed of having their hair cut. The look was fabulous on her. She had very pretty eyes, and the length of the hair accentuated them, with the turned up ends of the hair lying on her cheek. They were all astonished and giggling, as they paid their bill. They couldn't wait to get back to the *Plaza Athenee* and let the men see them.

At seven o'clock they were all in the lobby of the hotel, dressed in their new finery. They almost missed their doctor friends, as they were all dressed in suits and ties, and none of the nurses had ever seen them look so handsome. It appeared that each of them had also treated themselves to haircuts and shaves. Lily secretly wished that one of them were Kit Claybourne. However, she vowed to make the evening perfect, and all thoughts of Kit were cleared from her mind. After many compliments, the eight of them piled into two taxis and headed for *La Tour D'Argent.* The building was six stories tall, and there was lots of glass. Their table was by the window on the sixth floor. It was the most spectacular view any of them had ever seen. Although the famous lights did not twinkle, due to the war, they looked straight across at Notre Dame and the Seine River. It was breathtaking.

It was a round table for eight, and the men and women were seated odd and even. Lily found herself next to Major Phillips, a good-looking doctor from Yorkshire. On her other side was John Garrett, whom she, of course, knew well. On his right was Gena, looking absolutely beautiful. Then to her right was Captain Hewitt, from London. Next came Poppy, and then Roy Porter from Lincolnshire. And last was Maddie. They were all good looking people, and it made a handsome table. The waiter, dressed in formal wear, placed their napkins in their laps, and then gave the men the wine list. It was as large as an Atlas! Lily was glad she wouldn't have to do the choosing. They all ordered martinis before dinner, and the men studied the wines. Everyone raved about the duck at *Tour d'Argent,* so they all decided they would have to order it. John ordered two bottles of white Pouilly Fuisse and two bottles of red St. Emilion. The service was incredible. After every course, the waiter replaced their napkins. The food was divine, and they laughed and laughed. They all vowed not to discuss the war. They hadn't come to *Paris* to speak of the same things they did back at the Field Hospital. Instead they talked of their homes, their schools, their favorite pastimes, brothers, sisters, parents and pets. They told stories of happy times in the past. Lily noticed that Gena and John were deeply engrossed in their own conversation much of the time. She was very hopeful that a romance was going to develop between the two of them. Gena had been interested in him for such a long time, and John now seemed equally interested. Major Phillips made a couple of comments that Lily might have picked up on and gone further with, if she'd wanted a relationship, but she didn't. She told him that she had someone waiting for her back in England. She hoped that was true. He didn't seem to mind, and undoubtedly had a girl waiting for him too. Lily knew that both Poppy and Maddie were totally available, but hadn't a clue about Roy Porter or Captain Hewitt. She would learn when they returned to the hotel.

They were all completely stuffed when the dinner ended. It had been a long day, but so filled with excitement, that fatigue hadn't caught up with them yet. John paid the bill, and they walked out of the restaurant. It had started to mist a bit, but no one cared. It was also bitterly cold, but Poppy took off her shoes and skipped down the sidewalk. "I always said if I ever came to *Paris*, I'd take off my shoes and walk in the rain," she laughed. The other girls were laughing so hard, and they followed suit. Each took off her shoes, and skipped along with Poppy. The looked like children. None of them cared if people were laughing. It felt so good to be carefree and young again. They were skipping for all of the boys who would never feel young again. The streets were really quite empty anyway. Many of the smaller shops were boarded up, with signs that said 'Closed for the War'.

They stopped a few blocks from the restaurant, and went inside a small, quaint café. There they ordered after dinner drinks. They discussed what they would do the next day, and decided to see as much as they could of Paris.

John and Maddie were both familiar with the subway system, which was by far the fastest way to get around. They made a list of the places they wanted to visit - the Louvre, the Eiffel Tower, Napoleon's Grave at Les Invalides, The Tullieries, Notre Dame Cathedral, Montmartre, the Sacre Coeur, and Malmaison. It would be a full day, and they would have to start early. It was nearly midnight, so they decided it was time to head back to the *Plaza Athenee.* Taxis were again hailed, and before long, they were back in their elegant rooms. Quick kisses on the cheek were exchanged at the door, and then they were in the drawing room, shoes kicked off, and gloves on the tea table.

"Well, who's in love?" asked Poppy.

"Poppy, what a cheeky question," Gena scoffed.

"No it's not. I don't mean really in love. Maybe just for the weekend. It's *Paris*, after all. I think Captain Hewitt is smashing. I never paid much attention to him at the hospital, but he's so different away from there. I don't know about love, but I like him a lot," answered Poppy. "So, what about you, Lily?"

"Nope. I established that I had someone I was interested in at home. Bill Phillips seemed perfectly all right with that. We're just here to have a nice time."

"Oh Lily, you're a spoilsport," Poppy laughed. "What about you Maddie?"

"Roy is very sweet. He's very easy to be with. I like him."

"Okay," said Poppy. "That leaves you, Gena. I couldn't help but notice that you and John Garrett were deeply engaged in conversation."

"Well – to tell the truth, I am rather smitten. He told me that he's been interested in me for a long time, but that he's never had a chance to be alone with me. I've felt the same way. So, who knows?"

"Oh Gena. I just knew that you two would click. I really hope something comes of it," Lily answered.

"Me too" the rest of them chimed at once. Then they all burst out laughing.

"Well, we'd probably get to bed, if we think we're going to do everything on our list tomorrow. It's one o'clock now. What say we set the alarm for seven?" said Poppy.

"You have to be joshing. Let's make it nine," Lily suggested.

Everyone else agreed. "All right. Nine it is. That will give us all eight hours of sleep. See you all in the morning," answered Poppy.

The girls paired off and went to their rooms. They were all asleep as soon as their heads hit the pillows.

19

They started at the *Louvre*, were disappointed in the size of the *Mona Lisa*, continued on with their list and lunched at the *Eiffel Tower*. Running out of time, *Malmaison* was scratched. By the time they returned to the hotel, everyone was exhausted. They all agreed to have a lie-down before enjoying a long bath and dressing for dinner.

Lily noticed that throughout the day, Gena and John paired off, and lagged behind the others. It was becoming obvious that a relationship was forming. Lily was terribly happy for both of them, and hoped it developed into a real romance. She couldn't help but think about how much she'd have loved to see *Paris* with Kit. Would she ever forget him? Gena was sharing the room with her, and she was already fast asleep. Lily tossed and turned. She was having a wonderful time, but she also felt lonely. *Paris* was a city to share with someone special. Everywhere she looked, she saw couples holding hands, and stealing quick kisses. And while it was marvelous to get away from the depressing atmosphere of the hospital, there were still plenty of reminders of the war. Primarily, there were wounded soldiers hobbling about on crutches, with sleeves and pant legs pinned up, where once there had been arms and legs. She hoped someday she might return to *Paris*, when there weren't such dreadful sights; when all of the lights were twinkling; all of the shops busy, and the streets filled with fashionable, posh people.

The telephone next to the bed rang, and it was John Garrett. Lily knew that he would rather have talked to Gena, but she was still soundly sleeping. Lily spoke in a low voice, so as not to wake her.

"Hello, John. If you're looking for Gena, she's practically unconscious. I guess she really needed the rest. Can I have her ring you?"

"No, that's fine Lily. I just wanted to discuss plans for dinner. Do you think everyone would like to go to *Maxim's*?"

"*Maxim's*? Is that even possible? It's so famous. Can we get reservations?" she asked.

"Yes. I know Eugene Cornuche, the owner. Actually, he's quite a friend of my father. We dine there whenever we're in *Paris*. I'll ring him up. If I tell him I have four gorgeous women that will do the trick. He fills the restaurant with lovely ladies. That's the secret to his success."

"Oh, John. Don't tell him that. We'll probably be thrown out when we arrive and he learns that you didn't tell the truth."

"Tell me, Lily. Which one of you isn't beautiful?" John laughed.

She was speechless for a moment. She didn't want to point the finger at any of her friends, and anyway, she felt that they were all beautiful. "Well, probably me," she chuckled.

"Ha! You, my dear, are the loveliest of the lot. Don't tell Gena I said that."

"Speaking of Gena," Lily said, wanting to change the subject. You two seem very cozy. Is this turning out to be more than just a friendly trip to *Paris*?"

"So far, so good. I do care for her. Of course, one weekend isn't time enough for us to develop a serious relationship. But, it's a beginning. She is a wonderful girl."

"I'm not surprised you think so. I adore her. Knowing her as well as I do, it seems to me that the two of you have a lot in common."

"Yes, we do. Plus, we have a lot of fun together. And the chemistry is right, too."

"That pretty well covers everything, doesn't it?"

"Yes. But, don't make too much out of this yet, Lily. And please don't say anything to her about what I've said. I wouldn't want to hurt her for the world. For that matter, I don't wish to be hurt, either."

"I won't say a word. I hope your relationship continues to grow." There was silence for a moment. "All right. So its *Maxim's* is it? That's thrilling. What a wonderful way to end out trip to *Paris*."

"I'll ring Monsieur Cornuche. I'll try for eight o'clock. If that doesn't work, I'll ring you back."

"I'm over the moon. Thanks so much, John. Goodbye."

Lily placed the receiver back in its cradle. Gena turned over and stretched. "Who were you speaking to?" she asked.

"John. And, you'll never guess. He knows the owner of *Maxim's*, and that's where we're going for dinner tonight. Can you believe it? He is utterly amazing."

"I know. Oh, I've heard about *Maxim's* forever. John seems to know everyone. How can he possibly be interested in me?" She sat up, and placed the pillow behind her head.

"Gena! What a thing to say. You are beautiful, sweet, and intelligent, that's why," Lily responded.

"Perhaps. But, I'm not sophisticated and worldly. I'm surprised I don't bore him." Gena played with a lock of her hair.

"Silly girl. I can't see John wanting a worldly, erudite woman. That wouldn't be his style at all."

"I hope you're right. I'm really beginning to care for him, Lily."

"You make a handsome couple. Just be yourself. I have a feeling everything is going to work out just splendidly," Lily answered. She got up off the bed, and went to the closet. She took out her new dress from *Printemps*, and laid it on the bed. She didn't really like having to wear the same thing two nights in a row, but there was no choice. Anyway, it was a lovely dress. "I'm going to have a bath. It's six o'clock now, so we have about an hour and a half before we leave here."

"Right. Then I'll rest some more until you've finished with the tub" Gena replied.

The taxi-cabs took them to Rue Royale, where the restaurant known for its elegant clientele stood. The owner himself welcomed them at the door.

"Ah, Jean Garrett. Bienvenue, a Maxim's. Je vois que vous etes en compagnie des quatre beautes extraordinaire. S'il vous plaît me presenter," said Eugene Cornuche.

"Yes, of course," answered John. "These are the Misses Lily Barton, Gena Weatherford, Penelope Paulson, and Madeleine Brooks. We've come to Paris on a weekend furlough to have a rest – an escape from the agony of war."

"Oui. I understand. It's good to see you, my friend. And to meet your friends. Please follow me, and I'll take you to your table," Monsieur Cornuche replied.

They all followed him to a perfect table next to a window. It was set with lovely china and silver. The restaurant was an art nouveau masterpiece. And true to the legend, there were beautiful ladies sitting by several windows that looked out on the sidewalk, so that patrons could see them as they strolled by. The nurses in their group added to the ambiance, for they were just as pretty. The room gave off the impression of lace, ribbons, velvet and diamonds.

It was another exquisite evening. Gourmet food served in an elegant environment, made even more perfect because of the delightful friendship they had formed. Since they knew it was their last night, nothing was spared. They drank the finest wines, the best champagne and exotic after-dinner drinks. Everyone was more than a bit tipsy when the night came to an end. Bill Phillips had demonstrated how to perform a tracheotomy using a butter knife and a melon, Poppy bored everyone to tears with a long, drawn-out explanation of the reasons for low blood sugar, and Maddie told a story about having dropped a bed pan filled with urine on the shoes of the Nurse Matron, while she was in training. They were all hysterically laughing when she reached the end. Lily noticed that John had his arm about Gena's shoulders, and occasionally he placed his hand over hers.

Finally they settled the bill, and thanked Eugene Cornuche for a spectacular evening. As they walked out to the sidewalk, they realized that it had begun to snow. The city looked like a fairyland. It was also very cold, and there weren't any taxis in sight. As the snow started to come down harder, their laughter turned to concern. Within a few minutes they found themselves in the midst of a true blizzard. It grew more and more difficult to see where they were going. The girls were having a particularly hard time walking on the snow-filled sidewalks in their high-heeled shoes. Soon the street signs were covered with snow and it became impossible to read them. Those who were the most familiar with Paris tried to ease their friend's alarm.

"Don't worry. I'll get my bearings in a moment. I'm just a bit confused about direction. The snow is nearly blinding," John said. "If necessary, we'll find a tube station and grab the underground. Paris is laid out in concentric circles. It's hard to be certain about what direction we're heading. I need a familiar landmark"

They stumbled on for what seemed like an hour, but was, in reality, about fifteen minutes. The night's alcohol intake didn't enhance the group's ability to figure out where they were. Gena started to cry.

"I'm frightened. There's no place open – no lights, except street lamps. What are we going to do?"

"It will be all right, Gena. Let's stop under an awning, and get out of the snow for a minute," John replied. He was holding her hand.

They stopped under an awning on a large building. "*LaBree et Fils, Avocet's*" was etched onto a brass plate on the side of the stone wall.

"What does that say?" asked Gena.

"Nothing helpful." John answered. "It means LaBree and Son's, Barristers."

"Oh, why can't it be a hospital or police station?"

Although it didn't seem possible, the snow was coming down even more heavily. The wind had picked up and was burning their cheeks.

"Jesus. My face is numb," Bill Phillips called out.

"So is mine, and my hands are too," cried Poppy. Her voice sounded panicky.

"Listen everybody. Stomp your feet up and down and keep moving about. We don't want anyone to end up with frostbite," said Roy Porter.

"We're in quite a muddle. I think we have two choices," yelled John. "We can either continue walking, hoping that we come upon an underground station, or we can try to break the window in this building."

"God Almighty. Break the window? We'll end up in a *Paris* Prison," yelled Tom Hewitt.

"That's better than freezing to death on the *Paris* streets," cried Gena.

"Let's break it," answered Lily. "But, wait. Let's go round to the front and see what the entrance is like. It might be easier to break down the door."

"Good thinking, Lily," answered John. "Let's all link up and crocodile around the corner."

They grabbed one another's hands and held tightly. Then staying close to the wall, they inched their way to the entrance. Shielding his eyes from the blowing snow, John saw that there were two large doors, each with a pane of glass in the top portion. "This is better," he called. "I think we can break a door down. All of you ladies need to stay together. Keep holding hands, and stay under the awning. We chaps will form a straight line facing the doorway. The left one. On the count of three, we crash into it with all of our might. Use your shoulders."

The four men prepared themselves for the exploit. "One, two, three." They threw themselves forward. There was a sound of splintering wood, but the door held firm.

"Let's try again," shouted Roy.

Once again they counted to three. This time when they attacked the door, they could feel it give. They gave it a third try, and it fell inward, with the glass shattering. A cry of relief rose from the group, as they scrambled to get into the building. Heat poured from radiators on the inside wall. Once safe, all of the women began to sob. Each man put his arms around a weeping nurse.

"We're going to be fine now. It's all right. Calm down," Roy said as he patted Lily's back.

"There's a telephone over on that desk. We'll call the hotel," Tom Hewitt said as he comforted Maddie.

"There, there, Poppy. You'll be back in your lovely hotel room in no time at all," Bill said soothingly.

"Gena, don't cry. We're all safe. We just had a bad scare." John Garrett murmured as he held Gena.

Gena wiped her nose with her sleeve. "How will we get back to the hotel?"

"We'll call the police. They'll get us back," answered John. They were all standing in a large foyer. In the middle of the space sat a square counter, where a clerk probably sat during the daytime. A telephone sat on its top. Since John spoke French, Poppy nudged him away from Gena and pointed him toward the desk. He picked up the receiver, while Gena still held his other hand. An operator's voice came on the line. John explained the situation and asked that help be summoned. The operator assured him that aide would be sent at once.

Two taxicabs and a police auto pulled up in front of the building in under ten minutes. After an explanation was given to the authorities, two foursomes crawled into the taxis and crept off through the snow-covered streets toward the *Plaza Athenee* Hotel.

Once they arrived, they immediately headed for the elevators. All except for Gena and John. No one even noticed their absence, since everyone was in such as hurry to get to a warm room, and a hot bath.

John went to the desk in the lobby and spoke to the clerk. Gena sat down in a small chair in a corner. After just a few moments, she and John also got into an elevator. But, they didn't return to their usual rooms. John held the key to a separate room, and together they disappeared behind its door.

Lily didn't even wonder where her roommate had gone. She assumed Gena was saying goodnight to John. So, she quickly undressed, and ran the bath. The water felt so glorious and she laid her head back, and relaxed. What an unpleasant experience it had been. She vowed never to go out again without checking the weather report. She'd had no idea that it snowed so hard in Paris. There was a wireless in the bathroom, and she had turned it on when she entered. The announcer was talking about the awful blizzard, and warning people to stay off the roads. Lily did not speak very good French, but she understood enough to comprehend that it was a very bad storm. She felt fortunate that they had made it back safely.

After a good, long soak in the tub, she finally drained the water, and wrapped herself in a giant, fluffy bath towel. When she was dry, she slipped her nightdress over her head. Emerging from the bathroom, she was surprised that Gena had still not returned. It didn't concern Lily as she was certain that her friend was with John. It just seemed a bit odd that she hadn't hurried to get out of her wet clothing. Perhaps she had come into the room and changed while Lily was bathing. "No matter," she thought, as she pulled the covers back on the bed, and snuggled beneath them. In no time at all, she was fast asleep.

When Lily woke in the morning, she was very surprised to see that Gena was not in the room, nor did it appear that she had returned the previous night. She checked the adjoining parlor, and the other bedroom. Both of the other nurses were still sleeping in there, but there was no sign of Gena. Now she was alarmed. She picked up the telephone and rang John's suite. Tom Hewitt answered the phone.

"Tom, it's Lily. Gena never came back to our room last night. Is John there? I need to speak to him."

"No Lily, John isn't here either. He came in and changed clothes after we returned last night, but he never came back."

"Alright. I have a hunch that they were together somewhere. I don't want to cause an uproar. They know what time we need to leave for the station. I'm going to start getting ready, and hope she comes back soon."

Just as Lily hung up the receiver, the door opened, and Gena came in. She was blushing furiously, but also smiling.

"Gena! Where in the world have you been? I was beginning to worry. I just rang John's suite, and Tom answered. He said John was there after we came back to the hotel, but that he left again," said Lily.

"Yes-well-yes, he was. I was here while you were bathing. We, um, John got another room when we arrived here last night. We stayed there," answered Gena.

"Oh my God! You slept with him? You've always been so prim and proper, Gena."

"Yes, I know. I've always vowed I would save myself for marriage. But, Lily, I've seen so much death and loss since I've been in the V.A.D. I decided that people should grab happiness while they can. John and I love each other. We are going to marry, if we ever get out of France, but last night may have been our only chance to be together until then. I'm not sorry." Gena headed for the bath, and hung her traveling dress on the door.

"I'm not criticizing you, Gena. I actually can see your point. I'm just surprised, that's all."

Gena walked back across the room to Lily. "Remember when I told you that sometimes it might be better if people didn't think so much? Well, now I can tell you that's true. Last night I didn't think at all. I just acted on my feelings." She smiled again, and disappeared into the bath.

Lily sat down on the bed. She was filled with awe. "I wish I had followed that line of thinking when I still had a chance with Kit," she murmured to herself.

There wasn't much talk as they waited at the *Gare du Nord* later that morning. It had stopped snowing sometime during the night, but they had to leave for the station much earlier than planned. The streets were icy and piled high with drifts on either side. The taxis crawled at a snail's pace. The rail tracks had been cleared, but all of the trains were running late. It would be a long ride back to *Aubigny*. Everyone in the group was feeling a bit down – even Gena and John. There was a myriad of reasons for sad feelings. Perhaps the primary one was the fact that they were returning to the Field Hospital; back to rank odors and gruesome sights; bland food and uncomfortable sleep; thunderous artillery and men's voices crying out for their mother's arms. They were also rather the worse for wear due to heavy alcohol consumption at *Maxim's*. The men ached from head to toe due to their heroic endeavor smashing in the doorway *at LaBree et Fils*, and the girl's feet were swollen and sore from walking too far through heavy snow in high heeled shoes. The laughter of the past two days seemed far removed from this solemn, Sunday morning. Gena and John, who should have been over the moon after a romantic night of first time passion, felt downhearted because upon their return to Aubigny they would have to pretend that they weren't lovers. All in all, the group was a miserable lot.

Finally the train ground to a halt on the track where they waited. Doors opened and people spilled from the cars; businessmen, posh women, and soldiers; one armed and one legged soldiers, some on crutches and others in wheel chairs. There were a few who walked and appeared to be whole, at least on the outside. At the sight of so many pathetic souls, the moods of the traveling doctors and nurses lifted. Not because their hearts didn't ache at the pitiful sight, but because all realized how very fortunate they were. Their complaints of moments before turned into foolish trivia. Could the men in uniform imagine returning from a magical weekend in Paris, instead of muddy and blood soaked trenches? Of course, no one laughed, or even smiled at this realization. But, they exchanged understanding glances and felt ashamed of their childish feelings. When the conductor called 'All Aboard', all eight climbed onto the train, praying that the war would soon come to an end.

20

The holidays at *Claybourne Court* were a dismal affair. The only thing that made them the least bit bearable was that Win was going on three years old. It was his second Christmas and Kit spent almost all of his time with his son. Win was the delight of Kit's life. He'd never allowed a nanny to be hired as a replacement for Lily, since her disappearance. He made every effort to keep Lily alive in Win's memory. When Kit was at *Sandhurst,* his good friend, John Garrett, who had already completed his medical studies, told Kit some fascinating information about the human brain. He'd said that many researchers were beginning to believe that everything that happened in a person's life was stored for eternity in the human brain. If that was true, then Kit hoped that Win still had recollection of Lily – or 'Ba', as he had called her, in his infant's attempt at saying 'Barton.' Kit talked to his son daily about Lily. He was quite certain that if she ever returned Win would know her. He would be a happy, little chap to have his 'Ba' back.

Naturally, Eleanor was infuriated when she heard her son babbling 'Ba' as he toddled about the nursery. Kit's refusal to employ another nanny was just one more bone of contention in their never-ending battle of wills. But, Eleanor spent much more time in front of her mirror, or down at the stables, than in the nursery. Kit and Lady Cynthia took turns caring for Win, and Kit even allowed the boy to go behind the baize door which led to the lower level, where the kitchen help was always waiting to give him treats, and spoil him. The entire household loved the little chap and he was seldom alone except for after-noon lie-downs, and at night when he slept. Kit moved his room directly across from the nursery, so that he could hear if Win cried in the night, and left Eleanor to her own devices in the master suite. Eleanor only seemed to remember that she had a son when a visitor came to *Claybourne Court*, which wasn't often. She liked to show him off. Even at those times, it was more about her. Win did take after his mother, with his great blue eyes, and silken blonde tresses. Thus, strangers usually commented on the resemblance, and often told Eleanor that her son was as handsome as she was lovely. Then she would utter an outright lie, and say 'I've just put my heart and soul into Win. I hope to have a little daughter to join him in the nursery before too long." When Kit heard such comments, he gritted his teeth.

He had tried in every imaginable way to convince Eleanor that their marriage was finished. He'd begun to think that she wasn't capable of understanding that he no longer had feelings for her. He might have been able to tolerate her selfishness and vanity, had she not said such vile, cruel things to him when he'd arrived home from France. To be told by your wife that you're a 'freak' was a painful blow after his desperate longing to return to *Claybourne Court*, and the misery he had endured while serving Britain in the war. It was simply inconceivable to Eleanor that there could be anyone who wasn't madly in love with her. Conversations with her were inane and hopeless.

"But, Kit," she'd cry, "I'm every man's dream of the perfect woman. Look at me. Do you believe you'd ever find anyone else who has my beauty and charm?"

"Eleanor, how many times must I say it? I'm not attracted to you anymore. Furthermore, I care nothing for your so-called beauty. You're vain, and you only care about yourself. You act like the world revolves about you, and perhaps, most importantly, you are not the lady I want to be the Countess of Claybourne. Nor, for that matter, do you show any interest in doing so. Can't we just agree to end this marriage now, with some dignity?"

"Dignity? What would you know about 'dignity'? Do you believe that it's dignified to chase around after a household servant?"

"Oh Eleanor. Rubbish! I've never chased after anyone – not even you. You threw yourself at me the moment I arrived at *Cloverhill.* I do wish you'd stop this foolish fantasy you have about Miss Barton. "

"Ha! Why did she run off in the middle of the night? Why should she have acted as though married people don't show their love to one another. What she saw that night was perfectly appropriate."

"No, it was not, Eleanor. It was a disgusting attempt to lure me back into your bed."

Eleanor's face turned scarlet with anger. "There isn't a man on this God's green earth who wouldn't give everything he has to share my bed." She stomped her feet and ran to her bedroom.

There was just no way to undo the ghastly mistake he had obviously made by marrying Eleanor. There were still no passenger ships, and now the house in London was in ruins. It was being re-constructed, but slowly, as there were not a lot of laborers to do the work. They were all in France. Kit did his best to keep his distance from his wife. The thought of spending the rest of his days with her was enough to drive him mad. He knew that she couldn't be happy either. He'd no real idea what had changed so drastically when the London house was bombed. Before that, she couldn't wait to leave *Claybourne Court.* Now, it was as though she'd always adored him, and never wanted to be parted. Kit, however, knew that wasn't true. It was apparent that the bombing at the London townhouse had frightened her. Thus, returning to *Claybourne Court* was a balm to her nerves. But, Kit did not believe for one moment that she loved him, or that she wished to assume the duties required of her as Countess of Claybourne. He suspected that she did not want to admit to her family the mess she'd made of her marriage. Kit knew her father, who was a good chap, and there was little doubt that he would have been appalled at his daughter's behavior. She had threatened to write to her father, but Kit wondered if she had done so. Either she was afraid to do so, or she had written and received a reply that was not what she had hoped it would be. Eleanor had embarked for England as the bride of a handsome English Earl, with her family as proud as peacocks, and her friends green with envy. It was understandable that she didn't want to return as a divorced woman, having to admit that she hadn't made a go of it. But, that was no concern of Kit's. What was done was done. As soon as the war ended he would put her on a ship if he had to carry her there himself.

A version of the above conversation between Kit and Eleanor took place every few days. In between times, Eleanor would join Kit, Lady Cynthia and Win, who sat in a high youth's chair, at the dining table. She would be dressed in fancy gowns, trimmed with ribbons and lace, smiling sweetly, and speaking in a little girl's voice. While the others were polite to her, she was generally met with silence.

It was a yearly tradition that *Claybourne Court* open its door for a Christmas Eve get together, wherein every resident in the village was welcomed. *Claybourne-on-Colne* was a small village, so there were really no strangers. Some were closer than others, but it was a cozy, close-knit hamlet. For most, Christmas Eve at *Claybourne Court* was a holiday ritual anticipated all year long. For others it was a relatively new experience. There had been no celebration the previous year, as the family was still in mourning over Sebastian's death. Kit dreaded the Christmas Eve gathering because Eleanor used such occasions to pretend to the world that the Claybourne's were a happy, devoted couple, just as she had after Sebastian's funeral. She stayed by his side the entire time, dressed to the nines in something much too youthful, and gazed at him like a love-struck maiden. Of course, whether they meant it or not, guests would complement him on his lovely wife.

Elisabeth and Will Morris were trying to decide whether or not they would attend the Christmas Eve gala at *Claybourne Court*. Elisabeth stood in the parlor of their cottage, holding the heavy, crème-colored invitation. It had only been delivered in the afternoon post.

"I'm not much one for such fancy 'do's Elisabeth. Also, there's that nasty business with Lily and Lord Claybourne. He's bound to ask about her. You know Lily doesn't want us to say anything about her." Will was sitting on the camelback sofa in the small parlor, reading the *London Times*. "What do we say to him, if that happens?"

"I understand how you feel Will. I don't really want to go either. But, everyone in the entire village will attend. Our friends and neighbors will wonder why we aren't there. I could say that one of us wasn't feeling well, but you know how much I dislike not telling the truth." She sat down next to him, turning the invitation over and over in her hand. "Oh, how I wish I'd never suggested Lily apply for that position," she sighed.

Will put the paper down. "Elisabeth, what happened wasn't your fault. You had no way of knowing such a thing would take place." He was silent for a moment. "You know, it was an odd thing. Lily never struck me as the sort of girl who would lose her head over a married man."

"She isn't that sort of girl, Will. I brought her up to be a lady and that's what she's always been. Lord Claybourne would never have known about Lily's feelings, if he hadn't told her that he loved her."

Will got up, went into their small kitchen and poured himself a glass of ale. "Can I bring you something, Luv?" he called to his wife.

"A cup of tea would be nice," she replied.

He returned with his glass and her cup. "Here you are, Luv." He bent down and kissed her nose. Then settling himself back next to his wife he sighed. "Oh Elizabeth, I wish Lily had taken a shine to David. He would have treated her like gold."

"Yes, Will, David's a prize. But there is no predicting why people do or don't fall in love. The heart has its reasons, I guess."

"I'm lucky your heart decided that I was meant to be with you."

"So am I, Will." Elisabeth smiled. "So am I. But, now that you've managed to change the subject to our own romance, we still need to decide about Christmas Eve."

"We'll do the proper thing, Luv. You're right. And, speaking of David, he and Jane will be there. I don't want them worrying about why we're absent."

David Morris had married Jane Marshall, the sweet girl who taught in the village school, the year before. They were expecting a baby in the spring, and Elisabeth and Will couldn't wait to be grandparents. At least one of their children was happy. Elisabeth prayed every night that Lily would return to *Claybourne-on-Colne* when the war ended. She knew that it would probably be better if Lily moved to London and nursed at one of the large city hospitals.

But Elisabeth dearly wanted her daughter close-by. She shared her thoughts with Will.

"Elisabeth, I hate to say this, but I worry that Lily will never know the joy of marriage. I know she'd make a wonderful wife and mother. She worshipped that little boy at *Claybourne Court.* But, this bloody war has taken an entire generation of our boys. Lily's a beautiful woman. Before the war, she could have had them lined up round the block to walk out with her. But, there are few chaps left to line up. And any who are left, are disabled or ten years older than I am." He slapped his hand down on his thigh. "A bloody waste," he exclaimed."

Tears welled in Elisabeth's eyes.

"I apologize for swearing, Luv. I just get so angry at so much devastation."

"We all do, Will. I pray every night that Lily will find a good man. Lily isn't only beautiful. She's generous, compassionate and kind-hearted. She has so much to offer."

Will patted his wife's shoulder. "I believe life happens the way it's supposed to. Lily will find her soul mate."

It was Christmas Eve, and *Claybourne Court* glittered like a diamond. Special permission had been granted by the village council and the War Department for every light in the mansion to be lit. Zeppelin strikes had dwindled to none, and the chances of the German's deciding to bomb a great house in the Cotswold Hills were remote. Two immense pine wreaths, each sporting a large, red, plaid bow, hung on the entry doors. As visitors entered, they were welcomed by Lord and Lady Claybourne, along with Lady Cynthia. Even young Win stood next to his mother, dressed in a navy blue Eton suit with short pants and knee-high socks. He was holding his mother's hand, but it was anyone's guess as to how long that would last. Unbeknownst to Kit, Eleanor had threatened Win with a pinch on the leg, if he wiggled. His face already showed an obvious wish to be free. Eleanor looked like she was attending a cinema premiere. She wore a white taffeta gown, with a tiered skirt and sheer organza sleeves. There was a low-slung sash at her hips, and it dipped so low in front that her bosoms nearly showed. Her hair was dressed in the latest style - a mass of ringlets falling to her shoulders. Her eyelashes fluttered above a layer of thick mascara, and she had drawn a perfect bow on her mouth with dark red lip rouge. She resembled an American actress. Still, no one could deny she was stunning. Kit was handsome, in white tie and tails, and he presented a perfect picture of grace and elegance. Many of the guests thought his eye patch added even more style and class. One would never have guessed that he was an extremely unhappy man – one who considered the woman in white to be insufferable. Eleanor occasionally whispered in his ear and giggled, as if they shared some private secret. She superbly acted the role of The Countess of Gloucester. A lot of guests were fooled. The Claybourne's seemed a happy family, but many people had difficulty understanding how he could possibly have married her.

After the guests had finished with the receiving line, they were free to circulate throughout the magnificent home. The large fir tree dominated the drawing room, piled high with gaily-wrapped packages, meant to be given to each guest. Lady Cynthia had been responsible for that task, putting great thoughtfulness into the chore. Each gift had been especially selected for the person whose name appeared on the card. It had taken great time and attention for Lady Cynthia to get it all accomplished, and of course there'd never been an offer of help from Eleanor, who naturally took the credit. Lady Cynthia had reached the point where she loathed Eleanor.

A smaller tree stood in the Great Hall, in the curve of the staircase, with gifts for children tied to its branches. The dining table was covered with lovely Sterling silver serving dishes, each holding one of Mary's tasty recipes. Exquisite Wedgewood China plates of crème and gold, embossed with the Claybourne 'C', were ready for guests to help themselves to all of the mouth-watering delicacies. The footmen circled the room offering champagne in crystal flutes and egg-nog in silver cups. There was pink lemonade for the children, and trays of cookies on low tables so the small ones could reach. For those who didn't wish to drink alcohol, there were large urns of hot tea.

After only a short while, the crowd loosened up. Many gathered around the baby grand piano in the drawing room, singing carols and exchanging pleasantries. Win finally managed to escape his mother's grip, and toddled off to be with the other children. Eleanor added one last vicious pinch to the many others that she had inflicted upon him. He stuck his tongue out at her, but she was busy batting her eye-lashes at a young Australian soldier who had driven over to *Claybourne-on-Colne* from the aerodrome at *Aston Down*, near *Minchhampton*. He had brought Clara Thornton, the woman who Kit had hired to watch over the youngsters during the party. The Aussie's name was Richard Vincent, and he was from Melbourne. He'd not yet been to France. Eleanor was seen leaving the great hall with him on her arm, as if she intended to show him about the house.

Clara, from Minchhampton, had been instructed by Kit to give the children free rein, so that they could have fun, but also to keep an eye upon them, so no child got into the champagne by mistake. The smaller ones needed assistance with feeding too. She was someone who made her living entertaining children at parties, and depending upon the occasion, she dressed accordingly. Because it was Christmas Eve, Clara had chosen to be an angel, in a white gown, with wings on the back, and a hand-made halo. The children were enchanted.

Everything proceeded swimmingly. Kit was enjoying himself more than he expected, now that he'd managed to move himself to the other end of the house, away from Eleanor. He hadn't seen her stroll away on the Australian soldier's arm. It was nice to visit with people he didn't normally see. He'd been pleased to see Lily's mother and stepfather when they arrived. He had never met Mrs. Morris, but Will was a lifelong resident of *Claybourne-on-Colne*, and had known Kit since he was a small child. He shook hands heartily with Will Morris, after brushing Elisabeth's fingertips with his lips. It was the first time she had met him. When she's been married to Doctor Barton, they had never made plans on Christmas Eve, for fear that someone would need her husband's attention. Heavy drinking, auto accidents and domestic arguments were plentiful on that holy night. After Kit had kissed her hand, Elisabeth wondered if his marriage was as happy as it appeared. Elisabeth had always been a good judge of character, and she immediately sensed that something was amiss. Nevertheless, he seemed to be a very nice gentleman, and his little boy was an angel. She didn't care for Eleanor.

After she and Will had finished filling their plates, they sat down at a lovely round table in one of the receiving rooms and tucked into the meal. Jane was laughing at how darling the toddlers were – they were becoming more and more wound up. Kit joined their table, and took another champagne from Halsey. Clara told stories from the Bible about the angels who were seen on high, and asked the children to help in performing a little play about Jesus's birth. They also played games, such as Ring around the Rosy. The children were finally worn out, and some were a bit cranky. Their parents scurried about collecting coats, hats, mittens and gloves, and got ready to say their goodbyes. Win pattered his way into the room where Kit sat with the Morris's. He stopped abruptly when he saw Elisabeth Morris. "Ba!" he screamed. "Ba!" He ran over and threw himself into her arms.

"What is it dear boy," asked Elisabeth, confused by his behavior. He just kept crying, as he burrowed his head into her chest, saying 'Ba', 'Ba'.

"Oh my God", shouted Kit. "I do apologize Mrs. Morris. My son seems to think that you are Lily. There is a remarkable resemblance. He called Lily 'Ba', as he couldn't yet say 'Barton.' He worshipped her. I've tried to keep her alive in his memory, and apparently I've succeeded. Come here, Win, come to Daddy. That isn't your 'Ba.' I'm sorry little chap."

Win looked up at Elisabeth's eyes, and again cried 'Ba', pointing his finger at her. At just that moment, Eleanor entered the room, with the Australian soldier still on her arm. It was probably her intention to introduce him to Kit. She came to a halt, and stared at Elisabeth Morris, with her son sitting on her lap, crying. She marched across the room and grabbed Win by the arm. He screamed and flailed about, scrambling to get closer to Elisabeth. Elisabeth instinctively closed her arms tighter about him. This time, Eleanor grabbed him in the midsection, and dangled him like a doll. He began to kick and scream, and he knocked her champagne glass out of her hand. The golden liquid splashed all down the front of her white dress. She dropped the little boy on the floor. "You little brat," she yelled. Now he was howling, for he was undoubtedly surprised by her actions, and probably hurt too.

Both Elisabeth and Kit jumped to their feet. "Damn you, Eleanor. You've hurt him. What is the matter with you?" He bent down and picked up his son, but not in time for Win to miss the malicious kick Eleanor gave to the child. Kit cuddled him close and stroked his head. Through clenched teeth he said, "Eleanor. Pack your things and leave at once. You will never lay another finger on this boy, or so help me God I'll kill you."

"If people only knew how cruel you are to me. You're a devil in disguise", Eleanor sobbed. "You are the one who's cruel, not me. I'm sorry I lost my temper. But, it was almost more than I could take when I saw him on that woman's lap, calling her 'Ba', just like he did her wicked tart of a daughter."

Elisabeth Morris walked over to Eleanor and slapped her across the face. "Don't you ever make disparaging remarks about my daughter again. She makes ten of you."

Eleanor turned on her heel, taking the Australian soldier by the hand, and ran out of the front doors.

"Come on, Luv, let's be getting on home," said Will. He turned to Kit. "We didn't mean to cause any trouble. I never thought about how much Elisabeth resembles Lily. She does, of course. We had no idea the boy still remembered her."

"That's my fault, Will. I keep her in his thoughts. He loved her so. You can see that for yourselves. I'm also sorry that I lost my temper with Eleanor. But, I can't take any more. I've put up with her childishness and vanity, but when it comes to actually harming Win, I won't have it. I want her gone."

Lady Cynthia heard all of the uproar, and walked swiftly into the room. Win was still crying. "Whatever has happened to my little angel? Kit, why is he crying so? He never acts this way. Did he hurt himself? He's always the best little boy . . ." She reached over to comfort him. "Oh my God! Look at these bruises. They're all over his arms and legs. What could have caused them?" Lady Cynthia cried.

Jane Morris, who until then had been silent, got up and examined the marks closely. "They look like pinch marks. I teach school, and see this from time to time. Either the children pinch one another, or sometimes wicked parents inflict this sort of punishment."

Kit looked at his boy's arms and legs. "Win, can you tell me who hurt you there?" he asked, as he gently put his finger on the bruised spots.

"Mummy" his little voice replied.

"Mummy? Mummy did this to you? When? When did she do this, Win?"

"When the people came... And at night-night."

"Do you mean to say that your mother pinched you in the receiving line tonight, and that she also does it when you are in bed at night?"

He nodded his head, tears still streaming down his angelic cheeks.

"My God, Kit. She's a mad woman. She cannot be allowed to get near that child again," Lady Cynthia exclaimed. "You are going to have to do something."

"I already have. I've told her to pack up and leave. She disappeared screaming and bawling, with that Australian soldier who was here. Does anyone know who he is?" Kit asked.

"I think his name is Frank Vincent. He's from Melbourne. I spoke with him a bit," said David Morris. "He wanted to know what it was like to fight in France. I told him it was bloody awful. Sorry ladies. I didn't much care for him. He told me that he had connections in England and still had hopes that he wouldn't have to fight. I laughed and told him that if I had a shilling for everybody who thought they could get out of fighting, I'd be a very rich man."

"He sort of sneered and said that his connections were very high up."

"I don't like that sort of person in my home," murmured Lady Cynthia. "He sounds like a slacker."

"Well, we had best be on our way," Elisabeth whispered, as she pointed in the direction of Win. He was fast asleep with his head on Kit's shoulder. His cheeks were covered with the remnants of dried tears.

Lady Cynthia showed the Morris's out, along with any of the other remaining guests. Most had already left. Of course the story in the village the next day would be the terrible fight that had ensued between Kit Claybourne and his wife, along with details about the way Eleanor treated the precious little boy. Kit carried Win upstairs to the nursery. There was no sign of Eleanor, for which he was glad. He gently undressed him, and found more pinch marks on his tiny bum. Cursing under his breath, he put the boy into his night-dress, and laid him in his cot. He didn't wake up. Kit sat with him for quite some time, his own eyes wet with tears. How had he found himself in such a conundrum? Eleanor had to leave. That was all there was to it. He wanted her far away from Win. No matter what it took, he would never let her harm his son again. Finally, after he was certain Win was resting peacefully, Kit walked silently down the stairway and looked about for his mother. She was sitting in the drawing room, smoking a cigarette, which was something she never did.

"Mother, are you all right?" he asked. "You never smoke anymore."

"I'm just so angry, Kit. I felt like I needed to. How could a mother harm a child like that?"

"I don't know, Mother. But it will never happen again. I can assure you of that. Win is sleeping peacefully now, but would you go up and sit with him for just a bit? I don't want him left alone."

"Of course, Kit. But, where are you going?"

"Nowhere in particular. I just want some fresh air, to help me calm down. It's a nice night. I'm going for a walk. I won't be long."

Lady Cynthia went up to the nursery, and Kit grabbed his coat and got ready to leave. As he was heading for the door, Mrs. Briggs and Halsey met him near the entrance. "Are you all right, Milord? That was a dreadful scene. Is it our business to know what happened?"

"I can't go through all of the details now. I'm worn to a frazzle. I just want to take a breath of air, and go to bed. Suffice to say that I learned that Eleanor has been trying to punish Win by pinching him black and blue. Tonight she went further, and kicked him after she dropped him on the floor. She's hideous. A cat's a better mother than she is."

"Why, that evil woman! I'd put my own hands 'round her neck and strangle her, given half a chance. We all love that little one like he's ours."

"I know, Mrs. Briggs. I'm going to see that it never happens again."

"Can we help in any way, Milord?" Halsey asked.

"No, Halsey. Just make certain that Lady Eleanor isn't anywhere near Win. Tell me if you see her."

"Of course, Milord. Where is the boy now?" asked Halsey.

"In his cot. Lady Cynthia is watching over him. I won't be gone long. Feel free to lock up and go to bed. I have my key." With that, Kit left the house, and went out into the quiet, starlit night.

The only person in the house, besides the staff and his mother, was Clara Thornton, who seemed to be packing up her gear and getting ready to depart.

21

Kit woke with a start. He'd had a terrible dream. Or, was it a dream? Leaping from his bed, he raced across the hall to the nursery. When he opened the door, he breathed a sigh of relief. Win was standing on his chubby legs, holding on to the rails of his cot, smiling broadly. When he saw his Daddy, he reached his arms out to be picked up. Kit smiled and went to his son.

"How are you this morning, my fine son?" he asked, as he lifted him into his arms. He raised his little gown, and examined the bruises on his legs and bum. They were more pronounced than the night before, but didn't seem to be bothering Win. Kit felt about his rib area, where Eleanor had kicked him, and watched his son's expression. "Hurt Daddy," Win whined. He didn't cry, and Kit was certain no ribs were broken. However, he would have a medical person see him sometime that day, just to be certain. Kit carried him into the adjoining bath, and after removing the little boy's sleep wear, he placed him on the loo, washed his face, brushed his teeth and combed his hair. Then he dressed him in a sailor suit. It was Christmas Day. Kit had no intention of letting his loathsome wife ruin it for his son. He hadn't the slightest notion where she was, and what's more, he didn't care. Perhaps she'd spent the night with the Australian soldier? It didn't matter.

When Win was ready, Kit brought him across to his own room and allowed him to watch while Michael, the valet, shaved him, trimmed his hair, and prepared Kit's clothing. Then he and Win went down the staircase. Win couldn't negotiate the steps, but he scrambled backward on his hands and knees. Mrs. Briggs had the tree lights lit, and the smell of cinnamon buns wafted up from the kitchen below. She spied father and son in the great hall, and gave Win a morning cuddle. Then she rang the breakfast bell for Kit and Lady Cynthia, who arrived looking ladylike in a grey cashmere dress, tunic style, with long sleeves and a round neckline. She wore a triple strand of pearls and a diamond and pearl brooch. Another cuddle was in store for Win, as his grandmother bent down and kissed her grandson. Then the three of them entered the dining room. The sideboard was spread with a lovely array of breakfast selections. There were scrambled eggs, sausages, bacon, broiled tomato and kippers, as well as homemade scones, buns and freshly baked bread. Lemon Curd, strawberry preserves and orange marmalade graced the table in delicate crystal jars. There was hot tea for Kit and Lady Cynthia, and milk for Win. He was placed into his high chair, with a bib tied about his neck. Kit fixed Win a plate with all of his favorite things, and he eagerly tucked in. Lady Cynthia and Kit talked during the meal.

"I assume she didn't return during the night?" said Lady Cynthia.

"No Mother, not as far as I know. I suppose she could still be in bed, but knowing Eleanor, since it's Christmas, and she's such a child herself, I'd expect her to be up with the birds, acting as though nothing is amiss."

"Yes, that certainly sounds like her," his mother answered, while buttering a scone. After a few moments she continued. "Kit, you aren't going to let her weasel her way back into this house, are you?"

"Heaven's no, Mother. I don't think you'll ever have to deal with her again."

"How can you be so certain?"

"I just have a feeling. I think this time she realized how furious I was – that I'd had all I intend to take."

"Yes, actually, I have the same feeling. I think we may be rid of her at last. Did you get any sleep, Kit?"

"Not much. I took a long walk, and cleared my head. How did you rest, Mother?"

"Well, when you returned, I intended to go straight to the Dower house, but I too wandered about."

"I intend to write Eleanor's father later in the day, explaining everything."

Lady Cynthia and Kit then turned their attention to Win, and spoke to him about Father Christmas, and how he had come down the chimney during the night, and left gifts for him. Win clapped his hands with glee. The fact that his mother was missing from the holiday breakfast seemed of no consequence to him.

Downstairs the servants and Halsey were eating their own Christmas feast. The long wooden table was filled with the same foods that the Earl, Dowager Countess, and little Viscount were enjoying. Only the elegant table setting was different. Of course, the only talk among them surrounded the Christmas Eve gala. Every single person hoped they would never lay eyes on Eleanor Claybourne again. They'd never liked her. Not from the beginning.

"This was such a happy home before her arrival. Since then, it has been one thing after another. There is always something wrong. Either it is too hot outside, or too cold; too rainy or too dry. God help me if I forget to tell her how lovely she looks each day," exclaimed Mrs. Briggs. "She is so full of herself."

"Yes, and this lovely home is nothing compared to her plantation in Virginia. I wish she'd never left there," added Mary, the cook.

"She never did want our dear little Win, either. I remember when 'e was born. She actually said so. But, to actually 'arm him! Well it's more than a body can imagine. And 'e not even three yet. That witch never deserved everything 'er 'ad. Imagine Milord Claybourne 'aving to put up with 'er antics. Me 'usband would take a 'and to me," added Molly. "I'd not be blaming 'im either."

"Mr. Halsey. Are you thinking we'll be rid of her? I surely hope so. We've all been better mothers to that sweet boy than she ever was," added Mrs. Briggs.

"I surely do hope so, ladies," Halsey responded.

"My 'eart just bleeds for the Earl. 'E's such a good man. So kind and thoughtful. 'E never shoulda married 'er. She saw a good man and went after 'im," continued Molly.

"Where do you think she'll go now?" asked Cissy.

"Who cares?" answered Polly. "I hope she dies." She crossed herself. "I know that's an awful thing to be saying, but people like that just shouldn't be alive. Look at all of the folk she's hurt."

"All right, Ladies. I think we've had enough gossip for one day. Your feelings are understandable, but let's think no more about her. It's the Lord's birthday and let God take care of Lady Eleanor. I think he will. People usually get what they give," Halsey said.

In the Will Morris home, Elisabeth's roast was slowing browning in the oven. Jane was getting ready to add the potatoes and start preparation of the Yorkshire pudding. The table was set, and David and Will were in the parlor drinking eggnog spiked with rum while discussing the war and the happenings of the previous evening.

"Did you sleep all right last night after all of the uproar at *Claybourne Court*," Jane asked Elisabeth. "Gosh, I have to tell you how downright proud I was that you slapped that hideous woman across the face," Jane laughed.

"Well, it wasn't proper, I'm sure, but I'll not sit back and listen to someone call my Lily such vile names. I can understand now why Lily couldn't bear her. And imagine, her hurting her own, darling boy. I was stunned when she grabbed him out of my arms. And then – to drop him on the floor like a sack of potatoes and kick him! I wouldn't kick a dog. Never! That woman is pure evil," Elisabeth exclaimed.

"Yes. Didn't Lily tell you that she was very self-centered and spoiled rotten? You could see that. She acted like she was younger than Win," replied Jane.

"Poor Lord Claybourne. He seems like a good man. I don't know if I've ever seen a man as angry as he was when he told her to get out," Jane said.

"Well, any normal father would be. Will told me that he felt like slapping her too, but I got there first," Elisabeth laughed. "After we got back home and Will went to bed, I seriously thought about going back there and trying to talk some sense into her. I got as far as putting on my coat, and walking down the road, but then I figured I best let Lord Claybourne take care of it."

"That's funny. Well – I mean funny-odd. David thought about doing the same thing. I went on to bed, but he was furious at the idea that any woman would purposely hurt her own child. And you know he still cares for Lily, like he would a sister. He was fit to be tied at the coarse things she said about your daughter. David can have quite a temper when he gets his back up."

"He didn't go though, did he?" asked Elisabeth.

"No, at least I don't think so. I went to bed, as I said. But, I think he would have told me if he'd left the house – me being pregnant and all."

"Who was that dark-haired soldier that Eleanor was with?" Elisabeth wondered. "He watched Eleanor drop Win and kick him, and never said a word."

"You know as much as I do. David chatted with him a bit. He didn't care for him much. He's an Australian training to fly aero planes over at *Aston Down*, near *Minchhampton*," answered Jane.

"What was he doing at the Claybourne's? Who does he know in the village?" Elisabeth asked.

"I think he drove that lady who organized the children, and watched over them. I know she was from *Minchhampton*," Jane said.

"Well, she couldn't have had anything to do with it. She didn't even know the Claybournes."

22

All of the presents had been opened, and the boxes and wrapping paper cleared from the drawing room. Win settled down to play with his new toys, and Kit sat back smoking a cigarette and drinking a cup of tea. A blaze roared in the fireplace and the wireless was playing holiday carols. Kit felt more relaxed than he had in a long time. Perhaps there was going to be a good life ahead for him. As he sat in his comfortable chair, thinking of the future, there was a knock at the door. Halsey went to answer it. There stood two police Inspectors, who asked to speak with Lord Claybourne. Kit snuffed out his cigarette, and walked to the door.

"I am Lord Claybourne," he said politely. "What can I do for you chaps?"

"May we come in, Lord Claybourne. We need to speak with you."

"Certainly," Kit replied, as he held the door ajar. They glanced around the great hall and into the drawing room as they entered. Seeing Win playing on the floor, one of them asked if they might speak with Kit privately.

"Yes, of course," he answered. Kit called his mother in from her private writing room where she'd been occupied with penning notes to people who had sent Christmas gifts. She had also written out end-of-the year bonus checks to be distributed to the staff. Lady Cynthia was greatly appreciative of their loyal staff, as was Kit. He asked his mother to watch Win for a moment, while he tended business with the police. Of course, she agreed. He led the men to his library, told them to make themselves comfortable and offered refreshments. Both asked for a cup of tea. Kit rang for a tea tray to serve three people. Then he sat down behind his desk and asked again how he might be of help.

"Lord Claybourne, we have some rather unpleasant news. It's about your wife, Lady Eleanor. She is your wife, is she not?"

"Yes," Kit replied. For the time being, he thought. "What unpleasant news do you have concerning Eleanor?" he asked.

"Lady Claybourne's body was found this morning. She appears to have been dead some six hours. It's hard to be certain. Rigor Mortis had come and gone. She was found by the summerhouse on your property."

"On my property? How-when-by whom?" Kit stammered. Kit was genuinely shocked and upset. He didn't love her, and in that moment of anger, he'd even told her that he would kill her if she ever touched Win again. But people said things like that all of the time. That didn't mean he'd been serious.

"Your wife was found by one of your neighbors who was out walking, Sir. She had been murdered. Strangled, from what has been ascertained."

Kit put his head in his hands. "Oh dear God. Murdered?" He began to weep. It was his fault. If he'd not lost his temper, she'd be home, safe and sound. He should have made her stay, and figured out a way to send her to London with a new ladies' maid until the war was over. But it was too late now. She was dead.

"Can you give me any more details? I realize that you're in the midst of an investigation, but isn't there something more?" he asked.

The tea tray arrived at that moment, and Kit's hand shook as he poured three cups.

"Well, Lord Claybourne, your wife was found lying on the grass in front of the summerhouse. Her white dress was torn in several places. Her underwear was intact, and she had not been misused. She was on her back, and her mouth was open, as if trying to breathe, and her neck had deep red marks on either side. The eyes show evidence of petechiae, which are small blood vessels in the eyes which burst when one is strangled," the smaller of the two men said.

"Oh God! How perfectly ghastly. But this is a very quiet village. Who could have done such a thing?"

"That's what we intend to find out, Lord Claybourne. If need be, we'll call in Scotland Yard. Now, may we ask you a few questions, Sir?"

"Yes. Yes, of course," answered Kit, in a daze. "Before you begin, may I ask your names?"

The short, stocky man on the right, who appeared to be in his mid-forties, introduced himself as Chief Inspector, Malcolm McCarthy. The constable on the left was younger, better looking and more amiable. He was about six feet tall, with dark-red hair and blue eyes. "My name is Inspector Edward Reese-Jones. Now, may we proceed?"

"Of course," assured Kit.

"For the record, what is your full name and what do you wish to be called?" asked Chief Inspector McCarthy.

"My full name is Christopher Ellis Claybourne. I'm the eighth Earl of Gloucester. My title is Lord Christopher Claybourne or Christopher, Earl of Gloucester. I prefer simply 'Kit Claybourne'. If you must be formal, I'd prefer 'Sir'."

"And your birthdate, Sir?" asked the Inspector.

"November 7, 1885.

"Place of birth?"

"Here. *Claybourne Court* in *Claybourne-on-Colne*."

"Are you married?"

"Yes. To Eleanor Emily Evans. Her birthdate was June 8, 1892. She was born in Lynchburg, Virginia."

"Do you have any children?"

"Yes. One son, born April 15, 1915. His name is Winfield Edward Claybourne. His title is that of Viscount. We call him 'Win'."

"How would you characterize your marriage, Sir?"

"That's an odd question. Am I a suspect?" asked Kit.

"Everyone is a suspect until we solve the crime, Sir. The more honest you are, the more helpful it will be," answered the Chief Inspector.

"All right. I have nothing to hide. I'd characterize my marriage as exceedingly unhappy," answered Kit.

Both officers looked up from the notebook in which they were taking notes. "In what way was it unhappy?"

"In every way imaginable. I married her in Virginia. She was young and lovely. She swept me off my feet with what they call 'Southern charm', and she was greatly taken with the idea of marrying an English Earl. Her father breeds fine race-horses. That's how I met her. I traveled there to purchase a horse." Kit went on to recite the entire story of his marriage to Eleanor, explaining about her ghastly reaction when she saw his eye patch, and continuing with the harsh words that were spoken on Christmas Eve when she purposely harmed their little boy. "I couldn't take any more," he explained. "It was the last straw. I wanted a divorce and would have found a way to obtain one."

"Were you involved romantically with any other woman?"

"Not for a very long while, and never in a sexual way. A young lady I hired to be Eleanor's companion and nurse while I was away in France became close to me. When I returned from the war, she was compassionate and kind. While Eleanor was calling me a 'freak' and a 'monster' Lily – that's her name –was concerned about how she might help me. Lily was not just a servant, although I don't happen to think there is anything wrong with that class. Her father was a physician and she had dreams of attending medical school. She'd attended college, and had assisted her father in his surgery. I've heard she is in France now, nursing with the V.A.D. – has been since 1916."

The questioning went on for hours. They asked every conceivable thing they could think of concerning his life, and Eleanor's, and even Lily's. Of course, he was asked to repeat the incident on Christmas Eve over and over. He had to give the names of all people who were witnesses. They seemed suspicious about the late night walk he took. Where had he gone? How long? Did anyone see him?

Finally they closed their notebooks, told him an autopsy was being performed, and then the body would be released for burial. They left, telling him they would check his story, talk to witnesses, and speak to anyone else who did not care for Eleanor. That left Kit to plan a funeral for a wife he did not love. He spoke to the vicar of the local church where the Claybournes had worshipped for generations, and made arrangements for a private ceremony in the *Claybourne Court Chapel* and internment in the family cemetery. How Eleanor would have detested the thought that she would spend eternity under English soil.

Both the village newspaper and the *London Times* carried front-page stories about the murder. There was mention that the police would like to speak with an Australian soldier stationed at *Aston Down* who had attended the party at *Claybourne Court* on Christmas Eve. He was the last person to have seen her alive. Still, the number one suspect appeared to be Kit. They told him that he had motive, means, and opportunity. No matter how much he denied their accusations, it did no good. Everyone who'd been a witness to the drama on Christmas Eve was interviewed at length. They had a lot of possible suspects who had no solid alibis. Kit, of course, was number one on that list. The second person of interest was Lady Cynthia. It was clear that she also had motive, means, and opportunity. She had also taken a walk on the grounds that night and had no alibi. William and David Morris emerged as suspects when they admitted that they both considered returning to *Claybourne Court* to have it out with Eleanor about the scurrilous things she'd said about Lily. These people were lower on the list of suspects, however, as it was deemed that their motives weren't as great as Kit's and his mother's. For a while, Mrs. Briggs made the list, but then it was discovered that she had arthritis in her hands, and wouldn't have had the strength to strangle someone.

Frank Vincent, the Australian soldier, presented himself to the Chief Inspector after he saw his name in the newspaper. He said that he had gone out to the summerhouse with Eleanor, and engaged in some 'romantic' activity, but had then returned to the house to pack up the equipment he and Clara Thornton, the baby sitter, had brought to the party. He had then waited for her in the auto. One of the departing guests remembered seeing him sitting in the car. He said that Eleanor had said she wanted to sit outside and think about what she was going to do, and that he never saw her again. His story seemed to check out. Clara Thornton said that he had waited for her while she gathered up her belongings, changed into her regular clothing, and visited the loo. She also said that she'd been hungry and pinched a bit of food that was left on the dining table. She was not fingered as a suspect, primarily because she had absolutely no motive for wanting Eleanor dead. She hadn't even known her. The investigation went on for a long while. Practically everyone in the village was interrogated. Most were immediately ruled out. It was becoming an all-consuming mystery. Everyone in the village speculated on who could have committed such a strange murder. Nothing had been stolen. The victim hadn't been sexually assaulted. The only thing anyone could possibly assume was that someone had been very, very angry.

23

Finally, after seven long months, on July 25, 1918, Lord Christopher Claybourne was arrested for the murder of his wife. Everyone in the village was stunned. Lily's mother wrote to her daughter at once, telling her the entire story. Lily had been transferred to the base hospital at Calais a month before, when more nurses were needed there. It was a good sign, for Calais was a recuperative hospital, the last stop before wounded soldiers were sent home to England. Gone were the gruesome amputations she had attended, and having to assist the surgeons when they dug the shells out of the gaping wounds in abdomens. Now she saw to the bandages, and helped soldiers learn to negotiate artificial limbs. In fact, she was at the same hospital where Kit had been based with his Victoria Cross and one eye. It was beyond Lily's comprehension that Kit could have killed Eleanor. She knew full well that he did have the motive, but one had to know Kit to understand that no matter how over the top he might have been with anger at Eleanor, he could never have killed her. He hated having to kill in the war, and he even detested rabbit, fox, and deer hunting. He may have loathed Eleanor, but murder was out of the question.

Lily was knocked for six when she learned what had happened. Kit was in the village lock up, awaiting arraignment for the strangling death of his wife.

Where was little Win, and who was with him? Oh my God, she agonized. How was Kit? She couldn't imagine such a decent, honorable man being held in confinement for something he hadn't done. But what if he were found guilty? He would be hung! She got shivers up and down her spine. Was there anything she could do to help? She thought and thought, Of course there was! Lily probably knew the real Eleanor about as well as anyone did. She'd been with her night and day for nearly two years. She was present the day Kit returned from the war. Perhaps her testimony could help.

She immediately went to Matron Jeanette in the administrative hut. Explaining her plight as succinctly as possible, she requested termination of her duties with the V.A.D. Jeanette was a kind woman who cared about the nurses she supervised. She listened sympathetically to Lily's story. When Lily was through, Matron Jeanette patted her hand and agreed that of course she should return to her home and do whatever she could to help. She said she would sign the papers immediately and Lily could take the afternoon ferry to Dover. From there she would board a train to *London* and on to *Claybourne-on-Colne*. "Oh, Matron, thank you so much. This is so very kind of you. I'll never forget your thoughtfulness. The V.A.D. has been an incredible experience for me. More than anything, it's fostered my desire to become a doctor."

"You've been a first rate nurse, Miss Barton. I wish I'd had a hundred more like you. I wholeheartedly support your future goals. If I can help in the way of a letter of recommendation, I would be happy to write one. You went far beyond the duties required of you. You endangered your own life many times to save our brave soldiers."

"Thank you again, Miss Jeanette. I'll never forget you." She shook the Matron's hand, briskly turned and walked away with her head held high.

Lily was still in her uniform when she made her way from the train station to *Claybourne Court*. She hadn't even told her mother that she was coming home. When Halsey met her at the door, his normal solemn mouth began to tremble and tears welled in his eyes.

"Welcome home, Miss Barton," he smiled. "I can't tell you what a sight for sore eyes you are. Please come right in. Mrs. Briggs will bring you tea, while I summon Lady Cynthia."

Lily removed her cape and gloves, and laid them on the familiar settee in the great hall. She gazed around the beautiful home, and saw that there had been little change. There were still fresh flowers scattered in lovely arrangements, and everything was neat as a pin. Mrs. Briggs scurried into the hall where Lily waited.

"Oh bless you, Miss Barton! . Everything is just as bad as it can be. I assume you know all about Lord Claybourne's unjust imprisonment? Of course he's innocent, but his barrister can't find the evidence he needs to exonerate him."

"What sort of evidence do they lack?" Lily asked.

"The same evidence that would prove someone else guilty." They both sat down in Mrs. Brigg's familiar little office.

"Do you have an opinion about who might have done it?" asked Lily, smoothing back her hair.

"My own opinion is that the Australian soldier who was the last person to be seen with Eleanor is the killer."

"Have the authorities spoken with him?"

"Yes. Scotland Yard is involved. Pray they find the real murderer."

"What of Kit? How is he holding up?"

"Quite well, considering. Lady Cynthia has contracted with a superb barrister in London. He's supposed to be very good. He's studying all of the details of the autopsy report right now. He's moved his office here, to *Claybourne-on-Colne*."

"Is Kit allowed to have visitors?" asked Lily.

"Yes, he surely is. Lady Cynthia goes two days a week. You need to speak to her."

"Of course," Lily responded. "And what about precious, little Win?"

"He'll be a sight better now, Miss Barton. He's a sad, lonely little boy. We all do our best, but he misses his Daddy. His never mentions his Mum. But, he speaks of 'Ba' continually. He had a birthday on April 15. His Daddy was still here then. It was the last happy time we had. Your arrival will cheer him up. It will cheer up Lord Claybourne too."

"Win speaks of 'Ba'? I'm astounded that he should remember me after so long," answered Lily, with wide eyes. She leaned forward and placed her hands on the desk.

"Yes, indeed. Lord Claybourne kept your name in his memory- talked of you all of the time. You just wait and see."

"Well, I'm happy to know that. I wish I'd never left here, Mrs. Briggs. It was a mistake. I wonder if this would have happened if I'd still been here."

"Oh, Miss Barton. Don't you be blaming yourself. I don't know what made you run off like you did, but I'm sure you had your reasons," said Mrs. Briggs.

"Someday, I'll explain it all to you. But, I do think I made a mistake."

"It isn't my business. I'm just happy to see your pretty face back here again. You'll be a joy to everyone. Poor Lady Cynthia. Comforting her son, and trying to care for her grandson. It's too much for her. You'll bring a light to her eyes. Come, let me ring the Dower House. She'll be here in just a tick."

Lily and Lady Cynthia talked for hours in the drawing room. Lady Cynthia broke down and sobbed when she first set sight on Lily. It was something Lily had never seen before. Not even when Sebastian died. It wasn't just weeping, but great gulps of sobs. Her relief at having help by her side was overwhelming. Lily found herself in the odd position of consoling her. She put her arms about her, and let Lady Cynthia lay her head on Lily's shoulder. The strong Lady of *Claybourne Court* had broken down. She'd carried the fear and anxiety for so long. Lily knew that it was healthy for her to express her emotions. She held on to Lily like a lifeline, and begged her to promise over and over that she wouldn't go away again. At long last, Lady Cynthia told her to wait while she fetched Win from his lie-down. Lily sat alone, sipping her tea, and anxiously tapping her toe. After several minutes Lady Cynthia appeared with a broad smile on her face, holding Win by the hand. Win spied Lily and began to scream, "'Ba'." He put his arms out to her. Lily took him into her arms and cuddled him.

"Yes, darling. Your 'Ba' is back, and my how you've grown. Just look at what a big boy you've become."

"Why did you go away, Ba? I cried but you didn't come back," he said, in a pitiful little voice.

She was amazed that he spoke so well. Turning to Lady Cynthia, she smiled and said, "I'm astounded at how well he speaks. Does he have a new nurse, or a governess?""

"Oh no. Kit wouldn't hear of it. He wanted Win to remember you. Kit is the one who has worked with him on his speech. He reads to him constantly, and teaches him how to say words," Lady Cynthia answered. "Kit spoke very early too. I think it's the reading and speaking to children that makes such a difference."

"Why, 'Ba'? Why did you go?" he repeated.

"I had to go and help with something called the war, Sweetheart. I know you don't understand that, but I'm back now. I'm so proud that you remembered my name."

"Yes, I do too know about war. My Daddy taught me. The Germans are fighting against our Country. Did you have to shoot a gun?"

"Oh, no Win. I was a nurse. I took care of the soldiers when they got hurt."

"I'm glad you came home," he answered. "I need you more than the soldiers."

"Yes, dear. That's exactly why I came back," Lily said in a choked up voice.

"Daddy told me lots of stories about 'Ba', but now Daddy is gone. Is he a soldier now, too?"

"No, Win, not this time. He didn't want to go, but he has some important business to take care of. We're all hoping that he can come home very soon."

"When, 'Ba'?" he asked.

"I don't know for certain, Win. But I'll tell you just as soon as I do know. Until then, I'll read you your stories every night."

Win clung to Lily and put his head on her shoulder. She rubbed her cheek against his and smoothed his thick, shiny hair. She buried her face in his neck, and breathed his sweet little boy smell. God, she loved him.

"Let's take him back to the nursery. It's past his lie-down time. Perhaps you'd like to have a lie-down yourself. Have you any clothing with you? You can bathe and change, and then we'll pay a visit to Kit. Visiting hours aren't until three o'clock, so you've time for a rest," offered Lady Cynthia.

"What a nice idea, Lady Cynthia. That sounds divine. Yes, I have a piece of luggage that I left in the great hall. I came straight from the station. I haven't many regular clothes. Mostly uniforms. But I do have a couple of things. They'll do for now."

"I could loan you Eleanor's things, but I doubt you'd want to wear them," Lady Cynthia ruefully smiled.

"No. Never. When I get time, I'll purchase some new items."

"Suit yourself, dear. You can also borrow anything of mine. We're about the same size I would guess."

Lady Cynthia was almost the exact height as Lily, and she was small-boned and slender. Lily guessed that she was correct. "That's awfully kind of you. I would like to look special for Kit. The dresses I have are rather passé, and styles have changed so," Lily commented.

"I'll bring several frocks over and have them hung in your cupboard. After you're finished bathing and resting, choose whatever you wish to wear. If you like any of them, just keep them."

"Oh, Lady Cynthia, that is just too kind. I wouldn't feel right about that. I'll borrow whatever I need until I can visit the shops. Thank you so much for your generosity," Lily replied.

Then Lady Cynthia did something she'd never done before. She put her arms around Lily, and gave her an enormous hug, and kissed her on the cheek. "I'm so grateful to have you back here. You don't know what it means to me. Kit will be over the top. Perhaps with your good sense, we can figure out the mystery about who committed this crime."

When Lily woke, she opened the cupboard door and was amazed to see an enormous array of dresses. She couldn't believe her eyes. These weren't shop dresses, bought off the peg. Each was obviously hand stitched, and designed by well-known stylists. Lily had never owned anything like them. The gowns were all created for the proper season. After looking though them several times, and trying on more than a few, she settled on a mint green georgette crepe, made over a darker green silk slip. The dark green taffeta sash was exceedingly smart, and the organdie collar and cuffs edged with Valenciennes lace were charming last touches. She knew that green was a very good color with her auburn hair.

She laid the frock on the bed, and ran water in the tub. She hadn't had a bath since before she left Calais. It felt wonderful to soak in the warm water, scented with lavender oil. She was happy to be back at *Claybourne Court*, and surprised that she didn't feel at all like she was out of place. On the contrary, she felt like she'd come home. That reminded her of her mother and Will, and she knew she would have to ring them as soon as she was dressed. Feelings would be hurt if she waited much longer. She planned on staying at *Claybourne Court*, to give help to Lady Claybourne but also to be with Win. She didn't think her mother would have any objection to that. She also wanted to meet Kit's Barrister. She couldn't imagine what she might be able to add to the case, but she felt a need to go over everything with him. She had a strange inner sensation that she could add something to this mystery.

Dressed in the splendid green frock, she went downstairs and found Lady Cynthia playing with Win in the Library. There were toys scattered about the floor.

"Oh, how lovely you look, Lily. That dress suits you to a Tee. You really must keep it. I never liked it on me. Turn around so that I can see the back,"

Lily did as Lady Cynthia requested, and suddenly Win clapped. "You're booful, 'Ba'" he said. Lily and Lady Cynthia burst into laughter. "Well there's a boy who has good taste," said his grandmother. Lily reached down and gave him a cuddle.

"Well, we must be going. We want you to be able to spend every moment possible with Kit. Edward is waiting outside with the car," commented Lady Cynthia. "Win, you be a good boy for Mrs. Briggs. 'Ba' and I will be back very soon."

Edward, the chauffeur whom Lily had last seen on that dreadful night when she escaped from *Claybourne Court*, seemed pleased to see that she had returned. It wouldn't have been proper for him to show too much emotion, but he smiled broadly, and said "Welcome, Miss Barton."

Lily and Kit's mother settled themselves in the back seat, and Edward drove down the hill to the village, and across the bridge to the jail. Lily had never dreamed of going inside such a loathsome place. She could imagine how Lady Cynthia must have felt. It was a stone building that looked as though it had been built in the 1800's. There were several trees surrounding it, and she could see small windows, very high up on the sides. That was probably where the inmate's cells were. It was impossible to think that Kit was being held in such a place.

When they entered, an elderly gentleman was sitting at a desk by the door. "Good day to you, Lady Cynthia," he said, as if he was quite familiar with her. He was about sixty years old, and had a full head of grey hair. His face was kindly, which made Lily feel a bit better.

"How do you do, Mr. Fowler," said Lady Cynthia. "I'd like you to meet a close friend of mine, Miss Lily Barton," she added.

"How'd you do, Miss Barton?" he asked.

Lily replied that she was fine, and that she was pleased to meet him. He asked them to leave their pocketbooks with him and sign a sheet on the desk.

"Oh, it won't be necessary for me to do that today, Mr. Fowler. I've just brought Miss Barton to visit my son," said Lady Cynthia.

Lily was astonished. "But-but-Lady Cynthia, aren't you going to come with me?" Lily asked. She was a bit frightened.

"Not today, Lily. I think you should visit with Kit alone this first time. I'll wait for you right here. Mr. Fowler will escort you to the visiting room." She sat down in a chair against the wall.

Lily, nodded, scarcely knowing what to say. Then Mr. Fowler asked her to leave her handbag and required that she empty her pockets. Lily was taken aback, but Lady Cynthia smiled, and Lily complied. Apparently she'd been through the routine many times.

"All right, Miss Barton," said Mr. Fowler. "Follow me."

They walked along a narrow corridor and when they came to a door, he took out a key ring and unlocked it. Then they continued on until they came to a room which obviously was set aside for visitors. There were tables and chairs, and a counter where people could purchase cigarettes and tea. Mr. Fowler asked her to take a seat and said that Kit would join her in a moment. Lily maintained her composure, but was a bit rattled. She tried not to show it.

Her heart was beating faster than normal. Finally she heard footsteps, and Kit entered the room. He was dressed in the typical black and white uniform of a prisoner, and Lily's heart broke. But it was still Kit, and although his hair had been cut shorter, he looked as handsome as he always had. Lily had been warned there was to be no demonstration of affection, so she stayed on one side of the table and Kit went to the other. He grinned broadly, and had tears in his eyes when he saw her. She placed her hands on the top of the table, and he put one of his over it. She felt a warm squeeze.

"God, Lily, when did you return? I had no idea. I'd have put on my white tie and tails if I'd known," he laughed.

"You look elegant to me," she replied, smiling.

"Are you back for good, or is this just a visit?" he asked.

"I'm home for good, Kit. I'll be staying at *Claybourne Court* to help your mother, and of course to be close to Win."

"Bless you, Lily. Win must be over the moon. Is he running around screaming 'Ba'?"

"Something like that," laughed Lily. She was surprised at how smoothly the conversation was flowing. She'd thought it would be difficult after so long. "Is there no chance that you might be given bail?" she asked. "I don't see why you have to be kept in this hovel," she frowned.

"They don't release on bail when it's a murder charge," he answered.

There was silence for a moment. "Did you get the books that your mother had sent over?" she asked.

"Yes. Thank Mother for me. My idea of Hell is being locked up with nothing to read. The books help to pass the time."

"Is there anything else you need?" she asked.

"Not at the moment, unless you can manage to smuggle in a file," he laughed again.

"I wish I could, Kit. We all miss you so much. What do your barristers say? There has to be some evidence that you didn't do this ghastly thing," asked Lily.

"So far, none. But I agree. It wasn't me. I know that. One would think that whoever did it would have left some clue behind."

"Would you care if I spoke with your barrister? I'd just like to make certain that I understand all of the facts," Lily said.

"No, that's fine, Lily. Perhaps you can see something that the rest of us have missed."

There was a moment of silence. Lily and Kit looked each other in the eye, and both smiled, somewhat sadly. "Lily, I'm very sorry . . ."Kit began.

"Kit, I made a terrible mistake . . ." Lily said.

They both spoke at once, and then laughed together. Kit raised his hand, and waved her on. "You first," he smiled.

"Kit, I never should have left that night. I acted childishly. It was a shock, but I should have known that there was more to it than met the eye. I knew you didn't love Eleanor."

"Lily, I've wanted to explain it to you for so long. Eleanor came up behind me. I never even heard her enter the nursery. I turned, and there she was. You opened the door just as she kissed me. I was just as shocked as you were. I was completely off my guard. I didn't . . ."

"Shhhh, Kit. You needn't explain. I should have had more faith in you. I was so confused. So young and silly. Going to France was a great awakening for me. I saw and heard things that were indescribable. Of course you understand what I mean. Many a night I laid awake listening to the sounds of artillery fire while men died in agony. I grew up, Kit. I now know what real heartbreak, real pain is. Real suffering. Most of all, I learned the value of controlling one's emotions – no more impulsive behavior, and no more escaping from reality."

"But, Eleanor kissing me wasn't reality. You were my reality – you and Win. Do you understand that now?"

"Yes, I've understood for a long time. But I was so afraid to write to you, for fear you'd moved on with your life."

Kit smiled. "And, I was afraid you'd done the same."

Lily placed her hand on top of his. "That's all done now. I'm here. I still love you. Those feelings only grew while I was away."

"They never left me either. I wanted you so," Kit murmured.

"I'm here now," she whispered.

"Oh, but Lily, I'm here in this God-awful place. I try to keep a brave front for my mother, but I'm frightened. What if we don't learn who committed this murder? What if I have to stay here for the rest of my life? Or be hung?" He shuddered at the thought.

"I'm going to do everything in my power to find out who really did this. I'm going to ring your barrister when I leave here, and see him as soon as I'm able. You're innocent. I know that, and God knows that. I promise, you'll be home soon," Lily said firmly.

Kit smiled and shook his head. "You're an amazing woman, Lily Barton. You almost make me believe you."

"Oh, do believe me, Kit. I have no intention of losing you now," she exclaimed with tears in her eyes. "I have some sort of strange feeling that I can find the answer somehow. I know I can."

Lily sniffled and smiled at him. Suddenly, visiting time was over. Kit and Lily exchanged a longing look. They wished terribly that they could hold one another. A guard appeared and escorted Kit back to his cell. Lily called out to him, "I'll write you a letter every day." He turned and grinned. Lily left the visiting room and stopped at the main entrance to retrieve her pocketbook and Lady Cynthia. Then they walked out to the parking area where Edward was waiting to take them home.

24

Lily had lunch with her mother and Will the next day before her appointment with Mr. Poindexter, the barrister. Elisabeth was surprised and truly beside herself when she heard Lily's voice on the telephone. When she hung up, she screamed for Will, telling him that Lily was home, and that they would be seeing her the next day. She understood completely why her daughter had chosen to stay at *Claybourne Court*, and didn't argue with her decision. It was such a relief to know that Lily was back from France, and would not be leaving again. Lily made plans to see her mother for lunch at least once a week, and more often if possible. After a nice catch-up chat, Lily headed off to the barrister's temporary office in the village. His regular office was in London, but he had moved to *Claybourne-on-Colne* for the duration of Kit's ordeal.

She was shown into his office immediately upon her arrival at the cottage-like structure he had chosen for his interim workplace. It was quite a charming spot, with only the receptionist and Mr. Poindexter. She was impressed with him immediately. He was in his mid-fifties, tall, with mostly grey hair and a distinguished face. Lily liked his professional, yet friendly demeanor. He asked her to make herself comfortable, and his receptionist brought her a cup of tea. Lily sat down across from him, and settled herself in the leather chair. It was her intention to show him how adamant she was about helping to find Eleanor's killer.

"How can I help you?" Mr. Poindexter inquired of Lily.

"I want to know every detail you have about the case. I want to read the autopsy report and any statements the police took from those who were present on Christmas Eve. There has to be some clue, somewhere."

Mr. Poindexter smiled. He didn't seem the least put off by Lily's rather cheeky attitude. One might have thought that she herself was a barrister. "Do you have legal experience, Miss Barton?"

"No sir. I'm a nurse. But I'm not stupid, and I love Kit Claybourne. I know he's innocent, and I think a pair of fresh eyes never hurts. I know I can be of help to you if you'll allow it," she replied.

"I have no objection to your assisting me with research, if Lord Claybourne has none. I shall have to speak with him, of course."

"That's fine. Kit won't mind at all. I've already spoken to him. He believes I can help you."

"Well, I'll tell you what. Since he's already told me that he wanted me to speak with you and listen to what you had to say, I'll let you do some catching-up if you'd like. I'll need to have you sign a form promising to keep anything we discuss confidential, and I'll need to have Lord Claybourne sign papers to the effect that he agrees to you lending a hand. But, I'll give you the case notes I have to date. You read them over and get back to me."

"You have no idea how much I appreciate your confidence in me," said Lily. "I know it sounds silly for me to think I can add anything to your work, but I just have a strong feeling that I need to do this."

"Who am I to argue, Miss Barton? I'm not so full-of-myself that I think another person can't render a new perspective." He swung his chair around, and opened a drawer in his desk. He took out a folder marked 'Claybourne', and handed it to Lily. "I'm afraid I cannot allow you to take these out of the office. This is the only copy I have of everything. But, I have a small conference room set up here, and you're welcome to use it for as long as you wish. I'll alert the other woman in the office that you may be coming in and out, and that she's to provide you with the file on Lord Claybourne whenever you request it. Does that meet your expectations?"

"My Goodness, yes. It more than meets my expectations. I'm delighted. I'll make notes on anything I think might be pertinent, and then speak with you about the file."

"That will be fine, Miss Barton. I'm sure you're dying to get started, so I'll lead you to the conference room and leave you to it."

Lily read until her eyes were very tired. She had come to the office at one in the afternoon, and it was now six o'clock. Still, she wasn't quite ready to call it a day. The file was very large. She'd had no idea how much paperwork was involved in such a task. It seemed that every person who had attended the party had been questioned by the local authorities. Then there were more notes made by the inspectors from Scotland Yard who'd been brought in to help solve the mystery. They had re-interviewed many of the same people. The words 'Means, Motive and Opportunity' were written at the top of each page. Obviously, when all was said and done, Kit was deemed to be the only person who met all three criteria.

Lily read over the autopsy report and spotted an item she had over-looked before. There was a notation by the coroner that a white feather had been found on Eleanor's dress, which had also been white. The Inspector had written 'dress was trimmed in feathers' next to the notation. There was also a sketch of a feather which closely resembled that of a swan or some sort of large bird. What sort of feathers? Lily wondered. She speculated about the kind of feathers a fashion designer would use on a frock. "Hmmm," she wondered aloud. "I should think a designer would use marabou –the sort used on a boa." She gathered up the papers, and walked back to Mr. Poindexter's office. He was sitting at his desk, reading a book on trial preparation. He looked up as Lily entered the room.

"Have you finished for the day, Miss Barton?" he asked.

"Yes. I think so. My eyes are crossing. But, before I leave I have a question of you, if you have time?"

"Certainly, I have time. Sit down. What is it you wish to know?"

Lily explained about the notation and sketch of the feather and asked him if he had seen the dress.

"Yes, the police have it, but I was given an opportunity to examine it."

"Did you notice that it was trimmed with feathers?" Lily asked.

"To tell you the truth, I don't recall. I remember that it was white, and it was quite badly torn."

"Yes, but the feather bothers me. I've never known of a dress to have actual feathers on it. Perhaps actors in theatrical productions would have such a thing, but otherwise, I can't imagine. The only feathers I've ever seen on a frock are of the fluffy sort – like what they use to trim a boa. They're called Marabou. The sketch that was made isn't that at all. It looks like a swan's feather. Have you asked any of those present at the party if they remembered feathers on Eleanor's frock?"

"No, I haven't. But I certainly shall, if you think it's of importance. What exactly do you think the significance of a feather would be?" the barrister asked.

"Well, if they found a feather on her body, and the dress wasn't trimmed with them, then where did it come from? Did anybody else have something with feathers on it? A hat, or an evening bag?"

"Ahhh, I see. Of course, that's the sort of thing a woman would notice more than a man. Well, Miss Barton, you just may have stumbled onto a valuable lead for me to follow. I intend to explore this matter further before I leave the office tonight."

"And I'm going to ask Lady Cynthia if she recalls anything about feathers, as well as all of the staff at *Claybourne Court*."

"Good show. Be here first thing in the morning. We'll take it from there. Thank you ever so much, Miss Barton. It seems your hunch about being able to help might very well be correct."

"I hope so, Sir. I'll see you the first thing tomorrow." Lily gathered up her cardigan sweater and pocketbook, and left for a return to *Claybourne Court*. She didn't bother to ring Edward to fetch her, and simply took a taxicab. When she arrived at the great house Lady Cynthia was in the drawing room. Win was downstairs, being fed a jam sandwich by Mary.

"Well, how was your day, dear?" asked the Dowager Countess.

"Perhaps very, very good. I don't want to get my hopes up, but something significant may have turned up. I can't tell you everything, since I had to sign a form promising to keep what I learned confidential. But I believe you can be of help to me."

"Me? Whatever makes you think that? Of course I'd do anything in the world to help, but I can't imagine what it would be."

"Just answer this question for me. Do you recall if Eleanor's dress, the night of the party, was trimmed in white feathers of some sort?"

"No. I don't remember any feathers. I don't believe there were any. I inspected her dress very carefully before the guests arrived, as I was concerned about the impression she would make upon those attending the party. Eleanor's taste often left quite a lot to be desired."

Lily laughed. "Yes. Actually, it wouldn't have been surprising if she had been all decked out in feathers."

"I agree, but she wasn't. I'm really very certain. Why does that matter?"

"I'm sorry, Lady Cynthia. You know I would tell you if I could. Just suffice it to say that it might be the break we've been waiting for."

"I understand, Lily. Oh, I do hope you're right. I knew that if you came back we'd clear this mess up."

"Don't count your chickens before they hatch, but keep your fingers crossed and keep praying. Now I must ask the same question of the staff, and hope I get the same answer."

She did get the same answer. No one at all remembered feathers on Eleanor's frock. She spoke with all of the downstairs staff, including Cissy, Polly, Mary, Sarah, Molly, and Martha. All firmly said that they remembered no feathers. Both of the footman, who had done the serving while circulating the room, also said they didn't recall any feathers on Lady Claybourne's gown, although they admitted that they'd been very busy. Finally, Lily went up to Mrs. Briggs' office, and asked the same question of her. Mrs. Briggs spoke positively. "Absolutely not. I looked at the dress with careful eyes. It was tarty, but there were no feathers. But Miss Barton, I can surely tell you who did wear feathers."

Lily's heart began to beat very rapidly. She felt hot all over and as though she'd been running, and was breathless. "Who, Mrs. Briggs? Who did you see in feathers?"

"That lady Lord Claybourne took on to watch the children during the party. What was her name? I know. Clara Thornton. We chatted a few minutes before the guests began to arrive. When she first came, she was dressed in a plain, simple frock. Then she went upstairs and changed into a get-up for the party. I guess it was meant to be a special costume for the children. She was fixed up like an angel. She must have made the outfit. It was a floor length white dress, with long bell-shaped sleeves, and there were wings attached to her shoulders in the back. They were covered with feathers. Lots of them. When I inspected the house after everyone had left, the library was scattered with them. That's where she was with the youngsters."

Lily tried not to show her elation. "What sort of feathers were they?" she asked.

"Normal like feathers. Like a swan, or I suppose a duck. But I'd say more like a swan."

"Do the Claybourne's still have swans in the pond down by the stables?" Lily asked.

"No. They were here when you came the first time, but when Win started to walk, Lord Claybourne got rid of them. He was afraid Win would get a bite. Swans can be quite nasty creatures you know," answered Mrs. Briggs.

"Mrs. Briggs, thank you so much. You've been a great help. If everything turns out the way I hope, I'll tell you all about it, but I can't right now," Lily said apologetically.

Mrs. Briggs smiled and waved her hand at Lily. "Don't be apologizing to me. If you can't tell me, then you have a mighty good reason, I'm sure. I'm only glad I could help."

Lily exited the office. As she rushed by Lady Cynthia, she told her that she had to go out for a while. She grabbed a light sweater and rang for Edward, who immediately answered and said he would bring the automobile around to the front. Lily prayed that Mr. Poindexter would still be in his office. As she got into the back seat, she asked Edward to please hurry, as she had an important errand.

In no time at all, they were in front of the barrister's cottage. Lily asked Edward to wait, while she jumped out of the car and ran to the entrance. Mr. Poindexter was still at his desk. He glanced up and acted startled when he saw Lily.

"My Lord, Miss Barton. I wasn't expecting anyone. You put a good scare into me."

"I'm sorry Mr. Poindexter, but I had to see you right away. I've learned something that I think may solve this case!"

He pushed aside the papers he'd been working on and told her to sit down and take a breath. "Now then, start at the beginning. I'm assuming it has something to do with the feather," he exclaimed.

Lily told him the entire story. He pulled out Kit's file, and flipped through the pages of interrogations until he reached one with Clara Thornton's name marked on it. "Shall I read it to you, Miss Barton?"

"Oh do, please," Lily replied.

"Here it is, verbatim, he answered.

'My name is Clara Louise Thornton. I'm twenty-six years old, and live in Minchhampton, Gloucestershire. I perform. That's to say, I'm an entertainer. I took the job to keep children out of the way at a party Lord and Lady Claybourne had at their house, Claybourne Court, on Christmas Eve. My friend, Frank Vincent, drove me there. We got there about five o'clock. It's a very posh place. The Butler met me at the front door, then Mrs. Briggs, the housekeeper, chatted with me for half hour or so. She told me what I was to do - that being I was to watch over the small children who was coming to the party, so's they wouldn't get into mischief and the like. I done this sort of work before. After we finished our chat, Mrs. Briggs showed me the way to the room I was to use for a change to my costume. Sometimes I dress as a princess – other times like a big dog or cat. This being Christmas and all, I dressed as an angel. I make my own get-ups. This one was pretty fancy. It was a long dress with wings. I made a halo out of a clothes hanger and glued it to the collar. It looked right good, if I say so myself. When it come time to go, about midnight maybe, I went back up and put on my regular dress. I always bring lots of toys and the like, so they had to be put in my bag. I seen Frank go outside with the Lady of the house earlier and I went to find him to tell him to come help me clean up. I didn't see him, so's I come back in the house and finished my chores. Then Frank shows up, and I was miffed at him for having me to do everything, so's I tell him to wait in the motor. Then, I come out and got in, and we drove off home."

"Interesting," commented Lily. Now, what does this Frank Vincent's statement say?"

There was more rummaging in the files, and Mr. Poindexter finally found what he was searching for. "All right," he said. "Here's what Mr. Vincent has to say . . ."

"My name is Frank Walter Vincent. I'm in England because I'm in the Air Force. I'm from Australia. Melbourne. On Christmas Eve I drove Clara Thornton, a friend of mine, over to Claybourne-on-Colne so she could entertain youngsters at a Christmas Eve party at an Earl's house – Claybourne Court. It was a swell house. I've known Clara since right after I got over to England. I'm based at Aston Down aerodrome, near Minchhampton. It's an Aussie base. Anyhow, we got to the house about five o'clock. I went to the downstairs part, and the blokes who work there gave me tea. I stayed down there till the party was near over. When I came up the stairs, the lady of the house herself said she would show me round. A very pretty bird, she was. Then she got into a row with her old man. She grabbed hold of my hand and dragged me outside. She was awful upset, crying and all. I tried to comfort her, and she started kissing on me. I didn't want no trouble from her old man, so I went back in the house. Clara was mad at me for not lending a hand, so I went to the car. She told me to wait till she was ready to leave, and after a bit she came out and we left. I guess I waited about a half hour. Clara had to get out of the angel get-up, and back into her regular clothes. That's all my story."

"Oh my God!" Lily exclaimed. "Are you thinking what I'm thinking, Mr. Poindexter?"

"Yes, Ma'am, Miss Barton, I surely am. I'm not quite certain how it all fits together. Someone is lying here."

"Yes, and I think if you consider the feather, you'll have the truth. Can you interrogate Clara Thornton, or are the police inspectors the only ones who can do that?" Lily asked.

"I can do it. I'll call her in for a deposition. If she refuses, I'll have her formally subpoenaed."

"Oh, please do. Can you ring her now? I'm just so anxious to hear the true story."

The barrister ran his hand through his grey hair. All was quiet as he thought. Finally he spoke. "I don't see any reason why not. But not a peep out of you, Miss. I don't want her to hear your voice here with me."

"Of course not. I'll not say a word. I promise," Lily smiled.

He looked through the papers again and found her phone exchange. He put the call through and waited. After three rings, her voice came on the line. "Hallo. Clara Thornton here," she answered.

"Miss Thornton. How do you do? My name is Ralph Poindexter. I am a barrister, representing Lord Christopher Claybourne over in *Claybourne-on-Colne*. Have you a moment to chat?" he began.

"Well – yes. I guess so. What do you want to chat to me about?" Miss Thornton responded. Her voice sounded frightened.

"Well, you see Miss Thornton, I've been reading through all of the papers the police gave me, trying to get up-to-date on Lord Claybourne's case. I only took it on recently. I imagine you've heard that he has been arrested for his wife's murder."

"Yes. I did hear that. I can't say I'm awful surprised, what with the way they was carrying on and all."

"You believe he is guilty then, I presume?" Mr. Poindexter continued.

"I don't know nothing about it really. Just that there was a big row that night."

"Miss Thornton, it would be a big help to me if you could come to my office in *Claybourne-on-Colne* and let me ask you some questions. It's called a deposition. This is something I need to do with a lot of the people at the party, to prepare for a court appearance."

"Well – I guess I could manage that. When would you be needing me?" she inquired.

"As soon as possible. I am starting with the people who were at the house before guests began to arrive. That would include you. Do you suppose you could meet with me tomorrow, at your convenience?" he asked.

"Tomorrow? So quick like? I guess I could. I'm not performing at present," she said.

"What time would suit you, Miss Thornton?"

"What say about noon? I'll have to take the train over. Frank's on duty at *Aston Down*." she answered.

"Noon it shall be. And I thank you greatly. I'll look forward to meeting you. Can you find my office? Shall I give you directions?" he asked.

"No. I'll find it. That's a small village. I'll ask someone."

"All right. Goodbye, and thank you again."

"Goodbye," she replied.

The barrister hung up the telephone, and Lily jumped out of her chair, ran around the desk and hugged him. "Oh, Ralph. You did it. You did it. I can't believe she agreed to come so easily." Lily nearly screamed.

Ralph Poindexter put his head on the desk and laughed. "When did we go to a first name basis?" he chuckled.

"We haven't fully, until you start calling me Lily. Isn't it daft to be so formal with each other, when we're about to solve a murder case?"

"All right, Lily, my girl. But I warn you. She may shut her mouth like a clam when she sees where the questions are leading. I can't force her to talk, you know. I'll have to use every ploy I learned in law school to get what I hope to out of her."

"I can't be here, can I?" she asked in a melancholy tone.

"Well now. Let's see." He thought for several moments. "How would you like to be hired on by me as what we call a court reporter? Can you take notes quickly?"

"Mr. –Ralph – you are a tonic! Yes, I can. I learned Gregg Shorthand so that I could assist my father in his office. He was a physician, and I had to write down every word of conversations he had with patients," Lily smiled.

"Then you're hired, Lily Barton. Be at my office at eight o'clock a.m. I'll teach you about depositions. I'm going to put you on my staff until this case is resolved."

"What a perfect idea. You're a genius. Thank you so much. I'm so glad Kit's mother hired you," Lily answered.

25

Lily was at the barrister's cottage at eight o'clock on the dot. Edward dropped her off in front of the building and she told him she would ring him when she needed a pick-up. Entering the office, she found Ralph Poindexter behind the desk, sipping tea, and studying papers.

"Well, good morning, Lily Barton. I don't need to ask if you rested well. I know you didn't, any more than I did. I spent the night, into the wee hours, writing up the questions I intend to ask Miss Clara Thornton. I'm going to get the truth from her, no matter what it takes. I wish I had a photo of her, so I had an idea of how she looks. I don't like to be surprised by anything."

"I've never seen a photo of her either, but the housekeeper at *Claybourne Court* described her to me very well. She said that Miss Thornton is quite a large woman. Not necessarily obese, but large boned and sturdy. She's also tall. Mrs. Briggs, the housekeeper, thought she was a bit lower class. Well – you could probably tell that from her grammar skills. Not that such a thing matters, but it might mean that she'll be intimidated by a barrister. Or, she could also have a grudge toward the higher classes," Lily explained.

"Yes, it's hard to know how that affects her, if at all. Good to know, though." Ralph answered.

"Also, Mrs. Briggs said that Miss Thornton apparently has a bit of a crush on the Aussie who drove her from Minchhampton. Mrs. Briggs and Clara chatted at the beginning of the evening, before the guests arrived. She indicated that she is quite keen on him. She's hoping for a closer relationship, and marriage."

"Now, that's very interesting. Perhaps she was jealous of Eleanor. It sounds as though Eleanor latched on to him, showing him the home, and eventually going outside with her," Ralph pondered.

"Yet, she doesn't mention seeing him when she went out to ask him to come in to help her pack up," mused Lily. She twirled a pencil around in her fingers. "Nor did he mention seeing her, in the statement you read to me."

"Perhaps they just missed each other, or is someone covering for someone else?" he queried. "There's just something not right here. I swear, I'll get the truth."

"I believe you will, Sir. I'm anxious to see how you handle her," Lily said.

"Well, take the file and go into the conference room. Read up on the case again. You can't do that often enough. If any questions come to your mind while she's being depositioned, write them down and give them to me," he suggested to Lily.

"Yes, I shall," she answered. He handed her the case file again, and Lily moved on down the hallway to the conference area. She had been practicing her shorthand, and wanted to continue with that too. It was terribly important that she get down every word that Clara Thornton uttered.

The morning passed quickly. Lily was once again absorbed in the case. She asked Mr. Poindexter if he would give her some dictation and let her practice her shorthand a bit more. He gladly helped her and she felt confident that she would do fine. She was surprised that she still remembered her old skills. It was like other things in life, she thought. Once you learned them, they were always there, in the back of your mind. At eleven forty-five, Lily went to the loo and combed her hair, which had been cut shorter, falling into soft waves about her face. She freshened her lip rouge and said a silent prayer that the end of imprisonment was in sight for Kit.

Clara Thornton arrived at exactly noon. Ralph had given his receptionist an off day, and Lily was sitting at the desk in the entry area. When Clara opened the door, Lily glanced up, as though she'd been absorbed in work, and welcomed her. "Are you here to see Mr. Poindexter?" she asked.

"Yes, Miss. I've an appointment. My name's Clara Thornton, from Minchhampton."

"Oh, yes, of course, Miss Thornton. I'll tell Mr. Poindexter you've arrived. Would you like a cup of tea?" Lily asked, very professionally.

"Yes, Miss. I'd like that fine. Thank you," Clara answered.

Lily disappeared into Ralph's office and gave him a thumbs up. "She's here," she smiled. "I'm going to get her a cup of tea, so wait just a moment."

He nodded, and smiled. "That's fine, Lily. Does she seem nervous?"

"Yes, I'd say so. At any rate, she's being very polite." Lily went about preparing the tea in a small alcove at the back of the office, and carried it back out to the entrance. Handing it to Clara Thornton, she smiled encouragingly, and told her that she looked very attractive. Miss Thornton was dressed in a bright yellow frock that looked a bit too youthful on her. It had ruffles at the hemline and on the sleeves. She was not an attractive woman and Lily felt a stab of pity for her. Her hair was long and stringy, and she had spots on her face. Her fingernails were bitten to the quick. She was most definitely a worried lady. When Lily complimented her, Clara Thornton's face grew red, from the neck up. Poor thing probably never heard nice things about her appearance. Then Lily hardened her heart, realizing that this woman could be responsible for Kit's confinement.

Ralph Poindexter came out to the entrance, and introduced himself to Clara. He shook her hand, which Lily noticed was trembling a bit. "Won't you follow me, Miss Thornton? We're going to use our largest room, so we have better space to be comfortable. Miss Barton, whom you've already met, will be assisting me." He waved his hand toward Lily. Then she got up from the desk and motioned that Clara Thornton follow them down the hallway. When they reached the conference room, Clara was asked to make herself comfortable, which she did. She set her tea cup on the table, and occasionally sipped from it.

"I have an entire pot made," Lily said, "so if you'd like more tea, just ask, Miss Thornton."

"All right," Mr. Poindexter began. "Let's get started. Miss Thornton, may I call you Clara?"

"Yes, Sir. I don't mind," she answered.

"Okay, Clara. I'm going to ask you several questions, and when you answer them, Miss Barton will record them on her pad over there. Don't let that disturb you. I just need a record of the people I ask to come into my office to tell me about this case. Do you understand?" he asked.

"Yes, Sir. I'm ready."

"Fine. Let's begin. Clara, I won't go over everything about the night of the murder with you. I know that you were driven to *Claybourne-on-Colne* with your friend Frank Vincent, is that correct?"

"Yes. Only, he's a bit more than a friend. I'm hoping he loves me. I'm hoping to marry him," she blushed.

"Well, that's lovely Clara. He must be very excited at that prospect."

"Well, no Sir. He don't know me feelings yet. I'm sort of playing hard-to-get and all. But, I think he cares for me a lot. It's moving along."

"All right. Clara, what did you wear the night of the party?" Mr. Poindexter questioned.

"I worn me regular dress while we drove up to *Claybourne Court.* Then I changed to me get-up that I made 'specially for the party and that. My get-up was an angel costume. I put a lot of work into it."

"Really? Can you explain the angel costume to me? Tell me everything that went into it."

"Well – It's a long frock, all white. Made of heavy cotton. I used a sheet. Then I made some wings out of cardboard, to put on the back like. I meant to paint 'em white, but then I had a better idea. I live on a farm, and we got swans on a pond down near the meadow. There are always swan feathers laying about. I run down there and picked up heaps of 'em. They was all over. It took a long time. But I got enough to cover the cardboard with 'em. It was hard. I glued 'em on, one feather at a time. They looked real pretty. Then I made a halo thing out of a coat hanger. I paint it gold color and all, and glued it to the back neck part. You know, in a piece that sticks up over me head. After that, I made the hanger in a circle, so's it come straight up from the one in back. I looked like a true angel. Frank said so." Clara had her hands folded in her lap, very neatly, but they were shaking, Lily noticed.

"So, tell me Clara, did you ever walk outside of the house in your angel costume?" Ralph Poindexter questioned.

"Umm – no – not that I can think. There'd be no reason for such." Clara shifted her eyes around, and didn't seem to want to look Ralph in the eye.

"Clara, can you think of any reason why there would have been a white feather found on Lady Claybourne's body?" he asked.

"Well – maybe they got swans at *Claybourne Court*," she replied, very nervously.

"No, they don't own any swans, Clara. Do you think if we took the feather found on Lady Eleanor's body and compared it to the ones on your wings, we would find a match?"

"Are all swan feathers the same and all?" She looked down at the table then took a sip of the tea.

"No, I believe there are special tests that can be done to show if they match," Ralph continued. He wasn't at all certain that was true, but then again, it might be.

"Oh," Clara murmured.

"Clara, those feathers are from your costume, aren't they? Are we going to have to test them to prove it?"

"No sir," she said. "They was mine. I walked out there to find Frank, so's we could get ready to go and all. I didn't find him, so's I went back in."

"Frank told the Inspectors that he was out there with Lady Eleanor, in the summerhouse, and that she kissed him. He was frightened that her husband would catch them, so he went back into the house. Does that sound true to you?"

"Could be," she said. Her answers were becoming much less drawn out.

"Clara, let me suggest a possibility to you. Would there be a chance that when you went outside to find Frank, you did see him in the summerhouse, kissing Lady Eleanor? Could you have waited until he left, and then attacked her, out of jealousy? I could understand how that might happen," Ralph Poindexter conjectured. "Tell the truth, Clara. It will be the best thing for you if you do."

Clara Thornton broke into hideous, wretched sobs. "I didn't mean it. I never hurt nobody in me life. But, her was evil. Her even kicked her own little boy and all. She was trying to get Frank to fall for her. He never even kissed me, and there he was kissing on her. He didn't see me. He run from the summerhouse and I come round the corner and pinched her. I says to her

'There, Miss Toff. How do you like being pinched and that?' Then I kicked her. Just like her done to her boy. She slapped me in the face. I just lost me mind. I yelled that Frank was mine and her better leave him alone. She laughed at me. Just laughed and laughed. She said Frank wouldn't never be mine. That I was an ugly hag. A piece of scum. That no man'd ever want me. She made fun about the spots on me face." Clara stopped talking, and put her head on the table, weeping uncontrollably. She sounded like she was gagging on her tears.

"Please go on, Clara. I know it's hard, but you'll feel better after you've told it. Miss Barton here will hold your hand," Ralph Poindexter indicated to Lily. Lily was taken back. She didn't really want to hold Clara's hand, but if it would help to convict her, she'd do anything. She scooted her chair over close to Clara, and took her hand, squeezing it in a comforting way. Clara finally brought her head back up, and wiped her nose with her sleeve. Lily gave her a handkerchief.

"Well, I went crazy. Before I knew what I done, I'd grabbed her neck. I didn't mean to kill her. I just wanted to stop her talking – saying such mean things. Her sort-of wrestled with me. Her was still laughing. We fought till we was on the grass, and I tore her frock. I never saw a frock like that one. I ripped and ripped at it. Her just kept laughing. I couldn't stand the sound. I put me hands about her neck again, and squeezed till her stopped laughing. She started trying to get out from me gripping, but I held tight. I hated her. When she was real quiet, I stopped and looked at her. I knowed her was dead. And, what's more, right then, I didn't care. People shouldn't laugh at other people. Course, I'm sorry now. I never meant to kill her." Clara was exhausted, and still weeping, but now the tears were just streaming down her face. Great, long streams.

"Lily, did you get all of that?" Ralph Poindexter asked. He shut the case file on the table, and wiped his brow.

"Yes, I got it," she answered. "I had to stop holding her hand, but I got it. I'm sorry, Clara. You're right about one thing. Lady Eleanor was evil."

Clara still sat with her head in her arms on the table. "What's to happen to me now?" she cried.

"I'm afraid we'll have to notify the Inspectors who are working on the case. You'll be taken into custody. I recommend that you get yourself a barrister."

"You mean they'll throw me in the lock-up? How long will I be there? You're a barrister. Can I be using you to help me?" she sniffed.

"Yes, Clara. You'll be in the lock-up. I don't know how long you'll be there. Probably quite a while. I'm sorry, I can't help you with your defense. It would be what's known as a 'conflict of interest'. The Court will give you a barrister, if you can't afford one. Barrister's are quite expensive," Ralph explained.

"I got no money. Just what I earn from me performing," she wailed.

"I'm going to have to call the constable's office. They'll tell you what will happen from now on. I want to tell you that you did the right thing in telling what happened. Didn't you feel terrible when you heard that Lord Claybourne had been arrested for Lady Eleanor's murder?"

"Yes. I guess I did. But, if he was dumb enough to go and marry her and all, well he's the one who brung her to England and that."

Lily and Ralph glanced at one another, and nearly laughed aloud. Clara Thornton had a point.

The authorities collected Clara and assured Ralph that she would have a barrister. They also said that Lord Claybourne would be released as soon as Miss Thornton was booked for the murder of Lady Eleanor Claybourne. After hearing the entire story, both Lily and Ralph hoped she would only be charged with manslaughter – unintentional murder. If that happened, she wouldn't spend her life in prison, or worse still, face hanging.

Of course Lily was over the moon. Kit would be coming home! She wanted to rush right over to the detention center and wait for his release. But Ralph recommended that she go on home. "It might take hours until he's processed out," Ralph explained. "Plus, I expect he'd rather not greet you in that dismal place. I feel certain that he's eager to see his home and his son, with you there as well. Give him the dignity of being dressed in his own clothing."

Lily agreed. Much as she was dying to see him, she knew that Ralph was correct. "Oh Ralph, how can I ever thank you. If you hadn't listened to me,

Kit might not ever have been freed. Not all barristers would have accepted my interference. I can never show my appreciation."

"No need. I'm the one who should be thanking you. I'd read through that autopsy once, and never thought about the damned feather. It took a woman to think about the fashion aspect of the case. So, I'm grateful to you. It's always been my contention that barristers should never ignore an interested party who wants to lend a hand. Especially intelligent ones. I can't help but feel a bit sorry for Clara. She's a pitiful soul. This is one of those situations where the victim really pushed the perpetrator to the edge. Eleanor was not a nice person, that's for certain," Ralph commented.

"No, she wasn't. I know that. I saw her call Kit every name imaginable when he returned from the war with an eye patch. She ran from him and called him a monster and a freak. I can sympathize with what Clara felt. I myself felt like slapping her then. Clara obviously has little self-esteem, and Eleanor knew it. I hope they don't charge her with premeditated murder. Obviously it wasn't. Perhaps they'll go easy on her," Lily said in a soft voice. "Well, Ralph, I must go. I've already rung Edward, the driver at *Claybourne Court*. He'll be here any moment. He may be outside now. Kit and I will ring you very soon, and have you to dinner." She paused. "Oh wait. Why don't you ride with me to *Claybourne Court*? I know Kit will be anxious to see you and thank you personally."

"Well, what a nice offer, Lily Barton. I'd be most happy to be there to welcome him home." He got up from his chair, and walked to the door with Lily. He turned out the light, and they both went outside. Sure enough, Edward was parked in front of the cottage. He jumped out and held the door for them, and they both slid into the back seat. Lily was bursting with joy. "Oh Edward. You'll never believe it. The barrister and I discovered who really murdered Eleanor. It was the woman who came to entertain the children that night. She confessed it all." Lily went on to tell the chauffeur the entire story as he drove them back to *Claybourne Court*. By the time they reached the great house, Edward had all of the details, and was over the top with happiness. "Miss Barton, would it be all right if I told the other staff the good news? They'll all be so pleased. We'll want to arrange a little something for a celebration to welcome Lord Claybourne home."

"I'm sure it would be fine. He'd want all of you to know as soon as possible. I don't know when he'll return, but hopefully it won't be too long," Lily replied. She climbed out of the automobile and almost ran to the doorway. Ralph followed behind, smiling. Lady Cynthia was in the great hall, along with Mrs. Briggs, and Win. "How did it go, dear?" asked Lady Cynthia.

"Better than any of us could have hoped. Kit will be home before nightfall. Clara Thornton admitted to killing Eleanor. Isn't that splendid news?" Lily could scarcely contain her excitement.

Ralph entered the house too. Lady Cynthia turned and welcomed him. "God bless you, Mr. Poindexter," she exclaimed. "I knew when I hired you that you were a very bright chap."

"It's Lily you need to thank. She figured it all out. We made a very good pair, if I do say so."

"How did it happen?" asked Mrs. Briggs. "Why did she do it?"

Lily went through the entire story. No one said a word, as she repeated word for word what Clara had admitted to. "Thank goodness the Inspector put a notation in the autopsy report mentioning the feather on her body. That's why I asked everyone here last night about Eleanor's dress. Oh, Mrs. Briggs, when you told me about Clara Thornton's angel costume, I nearly died. I wanted so badly to tell you, but I'd promised to keep it confidential. But now it's fine for you to know everything. Kit will be free – free! All of this will be a terrible nightmare."

Halsey appeared while they were all discussing Clara's confession. "Lady Cynthia, may I ask you a question?" he asked.

"Certainly Halsey. Do you wish to speak with me privately?" answered Lady Cynthia.

"No, Milady. I'd like Mrs. Briggs to know what's being planned. You see, we're all so over-the-top about Lord Claybourne's being released. We'd like to line up in front of the house to welcome him home. You know what I mean? Two lines on either side of the front of the house," Halsey explained.

"What a top-drawer idea, Halsey. Just perfect. Kit will be so touched. It will mean a lot. We'll need to know exactly when he'll be arriving. How do you suppose I can find that out?" She turned to Lily.

"Mr. Poindexter, you should be able to find out. I love the idea, Halsey."

Ralph excused himself and asked where the telephone was located. Lily showed him into the drawing room and pointed to it. Then she left him to make his call in private. A few moments later her returned to the great hall, smiling. "I just spoke with the authorities. He's been officially released, and a constable will be driving him home. I expect it will be in about twenty minutes," he pronounced.

"Do you mean twenty minutes until he leaves from the village, or twenty minutes until he arrives here?" Lily inquired.

"Oh – by the time he arrives here. I expect he's on his way now."

Lily shouted with glee. "He's on the way," she called to everyone. "Twenty minutes at the most. Oh, thank you so much, Ralph. You are such a treasure."

The entire group was massed in front of the house. "So, we're the welcoming committee, then," Ralph laughed.

"Yes," cried Lily. "Isn't it fun, Ralph? I never dreamed this when I left here this morning."

"Nor did I, young lady. Nor did I. Wait – I think I hear a car pulling into the drive," he murmured. "Yes, there's the auto." He motioned to the staff that Kit had arrived.

All of them lined up, the men on one side, and the women on the other. Lily, Lady Cynthia, Win and Ralph stood between the two formations. The constable's automobile pulled up in front. Before it had even come to a full stop, Kit leaped from the back seat. He was beaming from ear to ear. Dressed in the elegant suit he'd worn on Christmas day, he looked like he'd just arrived from a posh gathering at a private men's club. With tears wetting his cheek, he stood quite still for a moment and admired his staff. How grand they all looked. He felt so proud. Then he saluted all of them, and they returned the gesture. All of them broke into "For He's a Jolly Good Fellow." That caused more tears to spill over, but as they did, he continued to smile. When they'd finished, he walked up and shook each member of the staff's hand. Finally, he turned and walked over to Lily. In front of everyone, he took her into his arms, and kissed her with obvious passion. Again the staff cheered and clapped. Kit whispered in Lily's ear. "Will you marry me as soon as possible, my lovely, strong Lily?" Win stood by her side, looking up into his father's face and Kit stooped down and picked him up, giving him a big kiss too. Then he whispered to Win. "Would you like 'Ba' to be your Mummy?"

Win grinned. "'Ba'. 'Ba,' be my Mummy," he shouted.

Everyone laughed. Lily reached over and kissed Win's cheek. Then she turned to Kit. "Lord Claybourne, just tell me when I'm to be at the church, and I'll be ready."

They all gathered together and entered the house. It was the happiest day that anyone at *Claybourne Court* could remember. The only thing that might have made it better would have been for the war to have ended. Lily knew she wouldn't marry until she could have Gena, Maddie, and Poppy as her bridesmaids. But, she had another of her strong feelings that peace would not be long in coming.

OTHER BOOKS BY MARY CHRISTIAN PAYNE

The Somerville Trilogy

Willow Grove Abbey: Book 1 of the Somerville Trilogy
St. James Road: Book 2 of the Somerville Trilogy
Serendipity: Book 3 of the Somerville Trilogy

The Claybourne Trilogy

The White Feather: Book 1 of the Claybourne Trilogy
The White Butterfly: Book 2 of the Claybourne Trilogy
White Cliffs of Dover: Book 3 of the Claybourne Trilogy

The Thornton Trilogy

No Regrets: Book 1 of The Thornton Trilogy
No Gentleman: Book 2 of the Thornton Trilogy
No Secrets: Book 3 of the Thornton Trilogy

About The Author

Mary Christian Payne was highly successful in several management positions in Fortune 500 Companies, in New York City, St. Louis, Missouri, Orlando Florida, and Tulsa, Oklahoma. Her work included Grant writing, and designing and writing Training Manuals for Executive Training Programs.

She left the corporate world, and became Director of Career Development at the Women' Resource Center at the University of Tulsa, where she designed a program that enabled hundreds of adult women to return to college and better their lives. She received the Mayor's Pinnacle

Award in 1993 for this achievement. Mary left that position when the Center closed, and then opened her own Career Counseling Center. She retired in 2008.

Mary Christian Payne became a successful, best-selling author at the age of 71, with the help of her publisher, Tom Corson-Knowles. All of her life, she had wanted to write, and had received accolades for her unpublished work. She was encouraged in college, and writing was a significant part of the various jobs she held.

In 2013, she read Tom Corson-Knowles' book about publishing on Kindle. She wrote to him and he telephoned her. The rest is history. Since that time, she has published nine books, with more on the way.

Mary lost her husband in June, 2015, after 33 years of marriage. The grief process brought a lull to her writing, but she found that putting words on paper helped immensely. She is now in the process of writing her second novel since his death. She lives in Tulsa, Oklahoma, with her two beloved Maltese dogs.

Sign up for the newsletter to get news, updates and new release info from Mary Christian Payne:

http://bit.ly/MaryChristianPayne

One Last Thing...

If you enjoyed this book, I'd be very grateful if you'd post a short review on Amazon. Your support really does make a difference and I read all the reviews personally.

Thanks again for your support!